DEATHWATCH

"You go now," Kurosawa said softly.

Corrigan looked at him, bewildered. "What do you mean – 'go'?"

"Boat now property of Imperial Japanese Army. You go now. Not be hurt if you co-operate with Japanese soldier."

"This boat's mine. It's how I make my living. If you think you can waltz in here and take it, you can . . ."

Kurosawa glanced nervously at Tashiro and drew himself up to attention. "Tashiro-san say if you do not go now he must shoot you."

As if to emphasise the point Corrigan heard Tashiro click the safety off his revolver. Corrigan felt the anger boil up inside him, his hands balling into tight fists at his side. For a moment he wondered if it might be worth it. With one blow he could smash the brutish little face . . . he might even have time to grab the revolver and finish him off.

Then he shifted his gaze towards Kurosawa and the platoon of soldiers waiting on the wharf. Yes, he could perhaps get in one punch but it would be a hollow victory. It would be the last thing he ever did.

There was nothing he could do. Slowly, painfully, he picked up the passport, pulled himself up on to the jetty and walked away, silently promising himself that one day he would get even with First Lieutenant Tashiro.

Also by the same author, and available from Coronet:

Venom

About the author

Colin Falconer was born in London in 1953. He is a journalist and has written for many national magazines and newspapers. He has travelled widely in Europe and South-East Asia and now lives in Western Australia. He is the author of one previous acclaimed thriller, VENOM.

C O L I N

FALCONER

DEATHWATCH

CORONET BOOKS
Hodder and Stoughton

First published in Great Britain in 1991
by Hodder and Stoughton Ltd

Coronet edition 1992

British Library C.I.P.
Falconer, Colin
Deathwatch.
I. Title
823.914[F]

ISBN 0-340-56239-0

Printed and bound in Great Britain for Hodder and Stoughton Paperbacks, a division of Hodder and Stoughton Ltd., Mill Road, Dunton Green, Sevenoaks, Kent TN13 2YA. (Editorial Office: 47 Bedford Square, London, WC1B 3DP) by Clays Ltd, St Ives plc, Bungay, Suffolk. Typeset by Hewer Text Composition Services, Edinburgh.

This one's for John and Arthur
whose kindness got me started.

DEATHWATCH

Prologue

November 1939

"The Japanese can never take Singapore. It's impregnable."

The tall grey-haired man gave the slightly built District Officer in front of him a wry smile. "Of course. But we have to be prepared for every eventuality."

"Well you can count me in, sir. I'll do anything I can."

"Good man. I have a document here you might like to read. It sets out the basics of what we expect from each member of our Coastwatching team. There's some sheets here from *Jane's Fighting Ships*. They might come in useful for identification."

"Thank you, sir."

"Speed is of the essence in any operation of this nature. You'll have to set up a camp somewhere with a view commanding the western passages so that you can report what movements you see almost immediately."

"I understand."

"You won't be in any danger of course. If the Japanese do make a move the real battlefield will probably be in Malaya."

The District Officer was dressed in just khaki shirt and shorts but still the sweat glistened at his temple and in the hollow at his throat. It was unbearably humid in the tiny office.

He turned away and looked out of the window, at the

metallic blue waters of White Bone Bay. In the distance he could make out the white froth of the breakers on the reef.

It was the monsoon of 1939. The statuesque palms swayed gently against the invisible breath of the north-west winds, and in the diffused light the schooners and launches at anchor in the harbour seemed to drift above the surface of the ocean, their reflections glittering on the glassy waters of the bay.

In the garden swallows glided and twisted among the flame trees.

It was hardly conceivable that the war could touch these dreamy backwaters. "Do you really think this will happen, sir?" the younger man said at last.

"Let's hope not, Manning. Let's face it, it won't be easy for the British Empire to fight a war on two fronts. Not if this bit of bother in Europe is still going at Christmas."

"I won't let you down, sir."

"Good." The older man looked at his watch. "Now then, what about a drink? Then I'll try and explain a bit more to you about this blessed radio."

PART ONE

1

. . . it remains an enigma to me even now, that in men and women so disparate, one should find such resources of courage. It was the most terrible war ever to be fought in those idyllic islands, yet for a few moments a handful of people who otherwise hated each other found a common cause and were, for a brief moment in time, prepared to die for it. Why did they do it? For their country? They were hardly patriots, any of them. I doubt if I shall ever understand it. I doubt if they themselves ever really understood the maelstrom of emotions that engulfed them.

From the diary of Ian McLaren Manning, Coastwatcher,
Santa Maria, February–October 1942.

December 1941

According to Father Goode, the worst thing Corrigan ever did was impregnate his housekeeper during the Sunday service.

It was a hot morning during the monsoons of 1941. Inside the Catholic mission on Santa Maria the faithful were dragging themselves half-heartedly through another verse of Father Goode's favourite hymn.

"Onward, Christian Soldiers . . ."

Thump!

Outside something heavy had fallen against the bamboo wall of the church. Father Goode looked up from the piano, his forehead creasing into a frown. His fingers continued to hammer out the chords on the keys of the tuneless piano.

"Marching as to war . . ."

Thump!

Another bang, and the flimsy wall creaked ominously. Rachel Goode faltered in her leading of the hymn and her glance darted nervously to the side. The singing had died away to a murmur as the attention of the native congregation wandered to the strange noises coming from outside the church.

It seemed to Father Goode that several of them were anticipating a visitation from the Lord Himself at any moment.

"With the cross of Jesus, going on before . . ."

Bump, bump, bump . . .

Wide-eyed, the parishioners of Santa Maria fell silent. Even Rachel Goode's voice had dropped to a murmur. Only Father Goode, his hands crashing on the keys, his tuneless voice rising with his desperation, soldiered on.

"Christ, the Royal Master, leads against the foe . . ."

Bump, bump, bump . . . BUMP!

Father Goode suddenly realised he was the only one still singing. He was determined to finish. He vented his frustration on the keyboard of the piano.

"ONWARD, CHRISTIAN SOOO-OLDIERS, MARCHING AS TO WAR . . ."

BUMP, BUMP, BUMP . . .

Father Goode stood up from the piano and with a contemptuous glare at his congregation, strode purposefully towards the door. Whoever had interrupted the worship of God would feel the full extent of his wrath.

Stepping into the warm morning sunshine in his long black soutane, he squinted in the sudden glare and went to the corner of the church. He was prepared for anything except the sight that awaited him when he got there.

Just the week before he had accepted his housekeeper Mary into the fold of Christ, another dusky lamb saved from her sins. He had been immensely proud of the achievement, considering Mary's previous record.

He had washed away her sins with his own hands. It had been a moving occasion despite Manning's asinine observation that he ought to have used a scrubbing brush.

Now here she was, her skirts hitched up around her waist, her legs parted and gripped obscenely around Patrick Corrigan's bared buttocks. In a reflex action, Father Goode clutched at the silver crucifix at his neck.

They were fornicating. *On sacred ground.* Father Goode felt his throat constrict as an apoplexy of rage suffused his cheeks with scarlet. His mouth worked soundlessly and his fists clenched and unclenched at his sides.

Mary's face was turned towards him, her eyes closed, her pretty brown face contorted by passion. Her mouth was open. She was groaning.

Father Goode actually began to grind his teeth. She was leaning on his Church and she was groaning. *The harlot!*

"Jezebel!" he screamed. "The Lord shall strike ye down!"

Mary's face actually went pale. Her eyes blinked open and stared at him, in naked, undisguised terror. She yanked at Corrigan's hair. Finally Corrigan looked round and saw Father Goode. He also noted the priest's young niece was standing open-mouthed behind him.

Corrigan's face split into a slow grin. "Morning vicar," he said cheerfully, and then the bumping continued.

It was the last straw.

"He's a totally worthless tramp and an alcoholic. His continued presence here is a disgrace to the white community. His example seriously hinders our efforts to lead these primitive people out of the darkness and into the Christian light. I consider it your responsibility – no, your duty – to have him removed from this island by whatever means you deem necessary."

Ian McLaren Manning listened to this speech with growing irritation. He was not the kind of man who needed someone to point out to him his bounden duty. It was as much as he could do to keep his voice pleasant.

He gripped the cane arms of his chair in an effort at self-control and gave the priest a chill smile. "Don't you think that's a little drastic, old chap?" he said finally.

"Mr Manning. Was Jesus being drastic when he threw the money changers out of the temple?"

Manning laughed, a harsh sound, like breaking glass. "Whatever we may think of Patrick Corrigan privately, he's hardly a criminal. He has rights, the same as everyone else. We cannot hound him off the island because we do not agree with his personal standard of morals."

The two men were seated on the verandah of the mission, while the thick grey sheets of the monsoon splashed in deep pools around the coconut groves.

"Common assault is more than just a bad habit," Father Goode said. "This man is a danger to every woman in this community. Something must be done."

Manning found an ally from an unexpected source. "I'm afraid I agree with Mr Manning," Rachel Goode said, suddenly appearing behind them on the verandah. "I think you are judging Mister Corrigan far too harshly. There is good in everyone after all. You've said so yourself."

"God knows I have tried to help him as much as any man is able," the priest said. But in the face of his niece's gentle reprimand he subsided.

"So what happened to Mary?" Manning said.

"We gave her absolution and sent her back to her village," Father Goode said.

"Isn't that a bit harsh?"

"There were other circumstances," Father Goode said, his face flushing a deep crimson.

"She was going to have a baby," Rachel added.

"I see."

"You don't see at all," Father Goode said irritably. "If you did, you'd do something about it."

"I don't see that it's my fault, old boy."

"She claimed it was an Immaculate Conception," Father

Goode went on. "However it seemed quite plain that paternity did not lie with the Divinity but with your Mister Corrigan. While we prayed for his mortal soul, he was dragging one of our flock into the den of iniquity with him. May Christ have mercy on his soul."

"Amen," said Rachel.

They sat for a long time in silence, the only sound the steady drip, drip of the rain falling from the eaves on to the wooden steps, and the murmurous thunder of the monsoon as it cast its grey shroud over the jungles and the mountains to the north.

"Father, I came here today to discuss another, more serious matter."

"What could be more serious than sin?"

Manning ignored the remark. "I have received instructions to evacuate the island, should Singapore fall to the Japanese. It would be wise if you were prepared to leave in a hurry, in the unlikely event that it proves necessary."

"I shall not be leaving Santa Maria, Mister Manning. My life's work is here. I cannot abandon it."

Manning frowned. "I think you should consider more carefully. Should the Japanese get this far no one can guarantee they will respect your rights as a civilian and man of God."

"I have already given it my full consideration. The answer is still the same."

Manning nodded. Even though he found the priest irritating and tyrannical, he admired his integrity and courage. He turned to Rachel. "I take it you will leave, of course."

"No, Mister Manning, I'll be staying here with my uncle to help him in his work. These simple people are in our charge. We cannot run away from them at the sign of the first danger."

"Miss Goode, I strongly advise that you reconsider. By all accounts the Japanese advance across Malaya has been notable for atrocious acts of savagery. The Commissioner has advised that all women and children . . ."

"No, Mister Manning," Rachel interrupted. Beneath the soft voice Manning detected a will of iron. "In God's eyes we are all equal. I shall put my trust in the Lord."

Manning turned to Father Goode. "Father, you must understand . . ."

"We are here to do the Lord's work, Mister Manning. The fortunes of war do not concern us."

Manning shrugged and got to his feet. "I hope your complacency is not ill-founded, old chap," he said softly. "I'd better be getting back. Good afternoon, sir." He bowed slightly. "Miss Goode."

He put on his white topee and mackintosh and went down the steps where his bicycle leaned against one of the wooden posts. He climbed on and pedalled slowly through the mist of rain towards Vancoro.

The two figures on the verandah watched him till he was out of sight. Rachel Goode turned to her uncle.

"Are we really in danger here?" she asked softly.

Father Goode shook his head. "No, Rachel, of course not. Singapore will never fall. The war will never touch us here."

2

It was generally known that Rachel Goode had become an object of speculation and fantasy for every white trader and official who had ever visited Santa Maria since she was around seventeen years old. She was undeniably the most beautiful white woman on the island, although she seemed at times to do her best to disguise it.

Her raven-black hair was always pulled back across her head into a tight, hard bun at the back of her head, giving her the harsh, pinched look of an English schoolmistress. Although she was just twenty, it made her seem much older.

Whenever she ventured outside her face was kept in shadow by a veiled and wide-brimmed hat, which sometimes helped to disguise the natural beauty of her high, patrician cheek bones and a mouth that seemed curiously sensual on such a controlled young woman.

She habitually wore shapeless white gowns that buttoned high at the neck and descended to her ankles, so that the curves of her young woman's body remained a mystery to all men.

But although she tried to conceal her natural beauty, her eyes always betrayed her; they were as cool and as green as the shallow waters of White Bone Bay, which the mission bungalow overlooked; there was fire in them, and many of the plantation owners – and their wives – had sometimes looked at her and wondered.

But whatever passions lurked hidden behind those eyes, God and Father Goode kept them sternly in check.

Rachel Goode had lived in the care of Matthew Goode since she was ten years old. Both her parents had drowned one hot summer's afternoon while on holiday in Cumberland, in England's Lake District, swallowed up silently by the peaceful blue waters of Lake Windermere. They had taken a small rowing boat out on to the lake and they had simply never returned. Searchers never recovered the bodies. All that remained as testimony of their fate was her father's tweed cap, which Rachel still kept in a drawer by the side of her bed, with a solitary and yellowing family portrait taken in her halcyon summer of 1927.

At the time her uncle was far away in Africa, saving the souls of the descendants of Cetewayo. He had immediately sailed back to England to take care of his orphaned niece; and as there were no other relatives to lay claim to the girl, he had taken the duty of her future upbringing upon himself. Two months later he returned with the young girl to the Natal.

It was the last time Rachel had seen England's cool, green hills; she had lived on missions in hot, strange lands ever since.

Matthew seldom mentioned her parents. He had hinted to her on a couple of occasions that their demise was brought about by the wrath of God, and had made veiled insinuations that her father was a man of strong and unrestrained passions. (Rachel had never been quite able to comprehend why the Lord had seen fit to include her mother in his just retribution, but she had kept this thought to herself.)

At first she had devoted herself to her uncle's care, grateful that he had taken her under his wing at a time when the world had been a dark and lonely place. She had learned to imitate her uncle's devout application to his faith, becoming after a time cook, housekeeper, nurse and verger. But it had become clear to her lately that she had no vocation inside the church, and she began to question those beliefs that he had forced her to share.

Ashamed and desperate, she had begun to have dreams. Wild, satanic dreams that haunted her all the following day, and left behind a restless and shadowy longing that soon became a permanent companion. Indeed she sometimes wondered, in the dark and guilty moments of the night, if her father's passion had not somehow been passed along in the bloodline to his daughter, and she wondered when God's wrath would touch her also.

But the years passed in slow, lazy cadence in the tropics; and nothing happened.

The boiling inner flood of Rachel's emotions had not raised a ripple on the surface. She went about her daily chores as she had always done. She had proved herself an excellent nurse in the small mission hospital, and her ear for music had led her uncle to persuade her to select a choir of native children for the mission church. She supervised the cookboys and the houseboys with a firm but gentle hand and in his quiet, emerald-eyed niece Matthew Goode felt he had discovered the perfect helpmate for a celibate priest.

In his complacency, he was not aware of the *tsunami* bearing down on them both.

It was late afternoon. Rachel was sitting in a wicker chair in her bedroom at the rear of the mission when the messenger arrived. It was moist, sticky hot. Outside the monsoon rain dripped heavily from the eaves. The only other sounds were the soft moanings from the next bedroom where Father Goode lay struggling with another bout of malaria.

The musty smell of vestments mingled with the gentle fragrance of the frangipani blooms in the vase on the dressing table. A crucifix hung on the wall over the bed, and a lamp cast a soft glow over the room, reflecting on the carefully waxed hardwood floor.

A Bible lay open on Rachel's lap, and she turned the pages listlessly. Matthew had charged her with the choice of readings for the Sunday service, before he had succumbed to his latest round of fever.

Suddenly the new housegirl appeared in the doorway.

Rachel looked up surprised. "What is it, Lelei?"

"Man he come from Mamara, missus. *Luluai* he got bad sick. Say Mastah he come quick."

"Is it bad? My uncle is very sick also. He cannot leave his bed."

"Im he say mastah no come, *luluai* he die finis!"

Rachel looked beyond the housegirl to the door. A native youth stood miserably out on the balcony, rain dripping from the thick bush of curly hair. It was forming a little pool at his feet.

"How did he get here?"

"Im he come longa *kedi*, missus."

The *kedi* was the name the islanders gave to their three-man canoes. Rachel shook her head. It would have been a harrowing trip in this weather.

She rose slowly to her feet and went to the door. She

recognised the youth. His name was Wesu. His father was Kumasi, the *luluai* – headman – of his village.

"Kumasi is sick?" Rachel said to him.

Wesu nodded. "Me fright for him, missus. Maybe he die finis."

"What's wrong with him?"

"Belly b'long him sore too mus. Him he no savvy *kai-kai*," he answered her. *He has bad stomach pains. He doesn't want to eat.*

Rachel nodded. "Very well," she said, and went down the passage and opened the door to her uncle's bedroom.

Father Goode lay white and gaunt in his nightshirt under the mosquito netting, shivering and burning with fever.

It was his twelfth bout of malaria, the tropic fever that was the scourge of missionaries in the Equator.

"Uncle Matthew," she whispered, leaning close to the bed, "are you awake?"

Father Goode stirred slightly in his sleep. "The fiery pit. Cast them into the pit!"

She leaned closer. "Uncle, I have to leave. One of the natives in Mamara Point needs a doctor. You'll be all right here with Lelei."

Father Goode gave a long sigh. He turned his face towards her, his eyes open yet somehow unseeing. "The Lord shall have his revenge on sinners," he said. "Oh, Sodom." And he fell back into a deep sleep.

Rachel tiptoed from the room, closing the door behind her. Lelei was standing outside, waiting. "Get the Father's black bag and the bicycle. Hurry now."

Lelei rolled her eyes. "You go, missus?"

"When the Lord calls, we must answer Him."

"No, missus. Better you stay. Bimeby Guberment man he come in boat, you go longa him."

But Rachel was already struggling into her mosquito boots, and the ankle-length white drawers that would protect her modesty on a bicycle. "I cannot wait for

Mister Manning. He may be gone for days. I will ask Mister Corrigan to take me."

Lelei put a hand to her mouth as if Rachel had uttered a *tabu* curse. "No, Missy!"

Rachel gave her a patient smile of forbearance. She stood up, put on a wide-brimmed straw hat and tied the ribbon.

"There is no one else. Mister Corrigan has a launch. It will be much safer than travelling in the *kedi* in this weather."

"But Missy! Him no good too mus! Him debil-debil!"

"Lelei, stop this nonsense. Now do as I say and get the bag. Hurry!"

A few minutes later Lelei stood on the balcony watching her mistress cycle through the driving rain, the native boy trotting beside her, clutching the black bag.

She made the sign of the Cross as Father Goode had shown her and felt for the weighty assurance of the *poopono* gourd in her pocket.

Lelei experienced a sudden sense of deep foreboding. She knew that when the missus didn't come back she was going to be in big trouble.

3

As Father Goode never tired of repeating, Corrigan's Trader's Post at Vancoro was a disgrace to the white population on Santa Maria.

The bungalow had been allowed to crumble into disrepair, empty whisky bottles lay strewn in the grass, and several of the wooden slats on the verandah and on the front steps were broken or missing. The store had been

Patrick Corrigan's only home and livelihood for the last five years, and during that time he had crumbled to the ravages of the tropics in the same way.

Patrick Corrigan should have been an exceptionally handsome man. Although he had the face of a fighter, his nose having been bent and twisted in numerous fights, the square jaw and the row of strong, white teeth had remained unharmed by the effects of their owner's fierce temper. He had a thick black mane of hair which he continually pushed back from his forehead but an errant comma always fell back across his eyes. It lent him a devil-may-care look that enchanted the traders' wives and the native girls alike.

Whatever his considerable talents may once have been, he now seemed to make a point of concealing them. He rarely performed any useful work, spending most of his time gambling at Sam Doo's in Chinatown; he seldom bothered to shave or put on a clean shirt; he was almost always drunk. He seemed to be happily bent on a private orgy of self-destruction.

When he wanted to he could be utterly charming; at other times he was as belligerent as a bear caught in a trap. Manning once remarked that when he was angry, Corrigan had the face of the Devil himself, but when he smiled, you could forgive him anything.

Right now Corrigan did not feel like smiling. He was bored, and he was tired. Bored with the endless rain, tired of the tropics, tired of his life. He had had every girl worth having on the whole island, and there was no man left who dared challenge him to a fight.

In short, there was nothing to help him complete his degradation except a bottle of Gilbey's gin. And that, too, was nearly empty. There was more on the *Shamrock* but Sanei had refused to go out into the rain and fetch more for him, even after he threatened her with a beating. He might be forced to fetch it for himself.

He sat in a heat-drugged stupor in the back room, sipping the last few drops of the oily liquid from an enamel cup, feeling the tiny droplets of perspiration running freely down the back of his neck and under the sweat-stained arms of his shirt. The raw taste of the spirit matched his mood.

It was then he saw her coming, and his first surprise turned slowly to fascination. He heard the cheerful ringing of the bicycle bell as she emerged from the grey sheets of rain, one hand on the handlebars, the other holding a tattered black umbrella. A native boy in a *lava-lava* trotted behind her, carrying a large black bag.

She was wearing a long white calico dress, spattered with black mud, a voluminous straw hat and white drawers that reached to her ankles. He shook his head in wonderment at this apparition as he watched her climb off the bicycle and run up the steps on to the verandah, out of sight.

After a few moments he heard her banging on the front door.

With a sigh Corrigan hauled himself out of his chair and walked slowly down the passageway. He opened the door. Rachel stood in the porchway, water seeping from her dress on to the bare wooden boards.

Corrigan swatted ineffectually at a mosquito feeding at his neck.

"Well – what the bloody hell do you want?" he said.

Rachel drew herself a little straighter. She would not let his manners and his vocabulary upset her. "I have come to ask your help, Mister Corrigan."

He grinned, unexpectedly. "Don't tell me. You want me to preach at Sunday school."

He drew down the corner of his mouth and emitted a long, loud belch. Her nose wrinkled in disgust at the smell of the gin.

"I need to go urgently to Marmari. One of the natives is very sick."

Corrigan scratched at his three-day growth of beard to signal his disinterest. "So?"

"I would like you to take me there in your launch. I

cannot possibly travel in the native canoe in this weather. On the *Shamrock* we could be there in a few hours."

Rachel saw a willowy brown shape, dressed only in a *lava-lava*, move in the shadows inside the house. She knew Corrigan had been living with one of the native girls, Sanei, for almost two years now. She tried to hide her frown of disapproval.

Corrigan saw the direction of her gaze and grinned. "Now why would I want to help you?"

"If not for the good of your soul, then perhaps to save the life of some poor wretch."

"What's one more black man, dead or alive?"

"Perhaps I can offer you something a little more substantial then." From her skirt she pulled two damp one-pound notes and held them under Corrigan's nose. It was money the mission could ill afford. But as her uncle was fond of saying – God would provide.

Corrigan rubbed the palm of his hand across his chin, the bristles making a rasping noise. "You're a strange lot, you Holy Romans."

Rachel's lips compressed in a thin, white smile. "Will you do it then?"

"It'll be a rough trip." Corrigan stared at her, then at the money. "Oh well, if that's what you want to do. But it seems to be a lot of trouble over one blackbird."

Leaning on the wheel of the launch, Corrigan peered through the cockpit windshield. The mainland loomed ahead in the darkness, a dark shadow against the deep purple of the sky. He was already regretting his impulse to take this damned girl up to Marmari Point.

He glanced round. Rachel sat huddled in a corner of the cockpit, next to the native boy, her hands thrust determinedly in her lap, the knuckles white. It had been a rough passage, but she had borne it stoically; he had been looking forward to the spectacle of seeing her vomit over the side but so far she had denied him the satisfaction.

"You all right?" he said.

She nodded and got shakily to her feet, one hand gripping the rail.

"Are we nearly there?" In the ghostly half-light her face shone pale as marble.

"We're in the lee of the headland now. Another quarter of an hour I reckon," Corrigan answered. "You didn't sick up then?"

"I felt a little unwell at times."

"Gets a bit choppy in the monsoon season."

"We must thank the Lord for a safe crossing," Rachel said mechanically.

"Don't see why. He didn't have bugger all to do with it. I've seen rougher seas in Sydney Harbour."

She fixed her eyes on Corrigan at the wheel. "You are not a God-fearing man, Mister Corrigan?"

"There are only two things that frighten me. A man with a gun and a woman with a Bible."

Corrigan reached between his legs and found the bottle of Gilbey's on the narrow wooden shelf behind the wheel. He unscrewed the cap and took a long swallow.

"Mister Corrigan, don't you think it would be safer for both of us if you refrained from drinking alcohol while you're in charge of this vessel?"

Corrigan belched. The sound of it echoed around the cockpit like thunder. "You can get stuffed."

"Thank you, Mister Corrigan," Rachel said mildly and she went back to her seat in the corner and prayed silently for deliverance.

4

Corrigan brought the *Shamrock* to anchor in the shallow water of the bay of Marmari Point. The moon was still bright, lending an almost eerie luminescence to the shadowy huts of the village that sprawled under the canopy of the coconut trees.

The gentle murmur of the diesel engines echoed around the lagoon. On the beach he could make out the fires burning in the village and the silhouettes of the natives gathered along the shoreline.

Corrigan threw the anchor over the side of the boat into the soft sand and clambered over the side into the water. Hitching up her skirt, Rachel prepared to follow him.

"Careful. You'll break your bloody neck," Corrigan said. Before she could protest she felt a vice-like grip on her arms lift her clear of the launch and deposit her in the shallow water.

"Mister Corrigan," she gasped. The strength of the man surprised her. He had lifted her effortlessly, as if she were a small child. "I can manage by myself."

"Suit your bloody self then," he muttered and waded away from her towards the beach.

They walked through the silent crowd to Kumasi's hut. Kumasi's wife waited outside. She was perhaps thirty years younger than the old man; she was bare-breasted, but she wore a patterned *lava-lava* around her middle. She and another woman were preparing a shroud from blue-dyed tapa cloth on the verandah of the hut.

"Looks like they don't hold out a lot of hope," Corrigan said.

Rachel didn't answer.

Kumasi's hut was built in the style of the Europeans. It was raised on stilts a few feet off the ground with a verandah right the way round the building. There were five rooms, partitioned with walls of split bamboo, the roof thatched with sago palm.

Inside a gathering of Kumasi's family and friends stood around the old headman's sleeping mat, watching; they were subdued in the patient expectation of death.

The headman was about sixty years old. His face was gnarled and wrinkled, the creases ingrained with the smoky residue of years of smouldering cooking fires. He was lean with a sparse and pointed grey beard in the shape of a "W". It gave him the appearance of a thin and rangy goat.

He lay groaning on a bamboo mat in the centre of the room. He was only half-conscious and his body was shiny with his own sweat, like melting chocolate.

The group of natives parted to allow Rachel and Corrigan through. Rachel knelt down beside the old man to examine him.

Outside the doorway a fowl fluttered up the steps and picked its way fussily along the verandah, leaving its droppings on the split-bamboo flooring. Above her head a gekko pursued one of its amours through a small hole in the rough-hewn rafters.

It took just a few moments for Rachel to make her diagnosis. She had watched her uncle tackle appendicitis cases at the Mission hospital and she knew the symptoms.

Rachel turned to Wesu. "Sick long time?" she asked him.

"He for sick last time sun he up," he told her. "Im he for die finis?"

"No," Rachel murmured with little conviction. "No, im he no for die."

"Balls," Corrigan said, somewhere behind her.

Rachel searched through the battered black leather bag she had brought with her. There was ether and two scalpels, a little sulphonamide, forceps, some aspirin and a quantity of bandages and catgut for stitching wounds.

Hardly enough to tackle an appendectomy but she would have to make do.

She felt the man's distended belly. It was badly swollen; the infected organ might burst at any moment, spreading its poison right through the intestinal cavity. As she ran her finger over his abdomen the man gasped with pain, the muscles in his neck constricting like whipcord, his mouth forced open in a silent scream.

It might already be too late. She would have to operate straight away.

She looked around at the cluster of dark faces peering anxiously over her shoulder. The atmosphere was charged with expectancy, the tension almost a tangible thing. She suddenly felt terribly helpless and inadequate.

One face was missing. She pushed out of the hut and marched down to the water's edge. She found Corrigan sitting on the sand, the bottle of Gilbey's gin nursed in his lap.

"Mister Corrigan. I need your help again."

He stared at her belligerently. "What's the point? The old bugger's had it. Let's go home."

"Are you going to help me or not?"

"Why the hell should I?"

"Because if you don't you aren't going to get your two pounds! Now pull yourself together and come with me!"

Rachel turned her back on him and marched back up the beach. Corrigan's jaw fell open. It had been years since a woman had had the temerity to try and tell him what to do, and he was shocked. She was just a slip of a girl, fifteen years his junior.

He saw no reason at all why he should help her. After all, that hadn't been part of the bargain.

But without really knowing why, he got up and followed her.

"We will have to render him unconscious."

They stood together in the steamy heat of the hut. The air was murmurous with the insistent buzzing of flying insects. Rachel had ushered everyone except Corrigan outside the hut and dark faces clustered around the doorway, peering in with frightened eyes.

"That's easy enough," Corrigan said. "A good wallop in the guts ought to do it." He laughed raucously.

She ignored him. She had boiled her scalpels in scalding water and scrubbed her hands until the skin was red raw. A hurricane lamp had been brought from the *Shamrock* and she laid it gingerly on the flooring earth by the side of the old man.

She was ready to begin.

She handed Corrigan a thick pad of gauze and unscrewed the top from a small glass bottle of ether.

"Don't get too near the lamp. The fumes from the ether are combustible."

Corrigan thrust his big ham fists into his pockets and regarded her, truculently. "You mean this is dangerous?"

Rachel stared, and said nothing. Corrigan stared back. It took a full minute but Corrigan was the first to break. He took one hand from his pocket and took the bottle.

"Every time he stirs I want you to put a little of the ether on the gauze and put it over his mouth and nose."

Corrigan dabbed some of the liquid on to the pad and quickly replaced the stopper. He put the gauze over the man's face. After a few moments the spastic movements of the limbs subsided, and the man was quite still.

"Don't keep it over his mouth. We don't want to suffocate him."

Corrigan lifted the gauze, and grimaced. "You don't really think he's going to live through all this?"

"It's in God's hands, Mister Corrigan."

"Cut his throat and put him out of his misery. The bastard's got no choice. If he doesn't die from blood loss, he'll get an infection. Look at this place." He cast a disparaging eye round the hut.

"Life is sacred. We should do our best to preserve it."

"That's your opinion."

Rachel picked up one of the scalpels. It glinted yellow in the light of the lamp.

"I hope you don't have a sensitive stomach."

"I'm not worried about a little bit of blood if that's what you mean."

Rachel knelt down beside the bamboo mat, the scalpel poised in her right hand. She took a deep breath and cut deep, a single swift slash with the keen edge of the blade that sliced cleanly through the skin and tissue of the abdomen. Blood welled up through the incision in a rich red mass.

"Oh Christ," Corrigan said. Even in the dim light of the hurricane lamp Rachel saw that his face had paled to the colour of chalk.

Rachel pointed the scalpel at him. "You will not be sick," she hissed at him.

Corrigan nodded and turned away.

"Thank you, Mister Corrigan," Rachel said and bent to her work.

"If only my uncle was here. I'm sure he could have done a much better job." It was damp hot in the hut, and the warmth from the body drifted up and made the perspiration pour from her forehead, in tiny white blisters. A dewdrop of sweat trickled along her nose and hung there; she wiped it away quickly with the sleeve of her dress.

Her long pale hands were covered in blood.

"You're doing all right," Corrigan mumbled. Rachel straightened, flicked back an errant strand of hair with the crook of her other arm.

She bent down over her patient once more. With one hand she held the forceps to keep the wound open, and with the other she groped for the infected organ. The entrails made a wet sucking sound as she pushed them aside.

"I'll be glad when this is over," Corrigan said.

The appendix now lay exposed in the wound, a swollen angry red. Rachel knew she would have to cut carefully but swiftly. If she burst the sac the poison would pour into the abdominal cavity and the man would almost certainly die.

She pulled the retractors wide to give herself a little more room, the scalpel held lightly in the fingers of her other hand.

"Ah." A few minutes later she produced a long piece of tissue, smeared with dark congealed blood, in the manner of a magician producing a rabbit from a hat. She let it plop to the floor and began to plug the wound with cotton wool.

"Looks like a used French letter," Corrigan said.

Rachel felt her cheeks blossom scarlet but she kept her head down and kept working. A small moth with feathery wings, attracted by the light from the lamp, fluttered into the wound, its body making a tiny plopping sound. She carefully extracted it with the forceps.

"He'll be crapping butterflies for a week," Corrigan commented.

A muscle in the man's arm twitched. He groaned softly.

Corrigan tipped a few more drops of ether on to the gauze and held it over the man's face.

"Don't leave the top off that bottle," Rachel warned him. "The lamp will ignite the fumes. You'll blow us all up."

Corrigan scowled but did as he was told. "A lot of fuss over one blackbird."

"When you cut into a man's body like this, Mister Corrigan, you cannot fail to notice that it is blood and gristle and bone, the same as any white man. Moreover you can never cut away a man's courage, or his virtue, or his love. These are things of the spirit. It seems to me the important things in a man are those things you cannot see. His character, and his soul."

"I had a dog with character once. He's dead just the same. Anyway it's all right for you to harp on about us all being equal underneath. I saw the way you looked at Sanei."

Rachel felt herself blush. She didn't answer.

She knew he was right; or at least he had part of the truth. There was something in her prim English soul that rebelled at the thought of a white man living with a native. It was a reflex action of her upbringing.

But she had felt something else, also. Recently she

had become fascinated with the illicit; or as her uncle would have put it, "lured by the powerful seduction of sin". Like Sodom for Lot's wife, looking at Sanei held an almost hypnotic attraction for her, beyond her own understanding.

She lowered her eyes, feeling Corrigan watching her. She tried to put everything else out of her mind and concentrated on her work.

It was almost dawn when she put the final stitches in the wound. A pale yellow light crept into the hut.

"He is in God's hands now," she whispered, cutting through the catgut with shiny steel scissors.

Corrigan ran a hand across his face, tasting the bitter residue of tiredness and nausea and stale gin. There was a cold, clammy sweat on his forehead. "I'm glad that's over," he murmured. "First time I've ever seen an operation."

Rachel smiled a thin, tired smile. "If you must know, Mister Corrigan, it's the first time I've ever performed one."

5

It was past noon when Corrigan was sufficiently recovered from the previous night's experiences to pilot the *Shamrock* back to Vancoro. Rachel promised the villagers that her uncle would return in about a week to check on Kumasi's progress. The old man was still alive, but privately Rachel held out little hope.

Still, she had done all that she could.

She sat silently in the rear of the launch watching Corrigan's fumbled attempts to start the engine. The rains had gone, and it was a fine, blue day. The waters of the lagoon were a deep sparkling green, and a warm breeze drifted across the bay from the ocean.

Portuguese men o'war drifted past, fat and jelly-soft on the starboard side. On the shore Rachel could make out the bright plumage of parrots among the dull green of the shoreline.

Finally the *Shamrock*'s engine coughed twice, then hammered into a steady rhythm, shattering the blue silence of the lagoon. The single screw throbbed and bubbled beneath the stern. Corrigan hauled up the anchor from the sandy bottom of the lagoon and turned the *Shamrock* back towards the ocean.

"How long will it take us to reach Vancoro?"

Corrigan regarded her out of bloodshot eyes. "About three hours in this weather."

"Thank you."

Corrigan leaned over the wheel, and guided the *Shamrock* out to sea. Occasionally he stole a sly glance back over his shoulder. By Christ, she really wasn't a bad-looking woman. Good skin, pretty oval face. If she took her hair out of that ridiculous bun she would probably be a real head-turner. Corrigan wondered why she made such a concerted effort at making herself look plain.

He tried to imagine what she would look like naked. Impossible to tell really. He let his eyes slip to her ankles. Nice slim ankles but a bit puffy and red where the mosquitoes had fed on those blue English veins. But they really weren't bad.

He shook his head. Pity she was such a notorious virgin.

It wasn't that men hadn't tried. One of the pearling captains had told him last year that he'd been invited to the Mission for dinner with Father Goode and his niece. While the priest had spent most of the evening trying to lure the recalcitrant seaman back to the fold, he had taken advantage of a few moments alone with Rachel to try and lure her back to his lugger.

The attempt had been a disaster and Father Goode had sent him on his way before he had time to finish his coffee.

Corrigan smiled ruefully. She saw him and gave him a puzzled look. Corrigan turned his gaze back towards the ocean.

It was a magnificent day: the sea stretched out in front of them, a sparkling flat horizon, the islets and atolls small bulges on the calm, flat surface. The smell of salt mingled with the diesel fumes, and from the land the wind carried the warm tropic smell of decaying fruit.

The hot sun dominated the cloudless sky; a school of dolphins played round the bows as the boat cut through the sparkling blue waters and the surface of the ocean was only disturbed by the sudden darting movements of the flying fish. Seabirds glided on the air currents high above.

After a while Rachel got up and came to stand beside Corrigan at the helm.

"I would like to thank you," she said.

Corrigan shrugged. "What for?"

"You helped save a man's life."

"If you say so. Don't forget you owe me two quid."

"You know it amazes me why a man such as yourself should insist on debilitating himself with alcohol. I'm sure with a little discipline you could learn to live a good and useful life."

"Is that so?" Corrigan pushed the long lock of hair out of his eyes and turned his head away to hide his frown of irritation.

"Yes, I believe it is 'so'. In fact Mister Corrigan . . ."

Rachel never got to finish her sentence. Suddenly the engine coughed and the *Shamrock* veered violently to port. Rachel fell sideways against the side of the cockpit. Corrigan switched off the motor and ran to the stern.

Rachel clambered to her feet. "What's wrong?"

"How the fuck do I know?"

Rachel felt her throat tighten. It was as if he had struck

her. She couldn't help but feel an almost physical agony whenever he used one of his vile oaths.

Corrigan was leaning out over the stern. "Have to go down and have a look I reckon." He started to strip off his clothes.

Rachel watched him.

She was no stranger to the human body. She had seen men naked before, lying quiescent on the operating table or in a hospital bed, between dank wet sheets, struggling in the throes of malaria or blackwater fever. She was even more used to the black natives on the island, who seldom wore anything more than a simple *lava-lava*, the sarong of the islands.

But suddenly she was shocked and frightened as Corrigan pulled the cotton shirt over his head. She realised she had never been alone with a man who was not fully dressed and the sexual potential of the situation hit her like a body blow.

His body was tanned a deep mahogany brown, his arms and chest covered with a thick mass of black curls. She had imagined the years of drinking had left him flabby and wasted but his body was hard and corded with muscle.

She felt a sudden and bewildering desire to reach out and touch him.

She was almost overwhelmed with her own shame. A dizzy well-spring of excitement seemed to overflow inside her and her throat tightened. She felt confused and she leaned back on the gunwale, no longer trusting her own legs to support her.

Corrigan looked round at her and smiled, a slow knowing smile as if he could read her thoughts. "Better keep my trousers on," he grinned. "Don't want to dazzle you with all my glory."

He stepped back towards the gunwale.

"Be careful," Rachel said. "I'll say a quick prayer if you like."

"I'd rather you kept a good lookout for sharks."

He put his legs over the stern of the launch and lowered

himself gently into the sparkling warm water. He took a lungful of air and with a surprising fluidity of movement he dived for the bottom, his feet rising briefly as he executed a perfect duck dive. Then he was gone.

Rachel stood by the stern, watching his dark body through the clear green of the water, and squinting against the glare. A rash of white bubbles sparkled and broke on the surface.

After about a minute he came to the surface, gulping deep lungfuls of air. His thick black hair was matted across his forehead.

"What is it?"

"Piece of vine tangled round the screw," Corrigan said. He took another breath of air and dived again.

Rachel rubbed her eyes. They were already sore from squinting into the bright sun reflecting on the water. It was when she refocused them that she saw the shark.

The dark shadow cut swiftly through the water on the port side, fifteen or twenty feet below the surface. At first she thought she had imagined it; but then it re-appeared on the starboard side, impossibly huge and menacing. For a moment she tried to persuade herself it might be a dolphin or a porpoise, but as it circled again she glimpsed the prehistoric and unmistakeable snout of the hammerhead and it was as if her heart stopped in her chest. For a few moments all she could do was watch it with horrified fascination.

The hammerhead was perhaps twelve or fifteen feet in length, a big one. It was still circling the stern of the boat, sensing Corrigan's movements in the water. It circled again, closer this time.

"Shark!" Rachel yelled and began to paddle frantically at the water with both hands, trying to warn Corrigan of the approaching danger.

The shark felt the panicked vibrations in the water and it began to get excited. It circled again, even closer.

Rachel stumbled to the cockpit searching for something to fend off the creature. Nothing, nothing.

Panic gripping her now, she ran back to the stern in time to watch the shark veer towards the *Shamrock*, its fin and the sweep of its tail breaking the surface as it came.

"Mister Corrigan! There's a shark! For God's sake, Mister Corrigan!" Again she paddled frantically at the water. A few feet below her she could see him working at the tangled propeller with his knife, unaware of the approaching fish.

The first warning Corrigan had was a sudden motion in the water around him, and a large dark shape passed very close. Then he saw it, the grey rubbery skin and the distinctive monstrous head, with its extended lobes and small evil eyes searching the blue mist of the water.

As it came in for its pass the shark swerved away suddenly, confused by the dark shadow of the boat and the smaller shadow of the man. It circled again, cautiously.

Corrigan did not panic. He knew that sharks were cowards unless there was blood in the water. But they were also unpredictable. Although they would usually only prey on the sick or the injured, perhaps one in a hundred might attack suddenly and without reason.

Suddenly it nosed towards him again. Frightened now, Corrigan kicked out at it, the heel of his foot connecting with the fish's sensitive nose. Usually that was enough to scare any shark away, at least long enough to get out of the water. But this one just twisted its head and came again.

He kicked urgently for the surface.

On the surface Rachel saw him come, watched helpless as the long grey body of the shark arrowed towards him.

"Grab my hand!"

She leaned over the stern to clutch at his arms as he surfaced in a boil of foam. Half his body came out of the water; in one fluid movement he grabbed her hand, and Rachel almost tumbled into the water with him. But with his other hand Corrigan clawed on to the stern, scrabbling wildly at the woodwork with his fingers as he lunged upward with his right leg.

As Rachel fell backwards she saw the shark come half out of the water, its long grey body shimmering with water, the slit of its jaws gaping open, revealing the rows upon rows of razor-sharp teeth, glistening and bone-white. She glimpsed the black staring eye, cold and evil at the end of that obscene truncated head.

The terrible jaws snapped shut like a steel trap and the *Shamrock* juddered as the shark's massive body struck the hull. There was an angry splash as it fell back into the water.

Then her head hit the deck and she lay on her back, stunned.

She couldn't breathe.

Corrigan's huge bulk lay on top of her; his body was trembling and the breath raked into his lungs in long, agonised gasps. Suddenly he opened his eyes and she found herself staring at him, her face just inches away from his. For long moments neither of them moved.

She looked into his eyes and she was shocked by the sudden intimacy of the moment. She could never remember being this close to another human being. The sudden moment of fear and release left her feeling small and broken. She wanted to hug him.

It was Corrigan who broke the spell. He grinned at her. "Bet that's the first time you've had a man on top of you," he said.

Rachel struggled to her feet, the front of her dress was dripping wet. Inexplicably, she felt humiliated and betrayed.

"You imbecile," she hissed and went to sit huddled and trembling in the cockpit.

The hammerhead circled the *Shamrock* for almost two hours. With the vine tangled around the propeller head, they were effectively stranded, drifting south-east with the current. Corrigan faced the situation stoically. He returned from below deck with another bottle of gin, propped himself up in the stern and began to drink.

The sun was low over the darkening ocean when the shark finally cruised off in search of easier game. At last Corrigan decided it was safe to venture back into the water; it took him just a few minutes to free the propeller shaft from the remains of the vine.

Still dripping wet, Corrigan started up the engines and the *Shamrock* chopped through the sea towards the mountains of Santa Maria, now many miles to the south.

The first stars had appeared on the eastern horizon when the throb of the motors finally changed to a rhythmic *thump-thump* as they entered a small deserted bay, fringed with palms.

"Where are we, Mister Corrigan?" Rachel said.

Corrigan scratched at the mosquito bites on the back of his neck. "About ten miles north of Vancoro. That shark cost us two hours and had us drifting nearly up to Sara Passage. No way we'll get back to Vancoro now."

"But we must. My uncle will be worried."

"I'm not trying to get through the reefs in the dark. We'll stay here tonight. If we get an early start you can be back home before breakfast."

Rachel felt a twinge of fear in the pit of her stomach at the thought of spending a night alone with this man.

"But I can't," she said weakly.

"Got no choice. Come on, cheer up. There's no food but we've got another two bottles of gin. You can have a drink and loosen up a bit."

A few minutes later the sun set behind the vast expanse of the Pacific Ocean, leaving only the silhouettes of distant small atolls silhouetted against a lucent mother-of-pearl sky. The clouds on the horizon changed from pink to brilliant saffron, finally fading to a deep purple.

In a few more moments the sky had darkened to molten lead; and the sudden night of the tropics engulfed the *Shamrock*.

Corrigan swung the launch close into the shore, and

dropped the anchor off the bows. Then he clambered back and turned off the motors. He lit the mantle on the gas lamp and swung round to face her. He was grinning.

"Well, this is it, Miss Goode. Your first night alone with a man."

Rachel felt the colour go out of her cheeks. He was grinning at her like a satyr. She felt a terror she had not known since the night she had been orphaned. It was night and she was utterly alone.

She knew why they weren't going to Vancoro. It was obvious to her now.

Corrigan was inflamed with lust. She shouldn't have allowed him to lie on top of her like that. Her uncle had been right about him all along. He was incorrigible, a man with no moral sense at all.

She was totally at his mercy. There was no doubt in her mind what his intentions were.

He was going to rape her.

6

Ian McLaren Manning stood with both hands gripping the teak rail of the schooner *Tulagi*, staring out across the water at the mountains of Santa Maria. The warm monsoon wind ruffled his thinning light brown hair, and stirred the Solomons Protectorate flag that hung from the mast at the stern.

The District Officer for Santa Maria was a slightly built man in his late thirties. In England he had suffered continuous bronchial and respiratory problems; his posting to the Pacific had probably saved his life. He took deep lungfuls of the salt air as he searched the dark green line of coast for the entrance to Vancoro harbour.

The sea was flat, docile; but then, without warning, uprushing water pushed the *Tulagi* off course, spray crashing over the bows from a calm sea. Broken, precipitous cliffs, many fathoms down, produced unpredictable overflows and whirlpools here. To westward gouts of water leaped and crashed back into the sea. Closer on the port side, two flat outcrops of rock caused a sudden sucking, surging tide as the *Tulagi*'s master tacked away to starboard.

These were the Admiralty Rocks; two pinnacles of rock that had been blasted below the waterline after a number of gunnery exercises on one of His Majesty's warships. Scarcely visible even in daylight, they now presented an horrendous hazard to everything passing in and out of Vancoro.

Jackie Su'a, the schooner's captain, took the *Tulagi* on a course to the north-east. The long sleek schooner tacked into the wind, reaching the southern point of the island, pushed westwards by the current. Jackie shouted orders to one of the deckhands, and they tacked hard again, the huge boom creaking and groaning in the wind.

Just as the oily swell of the tide race seemed to be pushing them towards the hungry white coral and booming breakers off the point of the island an opposing current suddenly caught the *Tulagi* and pushed them eastwards.

It was a deadly game of wind and currents that every vessel entering the harbour was forced to play.

Suddenly they were in calm water again, steering leisurely for the natural harbour of Vancoro to the north; it was the largest settlement and also the District Station on Santa Maria. The *Tulagi* tacked inside the shelter of the harbour, with its strip of white beach, the palm fronds gracefully waving a welcome in the rush of the north-west monsoon.

Jackie brought the *Tulagi* in to follow the passage between the two reefs.

The wide harbour of Vancoro opened in front of them, a natural formation surrounded on either side by forested headlands. They passed the rotting hulk of the *Bellama*, the skeleton of another government schooner wrecked long ago on the treacherous reefs.

It was hard to believe this quiet backwater of the world might soon be torn apart by the thunder of guns.

The news was not good. The Japanese had overrun the Malay Peninsula and stood at the gates of Singapore itself. If Singapore fell . . . but that was impossible. Churchill himself had said she was impregnable.

Manning stared moodily at the water and mourned for England. In Europe the Germans held dominion of all of Western Europe, their guns pointed towards the Dover cliffs, Heinkels flying nightly sorties over the English coast. The beaches of Brighton were covered with barbed wire, the lights of London blacked out. It seemed somehow surreal, a nightmare of fantastic proportions.

His hands tightened on the rail. He felt a sharp pang of regret. They had told him he was too old to fight. The last time he had been too young.

He loathed his weakness; loathed his thin, frail body. He loathed it as a boy, too frail for football and athletics; he had hated it as he stood in front of the mirror as a pimply youth; he despised it as a man, when the frequent bouts of illness incapacitated him.

Now in time, he had come to despise himself. A middle-aged bachelor on a forgotten island. A wasted life.

To the north he saw the familiar outlines of the settlement. The stone prison building, standing high and alone on the northern promontory, its bare limestone walls stark against the green backdrop of the jungle; the mariners used it as a leading mark.

Below it, among the casuarina trees, he could make out the red-roofed bungalow of the Protectorate building, the white painted walls in vivid contrast to the lush green of the bay. On the small patch of brown stunted lawn a few yards from the front steps stood a white-painted flagstaff. From it, a Union Jack fluttered in the breeze.

As they sailed past the headland the rest of Vancoro came into view; first the police barracks and the trading store and beyond them, almost hidden among the coconut palms, the thatched roofs of the village itself.

A long jetty ran out from the shore, and a corporal and two native constables were drawn up to attention on the landing stage. With them was another figure, all too familiar in his white collar and black soutane, the crucifix at his neck glinting in the sunlight.

Manning groaned. He had been looking forward to a cold shower and a cold beer. He knew the appearance of Father Goode would change those plans.

Jackie Su'a brought the *Tulagi* round in a sweet curve, docking her gently alongside the wharf. At a roar from the corporal the waiting constables brought their rifles clumsily to slope. At another roar they saluted, executing a ragged present arms.

Manning drew himself up to his full height and watched Goode climb aboard. He took a deep breath and waited.

"Manning," Goode said, his voice shaky with emotion. "Thank God you're back."

"Whatever's wrong, old chap? You're as pale as a ghost."

"It's my niece," the priest said, "the most terrible thing's happened. She's been murdered. Raped and murdered."

7

By the time Corrigan weighed anchor a velvet blackness had fallen over the Pacific. He clambered over the side of the boat and Rachel heard a splash as he dropped into the water.

"Are you getting out of the boat, lady?" Corrigan said.

"I think I shall stay here," Rachel said, huddled in the cockpit.

Corrigan muttered something she couldn't quite hear and then he waded away in the darkness.

Rachel drew her knees up to her chest and shivered. She looked up at the gathering cluster of stars and the moon, very silver and very large, rising over the ocean.

A full moon, she thought, and trembled.

After a while she saw a small fire glowing on the beach. The rocking motion of the boat was making her nauseous. The fire seemed warm and inviting. She knew if she stayed where she was she would be violently ill.

She spent long minutes trying to make up her mind what to do. She felt safe on the boat. If she went ashore she was at Corrigan's mercy. On the other hand some forms of death are preferable to seasickness.

Still she hesitated. Finally the decision was made for her. She heard Corrigan again wading towards the boat. She huddled further into the shadows of the boat and listened to the splashing of the water as Corrigan reached the side of the *Shamrock*.

"Lady?"

"What do you want?" Her voice sounded shrill and taut. She saw one of Corrigan's hands grip the edge of the boat. It seemed unusually hairy in the moonlight. Suddenly a pair of eyes, cold and evil, stared at her.

"Pass me the other bottle of grog."

"I don't think you ought to drink any more."

There was silence. Corrigan's hand slipped on the edge of the boat and for a moment he disappeared. The boat rocked again as he pulled himself up to the gunwales.

"I don't want another lecture on the evils of drink. I want the bottle. Are you going to give it here or do I have to get it myself?"

Rachel decided not to infuriate him. God knows what a man would do for liquor. She went to the cockpit and found the other square-faced bottle, resisting an impulse to fling it into the sea. She handed it to him.

"Are you staying here?"

"No. I think I shall come to the beach now," she said. If the worst came to the worst she could make a run for it.

Gripping her skirt tightly at the knees she sat on the gunwales and tried to swing her legs over the edge without parting her ankles. Corrigan reached up and offered her his hand.

"I can manage, thank you."

"Suit your bloody self."

He began to wade back to the beach.

Rachel tried to swing her left ankle over the side of the boat but a seam of her dress caught on a rough nail and she toppled headlong into the water.

Corrigan threw back his head and guffawed.

"You ought to take those wet clothes off."

"I'm all right," Rachel said huddled by the fire. "I'm not cold."

She shivered, her teeth making chattering noises in the darkness.

Corrigan shrugged, muttering darkly to himself. He smelled of sea salt and gin; a strong masculine smell she found somehow terrifying and yet strangely compelling. His presence filled her with bewildering emotions. She was terrified of his size, and his strength; yet something in her found that strength strangely reassuring.

Her thoughts confused her. She tried not to think.

Corrigan unscrewed the cap from the bottle of Gilbey's and put it to his lips. He threw back his head and took a long pull. He wiped his mouth on the back of his hand, and drew a grubby sleeve across the lip of the bottle.

"Here, have a belt. This will warm you up."

"No thank you." He was trying to get her drunk.

"Medicinal purposes. You'll catch your death otherwise."

Rachel hesitated. She was cold and very hungry. A tiny drop wouldn't hurt. She hesitated, then reached out and took the bottle from him. She sniffed. It smelled foul. She put the bottle to her lips and tipped it back. Suddenly her mouth and throat were full of the strong, burning liquid. She gasped, and tried to spit it out but the vile stuff was already inside her. She stood up, gasping for air. "Oh . . . oh!"

"Careful!" Corrigan said. He made a grab for the bottle, before it dropped from her grasp into the sand. He waited till Rachel's coughing fit subsided and then gave her a rough slap on the shoulder. "Bit better than Communion wine, eh?"

It was getting cold. The wet calico clung to her skin, and the small warmth of the fire had done nothing to dry her out. The effects of the gin were wearing off. She had not meant to have any more after that first dreadful mouthful. It had tasted vile, but it had warmed her a little and Corrigan had persuaded her to take several more mouthfuls.

Corrigan was watching her, but she couldn't quite fathom his expression in the dim glow of the fire. The gin bottle was cradled in his arms like a baby.

"I think I'll find a place to sleep," Rachel said.

"Kip down here," Corrigan said. "It's as good a place as any. You can get under a blanket with me, if you like. I'll warm you up."

She bit her lip, and her fingers tightened on the blanket clasped around her. She tried to speak but her voice caught in her throat. She had to show him she wasn't afraid.

She got to her feet and staggered sideways against the trunk of a palm. She realised with horror that the gin had made her a little drunk. She wasn't used to strong drink.

Corrigan got up to help her. "I can manage," Rachel told him.

"So you keep saying."

She turned and made her way back along the beach. The silver flecked surf raced up the strand towards her, swallowing her footprints. She had never felt so totally alone.

She tottered fifty yards further along the sand. She looked back. This was probably far enough. Even her uncle would have approved. She huddled against the bole of a coconut palm, and drew the thin blanket over her.

It was so cold . . .

Her uncle's God, which had often seemed so irrelevant to her in recent months, took on a new significance. She began to pray.

From where she lay she could just make out the bulky shape of Corrigan as he sat by the fire, the gin bottle nestled in the sand next to him. He was rolling a cigarette. Occasionally he would look towards the spot where she sat and shake his head, stirring the coals of the fire with a stick.

The sound of his mumbled curses drifted to her on the night air, a low growling sound, like the chanting of a pagan rite. A gust of wind made the flames flicker suddenly, illuminating his face with burned amber, making it appear suddenly dark and satanic. She made up her mind to stay awake that whole night. Whatever happened, he would not find her sleeping.

She remembered again that morning outside the church when they had found him with Mary. The way Mary had looked, her face contorted that way . . . it was horrible, of course, but . . . she closed her eyes trying to chase the image from her mind.

She wished she had never seen it. It had haunted her ever since, a disturbing, shocking, exciting vision.

She heard a noise. Corrigan had got to his feet and now he was walking towards her, staggering slightly. Her breath caught in her throat.

She felt her cheeks flush hot as she remembered the strength of him when he had lifted her out of the boat at

Marmari. And those thick cords of muscle on his arms and chest when he had stripped off his shirt. She realised she could never fight him off. She was utterly helpless.

She wanted to run, but her legs refused to respond. He was getting closer now. Already Rachel began to compose the litany she would recite to her uncle when she reached Vancoro.

"He crept up on me while I was asleep. There was nothing I could do. I tried to fight him off but he was too strong. There was nothing I could do . . ."

Corrigan was standing over her, he seemed like a giant from where she lay, his silhouette blocking out the moon. "Are you cold?" he said.

"No, I'm all right." Her voice caught in her throat.

He squatted down next to her in the sand. "You don't want to sleep here all alone. Here, snuggle up next to me."

Rachel didn't trust her voice not to betray her terror at that moment. She didn't speak, didn't move.

His hand reached out for her. "It's not right for a beautiful girl like you to hide yourself away all the time. It's that bloody uncle of yours, isn't it? Well you don't have to worry now. He'll never know. How about a little kiss?"

"Mister Corrigan . . ."

Suddenly it was as if she had touched a live electric current. She felt his hand squeeze her breast and she gasped with shock and surprise and then she heard a sharp slap.

Oh, my God. She had hit him. She hadn't meant to, it was almost a reflex action. She gasped at her own audacity and shrank away from him, terrified.

"What did you do that for?" He sounded genuinely surprised.

"Please go away," she heard herself say.

Corrigan sighed. "Well, suit yourself. I've never forced myself on any woman that didn't want to," he said. He stood up, staggering slightly. "You're a bloody strange one, and no mistake."

He turned away. She heard his footfall in the darkness, the soft squeaking of the sand under his bare feet. Rachel stared after him, her whole body shaking uncontrollably.

The fire Corrigan had built further up the beach had burned down to a few embers. He kicked sand over the ashes, then bent down and picked up his blanket. He looked back up the beach towards her, muttering darkly to himself.

And then he started to come back.

Rachel felt her breath catch in her throat. What now? He had the blanket trailing behind him in the sand. Perhaps he intended to rape her and then smother her with the blanket so she could never tell anyone what he had done to her.

Her right hand clawed into the soft sand around her and closed around a large rock. It felt reassuringly heavy. She pulled it free of the sand and clutched it to her chest, ready. If he tried to force her, she would not give in without a good fight.

He was standing over her now, the blanket clutched in his right hand. After what seemed to her like an eternity, he leaned forward and threw it over her. "Don't get cold," he grunted, and then he trudged back up the beach.

Rachel let the rock slip out of her hand. She reached out for the blanket, and pulled it towards her, flooded with gratitude and relief. He had given her the only other blanket.

She saw Corrigan sink into the sand next to the ashes of the fire, and his dark bulk lay motionless on the sand. Rachel let her head fall back on to the sand, and she released her breath in a long, broken sigh.

Her breast still seemed to tingle from his touch. My God, Uncle Matthew would have a seizure if he ever found out what Corrigan had done. He had touched her, actually touched her breast. And so casually too. Almost as if he thought she might enjoy it. Her uncle was right. Corrigan was beyond redemption.

Relief was quickly replaced by outrage. The man had

no shame. To have actually had the temerity to suggest that she should want to . . .

She looked up at the canopy of stars above her, her heart still beating wildly in her chest, her whole body still trembling from fright and from the cold. Slowly she felt her sense of outrage ebb away, to be replaced by something else, an emotion as overpowering as it was unexpected.

Disappointment.

8

Manning sat in his office overlooking the bay and dabbed at his face with the handtowel he wore at his neck. Beads of perspiration shone like small gems on his upper lip. He listened to Father Goode's plaintive appeals with increasing frustration, his fingers drumming irritably on the desk top.

For two days and nights he had sat on the *Tulagi* in Kia lagoon writing receipts by lamplight until two o'clock in the morning, the decks of the sloop littered with scraps of paper and cloth and the lengths of fibre and fish twine with which the coin was packed away. Some of the natives had to travel huge distances to pay the tax money so he had received them at whatever time they had arrived, as they paddled alongside the government schooner in their canoes.

It had been a long trip. The *Tulagi* had pitched and swayed before the persistent north-west winds and Manning was wet, tired and burned by the sun. His nose had begun to peel.

"Wait a minute, old boy," he said at last, leaning back in his chair and tucking his hands behind his head. "There's no basis for these allegations you know. It's possible his launch has broken down."

Father Goode fixed his black pulpit eyes on Manning with an expression of scorn. "Then why haven't they sent a native back in a *kedi* for help?" He sat back in his chair with the air of an attorney who has produced the final damning piece of evidence. "No, I tell you he has raped her. Raped her and fed her body to the sharks!"

"Steady on, old chap."

Father Goode's eyes burned with messianic fervour. "Mister Manning, we all know the sort of man that Corrigan is."

"Yes, I'm aware of his proclivities, but that doesn't make the chap a criminal."

The priest brought his fist down on the desk, tapping out the rhythm of his reply. "A man who will rape a defenceless woman will not stop at murder."

"If you're referring to Mary, I don't think she was an entirely unwilling partner in the act."

A fleck of spittle appeared at the corner of the priest's mouth. "I gave that girl Holy Communion. I received her into the Holy Spirit myself. I tell you it was rape!"

"Well, if you can show me how a woman can be taken against her will on six separate occasions, old boy, I'll agree with you."

"I expect you to do your duty, Mister Manning."

Manning raised his eyebrows in an expression of mild surprise. "Oh yes?"

"You must go to Marmari straight away on the *Tulagi*. There may still be time."

Manning nodded and sucked thoughtfully on his front teeth. He was surprised to find his arm balled into a fist on the arm of his chair. He unclenched it and placed it carefully on the table in front of him as if he was unloading a gun. "Well, I shall certainly do that, old boy. As soon as the weather improves."

Father Goode dabbed impatiently at the perspiration on his forehead. "The weather's perfect."

Manning waved his hand lazily in the direction of the verandah. "Have a look, old boy."

The priest got up and went to the door of the bungalow. On the horizon a line of ink-black clouds were moving in swiftly from the north-west, the towering black anvils ominous against the blue sky.

Manning came and stood next to him. "Looks like we're in for a drop more rain, don't you think?"

When Rachel opened her eyes it was broad daylight. She sat up with a start, her heart hammering in her chest.

Her head ached. She felt suddenly nauseous and tiny droplets of sweat broke on her forehead. There was a mild but persistent drumming inside her skull. Then she remembered with a flush of guilt: the gin!

She looked down the beach. Empty. Where was Corrigan?

A few minutes later he stumbled out of the forest; he was carrying a large bunch of bananas.

Rachel's breath caught in her throat when she saw him. It was not just the memory of last night; he had been for a swim, and he was still stripped to the waist, the water still clinging to his body, like tiny sparkling jewels on a mahogany chest. His hair was wet, and the errant comma of hair hung rakishly over one eye. He grinned at her. She had to admit to herself that for a satyr and a moral reprobate, he was an uncommonly fine specimen of a man. "You all right?"

Rachel shook her head. "I think I have a touch of fever."

Corrigan laughed. "Hangover more like."

"A hangover?"

"Your sainted uncle would have a fit, wouldn't he? Here – want a banana?"

Rachel shook her head, feeling her gorge rise at the thought of food. She watched as Corrigan tore a banana off the bunch and began to peel off the thick yellow skin. He seemed cheerful and relaxed; it was as if the previous night had not happened. Or perhaps he has already forgotten, she thought. A man like Corrigan would not think of the incident as any more than a minor hiccough in a long sequence of sin.

"What are you looking at?"

She held up one of the blankets. "Thank you for the blanket."

"I didn't need it. It was a hot night," he lied. "Want a drink? There's fresh water in the boat."

"Yes, please."

"All right," he said. She watched him trudge down the beach to the waterline and felt a pang of regret. It was such a waste. Despite what her uncle said, Mister Corrigan did have some very fine qualities.

They had been at sea less than an hour when Corrigan went to the bow, squinting against the glare of the harsh sun. "See that," he said.

Rachel followed the line of his finger. "A storm?"

"Looks a long way off now but it could be on us in half an hour."

It hung just above the horizon, funereal and sinister, an ominous black border around the blue morning sky.

"I'd say a big wind was on the way," Corrigan said. "*Komburu*. The wild wind from the north-west. I don't want to be out on the open sea when it comes. We'd better get moving."

It came suddenly, like the tropic night, the towering anvils of the storm clouds passing over the sun while it was still rising in the sky. The shadows raced towards them over the open sea, turning the ocean to the colour of molten lead.

Whitecaps began to appear as the storm advanced, whipping salt spray on to the windshield of the cockpit.

"Better hang on to that fancy hat of yours," Corrigan said.

A sudden gust of wind whined in the antenna of the

mast, rattling the wires, and a huge wave struck the bows, sending a fierce shudder through the *Shamrock*.

"Shouldn't we radio a mayday call?" Rachel said.

"We could if the radio worked," Corrigan said. "Not that it would do any good."

Another wave crashed over the bows, and the *Shamrock* lurched heavily in the water. There was a low growl of thunder overhead, as menacing as the roar of a tiger in the night. The *Shamrock* staggered on through the mounting waves, as the first spots of rain began to splatter on the windshield among the crusted salt.

"Tie this round your waist," Corrigan said, grabbing two coils of thick rope from the deck and throwing one at Rachel. He looped the other rope around himself, and lashed them both to the wheel.

A huge wave broke on to the bows and the *Shamrock* shuddered in dismay, before staggering on to meet the next onrushing wave. Under the howling fury of the wind the calm blue of the ocean had been transformed into a grey churning monster in just a few minutes. The sea was breaking over the small boat now with such force that it was driving the bows under in a boiling spray of white foam, blanketing out the sky so that for long moments the world became a huge terrifying wall of water before the tiny launch picked up her nose to plunge upwards through the next crest.

"You still reckon this God of yours is any good?" Corrigan shouted.

Rachel's face was grey-white in the eerie twilight of the storm. "Do you want me to say a prayer, Mister Corrigan?"

"Yeah, you'd better," Corrigan shouted back, as spray from the next wave smashed against the windshield, "and you'd better make it a bloody good one."

It was dark now, the sun blotted out by thick black cloud, the whitecaps glowing like phosphorous. Time was measured by the instants between each wave; the few precious seconds in the troughs of the breakers as Corrigan fought to turn the bows back into the waves before the terrible crashing thunder of the sea could smash over them and turn the *Shamrock* on to its keel.

Each time it seemed the next wave would surely tip them over, but somehow the *Shamrock* would come straining out of the sea with foam spuming from its bows, creaking and groaning under the weight of the water pouring over the gunwales.

They were ankle deep in seawater now. Rachel gripped the rail in front of her in terror, her knuckles almost translucent through her wet skin. Another wave crashed over them and for a moment the raging sea covered the decks. It seemed like an eternity before the *Shamrock* finally recovered and pushed up through the next crest.

"Where's that God of yours now, Miss Goode?" Corrigan roared and threw back his head and laughed like a madman.

The mountains of Santa Maria were very close; they could make them out huge and black between the breaks in the cloud.

The pumps were useless now. Corrigan had Rachel bale frantically with an old treacle tin, a futile, desperate gesture Corrigan knew, but it helped to take her mind off the fear. She worked beside him feverishly with chilled and trembling hands.

Corrigan looked anxiously for the Admiralty Rocks; he sensed they were very close. So far the plucky little *Shamrock* had weathered the storm, but the worst was to come as they made their dash for Vancoro harbour. The tell-tale spray of the rocks was lost in the angry lather of the sea. Another swell slid beneath them, and the mountains of Santa Maria were lost from view.

Then he heard them; under the howling wind he could make out another sound, deep and regular, like cannon fire. The Admiralty Rocks! But where, where?

He strained his eyes against the gloom and the driving rain. The sea towered around them like a massive grey wall, limiting vision to no more than fifty yards. The booming of the reef was closer now.

Christ, Corrigan thought. We're almost on top of them!

The *Shamrock* was suddenly thrust high on the top of a swell; and in that instant the lightning flashed, a jagged fork that speared into the horizon in the south-west. He saw them then, the slippery grey rocks and the high fountain of surf around them, just a hundred yards ahead of them. Then they were gone, hidden once more behind the walls of boiling grey sea.

Instinctively Corrigan threw the *Shamrock* to starboard, not daring to turn too hard and take the next wave side on. The long swell passed under them and then they were cascading down the lee of the wave into a huge trough.

"Dear Jesus!" Rachel yelled, sprawling headlong on to the deck.

Corrigan saw the gleaming grey jaws of the reef slide by the port gunwales almost close enough to touch. Then the next wave crashed over them and the *Shamrock* rocked and shuddered up the face of it. Corrigan fought to hold the rudder steady, expecting any moment to feel the terrible crunching of jagged rock tearing open the hull.

Now!

Corrigan held his breath.

Suddenly they were pitching and sliding down the next swell and Corrigan turned and saw the spray from the rocks slide by behind them.

They'd made it. They were through.

But he still had to find the passage through the harbour mouth.

He brought the *Shamrock* about in the lee of the island, and for a few moments the tiny launch rolled on the swell. It was a brief and blessed relief from the hammering of the waves. Then the surf picked them up and they were hurled forwards by the tremendous following seas, the bows singing up through the spray as the crests passed beneath her.

They swept past the southerly part of the island, carried

along in the monster jaws of the storm. Corrigan waited for a moment's lull in the seas, then took her around again to go with the current into the harbour mouth.

But the *Shamrock* was heavy with water now. She responded too slowly.

In a few seconds, the surf rushed over her, plunging into the cockpit and foredeck, turning the launch on its beam.

Corrigan heard a scream as Rachel was hit by the rushing wall of water, and his own cramped fingers hooked around the wheel as the *Shamrock* was swamped over on to her port flanks.

"This is it," Corrigan thought. "We're going over. We've had it."

But then the swell dipped beneath them and the *Shamrock* struggled upright again, like a bull in the corrida, refusing to die.

"That's a girl!" Corrigan shouted. "Never knew a woman yet who wasn't a fighty little bitch at heart!"

He laughed in triumph and looked around for Rachel.

But the cockpit was empty.

She was gone.

Rachel hit the water on her stomach, with a stunning ferocity that hammered the breath out of her. Almost at once the sudden silence of the sea rushed over her. She surfaced choking and gagging. The first thing she saw was the *Shamrock*, its stern wallowing in the foaming seas, turning to face the next onrushing wave.

She tried to swim towards it but it was useless. She felt the current begin to drag her under, sucking at the long wet calico of her dress. It was impossible to fight it. She didn't have the strength left in her arms.

She thought of Lake Windermere. Was this what it was like for her father and mother? Then the water flooded into her mouth and in the terror of near-death she made a last final effort to reach the surface.

For a moment she broke free of the sucking, clinging

water but then another wave broke over her head and she knew she was beaten. "God have mercy on my soul," she prayed silently, and she gave herself up to the raging sea.

9

Rachel felt the strain at the rope at her waist, dragging her up through the water. Suddenly she was gulping the sweet air into her agonised lungs, and through the mists of the suffocating pain she saw Corrigan, one hand on the wheel, the other pulling at the lifeline, hauling her back towards the boat.

She was just a few feet away from the *Shamrock* now. She slapped ineffectually at the water with exhausted limbs as Corrigan dragged her back towards the starboard gunwale.

"Grab the rail, you bloody woman!" he roared.

Somehow Rachel was able to close her fingers around one of the steel rails. She felt herself being pulled out of the water. She fastened her other hand round the gunwales and pulled, rolling on to the deck of the launch with a jarring lurch. Painfully she crawled back into the cockpit, and lay gasping on the flooded decking, choking seawater through her mouth and nose.

They were between the heads now, and the crashing of the breakers and the howling of the wind had begun to fade. Wallowing in its own bilge, the *Shamrock* limped between the reefs into Vancoro harbour.

Rachel struggled to her feet, peering out through the windshield. A fine salt spray was blanketing the headland in white gauze, but through it she could make out the tiny settlement of Vancoro.

"Thank God," she murmured. Her knees were trembling, and she had to grip on to the rail for support. She looked around at Corrigan. He was grinning.

"Well, lady, you really got your two quids' worth, didn't you?"

Rachel lay in bed in a long white cotton nightgown, fanning herself gently with a handkerchief. Her uncle sat on the bed beside her, his high forehead creased into a frown of confusion and concern. He was yet to satisfy himself that his niece's virtue remained intact; a condition he prized almost as highly as the early Christian fathers.

It was the morning after the *Shamrock* had made her surprise appearance into the storm-swept bay of Vancoro. The cyclone had swept on towards the south-east; today the islands reposed once more in the tropic sun, as if the big wind had never been.

It was sticky hot in the room, the air as thick and suffocating as warm treacle.

"You mean to say you were alone with him – all that time – and he never once tried to lay a hand on you?"

Rachel shook her head and continued to fan herself with the flimsy piece of cotton. It was a small lie; although Corrigan had tried, he had not succeeded. Well, not for more than a fleeting second, anyway.

"Let the Lord be praised," Father Goode muttered and dabbed ineffectually at the beads of perspiration on his neck and cheeks.

"Amen."

"I must say, Rachel, I find your actions ill-advised to say the least. I think you have tested the mercy of the Lord most unreasonably."

Rachel took the rebuke stoically, gazing back at him with an expression of meek contrition. "Yes, Uncle Matthew," she said.

"I shudder to think what could have happened," he said, encouraged by his niece's manner. "Mister Manning was convinced you had been murdered."

He patted her hand gently, satisfied that he had impressed on her the magnitude of her folly. "I know you did what you thought was best, and in good faith. But you fail to appreciate what sort of man Mister Corrigan is."

"Oh, but Uncle, I think you've misjudged him."

Father Goode raised an eyebrow, surprised if anything by the vehemence of her reply. "Mister Corrigan is a disgrace to the civilised community on this island and an abomination before God," he said, reciting his personal catechism.

"Oh, I know he has his faults," Rachel said mildly, and her uncle shook his head in shock at this understatement, "but deep down he is a good man. He's an uncut diamond."

Rachel sat up in her bed, her green eyes shining with sudden fervour. "If only you could have seen him during the storm," she said. "He saved my life. He was . . . magnificent."

She realised what she had said and blushed crimson. Her uncle shifted uncomfortably on the edge of the bed. His niece's faith in the inherent good of this man was disturbing.

"Your experience certainly seems to have left a deep impression on you," he observed.

He studied his niece. She had changed somehow. In what way, he couldn't be sure, but there was an indefinable something . . . her eyes shone a little brighter, there was a certain lightness of spirit that had not been there before. It was a bad sign, he was sure of it. He would have to question her further.

But at that moment the door burst open and Lelei burst into the room, her eyes wide and terrified.

"Lelei?" Father Goode said. "Whatever's wrong, girl?"

"Mastah, better come. Quick."

"What is it?"

"Mastah Corrigan. Woman b'long im she killim bad!"

Father Goode was on his feet in a moment. He rushed

to the mission steps. "Oh, my goodness," he said, uttering the strongest oath that came to his mind.

He stopped and stared. There face down on the verandah lay Patrick Corrigan. He was groaning and was surrounded by a pool of his own blood.

10

The knife had entered the flesh of Corrigan's arm just below the shoulder joint, glancing off the bone and embedding in the thick band of muscle around his upper arm. It was an ugly gaping wound two or three inches across and the flow of blood had made it seem even worse. Fortunately for Corrigan, no arteries or tendons had been severed.

Father Goode and Lelei dragged him into the Mission's medical room, where the priest cleaned the wound, injected a local anaesthetic, and begun to stitch the ragged edges of skin and muscle together.

"How did it happen, Mister Corrigan?"

"None of your damned business."

"If you wanted it to be none of my business you shouldn't have come here for me to stitch you back together."

Corrigan grunted. He was lying face down on the table, his head cradled in the crook of his right arm. Finally he said: "It was Sanei."

"A woman did this?"

"Little bitch. I'll tan her arse when I find her."

"I suppose you're not going to tell me why?"

"You suppose right."

Father Goode shook his head. He couldn't understand what good his niece could see in the man. He smelled like a wine vat. Still, he thought, the Lord rejoices more over one sinner who returns to the fold than ninety-nine others who haven't strayed away. It was his duty to try. After all, he would never have a better opportunity.

"Mister Corrigan. Have you ever thought of returning to the Christian faith?"

"No."

He decided to try another tack. "I take it you know of Heaven and Hell?"

"You've mentioned them to me before."

"Which place would you rather be?"

"I'd rather be in Heaven than in Hell."

Father Goode beamed. Now they were getting somewhere. "Ah, but you must be a Christian before you can get into Heaven."

"Is that so?"

"'If any man will come after me, let him deny himself, and take up his cross, and follow me.'"

"That's 'Matthew', isn't it?"

Father Goode stared at Corrigan in astonishment. "Mister Corrigan. I didn't know you knew the Bible."

"I had the Gospels rammed down my throat for seventeen years. My father was a very religious man."

"Then you must surely understand how important it is to live a Christian life. It is the very pathway to Heaven."

"Look, I know the pathway to Heaven. And I wish I had a glass of it right now."

Father Goode cut the last of his stitches and moved to stand in front of Corrigan. It frustrated and puzzled him why other men could not understand the basic mathematics of life. "Strong drink is not the answer, Mister Corrigan."

"That depends on the question."

Father Goode gave Corrigan a withering stare, the beetle-black eyebrows knitting in a frown of righteous anger. "Do you believe in Hell, Mister Corrigan?"

"Oh yeah, I believe in Hell all right. I reckon I know more about it than anyone who listens to you spouting your crap every Sunday."

The priest paled and swayed slightly on his feet. The blasphemy reverberated in his ears like a blast. "Mister Corrigan!"

"All you lot are the same. You talk about suffering but you don't seem to do a lot of it."

"Jesus suffered on the cross."

"Only for nine hours."

Father Goode discovered he was actually close to tears. "That's a blasphemy, Mister Corrigan," he said, his voice sounding strained and hoarse.

"Look, I reckon the islanders have got the right idea. They say a man's led a good life if he obeys his chief, respects older people, and looks after his own kind. That doesn't seem such a bad idea to me. It doesn't need all your palaver to make a good man any better. And if he's not any good, he deserves all that's coming to him, in my opinion."

"The power of God can absolve all sins."

"That's what my old man used to say. He'd come back from the church, all his sins forgiven, and lay into us with the belt again. He was a bastard, and no amount of praying and preaching ever changed that."

Father Goode shook his head. "Mister Corrigan, you are damned for all time!"

Corrigan stood up from the table. "You're probably right. In fact I know you are. And to tell you the truth, Father Goode, I reckon that's the way it ought to be."

"But Jesus loves you!"

"Then He's a bloody fool."

Father Goode's lower lip began to quiver. He felt his control slipping away. He turned on his heel and hurried out through the French windows and on to the verandah to compose himself.

Corrigan heard the rustle of cloth behind him. Then a voice said, "You must forgive my uncle. He is sometimes a little highly strung."

Corrigan span around. It was Rachel. She was wearing a long white frock, and her long black hair, instead of being tied in a bun at the back of her head, cascaded freely around her shoulders. Corrigan thought he could detect the faint aroma of perfume.

"How long have you been standing there?"

"I was worried. I thought you might be badly hurt."

Corrigan picked up his blood-soaked shirt from the floor. He reached into his pocket and threw two one pound notes on to the bench. "I'm all right. Here, better give old Blood and Thunder this. Didn't expect him to fix me up for nothing."

Rachel stared at the two crumpled notes. She felt that perhaps she recognised them. "But this is too much money."

"That's all right. I charged you too much money to go to Marmari."

Rachel looked at the heavy bandage on his shoulder. "What happened?"

"Sanei. Damned woman took to me with a knife. Wait till I find her. I'll give her a hiding she won't forget."

"But why did she do it?"

"Well, she's got a funny set of morals, see? Doesn't mind me carrying on with any of the local girls but I suppose she thought you were a threat to her."

"Me?" Rachel blushed. "What do you mean?"

"Better ask her. It's a bloody silly notion, but that's women for you." Corrigan stamped out and Rachel listened as his footsteps clattered on the wooden steps and were gone.

A few moments later Father Goode came back into the room. "That man is damned for all time to the fires of Hell," he muttered. "And my sympathy for the Devil."

"You're wrong," Rachel said.

There was an uncharacteristic note of irritation in her voice. Father Goode looked at his niece. Two fat tears were trickling down her cheeks.

"Rachel? What's wrong?"

"Nothing. Nothing is wrong. Everything is just the same

as it always is," she said and turned and left the room.

Father Goode sighed. His niece was sometimes a mystery to him. He supposed it was because she was a woman.

Ian Manning looked out through his binoculars across the glittering blue waters of White Bone Bay and the fifty miles of shimmering ocean to Cape Tavu.

The recent storm had swept away the thick cloud that perennially covered the distant island, which was defined now in vivid contrast to the virgin white background of cumulus, and the stark indigo hues of the ocean.

Manning was perched high on the trunk of a tall banyan tree. It was huge with a smooth bark and shiny leaves. Roots hung down from the branches to the ground in grotesque profusion, some as thick as the trunk of a sapling. Manning wrapped one arm around the limb of the tree, the binoculars held to his eyes with the other.

"This will do," he muttered softly to himself, "this will do nicely."

He was selecting his sites with exaggerated care. If he ever needed to use them, he knew his life would depend upon how well he had chosen.

Already he had begun to shift stores to secret caches in the hills. There was tinned food, bags of rice, kerosene, trade goods, drums of benzene and even a case of whisky. He and his native police would be able to survive for months – perhaps indefinitely, with help from the natives.

Manning began to pick his way carefully back down the tree. At its base he was enveloped once more in the steaming and gloomy miasma of the jungle. Immediately small rivulets of sweat started to pour down the flushed lines of his face, from the wellsprings of sweat in his scalp and forehead.

He sank to his haunches, wheezing from the effort of climbing the tree, but his mind now fully absorbed with his plans.

The site he had chosen would offer uninterrupted views

of The Slot, the narrow deep-water channel between the Solomons. If the Japanese came, this was the highway they would use to push their war machine to Australia and New Zealand.

The path leading up led along a streambed of bare wet rock that would leave no tell-tale footprints. The clearing itself was gloomy and dark; it would aggravate his bronchial complaints of course, but it was the price he would have to pay for the security of the trees. From the air the site would be invisible, hidden behind the endless green canopy of the jungle.

The clearing itself was surrounded by dense growth, twisting lianas, white orchids and dim creeper-strewn passages, dappled with pale sunlight. If the Japanese came looking for him – and Manning didn't doubt that they would – they would have to walk right into the clearing before they discovered him.

It all seemed unreal, a fantasy game. After all, Singapore stood in the way of the Japanese, with 80,000 British troops and guns. It was surely the rock on which the tide of the Japanese advance would break.

But if it didn't, Ian McLaren Manning would at last prove his worth to Mother England. He would not let her down. He had waited too long a time for the opportunity.

The Chinatown in Vancoro consisted of a cluster of flimsy wooden shacks with coral jetties leading out to the deep water. The schooners lay at the end of the piers, their holds crammed with trochus shell and copra and trade goods.

Along the wharves was the ramshackle huddle of shophouses, filled with cheap lamps, fish hooks, beads, pipes and gaudily labelled tinned food. From inside came the sibilant chatter and clatter of counters as the Chinese bartered and squabbled and gambled at fan tan.

Europeans came to the Chinatown for just two things; to bargain with the gaggle of Chinese in their too-long shorts and dirty white vests, or to drink at Sam Doo's Drinking Palace.

Sam Doo owned a store near one of the piers, a corrugated iron building with a green tin roof. In contrast to the glaring sunshine outside it was always cool and dark inside. At the far end of the store, past the tangle of ships' gear, the coils of rope and the galvanised anchors, there was a cluster of old tables and chairs where Sam Doo tended bar.

The walls were covered with dusty whisky and beer advertisements and gaudy prints of scantily dressed girls, all coated with a fine gauze of dust. There was also Sam's collection of island trophies; clubs, shields, and stone-head axes, clam shell arm-rings and a chief's insignia crafted from an intricately fretted turtle shell. The only decoration consisted of two decaying paper lanterns that hung in gaudy splendour over the bar and a picture of the King that hung on the far wall.

A waltz tune was playing scratchily on the gramophone. Sam Doo was immensely proud of it, despite the fact that he had only one record. It was "Always".

Sam was a little Chinaman with long black hair and a wizened monkey face; he had a mole on the left side of his chin from which long grey hairs protruded in a straggly kind of beard. He always gave his customers a cheerful welcome and the benefit of a broad gold-toothed smile; but today his mood was darker and less benevolent.

And with good reason.

In fact Sam Doo groaned when he saw Corrigan crossing the street towards his hotel. On any other day he would have been pleased to see the big Irishman; he supported a big thirst, and Sam was always happy to take his money.

But not today; not with the planter Heydrich sitting on the other side of the room, in such boisterous mood. There was bound to be trouble. The hotel wasn't much, he knew. But it was all he had, and it was the only one in Vancoro.

Wolfgang Heydrich gazed at the picture of King Edward

VII and raised his glass of gin in an ironic toast. He felt better than he had felt in years. In fact he was thoroughly enjoying the spectacle of seeing the English soiling their creased white trousers as they contemplated the Japanese advance down the Malay peninsula.

In Europe his own countrymen had brought the mighty English to their knees, and the Wehrmacht was baying at the portals of England herself, like a *Pinscher*, eager for blood. If only Hitler would let them off their leash, he thought eagerly.

In an expansive mood he was about to order another bottle of gin when he saw Corrigan.

Heydrich and Corrigan each nursed a profound dislike for the other. Perversely, they attempted to conceal it beneath a veneer of cordiality, only in order to foster their distaste for each other a little more. Their lives were easy and they were bored; their mutual contempt gave them both an opportunity to release a little of the *ennui* that afflicted them.

Heydrich had made a number of clumsy attempts to lure Corrigan's native girl away to his own plantation at *Marakon*. Not only was she the most beautiful native girl on the island, but it would also have been a satisfying psychological victory.

For his part Corrigan pretended not to notice. He knew Sanei would never leave him and he enjoyed the fat man's jealousy. He fed it at every opportunity.

"Corrigan!" Heydrich roared, as if he was greeting a long absent friend. "Come and have a drink with me!"

Corrigan stood in the doorway, his hands thrust deep into the pockets of his shorts. It was not midday and he was already drunk. He swayed uneasily on his feet.

"All right," Corrigan said, and he tottered over.

If Sam Doo had anticipated trouble earlier, he was convinced of it when he saw Heydrich get out the playing cards.

"Just a friendly game," he heard Heydrich saying, "but we might as well make it interesting."

And he pulled a bundle of notes from his pocket and slapped them down on the table.

They had been drinking solidly for almost two hours, but Heydrich had been sober when they had begun, which gave him an advantage. Sam Doo continued wiping glasses from behind the protection of the bar, and watched as Corrigan grunted and pulled some crumpled notes from the pockets of his shorts and slapped them down on the table.

Sam Doo started to put away the bottles lining the shelves behind him, hiding them away in the cupboards under the bar. It would be less to be broken later.

Corrigan won the first two games, without taking a lot of money from Heydrich. He dealt himself two pairs and a flush, and the German had thrown in his hand both times.

But on the third game, Sam Doo realised what was going to happen and he started to put the glasses away as well.

Corrigan picked up his cards. He had two aces. He threw away three cards and picked up a ten, a five, and another ace. Three aces.

He reached to the side and picked up two one-pound notes and let them fall in the middle of the table. Heydrich smiled.

"A good draw, Corrigan?"

"Let's get on with the game," Corrigan said. He was slurring his words.

Sam Doo moved to the other end of the bar to watch. From his position he could see Heydrich's cards. Two kings and the other ace, a nine and a three. He threw away the two low cards and drew two more from the top of the pack.

A king and another nine.

Heydrich sneezed, pulling a voluminous white handkerchief from the pocket of his cotton jacket. He made a pantomime of blowing his nose and when he replaced the handkerchief in his pocket he had a full house. The nine had gone and had been replaced by yet another ace.

It had been clumsy but Corrigan was too drunk to notice the ploy.

"Hurry up and bet," Corrigan muttered.

Heydrich dropped a large five-pound note on the table. "I dare say you have a very good hand, Corrigan. But what the hell, eh? A gamble is a gamble."

Corrigan sat for a long time without moving. Finally he picked up the few notes from the pile beside him and dropped them in the middle of the table. "Cost you another two to see if you're right."

Heydrich smiled a soft gloating smile and pushed another large blue note into the middle of the table.

Corrigan looked down at the small pile of coins beside him. His eyes were glazed from the effects of the alcohol. "I thought this was supposed to be a friendly game. You know I can't match that."

"You don't have to use money. What about the girl?"

"Sanei?"

"The islanders buy and sell them all the time. Don't tell me you've grown fond of her?"

"Take the money, I'll not use someone as a stake in a card game."

Heydrich looked disappointed. "I was wrong about you, Corrigan," Heydrich said laughing. "I always said you had no morals. All right then, I'll take a marker."

He pulled a pen and a piece of paper out of his jacket and passed it over to Corrigan. He scrawled the amount and his signature on the bottom.

Heydrich examined it carefully, and then, without taking his eyes from Corrigan's face, he laid his cards down one at a time.

"Three aces and two kings," he said slowly. "Full house."

Heydrich scooped the pile of banknotes towards him. Corrigan watched him, and Sam Doo wondered if perhaps the big man was too drunk to realise what simple logic should have told him straight away. Heydrich's full house made five aces in the pack.

In fact it took some moments for it to sink in. But then Corrigan lurched forwards and grabbed Heydrich by the shirt front, one of the buttons ripping away. Sam Doo heard the gentle click as it hit the wooden floor.

"You fat German slug."

Heydrich's face flushed scarlet. "Get your hands off me, you English pig."

Sam Doo started to run. As he reached the end of the bar he heard a wet, slapping noise, like someone punching their fist into a cabbage. He turned round in time to see Heydrich tumbling backwards off his chair, blood spurting from his nose.

11

The next morning Manning sat in his office, finishing off his paperwork and preparing himself for one of his more stressful duties. He opened the court record book to a fresh page in front of him and laid out his pen neatly on the right-hand side of the thick ledger.

Then he sighed and leaned back in his chair.

He gazed out of the window, and marvelled once again at the vista spread before him. He never tired of it.

Below him he could make out the police barracks, the Catholic Mission and the tiny hospital annexe. The houses of the village were mostly hidden by the palms as the bay swept round towards the headland. The harbour was dotted with small emerald islands, the water flecked with specks of white water driven by the north-west monsoon.

In the garden hibiscus bushes with flowers of vermilion, white and orange clustered around the window. A crimson pygmy parrot landed on one of the bushes to peck nervously at the flowers.

A white orchid was in full bloom on the other side of the garden under a flame tree, its branches a mass of bright scarlet. A black and white hornbill settled heavily onto the branches, disturbing a small flock of white cockatoos who took to the air, screeching their complaint.

As he watched an enormous butterfly flew across the lawn, and landed on the sill; it was fully eight or nine inches across, its wings a breath-taking combination of electric blue and yellow.

Manning sighed with something like content; it was at times like this that he knew he loved these islands.

Suddenly the door to the office flew open and Sergeant Lavella burst into the room. He stamped his feet to attention, and the flimsy bamboo flooring of the office jarred and shuddered in protest. The poles, Manning knew, were ant-ridden; one day Lavella would bring the whole lot down on top of them.

Sergeant Lavella was an extraordinary individual. Many of the islanders had a good physique but Lavella was exceptional. He wasn't tall, but the muscles on his shoulders, chest and back stood out in thick bands under his skin. When he walked, his *lava-lava* was stretched tight against his thighs.

In contrast to his perfect physique, Lavella had the face of an all-in wrestler. Of indeterminate age, he had a busby of grizzled black hair, a squat nose, wrinkled face and a gap-toothed smile. Those teeth that remained lolled in his head like old tombstones.

Like most native constables he wore just a simple *lava-lava* with a leather belt and buckle. His most treasured possession was the Lee-Enfield bolt action rifle that he carried on his shoulder as he patrolled the island, marching with the fierce pride of a Coldstream Guard in Whitehall.

It was for him a symbol of the government's authority,

and by logical extension, his own. But although he loved firearms, he did not understand them; to Manning's constant chagrin and despite his constant urgings, Lavella rarely remembered to clean the gun. Manning doubted whether the damned thing would work if it was ever required; perhaps, Manning thought, knowing Sergeant Lavella's lack of self-control, that could be a good thing.

Lavella stood watching him expectantly. Reluctantly, Manning forced his thoughts back to the matter in hand. The previous afternoon there had been a fight at Sam Doo's Drinking Palace in the Chinatown.

It was the haunt for all of the colony's black sheep, as well as the native sailors and traders from other islands. It was there that Corrigan and the Austrian planter Heydrich had started their brawl, and it had taken Sergeant Lavella and four of his men to finally drag them out of the bar and into the prison, still spitting and cursing at each other.

Manning rubbed his eyes wearily as Lavella cleared his throat impatiently. It was another of the problems Manning had with Sergeant Lavella. He was impertinent.

"You want for lookim prisoners now *kiap*?" he said.

Manning sighed. "Yes. Me lookim now Sergeant."

Lavella disappeared outside and a few moments later two of his men came in with Corrigan and Heydrich.

"Hello, Manning," Corrigan greeted him cheerfully.

Manning frowned. The two men stood in front of the desk, dirty and unshaven, like a couple of truant schoolboys fiddling with their shorts. Corrigan even looked genuinely embarrassed.

"What is it this time?" Manning said. "Drunkenness or fighting?"

"Both," Corrigan grinned.

Manning leaned back in his chair and examined the two men. Corrigan was unshaven and his shirt was ripped and smeared with bloodstains, but with that devil-may-care smile of his and his dark blue eyes twinkling in that handsome face, it was hard to summon up the appropriate degree of wrath. Even so, Manning felt a prickle of impatience for a man who could waste his life in such a way.

Heydrich was a different matter. He was a short, gross man with lank blond hair and an odd, mis-shapen face; it was as if the two halves didn't quite match. The effect had been aggravated by the close attention he had received from Corrigan's fists. One eye was a swollen purple lump, his lips were cracked and one of his lower teeth was missing.

He looked a slightly comic figure as he stood there now, shivering with outrage.

"All right," Manning said to Sergeant Lavella, "read out the charges."

Sergeant Lavella drew himself up to his full height and began to recite the previous night's events.

"Longa sundown me fella police we go longa Sam Doo, bigfella crashim inside, me fella police all go in. Dis fella black hair he have dis feller white hair on table right up close and he smackim head this way." And Lavella demonstrated with his fist in his palm. "White hair he yell, like this, 'Aaagh! Aagh!' Me fella police we go bang bang on dis feller black hair, we fright for he killim white hair finis. More police he come, we all go bang bang dis feller, he yell, he punchim all, very bad."

Lavella finished his short pantomime and Manning shifted his attention back to Corrigan. "Do you have anything to say for yourself?"

Corrigan did not seem unduly perturbed by Lavella's allegations. "I guess what he says is right. I'm a bit hazy. I had a bit to drink."

Manning tried to look stern. "You're telling me drink is to blame for this unsavoury episode?"

Corrigan straightened up, jutting out his jaw defiantly. "It weren't the booze. This little arse insulted me."

Heydrich could hold his tongue no longer. "Lies! He attacked me! There are witnesses! He is crazy!"

"Crazy? You little slug . . ."

"Shut up! Both of you!" Manning was finding it difficult to contain his impatience. Sergeant Lavella's hand went nervously to the gun in his holster. Manning chastened him with a stare. The last thing he needed was a gun battle in his office.

Clearly terrified of Corrigan's temper, Heydrich subsided and moved away out of the range of Corrigan's fists. "Suppose you tell me your version of the incident," Manning said to Corrigan.

"We were playing cards. We'd both had a bit to drink. He started raving on about Hitler and we got into an argument. He called me an English pig so I let him have it."

"Because he called you a pig?"

"I didn't mind that. But I'll not have anyone calling me English."

Manning pursed his lips thoughtfully. "What did Mister Heydrich say about Hitler, Corrigan?"

"He said he was some sort of superman and he was going to walk all over Europe. That's when I said balls and he called me an English pig."

Heydrich's face suffused with purple rage and he started to quiver. "Lies! He's making it up! We are playing cards and he attacks me because I am winning! He's out of his mind – he should be locked away!"

A fine spray of spittle glittered like diamond chips on Manning's desk. He examined them with distaste. As an Austrian national he had naturally watched Heydrich's behaviour very closely. But now with the Japanese on the doorstep he wondered if it might be wise to have Heydrich interned in Australia for the duration.

After a few moments Manning stirred and looked at Lavella. "Any witnesses?"

Lavella nodded and went outside. Over the next half an hour no fewer than five of Sam Doo's customers swore they saw Corrigan throw the first punch. Sam Doo, the proprietor, had been especially vehement in claiming damages, although Manning couldn't be sure that much of the havoc hadn't been wrought by Lavella and his policemen. But there was little doubt about Corrigan's guilt.

Manning rested an elbow on the desk and looked at the big man with the patient forbearance of a teacher with a wayward pupil. "What am I going to do with you, Patrick?"

As Deputy Commissioner for the Western Pacific, Manning had sweeping powers. He performed the functions of magistrate, chief of police, head gaoler, coroner, treasurer and customs officer. On Santa Maria his word was law and his prestige somewhere approximating that of God. He could put Corrigan in jail for three months if he wanted to. Of course Corrigan could appeal to the Commissioner in Fiji but by the time the ruling was overturned the three months would be up.

"The case is clear," Heydrich said, interrupting Manning's deliberations. "It is your duty to punish this man!"

This was the wrong approach.

Ian McLaren Manning was not the sort of man who enjoyed having his duty pointed out to him, and this was the second occasion in as many months that someone on the island had had the temerity to propose it. A quiet man by nature, Manning was none-the-less a man of his own mind. More importantly, he did not approve of Germans, and Heydrich's claim to Austrian nationality seemed to him no more than a matter of semantics.

Manning's father had been killed on the Somme.

"I beg your pardon," he said icily.

"He has broken the law. You must put him in prison."

Manning sucked his teeth thoughtfully. Corrigan was undoubtedly a drinker and a gambler and a womaniser, but there was a certain charming roguishness about him that Manning admired in spite of himself. The thought of giving Heydrich the satisfaction of seeing Corrigan in prison filled him with repugnance.

Manning's decision was based more on impish impulse

than reasoned judgment and Manning almost smiled as he spoke.

"Case dismissed." Triumphant, Corrigan threw back his head and guffawed.

"But you can't," Heydrich spluttered. "He is a criminal. Where is the justice?"

Manning waved his hand lazily in Heydrich's direction. "Get rid of them," he said to Sergeant Lavella.

"I will report this to your superiors!" Heydrich shouted as Lavella pushed him outside. "This is an outrage!"

The door slammed shut behind them.

Manning's gaunt features creased into a wry grin. It was not often that a job allowed one to dispense justice without due regard to the facts. It was one of the compensations of being a big fish in a tiny pond.

Just then he heard a meaty thud on the verandah and more shouts from outside. Manning leaped to his feet and ran out of the door. Heydrich lay at the foot of the bungalow steps, a froth of red bubbles pouring from his nose.

"Bloody krauts," Corrigan said, standing over him, "think they own the bloody place."

Sergeant Lavella had his revolver out. Manning grabbed it and threw it in the bushes. Grabbing Corrigan by the arm he pulled him across the compound towards the path that led up to the prison building.

"Seven days," he said, pulling Corrigan meekly along behind him, "and you really are a damned idiot."

12

When war had broken out in 1939 Ian Manning had applied to join the Armed Forces, but because of his age and his bronchial condition, he had been rejected. But shortly afterwards he had been approached by the navy and given the rank of captain as part of a new unit called the Coastwatchers.

As part of a network around the British Protectorates in the Pacific, his job would be to work behind Japanese lines, monitoring enemy movements along the coast, should the island be invaded. When he had been first given the appointment he had thought it was a sop to his pride; but now it was suddenly terribly real.

He sat in his office overlooking White Bone Bay, holding the radio message loosely in his right hand. It had arrived almost a week ago and he had re-read it scores of times, but the purport of its message still seemed unreal.

Singapore was about to fall. He was to evacuate all the Europeans from the settlement immediately. They were to be taken aboard the Levers Brothers' ketch *Melinda* to Tulagi and then on to Sydney.

The speed of the Japanese advance had taken everyone by surprise. On Christmas Day the armies of Nippon had marched into Hong Kong. On 3 January they took Manila. On the 23rd New Britain had fallen.

By the first of February they were at the gates of Singapore itself, the impregnable fortress of Asia, the symbol of colonial supremacy in the Far East.

Astonishment was quickly replaced by fear, as traders, planters and officials rushed to get away from the tide of the Japanese advance. Rumours of Japanese atrocities filtering through from Malaya caused a ripple of panic through the white population.

Now the *Melinda* lay at anchor at the end of the jetty, lost in a bobbing mass of smaller craft that had hurried from settlements all around the island to meet her. Piles of luggage littered the pier, and the wharves where groups of curious and bewildered natives had come to watch the spectacle.

This morning the mood on the pier had boiled over into hysteria. There had been arguments about how much luggage could be brought on board and twice fights had broken out. A planter had had his nose broken by a missionary and the captain of the ketch had been assaulted by the wife of an engineer.

For Ian Manning, who had been brought up to believe that self-control was the greatest human virtue and that an Englishman should behave like one regardless of the circumstances, that morning's events had been a salutary experience. He had never had to deal with naked terror before and he quickly learned that it was beyond his control.

After almost fifty years the British were leaving the Solomons and the sight filled Ian Manning with disgust.

He had finally washed his hands of the affair and left the pier, leaving the panicked settlers to the chaos they themselves had created. He had his own problems to take care of. He had retreated to his office where he could still hear the screams and curses carried up to him by the sea breeze.

Manning shook his head. He wondered what the natives thought of it all.

Tomorrow all the Europeans would be gone. Well, almost all, Father Goode and his niece had resisted all his entreaties to reconsider. Corrigan too, had remained recalcitrant, but for different reasons. He didn't give a damn about anything, least of all the war. And then there was Heydrich, skulking on his plantation at Marakon. Manning wished now that he had had him interned when he had the chance.

For all the others it was an ending. But for Manning, the war had suddenly begun.

He had chosen three possible camp sites and there were caches of stores secreted away in caves in the hills and mountains to the north. Soon he would be on his own.

The months stretched ahead of him now, uncharted, filled with danger and loneliness. He realised his chances of survival were minimal and deep in the pit of his stomach he felt an oily tingle of fear and excitement.

At last he was going to war.

He went to his desk and took some photographs out of the drawer. They were yellowed and creased with age. His mother, two brothers in Chelmsford, a sister in Southampton. He carefully tore them up and threw them in the wastepaper basket.

The code books and all the files would have to be burned of course. But the biggest problem would be the radio. It was a type 3B transmitter, receiver and loudspeaker. It would have to be packed in three metal boxes, as big as packing cases. It ran on a car battery, and was powered by a small motor engine, all in all nearly seventy pounds in weight. Somehow it would all have to be transported up to the hills.

He was still lost in the details of the logistical problems when he heard the distant drone of an engine. The throbbing sound of motors rose and fell in cadence with the wind. At first he thought it was another launch heading into the harbour, but then he realised that the sound was coming from the north.

He went out on to the verandah, and looked skywards, one hand shielding his eyes against the glare of the noon-day sun.

A pathway led up through the flame trees towards the residency; behind it the land rose steadily towards the heavily wooded hills. A few hundred yards beyond the bungalow a group of a half dozen labourers were planting the barren red hillside with casuarinas and digging drains to carry off storm water. They too stopped and looked up at the sky at this unexpected intrusion.

In the far distance were the mountains, the spines of basalt that ran the length of the island. Above them Manning could make out a black speck moving towards Vancoro.

Gradually the speck took shape, formed into the ugly and unmistakable silhouette of a flying boat. At first

Manning thought it must be an RAAF Catalina, but then he realised that was impossible. The nearest Catalina base was at Tulagi, far to the south. The flying boat was approaching from the north-west.

Suddenly it dipped its wings and began to drop towards Vancoro and Manning realised what it must be.

"Oh, my God," he moaned and leaped from the verandah in one jump and began to run down the pathway towards the harbour.

13

By the time Manning reached the harbour, the Kawanisi was banking over the coconut fronds lining the bay and had begun its bombing run, approaching Vancoro from the south-west. The islanders watched it come with happy curiosity.

"Run!" Manning shouted at the crowd of natives lining the water's edge. "For God's sake, run!"

They stared back at him, uncomprehending.

On the pier the Europeans who had been milling around the gangway of the *Melinda* suddenly began streaming back down the jetty. Manning heard screams and saw the woman who had tried to assault the *Melinda's* captain being jostled out of the way and fall headlong into the water.

Manning ran over to a group of the islanders and began to push them back towards the row of casuarina trees. "Run, damn you!" he screamed at them.

Bewildered, several of them jogged away towards the trees, still peering over their shoulders at the flying boat.

Manning realised the Japanese would attack the ketch

first. It would be easy prey, unarmed and with the Union Jack fluttering over the stern. Then, unexpectedly, Manning heard the chatter of machine gun fire.

Incredibly, someone in Tulagi had had the foresight to equip the ketch with an ancient Vickers machine gun. Two of the *Melinda's* crew still remained on board, manning the gun, and Manning saw fabric from the flying boat's starboard wing being torn away by the shells.

The roar of the Kawanisi's engines was deafening now. Then there was a new sound, a shrill screaming whine as the clutch of bombs began to fall.

Manning looked up. He could make out the silhouette of the pilot behind the controls.

"You bastards!" he shouted. "You bloody bastards!" but his voice was drowned out by the scream of the engines.

The first bomb struck the wharf just a hundred yards from where he stood, and threw him to the ground. Until then he had never realised that a sound could cause actual physical pain, but as it exploded the concussion sent such a sharp searing agony through his eardrums that he screamed and put his hands to his ears to try and shut out the sound of the explosions. He felt the ground below him tremble as if the earth itself was about to crumble away beneath him. He felt a stinging spray of earth and fine stones on his back and legs.

He clung to the ground, his face pressed hard against the dirt. The quayside shuddered as the rest of the bombs fell and then he heard the inevitable screams of fear and pain, close by.

When he looked up again the jumble of tin and corrugated iron buildings that made up the Chinatown were either flattened or burning. The quay was strewn with bodies. One of the bombs had exploded in the middle of the bund, scything down a group of islanders who had been fleeing towards the village. Most of the tall palms had snapped like twigs, and now lay across the road or half submerged in the water.

Manning rose to his knees. Through the drifting black smoke he saw Sergeant Lavella running towards him.

"Get everyone away from here!" Manning shouted. "Hurry!"

Sergeant Lavella nodded and trotted away, firing his revolver wildly in the air to attract attention.

At the far end of the bay the Kawanisi flying boat turned slowly, short and snub-nosed, and prepared for a second pass. Manning watched it, in hatred and fear.

Suddenly he remembered the aerial, on top of his office. It would give away the position of the teleradio. There was a chance that the pilot hadn't seen it yet.

He leaped to his feet and started to run back up the path towards the thatched bamboo hut.

Manning heard his own blood pounding in his ears, every breath forcing its way into his lungs like fire. He staggered, his leg muscles protesting the effort it had taken to run back up the pathway. He gasped another breath into his lungs and kept going.

He was still fifty yards away from the residency when the bomber came back for its second run. The roar of the Kawanisi's engines echoed around the hills. It raced over the green canopy of the jungle towards him, with unbelievable speed.

Suddenly he realised he wasn't going to make it. He would be caught out in the open directly in the bomber's path. He had to get under cover.

Already puffs of red dirt kicked into the air twenty yards in front of him. They were strafing. Manning felt himself freeze where he stood, his legs paralysed with sudden cold fear.

He watched, fascinated, as the whirling devils of flying dust got closer, like a quick burning fuse.

Closer. Closer.

14

Something hit Manning hard in the chest from the side, and then he was hurled through the air into the bushes. He rolled over and over through the undergrowth and the flying boat roared overhead, its machine guns clattering.

He blacked out.

It was perhaps only a matter of seconds. When he opened his eyes, he was lying on his back staring up at the empty sky. He couldn't breathe.

Somewhere a voice was shouting at him.

He forced another deep lungful of air into his chest and rolled over on to his side. He found himself staring into a strangely familiar face.

It was Corrigan.

"You all right?"

Manning nodded, unable to trust his own voice. He raised himself on his elbows, and looked back towards the harbour. As he watched, the Kawanisi made a slow sweeping turn over the harbour, and then flipped its wings and headed back to the north. Glycol vapour was streaming from one of the starboard engines; the sailors manning the Vickers had exacted a small measure of retribution at least.

Manning turned to Corrigan. "You saved my life."

"Don't thank me."

"I wasn't going to. I was going to ask you what you were doing out of jail."

It was early afternoon. A haze of acrid black smoke hung over Vancoro. The Chinatown section had been razed; there was nothing left but a smouldering mass of warped metal and timber.

Miraculously the *Melinda* had suffered only minor damage. Perhaps diverted by the unexpected machine gun fire the Japanese had dropped their clutch of bombs long. Manning's ketch *Tulagi* had been strafed, but was still navigable.

But the life of the *Melinda* had been expensive. Thirteen islanders lay dead, and two Chinamen – caught, already in a state of oblivion perhaps – in Sam Doo's store.

It was the men on the Vickers gun that had perhaps also saved the teleradio; although the bamboo office was riddled with machine gun shells, the radio itself was undamaged. The damage to the starboard engine had forced the Japanese pilot to abort the attack.

The courage of the two men on the gun had cost them dearly; they too now lay on the jetty beside the *Melinda*, their bodies covered with a bloodied tarpaulin.

Another fifteen islanders had been wounded in the attack and Manning had had them put on board the *Melinda*, so that they could be cared for in Tulagi. The sudden appearance of the bomber had expedited the evacuation. The *Melinda* was already preparing to sail, leaving piles of boxes and luggage abandoned on the wharf.

Manning turned away from the window. The wind whistled softly through the gaping holes in the slatted bamboo walls of the office where the bullets had ripped through.

"Want a drink?" Manning said.

Corrigan grinned. "Got any gin?"

"I can do better than that." Manning reached into his desk and took out a bottle of Glenfiddich Scotch malt whisky. He had bought it from a trader a year ago. He had been saving it for a special occasion.

He poured three fingers into two thick glass tumblers and handed one to Corrigan. He felt strangely elated. The terror of a few hours before had left him exhilarated and relieved; he had always been afraid that in a sudden crisis his courage would fail him. Instead he had found a recklessness in himself that had astonished him.

"Your health, Patrick."
"And yours. For all the good it will do you now."
Corrigan swallowed the whisky in one swallow, like it was a flat beer. He grimaced and held out his glass for another.
"I don't want to seem churlish, Patrick," Manning said. "But how did you get out of the jail?"
Corrigan shrugged. "I've got a key."
"I see."
"You don't seem very surprised."
"Nothing you do shocks me any more."
"When a man spends as much time as I do in the can he can't afford not to let himself in and out occasionally. Some nights I need to slip out for a drink, you know? So a few months ago I told Sergeant Lavella I'd thump him if he didn't give me a spare key. So he did. You know these blokes. They're not used to saying no to a white man."
Manning smiled, despite himself. "It's a good job you did. Or I wouldn't be alive right now." He handed Corrigan another glass of the whisky. "Well, it looks like the war has finally caught up with us."
"Looks like it."
"What are you going to do?"
"Nothing, why should I?" He took another long swallow from his glass. "It's not my bloody war. Anyway, I'm a pacifist."
"I didn't know that."
The irony in Manning's tone was lost on Corrigan. "Nothing's going to change. If the Japs don't bother me, I won't bother them." He downed the whisky. Manning shook his head. The man had a remarkable tolerance for strong drink.
"You've had no second thoughts about staying on?"
"Why would I?" Corrigan answered. "And what about you? I've heard a little rumour you're going bush."
"Shouldn't believe everything you hear, Patrick," Manning said cheerfully. He handed Corrigan the bottle of Glenfiddich. "Here. You might as well have this."

Corrigan's face split into a broad grin.
"I always said you were a generous man, Manning." He took the bottle and extended one huge hand. "The best of luck to you," he said and shook Manning's hand and headed back down the hill towards Vancoro.

It was just after dawn. Manning was ready to leave.
Sergeant Lavella had wanted to bring all the office files, even the carbon copies. By Lavella's reckoning the rifle and the carbon copy were equal symbols of power and authority; it was as unthinkable to allow a duplicate copy of a 1936 court case over a Rendova woman who had insulted a Marmari girl's parrot to fall into Japanese hands as it would be to hand them the defence plans for the South Pacific.
Manning had calculated that it would have required fifteen native carriers to transport the boxes of useless documents; almost as many as he needed to carry the precious teleradio. For the sake of morale Manning had decided to compromise, and so he arranged for the boxes to be buried in the hillside above Vancoro, safe from the inquisitive eyes of the Japanese.
Manning then focused his concerns on the teleradio.
It was a 3BZ type AWA transmitter. It could be carried in four separate boxes, but extra carriers were needed for the batteries, the charging motor and the benzene. It was heavy and cumbersome; Manning had needed to recruit at least a further dozen carriers to transport it.
But finally the procession was ready, Sergeant Lavella had his six bronzed constables to attention, closed up and their rifles at slope; even Chomu, the cookboy, his pots and pans slung over his shoulders, stood stiffly erect. They all waited patiently for Manning's command to leave.
Manning stood on the lawn and watched as Sergeant Lavella lowered the Union Jack from the flagstaff for the final time. Solemnly he handed it, neatly folded, to Manning.
Manning packed it carefully and then walked down the

path a little way and looked out over the bay. Piles of boxes and luggage were still strewn across the pier and the wharf where they had been left the previous day after the *Melinda*'s sudden departure.

Two massive bomb craters gaped open along the wharf like ulcers, and on the other side of the village Manning could make out several pathetic bundles lying on the ground outside the mission hospital, their bodies covered over with blankets.

Manning felt stricken with grief; he wondered what would happen to the simple people of Santa Maria. They had no knowledge of the white man's way of making war; they had no forewarning of how terrible it might be.

He turned his back and with a swift nod to Sergeant Lavella, he gave the order for his little procession to start the long march into the hills.

After almost fifty years, the British were leaving Vancoro.

PART TWO

15

The grey compact lines of the destroyer were silhouetted against the velvet blackness of the Pacific sky, and the small white moustache of the bow wave glowed with a ghostly phosphorescence in the moonlight. On the starboard rail Lieutenant Mashita Tashiro looked out at the eastern horizon towards the distant Solomons Islands, and the first violet stain of dawn.

In a few hours the destroyer would leave the convoy and take them towards the island of Santa Maria. At last he would see action!

"Soon, Kurosawa-San, soon," Tashiro said, and his lips split into an eager grin. "After all this waiting, we will soon be in battle."

Noriko Kurosawa stood at the rail with him; he was younger than Tashiro and too cautious to be a true warrior, Tashiro thought. Kurosawa removed his spectacles and cleaned them studiously with a handkerchief. It was his way of thinking; he would not reply until he replaced them on his nose.

"You are very eager, Tashiro-san."

"Every young man should be bloodied in war. Do you not feel the world turning?"

Kurosawa nodded slowly. "Yes, I feel it. But we must not underestimate the Americans. So far we have taken them by surprise. But somewhere they will gather their forces and make a stand. They are a worthy enemy and the battles will be bloody."

"We will crush the Americans as we crushed the British at Singapore."

Kurosawa fell silent, guarding his thoughts. For a long while they stood looking towards the far horizon. Dark clouds were spread across the entire sky, thick layers piled upon each other. Gradually streaks of infinitely delicate yellows tinged the clouds as the sun began its climb towards the sky.

A shaft of gold suddenly split the pale violet of the sky; pastel shades of blue, grey and purple burned into the cumulus clouds that lay on the dark of the ocean. Thick golden shafts split the horizon, like orange search-lights seeking out every corner of the sky. The pastel colours disappeared; and suddenly a flaming sovereign red appeared on the far horizon. The whole world was momentarily bathed in the colour of blood. The crimson stained the bow wave, the grey steel of the ship's hull, the gun turrets, the gangways; their faces.

Slowly it rose over the island of Bougainville, its bloody fingers creeping up into the pink towering banks of cumulus.

"Look," Tashiro whispered. "It is an omen. The Rising Sun!"

For almost five months the war that had been raging around the South Pacific had ignored the little settlement at Vancoro. Occasionally a Kawanisi or a Zero, the distinctive red sun emblazoned on the silver fuselage, would pass low overhead. But otherwise life there had changed little.

But that morning it was to change for ever. As dawn broke over the island the silhouette of a Japanese destroyer lay grey and forbidding against the deep blue waters of the lagoon. The war had finally come to Santa Maria.

A company of Japanese soldiers landed on the foreshore in two sampans. They marched up the path between the casuarina trees to the Residency. There they raised the flag of the Rising Sun over the unkempt lawns of the bungalow, where for fifty years the red, white and blue Union Jack had flown in the breeze.

Patrick Corrigan watched them with fleeting interest. Then he ambled down to the wharf, as he had done every morning for almost a fortnight, to tinker distractedly with the Gardner diesel engine on the *Shamrock*, and waited for the Japanese to seek him out. At the Mission, Matthew and Rachel Goode prepared themselves for the visit also.

They didn't have to wait long.

Father Goode greeted the Japanese dressed in full canonicals.

He counted eight uniforms; six soldiers and two officers. They wore the distinctive tropical field caps with havelocks, khaki tunics, shorts and puttees. The soldiers marched two abreast, as if they were on the parade ground, their rifles slung over their shoulders.

Father Goode studied the officers. One had a smooth, almost bronze face, passive beneath the dun-coloured cap. His head had been close-shaved and he wore thick horn-rimmed spectacles. He resembled one of the cartoon caricatures Father Goode had seen in the newspapers he had sent out from England, except for one thing; there was a calm intelligence written on to the face, and almost at once he sensed a possible ally.

The other officer was almost a head taller. He walked with exaggerated arrogance, his back ramrod-stiff. He wore a sword at his hip, and one fist was clenched around the hilt.

The taller man was clearly the senior of the two officers. He walked half a pace ahead, his eyes fixed on the priest. He barked out a command and the column of soldiers halted a few yards from the front steps of the bungalow.

Father Goode affected the slightly patronising smile he wore at Sunday service and went down the steps to meet them.

"I am Father Matthew Goode," he said, his hands clasped in front of his chest in an attitude of devotion.

"We have been expecting you. My niece has made some morning tea. Would you like to sit down and join us?"

If Lieutenant Mashita Tashiro had understood this little speech he may have perhaps betrayed some astonishment. As it was, he brushed past the priest and marched ahead into the bungalow.

Father Goode watched him go inside with an expression of pity and disdain. It was as he had anticipated.

Utter barbarians.

Rachel came to stand beside him. "What is he looking for?"

"My dear, I have no idea."

"Please excuse," Kurosawa said in English. His gently accented voice was soft, like a woman's. "Is necessary. So sorry."

Father Goode smiled at him, with a mixture of relief and condescension. He had not expected to discover a Japanese with any mastery of the tongue which he regarded as the universal language.

"Ah, you speak English."

"I study one year at University in America. Michigan."

"Then perhaps you could explain to the other gentleman, when he comes out . . ." Father Goode nodded towards the bungalow. "I am a man of God. The war is of no account to us here."

Kurosawa did not reply. He stood stiff and ill at ease, the hot noonday sun reflecting in the thick lenses of his spectacles.

"Perhaps you would like to have some tea with us," Rachel asked him. They had already determined that on no account would they allow the Japanese to intimidate them. Father Goode had told Rachel that they should extend the same courtesies to the Japanese as they would to any new visitors to the island. "Besides," he had added, "fear will only arouse their brutal instincts."

Lieutenant Kurosawa hesitated. Although he had overcome his initial amazement at this unexpected greeting, he was not sure whether Tashiro would wish him to accept the offer. However he felt it would be impolite to refuse.

"It's too hot to stand out here," Father Goode told him. "Come and join us on the verandah."

"Thank you," Kurosawa said and followed the priest up the steps to where four cane chairs and a small wicker-work table had been neatly arranged. On the table was a silver salver with half a dozen egg-yellow scones, a glass dish filled with rich currant jam and a delicate china teapot.

From inside the bungalow Rachel heard a drawer crash to the floor. She exchanged glances with her uncle. It seemed Tashiro was conducting his search of the Mission with unnecessary ruthlessness.

"Please sit down," Father Goode was saying. "My niece made some scones. Would you like one?"

Lieutenant Kurosawa sat stiffly to attention in the cane chair between Rachel and Father Goode, his cap gripped in one hand, a cup of scalding hot tea in a rose china cup in the other. A meticulously polite man in private life, he was unsure how to behave as a conqueror.

When Tashiro re-appeared on the verandah Kurosawa hurriedly replaced the tea on the silver tray, and jumped to his feet.

Tashiro looked down at the plate of food, picked up one of the scones and bit off a mouthful. Finding it not to his taste he immediately spat it on to the bare boards of the verandah.

The priest regarded him in shocked silence.

"Who are they?" Tashiro asked Kurosawa in Japanese. "English?"

"He is a Catholic priest. This is his niece. They say they wish to remain neutral."

"What about the English *kiap*?"

Kurosawa turned back to Father Goode. "Lieutenant Tashiro wish to know hiding place of English *kiap*. Some native say he is still on island."

"Not to my knowledge," Father Goode lied. "As far as I know he left on the *Melinda* back in February. Mister Corrigan and the Austrian Heydrich are the only other white men left on the island." He lowered his voice to a conspiratorial whisper. "It is likely what the natives are telling you is what they wish were true. They were rather fond of him."

Kurosawa translated this knowledge to Tashiro. The young officer considered this a moment. "Tell them they are on parole," he said, and turned and marched away down the path.

"What did he say?" Father Goode asked Kurosawa.

"Tashiro-san say you are on parole."

"What does that mean?" Rachel asked.

"You not be harmed if you co-operate with Japan soldier. You are subject of Emperor now."

"We have only one Lord," the priest told him grandly. "And He is not of this world."

"Emperor is God also," Kurosawa told him, bowed, and smartly replaced his cap. As he hurried after Tashiro Father Goode ruminated on the blasphemy he had just heard.

"Pagans!" he spat. "They are no better than these poor natives they have conquered."

"It's not the natives they have conquered," Rachel reminded him gently. "It's us."

Father Goode scowled and watched the troop of soldiers march away. "I wonder where they're going?" he said.

"Towards the foreshore," Rachel said. "It looks as if they are going to visit Mister Corrigan now."

"Well, they won't get any tea and scones there." Father Goode sniffed, and he went back inside the house.

16

Out on the bay, frigate birds wheeled high overhead, occasionally swooping down on the blue-green waters to take off a fish. A kingfisher joined them, its feathers pure white and metallic green, vivid against the backdrop of the cobalt sky. It gave a convulsive twist and plunged into the water in a flash of silver spray.

The *Shamrock* was moored at the wharf, a gentle breeze slapping small waves against the hull. Corrigan had removed some of the deck planks and was bent over the engine cowling holding a 5/8 spanner and an oil-soaked rag. He squinted against the glare of the sun and caught sight of them coming down the hill from the Mission. He swore softly underneath his breath and leaned on the rail to wait.

There were half a dozen soldiers, and two officers. They marched in double file on to the jetty, their boots clattering on the wooden planks. Corrigan straightened and spat into the oily water. He wiped his hands on the greasy rag and threw it in the scuppers.

Corrigan had never liked any man in a uniform, regardless of the colour of his skin, and the men he saw that morning did nothing to dispel his prejudice. Especially the officer at the head of them. One fist clutched the ceremonial sword at his hip, and his face was a tight mask of controlled violence. Corrigan recognised the type at once and sensed danger.

At the officer's staccato command the platoon came to attention a few yards from the *Shamrock*.

"Good morning, you little yellow turds," Corrigan said cheerfully.

The shorter of the two officers stepped forward and said in English: "You are Corrigan?"

Corrigan grunted. "You speak English then?"

"My name Lieutenant Kurosawa. This Lieutenant Tashiro, of Imperial Japanese Army. We come on your boat now."

"I can't stop you."

The one called Tashiro jumped down on to the deck, landing easily on the balls of his feet, still clutching the sword at his hip. He strode up to Corrigan, his eyes black and cold beneath the peaked cap.

"Welcome aboard," Corrigan said.

Kurosawa jumped down beside Tashiro. "We now take possession of island in name of Emperor. You now Japanese subject."

"I'm touched."

Corrigan turned away from Tashiro and studied the one called Kurosawa. He looked nervous. He's a scholar all right, Corrigan decided. Not much to worry about there. It's the other one you have to be careful of.

Tashiro turned away from him and went inside the *Shamrock*'s tiny saloon.

The *Shamrock* had a single cabin below the wheelhouse. It was cramped, the air thick with diesel fumes and the taint of the bilges. There was a single bunk, unmade, and a small desk in the corner. The desk was strewn with papers and empty bottles of gin rolled around the floor.

Tashiro wrinkled his nose in disgust.

Corrigan watched him, his arms folded in truculent indifference. "Your friend looking for something?" he said to Kurosawa.

"Tashiro-san look for gun."

"Haven't got any. I'm a pacifist."

"You are English?" Kurosawa said.

"No, I'm not bloody English," Corrigan said fiercely. "I'm Irish."

There was a crash from the direction of the saloon.

Tashiro had taken the drawers out of the desk and tipped them on to the floor.

"I hope your friend's going to tidy up afterwards."

Kurosawa didn't answer him. Corrigan watched as Tashiro rifled his papers and his logs, giving them perfunctory attention before scattering them on the deck of the saloon. Corrigan clenched his jaw, trying to contain his rage.

Finally Tashiro stepped back on to the deck, and stood in front of Corrigan. He stared up at him, his face taut with contempt. Corrigan returned his stare, the stubbled chin creasing into a boyish grin.

"What can I do for you, short arse?"

The blow came so suddenly and so quickly that Corrigan was taken completely by surprise. He caught only a glimpse of the revolver in Tashiro's hand before it came up between his legs and into his groin.

Corrigan fell gasping on to the deck.

The pain seemed to take over his whole body. He couldn't breathe. He curled into a ball on the deck, gasping, trying to control the waves of agony shooting through him.

He heard voices shouting, close but somehow very distant. He realised Kurosawa and Tashiro were arguing.

It was some minutes before he opened his eyes. Tashiro was still standing over him, the revolver hanging loosely in his right hand. His eyes were bright with excitement.

He barked something at him in Japanese.

"You must get up now," Kurosawa repeated behind him. He looked frightened.

Tashiro nudged him with his foot.

Corrigan rolled on to his knees and slowly lifted himself to his feet, his hands clutching for the gunwale rail of the *Shamrock*. He felt the sudden clammy hand of nausea wash over him. He thought he was going to be sick, and fought it back. He wouldn't give the bastard the satisfaction.

He climbed shakily to his feet. "Your friend's a real hero," he said to Kurosawa.

"Very sorry," the Japanese officer said and Corrigan realised that he meant it. "Tashiro-san very strict man. He say he must teach you respect for Japanese officer."

Corrigan staggered into the saloon and rummaged through the papers scattered around the floor. Every movement made him grunt with pain. He found what he was looking for and came back on to the deck.

"My passport," he grunted. "I'm Irish, damn your bloody eyes." He glared at Tashiro. "A neutral, understand? I've got nothing to do with your bloody war."

Tashiro snatched the passport from him and studied it briefly. He threw it on the deck and barked out a command to Kurosawa.

"Tashiro-san wish to know where English *kiap* hide."

"Sydney, I think."

"Bullshit," Kurosawa said.

"Nice English teacher you had."

Kurosawa shook his head. "English priest also say he run away. But some native say *kiap* still on island."

"I'd take the priest's word if I were you. Man of God wouldn't lie."

Kurosawa turned to Tashiro and told him what Corrigan had said. Tashiro turned to Corrigan and then spat out another command.

"You go now," Kurosawa said softly.

Corrigan looked at him, bewildered. "What do you mean – 'go'?"

"Boat now property of Imperial Japanese Army. You go now. Not be hurt if you co-operate with Japanese soldier."

"This boat's mine. It's how I make my living. If you think you can waltz in here and take it, you can . . ."

Kurosawa glanced nervously at Tashiro and drew himself up to attention. "Tashiro-san say if you do not go now he must shoot you."

As if to emphasise the point Corrigan heard Tashiro

click the safety off his revolver. Corrigan felt the anger boil up inside him, his hands balling into tight fists at his side. For a moment he wondered if it might be worth it. With one blow he could smash the brutish little face . . . he might even have time to grab the revolver and finish him off.

Then he shifted his gaze towards Kurosawa and the platoon of soldiers waiting on the wharf. Yes, he could perhaps get in one punch but it would be a hollow victory. It would be the last thing he ever did.

There was nothing he could do. Slowly, painfully, he picked up the passport, pulled himself up on to the jetty and walked away, silently promising himself that one day he would get even with First Lieutenant Tashiro.

17

The Japanese had converted the Residency into officer's quarters. All the relics of British colonialism – like the books of poetry by Dryden and Shakespeare, the pictures of the King that had adorned the walls – had been thrown out and burned.

Barbed wire had been hastily erected around the compound, and a double line of guards had been placed around the perimeter as protection from saboteurs.

Manning's office was now Colonel Nakamura's headquarters. Nakamura was the commander of the small force of Japanese troops on the island. He was a bull of a man with black eyes, a small, dark moustache and the gait of a wrestler. A career soldier with combat experience in Manchuria he was eager, like Tashiro, for glory.

That first night Lieutenant Tashiro wrote in his diary:

"We have successfully subjugated Santa Maria. Everywhere our armies are sweeping across the Pacific, crushing all resistance. Nothing can stop us now . . ."

Later, clad only in shorts, the hard compact body glistening with sweat, Tashiro knelt on the bamboo mat in front of the picture of Emperor Hirohito that he had placed on the small cabinet beside his bed, and touching his forehead to the mat, he once more dedicated his life to the service of his Emperor.

His face was composed in concentration. He had finely chiselled bones, with the classic square jaw of a Samurai warrior. The eyes were deep set, liquid black pools that burned with a fever known only to those who have ever dreamed of glory. His coarse black hair, shaved close to the skull, gave him the appearance of a monk.

Mashita Tashiro was content. At last he had come to war.

All the time he was at cadet school he had been afraid that things would move too quickly; that the war would be over by the time he was drafted to the battlefront. His greatest fear had been that he would end up as just a spectator in Japan's greatest and most glorious hour.

He remembered that crisp winter's morning late in 1941 when he had heard Captain Hiraide's voice crackling over the radio in that hushed stillness that came just after dawn:

"Here is an announcement by the Naval Section of Imperial Headquarters. Today, December 8, before dawn, the Imperial Navy conducted a death-defying air raid upon the American fleet and air force stationed at Hawaii . . ."

He had been home on leave. That night he had dressed in his cadet's uniform and had gone with his father to stand outside the Imperial Palace in Tokyo. Thousands of children had converged through the streets on the palace gates to celebrate the news of the victory, each of them carrying a globe-shaped paper lantern, hung on a pole.

Tashiro had felt proud and envious. Proud to be a part of the Japanese military that had brought the Emperor so much glory; envious because he had not taken part in any of the battles.

Then in the middle of February, Singapore fell. One hundred thousand British, Indian and Australian troops surrendered, shattering almost two hundred years of Western domination in Asia. It was irrefutable proof to Tashiro of Japan's destiny in the shaping of the world and of the *Yamoto-Damashii* – the invincible spirit of Japan. After all, she had not tasted defeat in three thousand years.

Now, in his quarters in the Residency bungalow, he set about his nightly devotions. He carefully removed the black sandalwood stopper from the bamboo incense tube and placed a stick of incense inside it. He placed it beside the framed picture of the Emperor and lit it. Its sweet fragrance suddenly filled the room.

He fingered the incense tube lovingly and remembered the day his father had given it to him. It had been on the day of his last visit to his home, a few days before they had sent him to the Solomons with his unit.

His family lived at Ogama in Saitama prefecture, to the north-west of Tokyo. The metal rail cars of the train had been stifling hot that day, and the air was murmurous with the humming of paper fans as the women in their *mirokasa* urgently fanned their faces.

He remembered many of the passenger cars that day had no seats; even then the war had begun to strain the country's fragile economy, and the government was requisitioning whatever raw materials they could for use by the military. Tashiro had to squat on the floor of the train all the way.

His family lived in a wooden grey-tiled house. The sliding screen rattled as he drew it aside. His father was sitting cross-legged on the *tatami*, playing *shogi*. His face had betrayed no emotion when he looked up and saw him; he had risen gravely to greet him and they both saluted. Then Tashiro knelt at his feet and received his father's blessing, in the traditional Samurai manner.

His father was an imposing man; not tall, but with an aura of strength and discipline. Despite his seventy years he stood ramrod straight. He had long grey hair that he wore tied behind his head, and a long wispy beard. His face was stern and composed; Tashiro had never seen him any other way. He had heard that even when the great Kanto earthquake of 1923 had taken his first wife and a baby daughter, Tashiro-san had not shed a tear, or displayed his grief openly to anyone.

All his sons had worshipped him.

Even when Tashiro's two older brothers were killed during the invasion of Manchuoko, he never once saw the old man show any grief.

He was, after all, Samurai.

He had killed five Russians with his sword at the Battle of the River Shain in 1904. It was a Yamoto sword, made of the finest blue steel, and it still hung on the wall above the *kamidana* – the household Shinto altar. On the blade above the hilt was his name: *Hiroo Tashiro*.

Later Tashiro's mother brought them *sushi* with green tea and his father showed him the large coloured map of the Pacific he had pinned to the wall. Each new military conquest was marked with a small Rising Sun flag. They both studied it and marvelled; Guam, Luzon, Borneo, Wake Island, Manila, Hong Kong, Rabaul, Java, Singapore . . . the young Tashiro was filled with an almost overwhelming sense of passion and fervour.

It was his generation that was to be the greatest Samurai of them all.

The next day, when they bade farewell for the last time, his sisters and cousins and some of his father's friends all came out to the train station to see him off. His mother had handed him a thousand stitch waistband; the traditional belt of cotton cloth to which each of his family and friends had attached a single stitch with a five or ten yen piece and a short inscription for good luck.

His father was the last to say goodbye. His face was pinched and dark; he looked on the verge of some terrible explosion of anger. Tashiro guessed he was trying to suppress a great emotion.

Gravely he had handed him the incense bamboo holder for good luck; and then, almost tenderly he raised both his arms and gave him the Yamoto sword that had hung over the *kamidana* in their home for as long as the young Tashiro could remember.

He took it with a feeling akin to awe. And as the train pulled away from the station he waved goodbye to his father for the last time and heard again the song he and his brother officers had learned at the military college:

> *Faithful to the Five Teachings*
> *Lying a corpse on the battlefield*
> *From old the warrior's conviction*
> *Though not one single hair remains*
> *No one can regret dying for honour.*

The sword now lay on the bed beside him. He drew it from its scabbard, held it in front of his face so that the light of the candle reflected from it, lending an eerie luminescence to his eyes in that hot and darkened room; and once more he whispered the oath he had first spoken in Tokyo many months before, dedicating his life to the service of his Emperor.

While Lieutenant Tashiro dreamed of glory, Ian Manning was thinking of survival. He had been living in the hills overlooking Vancoro for three months, driven away by an invasion that had not come. Finally that morning he had seen the first Japanese warship enter Vancoro harbour and he wondered how long it would be before they came looking for him.

Until now Manning had continued with his work as District Officer as if nothing had happened. He still visited the outlying districts, settling disputes, and enforcing government laws. At every opportunity he had warned the islanders that should the Japanese come to Santa Maria, they were to have nothing to do with them.

Time alone would tell how effective his warnings had been.

Every morning and evening he sent regular reports of Japanese movements over the Coastwatcher's frequency, but increasingly Manning sensed the futility of what he was doing. The Allies were yet to deploy any forces strong enough to make use of the information he was passing on. The Japanese were sweeping all before them.

Manning's radio picked up the news broadcasts from Australia and the news was mostly bad. Although sixteen American B-25's had carried out a largely successful daylight raid over Tokyo, elsewhere the situation was bleak. Rabaul had fallen; the Dutch had capitulated in Java; and worst of all, the Japanese had captured Corregidor and with it, crushed the last resistance in the Philippines.

Despite these setbacks, Manning had decided he would stay on the island for as long as he possibly could. Some day – who knew how soon? – he might be needed.

Sergeant Lavella and his six constables had remained loyal to him, as had his cookboy, Chomu. They had built three huts in the clearing, made from vines and poles hacked from the jungle, with kunai grass and palm leaf for the walls and roofs. One of the huts served as Manning's quarters, and housed the teleradio equipment; the other two were quarters for Lavella's men and a kitchen.

They had plentiful supplies and Sergeant Lavella went down to the shore every few days and always returned with a plentiful supply of fish. They used their trade goods to barter with local villagers for vegetables and fruit from their gardens. Occasionally Manning hunted for wild pig.

Manning had also taken the precaution of bringing the contents of the island's Treasury; although the currency was theoretically worthless now, the islanders still used it for trade, and would continue to do so, no matter who controlled the island.

Manning knew that until the Japanese came looking for them, they could survive indefinitely.

Their worst enemy was the jungle itself. Manning suffered continuously from prickly heat. It would strike at his back, behind his knees, or across his chest. A red rash would form, where acid perspiration had eaten away small flakes of skin. When new sweat ran across these raw patches, Manning would grit his teeth and swear silently to himself. It was as if someone had suddenly stuck a handful of pins into him.

After a while the constant stream of perspiration caused little sores to develop on his body. The islanders called it jungle rot. His crotch and armpits were gouged with little blisters that broke and left small holes that would not heal.

But Manning was prepared to endure any hardship. In his own way, he had dedicated himself to his own king. There was no power, and no glory in his vision. Just an aching longing to survive and prevail, and to prove to himself and his long dead father that he too was a man.

18

"It's an abomination. These people are nothing more than barbarians! Their treatment of the people here is shameful. Several of the women have complained to me they have been raped by Japanese soldiers. The men are used as beasts of burden. It cannot continue!"

Father Goode paced the verandah outside his bungalow. He had worked himself into a frenzy. As he paced up and down, his hands worried the large silver cross at his neck. He was becoming hysterical.

Rachel watched him with growing concern. It always frightened her to see him like this. There was no knowing what he might do. She took his arm and led him to the cane peacock chair and sat him down.

"Sit down, uncle. Please. You'll bring on another bout of the malaria if you go on so."

Father Goode allowed himself to be led to a chair; within moments he was on his feet again, pacing from one end of the balcony to the other in the grip of his dilemma.

"I must do something, Satan is amongst us. We cannot sit idly by and do nothing!"

"Uncle, there's nothing we can do. Let us thank the Lord they have left us in peace here. They could shoot us and burn down our church if they wanted to."

Father Goode turned on her, his eyes ablaze with righteous wrath. "All these years of work. These are my people! I cannot stand by and leave my sheep to the ravages of these wolves!"

Once again Rachel took her uncle by the arm and led him to the chair. The last few months had exacted a terrible toll on him. The Japanese had left them alone – so far. As missionaries they were considered neutrals by the Japanese army. But it was an uncertain truce. Every day Rachel wondered when the hiatus would end.

"We can be of no service to the people in a Japanese prison," Rachel said.

"It is a test of our will, and of our faith. It is not for us to reason these things. Remember our Lord in the garden of Gethsemane? Even He faltered then. It was His final test. If the heathen put us to the sword, better that than fail in our duty to God!"

It seemed to Rachel that the Lord was being a little unreasonable, but she kept her silence. She knew better than to provoke theological argument when her uncle was in this mood.

"We will pray about it," she told him. "God will tell us what to do."

Rachel didn't believe it for a moment, but she hoped

it might serve to pacify her uncle for a time. She knew only too well the result of taking their protests to Colonel Nakamura.

Father Goode hung his head in his hands. "You don't think I've been praying these last few weeks? I have hammered with my fists on the doors of Heaven pleading with Him to deliver these people from this purgatory. The answer is always the same."

Rachel put a hand to his forehead. "You have a fever. You have another attack of the malaria coming on. Let me put you to bed."

The priest pushed her hand away angrily and jumped to his feet. "Stop fussing over me, child. I know what you're up to."

Rachel's hold on her patience finally broke. "All right, go down to the Japanese Commander and give him the Sermon on the Mount and see what good it does you! And after they've tied you up and shot you down like a dog, what's going to happen to me?"

The priest looked sadly at his niece. So young. So helpless. He thought of what the Japanese soldiers might do to her if he was no longer there to protect her and he was forced to close his eyes to block out the vision.

"Very well," he muttered.

He eased himself back into the chair and they both fell silent to their own thoughts. Father Goode immersed himself in the composition of dark and brooding soliloquies against the iniquities of Man; Rachel wondering how much longer she could continue to stall the inevitable.

"He wants to be a martyr," she thought bitterly. "One day he's going to get his way."

She sat on the cane chair next to the door, and watched the shadows inch across the bare patch of lawn towards the verandah steps. The sun was getting high in the sky. It was going to be another hot day.

Her uncle shifted irritably in his chair. "Where is that damn Lelei? It's time for morning tiffin."

Rachel got up quickly. "I'll fetch it."

But he was too quick for her. He jumped to his feet and blocked the way towards the kitchen. "Why should you fetch it? You're not a maidservant."

He turned and strode down the verandah towards the kitchen, the black hem of his soutane flapping around the worn brown leather of his sandals.

"Lelei!" Then, roaring: "LELEI! Where is the blessed girl?"

Suva, the cook-boy, hurried out on to the verandah, wiping his hands on the apron at his waist. "I help for you, mastah," the boy said, bowing quickly. "I get im tea for you."

"I want Lelei. Where is the blessed girl?"

Suva looked over Father Goode's shoulder at Rachel, his head bobbing obsequiously. The priest immediately understood the conspiracy of glances between them.

"What's going on?" he demanded.

"Lelei she go," Suva said.

"Gone? Gone where?"

Again Suva looked at Rachel. She shrugged her shoulders in capitulation.

Suva lowered his eyes. "She go stay longa *Japoni* boss," he mumbled. "*Japoni* boss he say he kill her finis she run way longa you."

For a moment Rachel thought her uncle was going to explode. His face flushed a deep maroon, and he seemed to be having trouble breathing. He turned away, beating his fist into the palm of his other hand in silent rage.

Rachel nodded to Suva and he gratefully backed away out of sight into the house.

Father Goode turned to his niece. "You knew about this?"

Rachel nodded.

The priest seemed suddenly to make up his mind. Gathering the hem of his cassock he stormed back into the bungalow, the screen door slamming behind him. Moments later he re-appeared, a large straw hat thrust firmly over his head. He jumped on the bicycle that was propped against the verandah steps.

"Where are you going?"

"I am not going to allow that child to be forced into prostitution by that monster!"

Rachel stamped her foot petulantly on the top wooden step. "Don't be so damned stupid!"

But for once her uncle let the oath go unchastised. With a little wobble he began pedalling away in the direction of Vancoro. He had made up his mind. There was no power on earth that was going to stop him now.

Two barbed wire fences, spaced at fifty yards apart, had been strung outside the District Office, now Colonel Nakamura's headquarters. The path leading up to the bungalow from the village passed between these two fences, and there was a sentry posted at each entrance.

It was along this pathway that Father Goode came that morning on the old and rusted black bicycle. He cycled slowly and imperiously, as he had done on so many previous occasions, to demand action or legislation from the District Officer over some matter concerning the spiritual welfare of the islanders – real or imagined.

This morning his bearing and demeanour were exactly the same.

The first sentry, a young boy barely eighteen years old, was perhaps too astonished to challenge him in time. He was also intimidated by the manner in which the priest rode past him without looking even once in his direction. It was as if he didn't exist. And when he was past him, it was already too late.

He had only two choices; he could either let him go or shoot him in the back.

The young soldier hesitated, his hand on the stock of his rifle. And in that position he stayed, unable to decide what he should do.

Meanwhile Father Goode cycled resolutely towards the thatched hut, secure in the knowledge that God was with him.

"*The Lord is my shepherd, I shall not want . . .*"

By that time he had already reached the second sentry, who had watched his progress first with bemusement, then panic. The first guard had let him through without even challenging him. Why?

He raised his rifle, and pointed it uncertainly in the direction of the priest.

"*Yeah, though I walk in the shadow of the Valley of Death . . .*"

Father Goode did not even spare a glance in his direction. His mind and heart were full of apostolic vengeance. He felt himself filled with the wrath of the Holy Spirit, as Jesus had been when he entered the temple to throw out the moneychangers.

The Lord was moving in him. Nothing could stop him.

The second sentry however was not aware that he faced such an unfathomable foe. He watched his compatriot fumble with his rifle then stared in confusion at the strange apparition making its way towards him, dressed in black in the heat of the day, the monstrous straw hat pulled down over the sickly pale face.

He decided something was very wrong. Unwilling to risk the wrath of Lieutenant Tashiro, he stepped forward, gun ready at his hip.

He ordered the priest to stop.

Father Goode, unfamiliar with the Japanese language, kept going. Even an exact knowledge of Oriental languages would have made no difference.

"*For Thou art with me. Thy rod and staff they comfort me . . .*"

Father Goode continued to recite his catechism and with a deft touch to the handlebars he steered neatly around the sentry and kept on going. He kept his eyes fixed on the hut, his mind already composing the speech he would make to Colonel Nakamura.

"*As the spiritual leader of the people I demand that you take immediate steps to ensure that . . .*"

The second sentry had been astonished to see the priest cycle past him, but surprise quickly turned to panic. He raised his rifle and aimed carefully.

"Stop! Do not go any further or I will shoot!"

"*. . . and furthermore, Colonel Nakamura, may I remind you that you are bound not only by common decency, but by the laws of the Geneva Convention . . .*"

Father Goode heard a loud crack and suddenly the ground seemed to surge towards him. Someone had pushed him off his bicycle so hard his face had hit the ground before he could throw up his hands to protect himself. There was a pain in his nose and mouth and someone had set fire to his left leg.

He tried to move but his whole body felt like lead. There was something warm and wet seeping through the cassock.

He groaned aloud and then blackness enveloped him.

19

The sound of the rifle shot brought Nakamura and Tashiro running out on to the verandah from the office. They found the priest lying face down on the lawn, his bicycle sprawled behind him, one wheel still spinning.

One of the sentries ran towards them.

"What happened?" Nakamura barked.

"He wouldn't stop, Nakamura-san," the soldier said. "I warned him twice. He just kept going."

Tashiro came down the steps, and strode over to where the priest lay. He turned him over with the toe of his boot.

"It's the English priest," Tashiro said contemptuously.

"Is he dead?"

Tashiro shook his head. "Leg wound," he said.

"What was he doing here? Is he armed?"

Tashiro frisked him quickly, expertly. He shook his head. "Unarmed. What do you want me to do with him, Nakamura-san?"

Nakamura shrugged. "Throw him in the prison house. We will interrogate him later," he said, and he went back inside.

Patrick Corrigan surveyed the night through the wrong end of a bottle of clear spirit, and toasted an uncertain future.

Ever since the Japanese had thrown him off the *Shamrock*, he had surrendered to the excesses of strong drink. Swallowed up by a fug of alcohol and despair he catalogued the litany of disasters that life had wreaked on him, and he stumbled through the house shouting slurred oaths at the Fates that had trapped him on a God-forsaken island with no way to live and no way to escape. He had become a prisoner of war in a war he wanted no part of.

It seemed no matter how fast or far he ran, trouble always caught up with Patrick Corrigan.

Sanei had been his only solace. He would rail at her, jeering insults as he struggled in the grip of another drunken rage; then he would chase her from the house, an empty bottle splintering on the ground at her feet as she ran. But the next morning she would always return, bringing him coffee and a meal of rice and spiced pork, as if nothing had ever happened between them. Sanei's soft loving slowly brought Corrigan out of the dark places of his own despair, until finally his spirits lifted and a new notion was born to him.

Although the Japanese had requisitioned the *Shamrock*, they had so far made no moves to appropriate Heydrich's schooner, the *Deutschland*. Perhaps it was because he was Austrian, and therefore the national of a close ally. More probably it was because Heydrich kept his boat out of sight in a neatly camouflaged boat shed on his plantation. Whatever the reason it represented to Corrigan a means of escape.

Heydrich's plantation was situated ten miles to the north, on the west coast of the island. To reach it by land, it would require a two-day hike through harsh mangrove swamp and jungle. But Corrigan was desperate, and he had resolved to do it.

He knew the boat would not be guarded. Once he reached the plantation it would be a simple matter to slip the boat free of its moorings under cover of darkness and head for the open sea. He would cling close to the shore and then plot a course to the west, for the Trobriand Islands, and then down to Townsville in Australia.

If they were stopped by a Japanese patrol boat, he could always produce the Irish passport and claim neutrality. The biggest risk was that they might be caught on the open sea by Japanese aircraft and strafed. But anything was better than sitting on Santa Maria, rotting away.

Corrigan located one final bottle of gin, just a quarter full, somehow overlooked during the binge of the previous weeks. Now he raised the bottle lovingly to his lips, as a final toast to the success of his venture.

It was then that he saw a familiar shadow on the verandah and he almost groaned aloud.

"What's that bloody woman want now?" he muttered.

He heard a faint tapping on the front door. Corrigan took another long gulp from the bottle and slid further down into the cane chair. "It's open," he croaked.

Rachel Goode crept into the room. She sniffed, walked across to the French windows and opened them.

"It smells in here," she said.

Corrigan watched her, fascinated. Whatever else you said about her, the girl certainly had a lot of nerve.

She was wearing a long white calico dress, and a broad-brimmed hat, tied underneath her chin with a bow. She untied the bow and took off the hat, and held it in front of her, agitated fingers working their way along the brim. Her eyes were puffed and swollen; she had been crying.

Corrigan grimaced. "If you want me to take you for another jaunt up the island you're wasting your time. The *Shamrock*'s the flagship of the Imperial Japanese Navy these days."

"That's not why I have come."

Corrigan shifted uncomfortably in his chair. "If it's my body you're lusting after, I'm already spoken for."

Rachel blushed bright crimson and Corrigan chuckled, a low indecent sound that came from deep in his chest. It seemed to Rachel that he enjoyed making her uncomfortable.

"It's about my uncle. He . . . he has been shot and thrown into prison by the Japanese."

"I heard."

"Is that all you can say?"

"Well, you know, we've all got our problems."

Rachel hated to beg, especially to Corrigan. Now she drew herself up to her full height. "I do not know what to do . . . or where to go. I . . . I hoped you might help me."

Corrigan stared at her open-mouthed. "Me?"

"You are a man of some resource. Why not?"

She stood there unmoving in the middle of the room, looking at him now down that proud and haughty nose. Her mouth had tightened in thin-lipped determination.

Corrigan got up from the chair and took two steps towards her. He was a head taller than the girl, and twice as broad. She stood her ground and returned his cool stare.

"What do I care if they tie the miserable old bastard up by his thumbs?"

To Corrigan's amazement a tear squeezed its way out of the corner of her eye and began its slow journey down her cheek. It hung there for a long moment; and the dull glow of the lamp reflected in it, making it sparkle like a gemstone before it finally splashed on to the collar of her dress.

She dabbed at her face with a handkerchief. "I don't suppose you do care. I'm asking you to do it as a personal favour to me."

He turned away. "You're out of your mind."

"I can pay you."

"How much?"

Rachel fumbled in her purse and threw a tiny bundle of notes on the table. "Ten pounds. It's all we have left."

"That money's no good to me here. Besides I'm not getting myself shot for ten pounds."

"There are other methods of payment if you prefer."

Corrigan eyed her coolly. He had no doubt what she meant and he was shocked. Shocked for the first time in many years. "The answer's still the same," he said huskily.

He reached for the bottle of gin and unscrewed the cap. Rachel stood and watched him. She had barely moved since she had entered the room.

"What are you looking at?"

"I'll not go till you agree to help me, Mister Corrigan."

Corrigan sighed. All he wanted was to be left in his own sort of peace, but now he could feel the cold tendrils of circumstance reaching out for him, drawing him in. He knew he should tell this damned girl to get out of his house right now.

"What the hell do you expect me to do?"

"I have no doubt that a man of your considerable resource and courage will think of something."

Corrigan sighed. All right then, he would do this damned girl one more favour. It wouldn't be that difficult after all, and when it was done he could get on with his plan to get off Santa Maria.

He screwed the cap back on the bottle and put it back on the table. To do what he was about to do, he'd better be sober.

*

Patrick Corrigan had lived on Santa Maria for almost five years and even he was surprised at how little he was taking away with him. He packed his passport, the little money he had left, some clothes and some food into an old canvas haversack and threw it across his shoulder. As an afterthought he went back for the gin.

"Medicinal purposes," he winked at Rachel.

Rachel said her uncle had a leg wound. We'll have to carry the old bastard Corrigan thought sourly. He threw down the haversack and vanished into the jungle that bordered the trading post. When he came back he had two lengths of bamboo, each as tall as a man. He took some lengths of coir rope and some flour sacks from the store and roughly fashioned a light, makeshift stretcher. Half an hour later he was ready.

Sanei waited sullenly on the front steps, staring at Rachel with dark, hooded eyes. Her face was drawn down in a sullen pout of disapproval. Corrigan came out of the bungalow and patted her head tenderly, as if she was a favourite dog.

He turned to Rachel. "She hates your guts," he told her cheerfully and walked past her into the night.

It was a warm night, and a gentle breeze drifted across the village from the bay, carrying the smell of salt. Cicadas kept up a deafening, throbbing symphony in the surrounding jungle.

A myriad of stars flared in the sky, the familiar winking pattern of the Southern Cross directly overhead. The moon rose slowly over the bay, the waves on the lagoon shimmering in its track like a gigantic staircase leading up to the heavens.

Rachel ran to catch up with Corrigan, now loping five paces ahead of her, gripping the stretcher under his right arm.

"Where are we going?"

"We're going to get your sainted uncle out of the blockhouse, like you asked me to."

"But you haven't told me how you intend to do that."

Corrigan grinned in the darkness. "Unlock the door I suppose."

"Unlock the door? What are you talking about?"

"I've got a key."

Rachel stopped in mid-stride and gaped at him. Once again she had to run to catch up with him. "You have a key?"

"I wouldn't be doing this if I didn't."

"But how?"

Corrigan didn't answer her. He grinned at her in the darkness and kept walking.

Wary of Japanese patrols he led them along a path through the jungle skirting the village. It was a full moon; like the night we spent together on the island, Rachel found herself thinking. It made it easy for them to pick their way up the gravel path that zig-zagged up the hillside.

All around them were the flickering glow of the fireflies and the rhythmic chik-chik of cicadas. Lamplight shone between the trees from the village far down the hillside to their left, and the air was scented with the heady aromas of frangipani and kerosene.

The lights of the Japanese sampans flickered at their moorings at the end of the jetty.

After a quarter of an hour the path got steeper as it wound its way up the headland around the District Office, the Residency bungalow and up towards the old prison building.

The gaol had been built on the promontory overlooking the harbour on one side, and the open sea on the other. The plateau had been cleared to make way for it, so that they had to stop on the fringe of the jungle, still some hundred yards away. The prisonhouse loomed ahead of them in the darkness, its limestone walls shining like old bones in the light of the moon.

Corrigan crouched down, creeping forward on his elbows and his knees, and signalled Rachel and Sanei to do the same.

There was just one sentry on watch outside, his silhouette illuminated by the single hurricane lamp that burned under the archway of the main door.

Obviously the Japanese were not expecting trouble.

"What are you going to do?" Rachel whispered in the darkness.

"We have a plan," Corrigan said.

He tapped Sanei on the shoulder. She nodded her understanding, and silently pulled herself up on to her knees and began to unbutton her thin cotton blouse.

Then, dressed only in the blue-dyed *lava-lava* around her hips, she got up and started to walk towards the sentry.

The Japanese sentry looked bored and unhappy. He knew that his was only a token presence, and that he faced a long and uneventful watch. The duty was also a slur on his standing within the company; the disgrace of being a prison guard was second only to being a prisoner oneself.

He had leaned his rifle against the wall, and now lounged on his haunches against the heavy main door, smoking a cigarette. Occasionally the glow of the cigarette illuminated his face and Rachel could see that he was very, very young.

He heard Sanei almost immediately. Crushing out the cigarette he leaped to his feet and grabbed his rifle, training it on the darkened jungle. But there was no question that he might pull the trigger; in truth he feared an inspection from First Lieutenant Tashiro more than he feared the enemy.

Rachel watched, confused and horrified. What was Corrigan planning?

The soldier barked out a command in Japanese. Sanei continued to walk towards him.

She moved very slowly, on the bare pads of her feet, with an exaggerated motion of her hips. Suddenly her shadow moved out of the darkness, and she was illuminated by the light of the hurricane lamp hanging over the door. Immediately the soldier relaxed as he saw the slim, half-naked body coming towards him.

He laughed once, a dry barking sound, and lowered his rifle. He had envisaged a long, dark night with only the night crickets for company but now it seemed his luck had changed.

He had heard from older colleagues that the women of the South Seas were free with their sexual favours. He had dismissed these stories at first and his first few weeks on Santa Maria had done nothing to dissuade him that they were anything but mischievous rumours.

But he was more than eager to revise his first impressions.

As Rachel watched, the young Japanese lowered the rifle to his side and took a tentative step towards the sleek-skinned girl coming towards him in the moonlight. Sanei put her arms around the young soldier's neck and her hips squirmed against him. The gun clattered noisily against the wall and on to the ground as the young *samurai* greedily clawed with both his hands at her body, perhaps in lust, or perhaps to convince himself that this apparition was real.

Already he was scrabbling at the belt of his trousers.

Rachel looked away, feeling her cheeks burning scarlet. She looked round at Corrigan, expecting to find him watching her with that infuriating, mocking smile of his. But Corrigan had other things on his mind.

With smooth and fluid grace, he tore off his boots, and took the knife with its heavy carved ivory handle out of the sheath at his waist. Then he started to crawl silently through the grass towards the prison block.

Hardly daring to breathe, Rachel watched him.

From the grass in front of the main door, the sounds of love-making were growing more intense. The soldier had dragged Sanei on to a small patch of grass and had rolled her on her back, stripping away the strip of cloth around her waist and murmuring endearments in his own tongue, all the time laughing with excitement and anticipation.

Meanwhile Corrigan had stopped, on the edge of the shadows, no more than thirty feet away.

Long seconds.

Suddenly he was on his feet, running across the clearing.

Rachel held her breath. The soldier had only to look up and he would see Corrigan coming. The rifle lay just a few feet away from him in the grass. He would have plenty of time to snatch it up and fire.

He was lying on top of Sanei now, his khaki pants around his ankles, the muscles of his buttocks clenched tight as a fist as he tried to enter her.

Sanei cried out in genuine pain.

Then she opened her eyes and saw Corrigan. Realising the danger she took the young soldier's head in both her hands in a display of mock passion, effectively blinkering him.

It was enough. It was only at the very last moment that the soldier saw Corrigan's shadow. He cried out in panic, and tried to reach for his rifle, but Sanei caught his wrist. He struggled and managed to pull his hand free but by then it was too late.

With an agility that belied his bulk, Corrigan sprang forward and brought the knife crashing down on the back of the man's head.

The soldier pitched sideways on to the ground and lay on his back, quite still.

Naked, Sanei jumped to her feet and kicked him once, fiercely, in the chest.

"Pig!" she spat.

Corrigan caught her by the wrist. "That's no way to behave on your first date," he chuckled. He picked up her sarong and threw it at her. "Get dressed. There's a man of the cloth in there, you know."

"I not make *pus-pus* with *Japoni* man again. Not even for you, Corrigan."

"You'll get a terrible reputation if you kiss and tell like this," Corrigan said. He turned towards the shadows where Rachel was hiding. "What's the matter with you, girl? Bring the stuff and get over here!"

Rachel picked up the haversack and Sanei's blouse from the ground beside her and ran across the clearing.

She looked down at the body of the soldier. "You killed him?"

"Of course I didn't kill him. I hit him with the blunt end. When he wakes up he'll think it was just a wet dream."

"But as soon as he comes round he'll alert the whole Japanese garrison."

"Not if we truss him up and gag him he won't. We'll throw him in one of the cells. It will give him plenty of time between now and morning to contemplate the terrible wickedness of women."

He fumbled inside the canvas bag and pulled out two large keys on a ring chain. While Sanei pulled on her blouse he put one of the keys in the lock of the main door and kicked it open.

The hurricane lamp hung on a nail hammered into the wall over the door. He took it down, and led the way inside.

The prison building had been constructed almost fifty years before, with hard-nosed British pragmatism. The original designers did not have the comfort and well-being of future inmates uppermost in their mind. There were few windows and the sanitary arrangements were spartan. From the cells came a dense aroma formed by years of mould and accumulated human waste. Rachel gagged.

"Many's the happy night I've spent in this little place," Corrigan said. "Enough to cure a man of drink. Now you know why I made Manning's little chocolate soldier give me the key."

Father Goode was the only occupant of the gaol. He was unconscious.

As they threw open the door of his cell a rat scurried away into the darkness, but in the lamplight they could see the open sore on one of the priest's feet where it had already gorged itself on his flesh.

Rachel's hand shot to her mouth. "Oh God."

The Japanese had not bothered to tend the bullet wound in the priest's leg. The lower part of the cassock was encrusted with dried blood from the wound; the exposed skin of his arms, feet and face was a mass of swollen welts where the mosquitoes had feasted on him.

Rachel ran forward and knelt down beside him, cradling his head in her hands. "Uncle Matthew," she murmured, "what have they done to you?"

Corrigan shone the lamp on the priest's face. "Is he still with us?"

Rachel felt for the pulse at his neck. She nodded. "He's lost a lot of blood. He needs medical attention."

"He's not going to get it here," Corrigan said. He handed the lamp to Sanei and bending down he hoisted the unconscious priest over his shoulder.

"We'd better get out of here before the last of the red hot lovers wakes up."

"Where can we go?" Rachel said.

"I've already thought about that," Corrigan told her. "I hope you've got your walking shoes on. We're going to pay a visit to my old pal Heydrich."

20

They made barely four miles that night.

Sanei led the way, navigating by the stars and some innate native sense, while Corrigan and Rachel struggled behind with the stretcher, scrambling and slashing their way through the clawing jungle and hanging liana vines, all uphill.

They had to stop frequently for Rachel to rest, her

uncle's dead weight almost too much for her. He moaned and tossed on the stretcher, his writhings several times tipping Rachel off balance and throwing her forward into the soft, moist earth.

They scrambled up the steep, jungle-clad hills, slipped down the shallow valleys, the dark brown vegetation crumbling and treacherous underfoot, then had to pick their way across moss-covered rocks in the creek beds.

Then the long climb up into the hills would begin again.

Just before dawn Sanei screamed in the darkness and Corrigan dropped the stretcher and ran to her. The girl writhed and thrashed in agony on the ground.

"What is it?" Rachel said.

"I don't know. She says she's been bitten. Maybe a centipede. I hope to God it wasn't a snake."

Corrigan cradled her in his arms, unable to help. Rachel squatted beside the stretcher, emotionally and physically exhausted, and began to doze, light-headed with fatigue. But half an hour later Sanei hobbled back on to her feet and Corrigan shoved Rachel roughly upright.

"We have to keep going," he said.

Whimpering with pain, Sanei again attacked the jungle with Corrigan's knife, carving a path through the creepers and the vines. Rachel gained a new respect for the native girl; without her, she knew, there was no way they would have found their way through the impenetrable night jungle.

By dawn they were all too exhausted to continue.

They rested in a clearing, the first yellow bolts of sunlight angling through the tall canopy of trees. The jungle was suddenly transformed by the morning into a paradise of orchids and ferns, with green and yellow and purple butterflies dancing around the brilliant red of a ginger plant flower. A flock of white cockatoos wheeled overhead, contrasted against the misty greens of the trees and the watery blue of the sky. Rainbow and Cardinal lorikeets screeched and squabbled in a nearby ailali tree.

Rachel forced herself to her feet. She tried to examine Sanei's swollen foot but the girl pushed her away, uttering a stream of curses in her native tongue. Rachel turned away with a shrug of despair and instead bent over her uncle who lay moaning and shivering on the stretcher, bathed in his own sweat.

Corrigan leaned over her shoulder. "How is he?"

"I'll have to operate," Rachel said.

He grunted. "I don't care if you cut his bloody leg off," he told Rachel, "as long as I don't have to watch."

"The fact is, Mister Corrigan, I need you to hold him down," Rachel said.

Corrigan shook his head. He looked down at the priest. His eyes were sunk back into his head and his face had the pale waxen quality of a death mask. The only colour on his skin was the swollen red lumps of the insect bites.

Rachel had ripped away the cassock, and the left leg lay exposed, livid-white and somehow obscene. The bullet wound was swollen and bloated and the flesh around it was a plum-coloured bruise. A scab had formed over the entry wound but pus oozed from beneath it. Corrigan turned away nauseated.

"Christ, woman," he muttered, "let's just shoot him and put him out of his misery. He hasn't got a chance."

"If we can get the bullet out, we can save the leg," Rachel said. "It's not deep."

"You haven't got any equipment," Corrigan protested.

"I'll use your knife," Rachel said, indicating the big ivory-handled knife Corrigan wore at his belt.

"Holy Mary, what kind of a woman are you?"

"I can't let him die."

He turned away. Sanei was squatting on the ground, her arms drawn across her knees in a distinctive native posture, watching their discussion with detached curiosity. She chewed noisily on a breadfruit, the purple stained juice dribbling down her chin.

Corrigan snatched it away from her suddenly and threw it into the undergrowth. "For God's sake," Corrigan

protested. "Go somewhere else and eat the bloody thing!"
Sanei looked at him in bewilderment.
Rachel did not take her eyes from him. "Will you help me?" she repeated.
Corrigan sighed. "I haven't let you down yet, have I?" he said at last.

Corrigan knelt on the priest's shoulders, facing towards his feet. One massive hand was planted on each of the priest's legs. Father Goode lay supine, firmly pinioned beneath him.
Rachel knelt by the fire, preparing the knife. She had sharpened it with a stone and heated it white-hot over the fire. Beside her stood half a coconut shell full of boiled seawater in which she had soaked long strips of her own skirt to wrap and bind the wound.
Corrigan watched her, one eye on the knife, the other on Rachel. Jesus, she didn't have bad legs under all that calico. He had stared with frank curiosity as she had torn up her skirt and his initial surprise had turned to admiration. A part of him wished she might start to tear up her blouse as well. He felt a familiar stirring in his groin. He realised with shock that Rachel Goode probably had a wonderful figure beneath the disguise of the flowing calico.
"Shame on you," said a voice somewhere between his legs. It was Father Goode. "Turn away your eyes, man. Have you no shame at all?"
"None to speak of," Corrigan said.
Rachel seemed oblivious to Corrigan's attention. Her mind was on the job in front of her. She cleaned Corrigan's knife with coconut fibre and seawater and crossed to the stretcher where her uncle lay, pinioned ridiculously beneath Corrigan.
"Ready, Mister Corrigan?" she whispered.
"Just get on with it."
Rachel knelt down, holding the edge of the blade over the wound. Suddenly she slashed with the knife and the

flesh split open like a ripe fruit. The thick pus bubbled up from the wound.

Corrigan swallowed hard and closed his eyes. Beneath him the priest bellowed and bucked like a wounded bull.

"Hurry up!" Corrigan shouted. "I can't hold him down for ever!"

Rachel slipped the little finger of her right hand into the wound and felt for the bullet. Father Goode screamed again, his whole body jumping and twisting like a marionette.

Suddenly Rachel twisted her hand and as she pulled her finger free a silver-grey object plopped on to the ground, followed by a thick rush of grey-green poison.

At the same time Corrigan bellowed and rolled aside into the grass, groaning and choking.

Rachel looked around. Father Goode lay quite still now. He had passed out.

Quickly she poured the brine over the wound and bandaged it with strips of her blouse. She wished desperately for some of the sulphonamide drugs they kept in the store at the Mission Hospital. But it was too late for that now.

Corrigan still lay rolling and groaning in the sand a few feet away.

"Mister Corrigan?" Rachel said, suddenly alarmed. "Are you all right?"

"He bit me," Corrigan gasped, in pain and indignation, "he bit me – on the balls!"

21

They reached Balo Balo around noon.

There had been no rain for several days and the carpet

of leaves crackled under their feet as they walked. On one side of the path someone had killed a big monitor lizard and a cloud of flies rose angrily from the pungent remains as they approached.

Sanei went ahead, while Rachel helped Corrigan carry the stretcher. Sweat glistened on her skin, soaking the ragged remains of her muslin skirt.

There was a clump of breadfruit trees on the outskirts of the village; past this the path widened into a grove of areca palms and Rachel glimpsed the thatched roofs of the huts, and the deep blue of the sea beyond.

Corrigan used his boots to drive off a scrawny yellow dog that yapped and tugged at his heels and they walked into the village.

A skein of blue-grey wood smoke curled into the still air from an open fire and the smell of freshly fried fish hung in the still air. Women with long bloodwood poles pounded grain in wooden mortars. A young man was lashing together a framework of sticks for a canoe; and beside him an older man with a pipe was casually repairing a fishing net.

Children played naked on the sandy ground outside the huts, staring at the party in surprise. One of the younger children ran wailing to its mother.

Corrigan stopped outside one of the huts and they laid down the stretcher. Father Goode was still unconscious, but in the last half an hour he had shown signs of recovering. He murmured and tossed on the makeshift stretcher.

Corrigan slumped down on the edge of a *keda* in the shade of a canoe house. A fish net hung from the rough-hewn rafters and naked children clustered around, staring at them with their steady, unabashed gaze.

Finally Sanei returned with an old man of about sixty and a young boy. Sanei introduced the older man as Ngatu.

Ngatu was an extraordinary sight. He had long pierced earlobes in which he carried his pipe and twist tobacco, and he had a strip of red cloth tied tightly around his lime-blond hair. Apart from the woven penis-wrapper, he wore little else except a long necklace made from the teeth of a flying fox. The red bandana and the sparse grey beard made him appear a little like a pirate.

The corners of his mouth were deeply ravined, and stained with betel nut juice.

"You like green coconut?" he asked.

"Yes, that would be kind," Rachel said.

"I'd rather have a gin," Corrigan said.

The old man said something to the youth with him. He disappeared into one of the huts and re-appeared with a small length of creeper worked into a loop. He went to the foot of one of the palm trees, gave it a sharp twist and passed his feet through.

Gripping the trunk with his hands and feet, and pressing on the trunk with the loop of vine, he reached up with his hands, at the same time drawing up his feet, repeating the action till he reached the top of the palm. He threw down two green coconuts and descended.

The headman slashed off the top of one of the coconuts with a machete and handed it to Rachel. She gulped thankfully at the tepid fluid inside.

He gave the other to Corrigan.

"We'll rest here tonight," Corrigan said.

"In the village?"

"In the old man's hut."

"That's very Christian of him."

Corrigan laughed. "That's got nothing to do with it. He and Sanei are from the same *tindadho*. They both share the same totem, the shark. He has to help her. It would bring him great shame to turn away one of his own clan, even a total stranger."

Rachel nodded. She knew about the tribal clans – pagan worship her uncle called it – but she still had little understanding of their importance in the island's society. Despite what her uncle said, it now seemed to her a very beneficial system.

Corrigan climbed to his feet and nodded towards the pale, twitching figure lying on the bamboo stretcher.

"Better move him into the shade. Looks like Sleeping Beauty is about to wake up."

"I refuse to leave this island. You can run away if you wish, Mister Corrigan, but my place is here with these people. They trust me. I will not skulk away like a coward in the night. It is my duty to stay and face the Barbarian in whatever form he may manifest himself."

Corrigan listened to this speech with growing impatience. His hands tightened into fists at his sides and his anger smouldered beneath the surface like lava under a volcano.

"Horseshit," he said finally.

"I would remind you not to use that sort of language in front of ladies."

This last rejoinder seemed so utterly incongruous, that Corrigan gave a guffaw of laughter.

"You consider ill manners and a foul mouth humorous?"

Corrigan punched his fist into one of the heavy bloodwood poles that rose from the centre of the hut in an effort to vent the rage that was building in him. The hut shuddered in protest.

Corrigan glared down at the pale wan figure on the stretcher. "No, it's you that's funny. What good do you think you're going to do staying here, you pompous little arse? The Japs are probably combing the jungle for you right now and when they find you they'll string you up by the balls and use the rest of you for bayonet practice. If that's the will of the Lord I'm Clark Gable. And while we're talking about manners, I don't recall hearing you thank me for saving your arse back there in that Jap guardhouse."

"I do not think it necessary to thank a man for taking the only reasonable course open to him. Surely you could not have considered standing idly by and leaving braver men to their fate?"

Corrigan laughed again, a barking sound without humour. Muttering under his breath he picked up one of the coconut husks that lay by the side of the charred fire. He threw it out of the doorway into the kraal with all his force; a fowl that was pecking at the foot of the steps shrieked and flapped in sudden terror.

Ngatu had given them an empty hut that was reserved for strangers. It was constructed of split bamboo and coconut fronds, and was raised a few feet off the ground. He had brought them a meal of squid and cabbage cooked in coconut cream, and had tended to them without question.

The priest's fever had broken soon after the removal of the bullet and he had recovered consciousness. He had even allowed Rachel to feed him some banana and had drunk some fresh coconut milk. Corrigan was already regretting the priest's resilience.

Now that the food and a little sleep had revitalised his spirits, Corrigan was eager to be on his way. They were still five miles from Heydrich's plantation, another day's march, perhaps two, weighed down as they were with the stretcher.

But Father Goode and his stubborn niece refused to go.

"I could be away from here by now," Corrigan cursed under his breath. "If it wasn't for you and your bloody niece I could be off this stinking island."

"All we're asking is that you help us find Ian Manning," Rachel said suddenly. "He and his policemen are somewhere on Santa Maria, we know they are."

Corrigan was unable to keep the sarcasm from his voice. "Is that all you want me to do? Find Ian Manning for you? How long would you like me to look? One year? Two?"

"Perhaps Sanei could find out for us," Father Goode said. "She's a native after all."

"A native, sure. She's not a clairvoyant."

"Well, we have made our decision. You must make yours. We cannot go with you. It's as simple as that."

"I can't just leave you here, can I now?"

Father Goode forced a rare smile. "Surely you wouldn't let a little thing like conscience bother you, would you?"

"He saved your life!" Rachel protested. "You can't talk to him like that!"

The priest lowered his head on to the stretcher, and closed his eyes. "Very well. 'By their works shall ye know them.' We are in Mister Corrigan's hands now."

Corrigan studied Father Goode with an expression of distaste. The priest's pomposity had been hard to stomach, even when he was dressed in the full glory of his canonicals. Now, with the flesh around his face shrunken in, leaving dark shadows under the sockets of his eyes and his cheeks, it was utterly grotesque. He was being lectured by a cadaver.

Corrigan sat with his back to them for a long time in silence, looking down towards the beach and the shimmering waters of the lagoon. Somewhere out there lay the Trobriands. Sanei watched him, unable to comprehend the moral dilemma that he was wrestling with.

Troubled, she got up, and sat herself down next to him, putting a slim, coffee brown arm on his shoulder.

Finally Corrigan turned back to Rachel and shook his head. "You don't know what you're asking."

"I'm sorry, Mister Corrigan," Rachel murmured.

"Sorry?"

"For involving you in all this."

"Lot of good that does me."

"Yes, but I'm sorry all the same. But if I had the time over again I would have done the same thing. I had no choice."

"Sure, I know the feeling well."

Corrigan stood up suddenly. It seemed he had made up his mind. "Do you think this miserable piece of religion and pomposity will make it?" he said to Rachel, pointing to the priest as if he were a piece of lumber.

Rachel nodded. "I haven't lost a patient yet."

"How many have you had?"

"The native Kumasi at Marmari Point was my first. Uncle Matthew is my second."

Corrigan shook his head. He hated them both, this monstrous priest and his cool-eyed, iron-willed niece. But he couldn't help but admire their courage. He just wished he'd never set eyes on either of them.

"What if he died?" he said, pointing to Father Goode. "What would you do? Would you still want to stay then?"

"Are you considering murder as a less painful alternative to abandonment, Mister Corrigan?" Father Goode asked him.

Corrigan ignored him. He looked at the girl for her answer.

"I don't know what I'd do," Rachel answered truthfully.

"At this point of time it remains a theoretical question," Father Goode said. "The more pressing question is – what *are* you going to do?"

"Manning may be dead, for all we know. The chances of finding him are a hundred to one. We certainly won't find him lugging the stretcher round with us."

"So what are you suggesting?"

Corrigan hesitated. Those cold tendrils he had felt the night before at Vancoro were embracing him now, their foul and clammy grip dragging him down.

But what other choice was there?

"You're right, Sanei might be able to find him. Maybe even some of the natives here in the village know where he is. Besides, she can find her way around in this country better than any one of us. We'll stay here in the village and I'll send her off to look for him."

"You have a reputation as something of a gambler, Mister Corrigan," Father Goode said. "What are our chances?"

"Of finding Manning? Hundred to one against. But if you're serious about putting money down, I'll give you ten to one on the Japs finding us first."

22

Sanei had been gone three days. By the third evening Corrigan had become fretful, pacing the hut with the long, restless strides of a caged tiger.

"The thing is," Father Goode was saying, "can we trust her not to go to the Japanese?"

Corrigan gave him a sour look. "For someone who professes to love these people, you don't seem to have a very high opinion of them."

"I'm a realist, Mister Corrigan."

Rachel stood up angrily. "She risked her life to save you, uncle. If you had seen what she . . ." She stopped herself. There was no point in elaborating on what Sanei had done to get him free. It would only inspire another speech.

"Very well, if you say she is to be trusted, I am willing to take your word." He laid his head back on the stretcher and closed his eyes, assuming the look of practised humility Rachel saw often on his face after he had given Communion.

Corrigan sat down against one of the bloodwood poles and looked up at the ceiling, watching a tiny pale gekko stalking its prey on the bamboo rafters. "What if she doesn't find him?"

"We must trust in the Hand of the Lord," Father Goode murmured.

"The Hand of the Lord. That's what you celibates use, isn't it?" Corrigan snorted.

Corrigan's ribald attempt at humour was lost on the priest. "Whatever happens we will stay here. There is no question of leaving."

"It's Manning I feel sorry for. He's got a tough enough job in front of him without having to take care of a cripple and a woman."

Corrigan heard a sharp intake of breath and turned to see Rachel glaring at him, her eyes aflame with sudden fury. "I may be a woman, Mister Corrigan, but I refuse to see how that is a liability. I do not recall breaking down in fits of tears at any time during the journey here."

"Well, I suppose there is that to it," Corrigan agreed sheepishly.

"Thank you."

"All the same, he shouldn't have put you in this damn position," Corrigan said to her, pointing at the priest.

"It was God's will," Father Goode said.

"No it wasn't. It was your bloody arrogance and stupidity. If you'd minded your own business instead of marching into the Japs' headquarters like Winston Churchill, none of this would have happened. I'd be on a boat to Australia and you'd still be playing hymns in Sunday school."

"Mister Corrigan, I have observed you for some time, and I have often wondered what it is you are running away from. It has struck me as an enigma that a man can be so obsessed with his own survival on one hand, and on the other work so hard to bring about his own destruction through strong drink and recklessness. The only conclusion that I can come to is that you are a physical and emotional coward."

Corrigan got slowly to his feet, his fists clenching and unclenching in silent rage. His face had darkened as if a shadow had passed across it.

Father Goode, his eyes still closed in pious contemplation, was not aware of him.

Corrigan stood looking down at him for a long time before suddenly stamping outside and marching away towards the beach.

"Sometimes you are an unspeakable thug," Rachel whispered close to her uncle's ear and his eyes started open in surprise at the venom in her voice. But then she was gone, running after Corrigan down the jungle path.

An hour later they returned. Corrigan had collected some bananas and a green coconut from Ngatu's garden. He divided up the meagre meal and they ate in silence. The priest's words were never mentioned again.

From the air, Manning's lookout, high in the branches of the tall banyan tree did not exist.

The platform and ladder had been expertly constructed by Sergeant Lavella and his men from bamboo and loia cane, and was lashed with vines and liana creeper. The roof had been covered in ferns so that even to an aircraft flying directly overhead, all that was visible was the endless green canopy of the jungle.

But from the ground the tree provided quite a different aspect. Cane loops had been nailed to the tree so that scouts could ascend or descend in less than a minute. There was a sentry high in the platform from dawn to dusk; he would lower a bucket for food, or water or to replenish his supply of betel nut.

The sentry was also armed with a conch shell. Manning had quickly learned that to the islanders all warships were "men o'war" – a hangover perhaps from the early colonial days – so that he knew he could not rely on his scouts alone for accurate information.

So that afternoon, when he heard the blast on the conch shell, he raced from his hut and began the long climb up the trunk of the banyan tree.

The field glasses were positioned on a tripod on a sturdy platform of bamboo. He paused for a moment to catch his breath, then bent over and focused them on The Slot, the deep-water channel that runs between the western and eastern islands of the Solomons.

Sweat trickled into his eyes from the wellsprings in his hair and on his forehead; he wiped them away with the shoulder of his thin khaki shirt.

It had been his third ascent of the banyan tree that day and he felt a thrill of fear and excitement; the war was getting closer. Out towards Cape Tavu he could make out the silhouettes of three destroyers and a half a dozen transports heading south towards Guadalcanal.

He knew from the Australian news broadcasts he picked up on the teleradio that the United States had started to hit back at the Japanese. There had been massive naval battles at Coral Sea and at Midway; although the details had been sketchy and the reports confused it had given him hope, the first real hope in many long dark months.

He had begun to tell the villagers that soon the white men would return; even though he was not sure he believed it himself.

The storms and low cloud of the monsoon months had given way to clear blue skies, perfect weather for Coastwatchers. For three days now he had been able to record every Japanese ship that had travelled up and down The Slot. It was as if he had a place at the Japanese High Command.

He noted the details of the ships he saw in his notepad. A resourceful individual in the Allied Intelligence Bureau in Townsville had torn out some pages of *Jane's Fighting Ships* and sent them to him back in December, when he had received his commission in the Coastwatchers. It had proved invaluable for his identification of the grey silhouettes he saw pass by each day along The Slot.

He clambered back down the banyan, into the dense green camouflage of the jungle. When he reached the bottom he waited, steadying himself against the massive trunk, until the roaring in his ears subsided and his vision cleared. The daily exertion of climbing the tree was taking its toll on him. But there was no question of easing up. His job was just beginning.

As he was walking back towards the radio hut Sergeant Lavella suddenly burst into the clearing, running with that distinctive loping stride of his.

He was holding his beloved Lee-Enfield in his right

hand, waving it wildly in the air to attract his attention.

At once Manning's first thought was that the Japanese had tracked them down. He felt his stomach turn to ice.

"Lavella! What is it?"

"White fellers!" Lavella gasped. "Maybe that feller Corrigan and that missus belong Jesus Christ. Come this way. Carry some fella longa bed."

Manning gaped at him, relief and astonishment mixed together. Corrigan? Rachel Goode? What on earth were they doing up here in the hills? And how had they found him?

Running now, he followed Lavella back to the track that led into the clearing.

Lavella and his scouts had spotted the little procession long before they reached the clearing. So it was almost half an hour later that Corrigan appeared, he and Rachel carrying the stretcher between them up the steeply winding path, Sanei ahead of them, Corrigan's knife in her right hand, slashing a path through the liana and hanging vines.

Manning waited for them at the top of the path, his hands thrust deep into the pockets of his khaki shorts, a curious twisted smile on his lips.

"Well, well, well," he said as Corrigan finally came into view. "Nice to see you again, Patrick. Come to help the war effort?"

Corrigan scowled. He didn't even answer him.

"How did you find us, Patrick?"

"The natives. Some fellow called Kumasi told Sanei where to find you. Even lent her a scout for most of the way."

"Kumasi . . . yes I know him. He's the headman at Marmari Point."

"That's him."

Manning frowned. "If you can find me this easily so can the Japanese."

"Come on, Manning. You know these people as well as I do, maybe better. They may not understand what's going on, but they're still loyal to the British bloody Empire, though I'm buggered if I know why. They know enough to realise the Japs aren't looking for you out of any concern for your health."

"It only takes one bad apple, old chap."

Corrigan shrugged. "Well, you're safer than you've any right to be, if that's any consolation."

Manning got up and went over to one of the boxes in the corner of the hut. He pulled off the lid and reached inside. He took out a bottle of Johnny Walker whisky.

"Time for a little refreshment after your hard journey," he said.

"You're a gentleman and a scholar."

Manning brought over two enamel mugs and splashed some of the amber spirit into each. Then he sat down on the packing crate opposite Corrigan.

"Your health, old boy."

Corrigan drained his mug, and held it out for another fill. "Your health needs a lot more drinking to than mine," he said grinning.

"Didn't think I'd ever see you again, Patrick," he said, pouring more of the whisky into Corrigan's cup.

"Make the most of it. I won't be around for long. I'm getting off this damned island as soon as I bloody well can."

"And how do you propose to do that?"

Corrigan winked. "Heydrich's going to lend me his boat. He just doesn't know it yet."

Manning stared into his cup. "I suppose it hasn't crossed your mind to stay and help the war effort?"

"No, it hasn't. And it's not going to either. So you might as well save your breath."

"I thought you might have had a change of heart, that's all."

"Oh, and what made you think that?" Corrigan said, holding out his cup again.

Manning raised an eyebrow. When Corrigan drank, he was like a camel at a waterhole. He poured another measure of whisky into the cracked enamel cup.

"Why else would you go out of your way to help the priest and his young niece? The Japs would have shot you if you'd been caught."

"They didn't catch me though, did they?"

"It was a very great risk."

"Blame it on my generous nature."

"It had nothing to do with the girl, I suppose?"

Corrigan drained the cup and slammed it down on the wooden trestle table next to the radio. "Don't be daft."

Manning shook his head. "I don't think I'll ever quite understand you, Patrick. I never quite know what you'll do next."

"You can think about it after I'm gone. I'll rest up here for a day or two if it's all the same to you, then I'm off." He got to his feet. "Thanks for the drink. I suppose you wouldn't have one of those to spare?"

Ruefully Manning handed him the bottle. "Plenty more where that came from. If you decide to stick around."

"Nice try, but my guess is you've only got one case of the stuff at the most. You'll run out in a week. Australia won't."

And he turned and walked out of the hut.

23

Ian McLaren Manning squatted on a packing box in the radio hut, and stared at the cards in his hands. The three of hearts, three of clubs, six of spades, six of clubs and the ace of hearts. Two pairs.

He smiled to himself.

"All right, old boy. See you two fingers and raise you two fingers."

"See you four fingers and raise you another two," Corrigan said.

Manning sighed. "Good God, Patrick. That's almost half a bottle."

"If you can't pay, don't play," Corrigan growled.

Manning had been cajoled into a friendly game of cards. As money was valueless, Corrigan had persuaded him to gamble with his fast dwindling supply of whisky. Already he owed Corrigan two and a half bottles.

"All right, I'll see you." He laid his cards triumphantly on the upturned crate. "Two pairs."

"Tough luck," Corrigan said, throwing down three queens and two jacks. "Full house."

Manning stared at the cards in surprise and confusion, then back at Corrigan. "That's impossible."

Corrigan's face flushed an angry red. "Are you calling me a cheat?"

Manning considered this question carefully. "Yes, Patrick old boy. I am."

Corrigan grinned unexpectedly. "Ah well, you're probably right. But you didn't see me, so it won't do you any good now." He checked the pad at his side, licking the pencil in his right hand and adding carefully. "That's three bottles and two fingers you owe me. We'll call it quits at three bottles."

Manning sighed and went over to the radio. He sat down on one of the crates and tuned the dial to 7 megacycles, listening for any interesting aircraft traffic. As he twisted the dial the hut suddenly came alive with the chatter of the US Carrier pilots and their ships.

"Good God!" Manning muttered.

Corrigan stared at him. "What in God's name is that?"

"I'm not sure," Manning said. "But it sounds like we're sitting in the middle of it."

*

At ten o'clock the blast from the conch shell sent Manning scurrying outside the hut. He looked up into the lookout on top of the giant banyan. Sergeant Lavella was leaning over the side, gesticulating wildly to the north-west.

"*Japoni* he come!" he shrieked. "*Japoni* he come!"

They heard them then. The distant buzzing of the engines grew to a deafening roar and several of the scouts started to shin up the surrounding trees to get a better look. Seconds later it was unnecessary.

A great formation of bombers raced across the empty sky just a few hundred feet above their heads. Manning caught a brief glimpse of the red discs painted on their fuselages, their propeller blades flashing in the sun. He tried to count.

A few seconds later, a second formation roared over them.

He ran back inside the hut and twisted the dial to the Coastwatchers' frequency.

Half an hour later, on the Australian cruiser *Canberra*, anchored off Guadalcanal, the captain piped this message over the loudspeakers:

"This ship will be attacked at noon by twenty-four torpedo bombers. All hands will pipe to lunch at eleven o'clock."

When the bombers arrived over Guadalcanal later that morning they found the transport ships had dispersed, the anti-aircraft batteries on the warships were manned and ready, and the fighters from the carrier escort were in the air and waiting for them.

Just after 2 pm, the sole surviving plane of the original force of twenty-four landed at Kavieng airfield. Manning had scored his first victory.

24

Dawn had thrown a pale golden aura along the ink-black border of the sea. Major James Mitchell strode across the khaki shamble of the tents and towards the dug-out on the edge of the airstrip.

Henderson Field had been carved through the razor-sharp kunai grass on the Lunga Plain. It consisted of a mud-black field with a gravel airstrip, already pocked with shell craters. In many places it had been hastily repaired with steel mats. The palms that surrounded the field had had their fronds blasted away by the constant shelling, and they stood now, ragged and bald. On the far side of the strip Corporal Cates was at work with the bulldozer, hastily digging a ditch for the bodies of Japanese snipers shot during the night, before setting to work on filling more of the bomb craters.

The first dirty light of the day silhouetted the makeshift skeleton of the control tower, no more than an elevated platform on the edge of the strip, and the unlikely oriental shape of the Pagoda, the operational headquarters that had originally been constructed by the Japanese. The American First Division had landed on Guadalcanal when Colonel Tei Monzen's engineers were within a few days of completing the strip. Ironically, the first planes to use the strip were the American Wildcats of Mitchell's own squadron.

The Japanese had been quick to respond. In the two weeks since the Marines had landed, the Japanese had thrown everything they had at Guadalcanal. The island was of paramount strategic importance; it was one of the few islands in the group with a plain wide enough to support an airstrip and so was vital to both sides. But it was also the first defeat the Americans had inflicted on the Japanese since Pearl Harbor, and it was becoming increasingly evident that the recapture of the island had become a matter of personal pride among the Imperial High Command. For the Americans it was fast becoming a symbol of resolve.

The night before Mitchell had landed on Guadalcanal the Japanese had attacked along the Ulu River, four miles east of the airstrip. The Marines, numerically superior, had won a crushing victory, but the ashen faces of the wounded as they filtered back into the camp told a different story. The Marines had been stunned by the ferocity of the Japanese attack; of eight hundred Japanese, only fifteen surrendered. The rest chose death, scythed down by the new American Browning machine guns in wave after wave of suicidal Banzai attacks.

Mitchell wondered how long the beleaguered garrison could hold out in the face of such commitment. The Japanese were landing troops unhindered on the western end of the island. An attack by a much larger force was inevitable.

Mitchell had reached the radio dug-out, which was hidden among the first row of stunted palms that surrounded the plain. The battered Japanese tent that stood nearby served as an office for the three marine radio operators who were on constant watch in the radio post. It looked ragged and forlorn in the grey half-light, countless jagged holes punched through the canvas by shrapnel.

The dug-out was no more than a narrow covered trench, fifty feet long and just five feet deep. No one could stand straight in it. It was roofed with coconut palm logs with decaying sandbags thrown on top. There was a ledge running along one side, scraped into the soft black earth, and it was on this ledge that the teleradio had been assembled.

By the side of the teleradio stood a pad and a field

telephone; from here the operator could instantly contact the operational headquarters in the Pagoda.

During a storm the rainwater soaked through the roof and dripped from the log beams on to the floor, forming a black, gluey mud which clung to everything. During these downpours the radio operators covered the precious equipment with their own waterproofs, protecting them from the cascading water while they themselves got soaked through.

Thankfully this morning there was blue sky overhead. A fine day for fighters.

As Mitchell stepped inside the dug-out a tall, gangly youth with bristle-cut hair and a blond fuzzy beard was already bent over the radio dials. There was a faint whine and crackle of static.

It was chill inside; later, in the furnace heat of the sun, the atmosphere would become unbearable. It was Corporal Shoup. He glanced up as Mitchell stepped inside.

"Nothing yet, sir," he said.

Mitchell sat down and took out a packet of cigarettes. He grimaced as he drew the smoke into his lungs; it was a Shikishima. There were no American cigarettes on the island. All they had was the supplies they had captured from the Japanese.

It was just one of the privations the Navy pilots had been forced to accept since they had landed on the "unsinkable aircraft carrier" of Guadalcanal. On the *Long Island*, there had been comfortable bunks, an air-conditioned mess and plenty to eat.

On Guadalcanal, there was the constant searing heat and torrential rain, voracious hordes of mosquitoes, and meagre half-rations. "If someone wanted to give the world an enema," Mitchell had heard one of his pilots mutter, "this sure would be a good place to stick the hose."

They slept in soggy, blacked-out tents, without floors. Their cots sank into the stinking black mud, as they snatched what sleep they could while around them there was the constant rattle of small arms fire from the jungle.

The Marines had learned to endure it with a stoic dark humour. Every afternoon at exactly one o'clock the Japanese bombers came to try and destroy what their engineers had so recently built. The Marines called it "Tojo Time". The Betsy bomber that came to bomb the airfield every night was "Louie the Louse". The Japanese destroyers that landed troops on the western end of the island, then lobbed shells on them from the blue waters of Iron Bottom Sound before sailing leisurely back up The Slot to Rabaul were the "Tokyo Express".

But for Mitchell and the rest of his squadron, the black humour was not so easy to accept. They were men who had experienced fear many times; men who knew combat and sudden death at close quarters in the skies at Coral Sea and at Midway. But shellfire was something new for all of them; during bombardment a man is helpless and in those long tense seconds when he first hears the whistle of the shell and waits for the concussion, he never knows just how close the shell will land, and whether he is seconds away from death. This was fear of a different kind, and already it was wreaking a toll on the pilots.

Someone observing closely would have noticed that Mitchell's hand shook very slightly as he lit his cigarette.

In fact Guadalcanal was effectively under siege. Within twenty-four hours of landing on Guadalcanal, the Marines had virtually been abandoned by the Navy. With the disaster of Pearl Harbor still fresh in his mind, force commander Admiral James Fletcher had chosen to withdraw from Iron Bottom Sound, taking most of the Marines' heavy artillery and half their supplies with him. The Marines on the island were left without cover from the air or the sea.

That was two weeks ago. By the time Mitchell landed at Henderson Field, he found a force of half-starved, angry men, the ghosts of Corregidor etched into their faces.

The arrival of Mitchell and the rest of the pilots from the *Long Island* was their first ray of hope. The nineteen fighters and twelve dive bombers they brought with them were the beginning of another of the Marine legends on Guadalcanal – the Cactus Air Force.

Mitchell leaned back against the wall of the dug-out and closed his eyes. He was a thick-set man in his early forties; one of those fortunate men whose quiet air of authority automatically commands respect from those around him. He had iron-grey hair, and a tanned, lined face that exuded a quiet confidence. He could have been a college professor if not for the eyes. They were cold and grey; the eyes of a hunter.

He looked slightly incongruous now in the battered blue baseball cap, with the shoulder holster bulging under the dirty leather flying jacket. But even in the ragged uniform that was to become the hallmark of the Cactus Air Force, Major James Mitchell somehow seemed to radiate assurance.

Ten minutes later there was a faint crackling sound from the loudspeaker and Mitchell's impassive face became instantly alert. He jumped up, dropping the cigarette on to the earth floor.

A human voice echoed faintly round the walls of the hut. It was a precise, slightly high-pitched voice. But very calm. It reminded Mitchell of the BBC newsreaders he had heard in London.

"Good morning, this is The Weatherman. I am speaking to you from the Upper Solomons. First the weather. There are clear skies here and over Bougainville, Choiseul and New Georgia. Nice weather for flying! It is now eighty-five degrees."

Mitchell and the corporal exchanged glances. The corporal scribbled furiously on the pad in front of him. The voice continued, clipped and precise.

"There has been a lot of surface activity in our region. I think you should anticipate reinforcements in your area late this afternoon or this evening. I have seen three carriers, five destroyers and a large troop transport heading down The Slot. They were making approximately ten knots. By my estimation they will arrive at Savo at between eighteen and twenty hundred hours tonight."

There was a pause. Mitchell leaned on the desk next to the corporal, the muscles in his jaw clenched tight.

"Now for you airmen . . . a squadron of torpedo bombers has just flown overhead from Kavieng headed your . . . wait a moment . . ."

The drone of aircraft engines was chillingly clear from the loudspeakers in the corner of the hut.

"Another four formations of three have just flown overhead. You probably heard them. Be prepared for twenty-four torpedo bombers, in two waves, coming your way. Be with you in about two hours. That's all for now. Good luck! Over and out!"

Shoup scribbled down the message and as soon as the transmission ended he picked up the telephone and called Air Control in the Pagoda. When he had finished he looked round for the major, but he was already gone.

Corporal Shoup let out a whoop and beat the table with his fists. At last. They had the information. Now they had the planes.

Now they could give the Japs a taste of what they'd been dishing out.

25

Corrigan had built a rough lean-to under a banyan tree from palm leaves and coconut fronds. It was only a temporary arrangement. Corrigan was eager to be on his way. If the Japanese found them, he'd be shot along with the rest of them.

He found himself thinking about Rachel. Christ, what a woman. He remembered the way she had stood beside him in the wheelhouse on the way back from Marmari Point. If she had been afraid, she certainly hadn't shown it. And the way she cut the bullet out of the priest's leg . . . she had a lot of spunk, you had to give her that.

What a waste. No wonder Father Goode had been hiding her away all this time. Corrigan smiled grimly to himself in the darkness. It was a pity he would not get to know her better.

A shadow fell across his face. It was Sanei. Silent as a wraith, she slipped inside the lean-to. He heard the rustle of fabric as she removed her shirt and the strip of tapa cloth at her waist and slipped naked under the thin blanket beside him.

She wrapped her thigh around him and then her fingers began to unbutton his shirt. He felt her warm breath on his cheek.

"Iris." It was her pet name for him. *Irish*. Only she couldn't pronounce it properly. He had always liked the sound of it before. Tonight it irritated him. He was surprised to find himself still thinking about Rachel. He pushed her hand away.

"Go to sleep."

She ignored him. He felt her tongue flick into his ear.

"Christ, it's like sleeping with a gekko. Get away, for God's sake, I'm tired."

"Make *pus-pus*," Sanei whispered.

"I don't want to."

Sanei's fingers went quickly and expertly to his groin. She found what she was looking for. Try explaining *that* away, Corrigan thought sourly.

"Make *pus-pus* longa me," Sanei whispered again.

Corrigan sighed. What the hell. Why not? It wasn't the time or the place to start getting sentimental over his choice of women. He rolled over towards the sweet brown body next to him.

Besides, if they made enough noise, it would upset Father Goode.

*

Wolfgang Heydrich took the battered straw hat off his head and mopped his face and hair with a voluminous white hankerchief. The thin white hair was soaked with sweat and clung in long wet strands to his head. It had been a long climb.

The planter had been born in the marshy flatlands of Flensburg, and even though he had lived in the Solomons for the past fifteen years, he still felt like a foreigner. He probably always would. He was prone to sweat and after two days in the jungle prickly heat struck at his groin and across his back and under his armpits.

Heydrich's plantation, *Marakon*, was built next to the sea on the west coast of the island and he rarely ventured away from it. He would only trek into the jungle for a very good reason. The hunting down of Ian Manning was, in Heydrich's mind, the best reason there was.

There had been rumours that Manning had not left the island with the other planters and miners on the *Melinda*. The Japanese were engaged in a constant, desperate search of the island, but they were hampered by two things. First, the natives were still loyal to the British, and Nakamura had been receiving confused and conflicting information from the islanders; secondly, the Japanese had committed their experienced troops to Guadalcanal and the soldiers on Santa Maria were mostly raw recruits, unskilled in jungle warfare.

Heydrich had one advantage over the Japanese; he was white. If Manning was still on the island, and the natives knew where he was, they might tell him what they would not tell the Japanese. And so he had decided to make the long hike deep into the hills east of *Marakon*, where the Japanese had so far not ventured.

He had set off three days ago. The hills rose steeply from the shores of Rolavo Bay and the orderly rows of palms on *Marakon* plantation; within a few miles the path from the coast was lost among the giant trees, and the tangle of ferns, creepers and twisting liana. By the end of the first day Heydrich was exhausted. But he kept on.

It was the third morning of their search. Gumu, his native guide, pushed doggedly on ahead. He was almost naked, except for the *lava-lava* at his waist, and his taut brown body glistened in the steaming heat. He had been born in these mountains, and he seemed to melt into them like a shadow.

Giant ferns, young saplings and clumps of bamboo crowded together at the foot of the towering trees. Thick lianas fell across the path and Heydrich often had to clamber over fallen trees, their trunks rotten and covered with white creamy fungus. Every hundred yards he had to stop to wipe the sticky cobwebs out of his face and hair.

They continued to climb for almost an hour. Heydrich felt his heart careening in his chest, and his face flushed to the colour of raw meat. His lungs were on fire in his chest. He gulped greedily from the water bottle and forced himself on.

He thought about the day the Japanese had first arrived in Vancoro harbour. Heydrich had toasted their arrival with a bottle of *schnapps* he had been saving for such a special occasion. After all, they were allies of the Third Reich, and just as importantly, they had put the English in their place. They were routing them out of their clubs and their pukka houses, shooting them down in their monstrous palaces all over Asia.

The next morning Heydrich had presented himself to the Japanese Colonel in Vancoro, and had been mildly affronted by the offhanded treatment he had received. He had offered his services, but Nakamura had perfunctorily examined his papers and told him to go back to his plantation and stay out of trouble.

They did not seem to realise his importance. But that would all change very soon.

Wolfgang Heydrich was now engaged in his own personal war.

He loathed the English. He hated their arrogance, their

clubs, their tea parties, their polo and their games of bridge. He hated the way they had always condescended to him at their tennis club, and he hated the way they and the French had humiliated and subjugated his country in 1919. He hated them for taking his father's legs at Verdun in 1916 and making him live the rest of his life a cripple, and he hated them because his mother died from tuberculosis in 1923, starved and impoverished; her legacy from the Treaty of Versailles.

It had taken him years of work and not a little luck – and yes, he had cheated, but why not? – to become their equal on this hot and fetid little island; yet even here they treated him as if he was a beggar.

Even before Adolf Hitler, Wolfgang Heydrich had hated them. Now, at last, the tide had turned. There was a new order in the world. And there was to be a new order on Santa Maria.

Suddenly Gumu stopped in front of him and pointed. "There!"

Heydrich made out the thatch and palm huts of the village between the trees. A tendril of smoke drifted up through the still twilight of the jungle. Already the natives' curs were howling in fear and rage as they caught the scent of the strangers.

It was a typical native village; it was surrounded by a tall bamboo fence, bound with lianas. Inside the kraal the reddish earth was packed hard, and dogs and pigs and small children scampered and crouched beneath the wooden stilts of the huts.

The headman of the village came out to meet them. Gumu told Heydrich his name was Tasimboko. He wore a thick belt of palm fronds over his carefully woven *lap-lap* so that he looked like a rooster when he walked. There was a thin string of trochus shells around his neck, and his teeth were blackened with betel. But he walked with a solemn dignity as he came out to greet Heydrich.

The German planter pushed Gumu ahead of him.

"Tell them I'm looking for the government *kiap*. Tell

them I have an important message for him and I have to talk with him."

Quickly Gumu translated what Heydrich had said. The headman exchanged worried glances with some of the other village elders who had come out to satisfy their curiosity.

Their view of the world was a restricted one. For as long as they could remember they had been ruled by the white *kiap*, and they had a certain filial affection for the British. But the war had come swiftly to the Solomons and it was difficult for them to understand what had happened.

They knew only that the white man had deserted the island, and had been replaced by the yellow soldiers. But they were confused because Manning was still somewhere in the hills, and he had come to the village and told them that soon white soldiers would come and throw the *japoni* off the island. They believed him. Already other white men – one of them wounded, and lying on a stretcher – had come to join the *kiap*.

But they were cautious; Manning had warned them that his hiding place was to be kept a secret.

Tasimboko considered carefully. The alliances of international politics was something quite beyond his knowledge; all that was apparent to him was that here was another white man who had come to join Manning in his refuge from the *japoni*.

So after some consideration, he pointed to the distant hills and told Gumu that Manning's camp was half a day's march away. He could take him there if he wished.

Gumu passed this knowledge on to Heydrich.

Heydrich almost laughed aloud. For three days he had sweated and grunted through this infernal jungle, visiting almost every village in a five-mile radius of *Marakon*. But it had been worth it. He was right. Manning was up there in the hills, and these people would lead him there.

The Japanese Colonel would be most grateful. He might even make Heydrich proxy governor of the island.

Heydrich turned to his native guide. "Tell them I will

be back in a couple of days. I will go with them to find the English *kiap* then."

As Heydrich set off back down the mountain he forgot the aching in his limbs and the fire in his lungs. Now he would revenge himself on the English.

And he would start with that little *Scheiss* Manning.

26

"He is somewhere on this island," Nakamura said.

"We cannot be sure, Nakamura-san," Kurosawa said.

"The natives say he is here."

"With respect Nakamura-san, there are many others who say he left with the other Europeans many months ago. We could be chasing a phantom."

"We have to be sure," Nakamura told him. "Our air force is taking heavy casualties over Guadalcanal. Whenever they fly a mission, the Americans are already in the air, waiting for them. The High Command believes they must be receiving advance intelligence of our attacks. Our forces have already captured two Englishmen with a transportable radio on Bougainville. There may be others on Choiseul or Santa Ysabel or even here on Santa Maria."

He turned to the map of the island on the wall of his office and stabbed a stumpy index finger on the thick, green-shaded area to the north.

"We will begin our search here. In the hills to the north-west."

Tashiro nodded. "He would have excellent views across The Slot. Our planes would be flying straight over his head from Rabaul and Kavieng. It makes sense."

"If he is there the natives in the district will know where he is hidden. They will lead you to him."

Kurosawa took the spectacles from his nose and began to polish them with his handkerchief. Even his colonel had by now learned to recognise this as a symbol of his dissent.

"You disagree, Lieutenant Kurosawa?"

Kurosawa replaced the spectacles on his nose and took a deep breath. He was afraid of Nakamura. "I do not think we should rely on the support of the natives, Nakamura-san. They have not co-operated with us so far."

"Why do you think that is, lieutenant?"

"Perhaps they are still frightened of the English."

The colonel looked at Tashiro. "Then we shall have to make them more frightened of us."

Tashiro grinned eagerly. "Yes, Nakamura-san."

"If he is there, we must find him. I charge it to you as your personal responsibility."

Tashiro bowed. "I will find him, Nakamura-san."

Kurosawa looked dismayed. Tashiro was far too confident. They could hunt for weeks in the jungles. If the natives were against them, they could inform the Englishman whenever they got close, and they would end up chasing their own tails. Intimidating them might only make things worse.

"Nakamura-san, may I suggest," Kurosawa stammered, "perhaps more troops might be necessary. A company of soldiers, conducting a systematic sweep of the area . . ."

"A company of soldiers? For one Englishman?"

Kurosawa lapsed into silence. Nakamura was a good soldier but this wasn't warfare. This was police work. What they needed was a system of informants. But while they continued to treat the natives as *kichibu* – beasts – then they would be fighting two enemies.

But he knew it was useless to argue.

At that moment the door opened and a guard stepped inside, saluting smartly.

Nakamura looked up impatiently. "What is it?"

"The German Heydrich is outside, Nakamura-san," the guard said. "He wishes to speak with you. He claims it is urgent."

Nakamura hesitated. "Very well," he barked at the guard. "Show him in here."

When Heydrich entered the room, an aroma of rank sweat came with him. He had not bothered to change his shirt since his return from the jungle. But beneath the grime that caked his face, his cheeks were flushed with excitement.

"Colonel Nakamura," he gushed as he was led in by the guard, "I have excellent news. It is about the English *kiap*!"

Nakamura regarded him sternly, saying nothing. He turned to Kurosawa. "What does he want?"

"He says it is about the Englishman, Nakamura-san."

Heydrich was delighted to see Nakamura's expression change from disdain to eager surprise. He savoured the moment as the three Japanese officers waited for him to speak again.

"Well," Kurosawa said, finally, "what about him?"

"I know where he is!" He grinned triumphantly at them. "I will take you to him – *ja*?"

27

Rachel watched Corrigan shove the tins of corned beef and beans that Manning had given him into the pocket of his rucksack. It was early morning and Corrigan was eager to be on his way.

"You're leaving us, Mister Corrigan?"

"Too damn right I am. I've no mind to stay here

and wait for those little yellow barbarians to come and shoot me."

"I wanted to thank you before you left. You saved my uncle's life."

"If that's what you think you're as crazy as he is. All I've done is win him a few extra days. The Nips are going to get him in the end. And the rest of you too."

"I dare say you're right," she said mildly.

Corrigan suddenly felt enormously sorry for her. She was, after all, just a girl. Barely twenty years old. She had attempted to wash the tattered calico dress, and while she waited for it to dry Manning had lent her one of his stiff-collared shirts to wear, many sizes too large for her. Her outfit was complemented with a native sarong. She looked at once both appealing and vulnerable.

"Look, you don't have to stay here," Corrigan growled at her. "If Blood and Thunder wants to die a martyr, you don't have to go down with him. Come with me. You'll stand more of a chance than you will up here."

Rachel gave him a soft smile. "Thank you Mister Corrigan. But I'm not only staying here because of my uncle. I love these people too, in my own way. I won't see them subjugated by the Japanese."

"You'd rather see them subjugated by the English."

"We all know evil when we see it, Mister Corrigan. Some of us run from it. Some of us stay and fight it. It depends on what you believe in."

Corrigan shook his head in wonderment. "I don't know where a young girl like you gets all these notions."

He hoisted his pack on to his shoulder.

"Are you going to say goodbye to my uncle?"

"You must be joking." Corrigan straightened and for a moment he hesitated. Then he held out his hand. "Goodbye, Miss Goode. You've got a lot of spunk, I'll give you that."

"Goodbye, Mister Corrigan. Good luck."

"Keep it for yourself. You'll need it more than I will."

Corrigan turned and made his way back down the path they had come a few days before, Sanei running to keep up with his long loping strides. Then the jungle closed behind him like an impenetrable green veil, and he was gone.

They reached *Marakon* at dusk. From the spur overlooking the plantation Corrigan could make out the splash of the red-roofed bungalow between the geometric rows of coconut palms. The boathouse was almost a quarter of a mile away from the house, built over the planks of a short wooden jetty that jutted out into the bay.

Corrigan hoped to reach the boat shed undetected, climb aboard the *Deutschland*, cast off and be across the reef before Heydrich realised what had happened.

"Nearly there," he grinned at Sanei. "This time tomorrow we'll be halfway to Australia."

The door to the crumbling old wooden shed creaked open with one lusty swing of Corrigan's boot. Corrigan slipped inside.

The stench of copra was overwhelming. Sacks of it were still piled up in one corner of the shed. In another corner Heydrich had stockpiled half a dozen drums of benzene, a furled mainsail, some kerosene tins and four new batteries.

But the *Deutschland* was gone.

Corrigan gave a grunt of frustration and surprise. He sagged back against the wall. The waves lapped against the wooden piles underneath him. The sound echoed around the empty boat shed, seeming to mock him.

Corrigan punched the wooden planking of the wall in rage, splintering and cracking the wood. The force of the blow ripped the skin from the knuckles of his right hand, laying them open almost to the bone.

"The boat she gone, Iris," Sanei whispered.

"Sure, and we can't go anywhere without it," Corrigan said.

He looked down at his hand. His knuckles were bleeding.

He swore at his own stupidity and stalked off towards the bungalow.

"Which way boat she go?" Sanei asked him.

"How do I know?"

"We go longa *kiap* now?"

"Now what would I want to go back to see Manning for? We're going to wait right here for Heydrich to come back with the boat."

A well-worn path threaded away from the boathouse through the close-planted palms to the thatched roofs of the copra sheds. Beyond them lay the bungalow.

Behind the sheds, set among the trees, a weak light shone from the labourers' huts. As Corrigan approached a naked child screamed and ran away to find its mother, a pug-faced creature with pendulous breasts and a soft flabby stomach that bulged over the scrap of cloth she wore at her waist. She was pounding taro with a wooden pestle.

"Where's Heydrich?" Corrigan demanded.

The woman shrugged. "He go longa Vancoro before sun he up," she said.

"Can't trust that fat slug to do anything right," Corrigan muttered and stalked off down the path towards the bungalow.

Corrigan vented his frustration on the servants. They gathered on the verandah and watched him march up the path with a mixture of astonishment and trepidation.

"Get me a drink, you bastards!" he shouted at the houseboy. "You've got a guest for the night."

Wolfgang Heydrich lived in all the opulent splendour that the tropics would allow. The bungalow had three bedrooms, a dining room, a drawing room, a study, and a kitchen. The verandah was shrouded in flaming red bougainvillea, and the gardens were redolent with the scent of hibiscus, azaleas and frangipani.

The floors were polished teak, and the walls were hung with expensive prints, imported from Europe. There were heavy leather bound books lining one wall of the study and in the drawing room Corrigan found a radio and a record player. He put a record on the gramophone and lowered the needle.

It was *Lili Marlene*. Corrigan threw it across the room.

In the study Corrigan found a photograph of Adolf Hitler on the bedroom wall, a black and white print taken during the Führer's address to a rally of *Hitler Jugend*. A flag with the inevitable swastika billowed in the wind behind him.

Corrigan went to the writing desk, found a pen and dipped it into the ink. With a few strokes of the pen the Führer's outstretched palm was no longer empty. It was holding something; something that was a part of Goebbel's anatomy, and was of a very intimate nature.

Chuckling Corrigan stood back to admire his handiwork.

Finally, in the storeroom, he found what he was looking for. It was a 1930 Mannlicher 65 rifle. Corrigan decided it might be useful if Heydrich decided to be difficult.

Then he settled himself into a cane chair on the verandah with a bottle of German Steinlager that the housegirl brought him. He laid the rifle down at the side of his chair.

"What's your name?" he said to the doe-eyed creature who had brought him the beer.

"Alice Melema'a," the girl said.

Alice Melema'a was Polynesian; taller and slimmer than the Melanesian girls of the Solomons. She was barefoot and there was an apricot hibiscus bloom in her long straight hair. She had a close-wrapped cloth around her waist with a gaily-coloured floral pattern on it.

Corrigan smiled. "Where do you sleep, Alice?"

The girl lowered her eyes and nodded towards the French windows at the end of the verandah. They opened on to Heydrich's bedroom.

"Well, that's where you're sleeping tonight as well. With me."

Alice Melema'a blushed, grinning.

Corrigan's considerable reputation had preceded him.

That night, with half a dozen bottles of Heydrich's good German Steinlager in him, Corrigan slept the peaceful sleep of the damned with Alice Melema'a tucked protectively under his arm, the rifle propped against the bedside table at his side.

Just after dawn Sanei woke him, shaking him roughly by the shoulder.

"Wake up, Corrigan! Wake up!"

Corrigan groaned and opened his eyes. "What is it?"

"Boat he come," she said, and Corrigan was instantly awake, leaping from his prone position to the French window in almost one motion.

"Holy Mary, Mother of Jesus."

He stood staring towards the path leading from the boathouse, his mouth hanging open in shock.

Heydrich was back all right. And he'd brought half the Japanese Imperial Army with him.

28

Corrigan screwed up his eyes against the glare of the bright morning, feeling his heart pumping wildly in his chest.

He leaned against one of the verandah posts for support as the effects of the previous night's bacchanalia with Heydrich's beer cellar hit him. It took him long seconds to react.

Then, like a man on a wildly pitching ship, he staggered back into the bedroom, grabbed the rifle, and threw on his shirt and calico trousers.

Alice had woken and she sat up in the bed, watching Corrigan's frantic efforts to put on his boots.

"You go?" she murmured.

"I'm going all right. As far away from here as bloody possible."

A few moments later, he stumbled back on to the verandah, the rifle slung over one shoulder, still pushing his left foot into his boot. Sanei was waiting for him, the rucksack slung over her back.

"Let's head for the hills," Corrigan told her.

Corrigan stood in the clearing, his hands on his hips, his chest heaving as he fought to catch his breath.

"Heydrich?" Manning was saying. "But how did he know we were here?"

"Same way we found you, I suppose. The natives."

"You think they betrayed us?"

"Maybe, maybe not. Heydrich's just another white man to them. They might have thought he was on your side."

Manning looked at the teleradio and the generator, and Father Goode lying semi-conscious in one of the huts. Moving through the jungle would not be easy. He wanted to avoid it at all costs.

"Are you sure the Japs are coming this way?"

"Look," Corrigan muttered irritably, "what do you want? A search warrant signed by the Imperial Emperor?"

Manning turned to Sergeant Lavella, who stood a few paces behind, anxiously fingering the trigger action of the old Lee-Enfield. "We must be ready to leave in an hour," he said brusquely. "Dismantle everything. Now – quickly!" He turned back to Corrigan. "I don't know what to say to you. You've saved our lives. Perhaps you've saved thousands."

"Yeah, I'm a real hero. Now I suppose you want me to help you shift all these boxes?"

Wolfgang Heydrich pushed the native boy along the path in front of him. Brilliantly coloured birds shot through the trees, darting in and out of the bright shafts of sunlight. A misty green haze filtered through the vast green canopy above them. In the jungle, it was always twilight; Heydrich could make out no more than a few feet in front of him through the dense growth of twisting lianas and orchids.

Mein Gott, a man could get lost in here and no one would ever find his bones.

The place was foreboding and oppressive and Heydrich cursed silently; better he had stayed behind and let Tashiro do his own dirty work. But the cunning little bastard didn't trust him. He had made him come with them.

He still hadn't recovered from the shock of finding Corrigan's calling card in his bedroom. The *Putz* had ruined his best pair of sheets and the photograph of Hitler his brother had sent him from Nuremberg. And a case of his best beer was missing from his cellar.

But Heydrich had not been given the time to dwell on the outrage. Tashiro had insisted that they immediately set out for the hills, to search for Manning. Heydrich had led them straight to Tasimboko's village.

Tasimboko had quaked with terror when he saw that Heydrich had brought the Japanese with him. Unable to deny knowledge of Manning's camp he was forced to give them his son Menazuni as a guide. Almost as soon as they had left, a terrible wailing had come from inside the kraal as the people of the village expressed their grief for what they had done.

Heydrich laughed out loud when he thought about it. Such loyalty!

Now as the small group struggled further into the hills, the heat became oppressive. The air was thin, and lungs laboured to extract life from it. Only Menazuni, leaping ahead through the undergrowth, seemed unaffected.

The path grew steeper. Heydrich stopped exhausted, mopping his forehead with a sodden handkerchief. Suddenly he felt a gun barrel nudge his spine. He turned. It was Tashiro.

Panting, he hurried on.

Sweat oozed out of the white pores of his skin, trickling off his fingers and dripping steadily from his chin on to his stained white shirt. His thin white hair was plastered across his skull in damp strands.

Suddenly Menazuni stopped in his tracks. He listened and indicated with his hands that the camp was very close. The Japanese soldiers pulled their rifles off their shoulders and held them ready.

Heydrich stepped back to let them pass. *Himmel*, they didn't expect him to fight as well, did they?

Kurosawa was at the rear. Heydrich smiled at him obsequiously.

The only civilised one of the lot of them, he thought sourly.

The young second lieutenant drew his revolver and pulled Heydrich up the slope with him.

The path became a trail. Menazuni pointed dead ahead and lay down in the grass. Tashiro tried to get him on his feet, but he refused to go any further. He managed to wriggle free and ran back down the slope. He brushed past Heydrich and was gone.

Tashiro shrugged. It was not important now. He drew his sword and motioned for his men to follow him.

As Heydrich watched, he was forced to quickly revise his estimate of Japanese soldiers. Quickly and efficiently they spread out into the jungle, moving silently as shadows.

He crept forward to watch. He hoped they would take Corrigan alive. He would prefer to see him die slowly. *Ja*, it would pay him for the sheets.

He licked his lips in delicious anticipation.

They were on the edge of a clearing. From where he crouched he could make out three thatched huts; smoke drifted towards the sky from a smouldering fire, but otherwise there was no sign of life. The silence was unbroken, save for the angry chatter of monkeys in the trees above.

Suddenly Tashiro gave a blast on his whistle and

immediately there was a burst of machine gun fire, very close, which sent the monkeys howling and scattering through the trees. Bullets smashed through the first two huts, ripping huge holes in the flimsy thatched walls.

Tashiro gave another blast on the whistle and the firing stopped, as suddenly as it had begun. It was the cue for the rest of Tashiro's men to rush from the surrounding jungle into the clearing, their bayonets drawn.

Screaming *banzai*s, they rushed into the huts, one of them firing his rifle from the hip. Seconds later they emerged, one by one, their rifles now held at their sides.

The acrid smell of cordite and charred wood hung in the air.

Heydrich got to his feet. "What is wrong?" he said to Kurosawa.

"English not here."

"But . . . they must be."

"No, not here," Kurosawa said mildly.

Tashiro, his sword drawn, stamped across the clearing towards the huts. He went into each of the huts, searching for anything that Manning may have left behind.

Nothing.

Enraged, he emerged into the sunlight and threw his sword into the soft earth in frustration. It clung there, shivering.

He turned to Heydrich. "You were wrong," he spat at him in Japanese.

Heydrich could only stare and shake his head.

"Corrigan must have warned them," he murmured.

Tashiro snatched up his sword. How much start did they have? "We must go after them," he said.

"We will never find them in this jungle without a native guide, Tashiro-san," Kurosawa said.

Tashiro said nothing. He knew Kurosawa was right. The muscles in his jaw rippled as he tried to control his anger. "Send that slug back to *Marakon*," he said, pointing at Heydrich, and set off.

*

Corrigan had won Manning the vital few hours he needed.

The Englishman had been preparing for just such an evacuation for months. He had already chosen a reserve site for his camp, in a jungle-covered gully on the slopes of Mount Tahunga, further north towards Marmari Point. It would be a long day's hike through steep valleys and along the ravined walls of Ngulinni river.

When Corrigan had re-appeared at the camp the previous evening Manning had hurriedly sent Sergeant Lavella to the nearest village to recruit carriers for the trip into the hinterland. There was no shortage of eager recruits; since the departure of the Europeans, the twist tobacco that the natives loved had been in short supply.

In the gathering dusk the transmitter and its generator were quickly packed in their crates and lashed with vines to long bamboo poles. Each stretcher was borne by four of the native carriers.

Other natives brought their supplies of rice, tinned meat, clothing and benzene. Two more carried Father Goode on the makeshift bamboo stretcher.

By the time they were ready to set off, the constellation of the Great Bear was glittering high overhead like a fistful of white diamonds. They hurried through the night, tripping over roots, stumbling in mud holes, slipping on wet leaves and grass as they struggled to put as much distance between themselves and the Japanese patrol as possible.

As they travelled deeper into the jungle, they attached small luminous fungi to their backs so they would not lose each other in the dark. Sergeant Lavella led the way, occasionally wading into shallow streams to help hide their tracks.

The moon had fallen behind the distant mountains when Manning finally allowed them to stop and rest. They slept huddled against the trunks of huge hardwoods, exhausted and soaked with their own perspiration, while the mosquitoes hummed and whined around their heads.

At first light Manning roused them and urged them on again.

The storm hit suddenly, soon after dawn, sweeping over the island from the south-east. The shadows raced towards them across the sea, and they looked up and saw the towering thunderhead clouds sweep in, blotting out the sun. In minutes the first rains broke over them, drenching the ground, and turning the earth into a glutinous porridge of mud. Every step became treacherous, the slime beneath their feet sucking strength from tired legs.

Manning had his police boys dotted through the line of carriers, while he followed close behind the men carrying the precious teleradio, worrying over it as if it was an only child.

When the squall struck, Manning had the carriers put banana leaves over the poles to deflect the rain from the canvas covers and keep the contents of the boxes dry. But the sudden downpour turned the mountain streams into torrents, and the carriers struggled to keep their feet on the slippery stones of the river beds, the turbid dirty water pulling and tugging at their legs.

The men Manning had entrusted with the teleradio were the strongest and the best of the carriers; if one of them slipped he would let his body fall but keep his arm quite rigid so that the stretcher he carried did not touch the water, and within seconds Manning would rush forward and take the weight of the pole until the man could once more struggle to his feet.

Progress was painfully slow in the torrential rain. But Manning wanted to be at the new camp by nightfall. Every hour he spent off the air was precious.

There was only one thing that was important to Ian Manning now.

Guadalcanal.

The rain slanted down in miserable grey sheets, and their legs ached from the cloying, dark mud. At midday they stopped to rest in the lee of a dark basalt ridge, and found fat leeches clinging to their legs, and even under their shirts. They burned them off with lighted cigarettes.

They laid Father Goode's stretcher in the overhang of the cliff, a sparse shelter from the torrents of rain. Consciousness had become a fragmentary thing for the injured priest; the journey had extracted a higher price from him than the others had anticipated. The constant bumping and jolting up the slippery track sometimes made him gasp with the shock of pain.

The malaria in his body had taken advantage of his weakened state to assault him once more; at times he burned with raging fever; moments later he was shaking and trembling with cold. The brief interludes of fitful sleep were a blessing.

He rested now, sweating in the cool damp of the shallow cave. His eyes flickered open and he saw Corrigan striding back down the path, a leather poncho over his shoulders.

"Mister Corrigan." To his surprise he found his voice was no more than a croak. "Mister Corrigan!"

Corrigan stopped, leaning into the cave. "So you're awake now, are you?"

"I wish to speak with you."

"Make it quick. We have to get going again soon."

"Please. Come closer."

Corrigan scowled but ducked his head under the overhang and squatted down next to the stretcher.

There was a pause as the priest deliberated over what he was about to say. It had been bothering him ever since the day that Rachel had gone with Corrigan on the *Shamrock* to Marmari Point. Now, sensing his own mortality, it had become important that he know the truth.

"Mister Corrigan, I must hear it from your own lips. Have you impugned my niece's virtue?"

"Talk English for God's sake."

"My niece. Did you take advantage of her?"

Corrigan snorted. "You can't think of anything else but sex, can you?"

Father Goode ignored him. "I'm waiting for an answer, Mister Corrigan. I'll know if you lie to me."

"No, I bloody didn't, for all the difference it makes. What on earth gave you that idea anyway?"

"I've seen the way she looks at you. She has sinned in the heart, if not in the flesh."

Corrigan looked away. "I don't know what you're talking about."

"I think you do."

"Look, I know what you think of me, and I guess you're right. If I could have, I would have. But I didn't. Now shut up. Get some sleep. We've still got a long way to go."

"Stay away from her, Mister Corrigan. She deserves better than someone like you."

Corrigan felt the anger flare in his belly. "I could say the same thing about you."

He turned and stalked out of the cave.

During that long afternoon's march he thought about what the priest had said. Christ, women! They were always trouble, whatever way you looked at it. It had always been easy with the island girls. You knew where you stood. They never tried to complicate anything with commitments. He knew Sanei loved him absolutely; there was no demand on him to feel the same way.

She knew he took other women. She understood about that. But with white women it was different . . .

He didn't want to think about it. He had his life as he wanted it, and as soon as he got away from this rotten island he would have it that way again.

Damn them. Damn the lot of them.

29

The evening closed around the island in a grey blanket. The rain continued to pour down in heavy sheets and leather boots were soon soaked through, the coating of mud and dead leaves making them heavy as lead. Even the natives with their strong splayed feet began to tire as they made their way up and down the steep valley slopes and boulder-strewn beds, slipping on the treacherous wet rocks and the greasy red mud of the highlands.

A premature twilight had settled over the mountains when they finally reached the Ngulinni. The site Manning had chosen was just an hour's walk along a trail that wound its way up the steep valley. To their right the valley fell away a hundred feet into the swirling brown waters of the river.

Manning stopped, looking back over his shoulder, straining to catch his breath. He waited for Corrigan to catch up. "Almost there, old boy."

"It makes no difference to me now. While I'm on this bloody island I'm not anywhere."

"There must be some way I can persuade you to join me. I could use a man of your talents."

"No thanks."

"Then what are you going to do?"

"I'm still thinking about it."

Ahead of them one of the carriers gave a cry of alarm. He had lost his footing on the patina of mud, and fallen on to his back, his right leg kicking frantically at the air as he tried to recover his balance. Terrified, he looked around and saw the hundred-foot drop below; he released his hold on the poles and clawed frantically at the mud.

The other carrier was battling desperately to keep his own footing, with the weight of the stretcher throwing him backwards. As his companion released his hold on the other end of the pole the stretcher and its load were twisted out of his grip.

Corrigan knew what was about to happen. "The batteries," he murmured.

"Christ, no!" Manning screamed.

In a moment he was scrambling up the path towards them. Corrigan raced after him.

Manning slipped and fell headlong into the mud. He could only watch as the first of the carriers slid over the edge of the trail, the bamboo stretcher and its load of batteries slithering after him.

Corrigan vaulted over Manning and made a desperate attempt to save the young islander. He lunged for the boy's outstretched arm. For a moment his fingers caught and gripped the man's wrist, and held him; with his other hand he fought for some purchase on the mud.

Then, inexorably, the boy's arm, greasy-wet with sweat and rain, slipped from Corrigan's grasp. Corrigan stared into his face, so very close, saw his eyes bulge in his head as the realisation of death came to him; then his mouth opened wide in outrage and terror as he fell.

He slithered down the slope and into the fast, brown waters of the Ngulinni. In a few seconds he had disappeared, the bobbing head carried away downstream and out of sight, the wreckage of the smashed stretcher still bobbing in his wake.

Nobody spoke. The only sound was the muted roar of the waters below. The other carriers stood and stared after him.

Manning lay on his belly, his face a mask of disbelief and horror. Finally he sank his face into the blessed oblivion of the cool wet mud. He tried to think about the poor boy who had just died, but he couldn't. All he could think of was the batteries. Without them the radio was useless.

It had all been for nothing. They might just as well have let the Japanese shoot them anyway.

30

It was dark when they reached the ridge and it seemed as if it was going to rain for ever. They all huddled together under a rocky overhang for warmth, tired, wet and dispirited. Unable to start a fire they ate a gloomy meal of tinned corned beef and cold beans by the light of a kerosene lamp.

There were leeches by their hundreds on the mossy trails, and after they had eaten Corrigan went around with a lighted cigarette, burning the ugly black creatures off their feet and legs. The only sound was Father Goode's muttered incantations, as he struggled and twitched in his delirium.

Rachel knelt beside him, trying to force a few drops of water between his lips.

"How is he?" Corrigan asked her.

"The journey's made him very weak. He is having another attack of the malaria."

"Manning's got some atabrine."

"It's too late for that now. He needs rest."

"Don't we all."

Rachel lowered her voice. "Mister Manning says the radio is useless without the batteries."

Corrigan nodded. "Like a boat without a rudder."

"So all your efforts were for nothing?"

"I don't know about that. You're still alive, aren't you?"

Rachel smiled at him. "Yes. You're a good man, Mister Corrigan."

"I couldn't do much else. The Japs were swarming all over *Marakon*."

"Come now, Mister Corrigan. You could easily have waited till they were gone, and doubled back behind them. Why didn't you?"

"Well, I suppose I could have done," Corrigan said. "But every man's allowed a little foolishness once in his life." He reached into his pack and took out the half bottle of whisky. He offered it to her. "This will help keep the cold out."

Rachel hesitated, then guiltily, she took it from him. She sipped from it, and handed it back to him. She made a valiant effort not to cough.

"You're getting better. We'll make a degenerate of you yet," Corrigan grinned.

"Thank you for the drink, Mister Corrigan."

"My pleasure, Miss Goode."

On the other side of the cave Sanei watched them, her eyes glittering in the darkness, reflecting the orange embers of the small fire. For the first time, she sensed real danger. He was looking at that white missus in a way she had never seen before. She had suspected before. Now she was sure.

She knew Corrigan had been with other native girls, but that did not hurt her. It was only sex and he was a white man after all. Sanei possessed him in a much different way.

She had lived her life for Corrigan and she had always known that one day he would marry her. Other planters had married native girls. She knew she could never be the same as a white missus, but it didn't matter. Among her own people it gave her respect.

Inside she knew he was no different to her; they were *one-talk*. She knew his violent temper and his lumbering gentleness. She had seen him at his worst when he was drunk, and when he withdrew into those dark moods that she knew had something to do with a past he could not shut away. And she had seen him at his best when he roared with laughter in that special way which seemed to infect everyone.

There were times when he took her, and he was rough and demanding; but there were other times when he treated her tenderly, as if she was a small bird in the palm of his huge hands, slow and easy.

She loved Corrigan. She loved his flashing eyes and his craziness and his crooked grin and the brown hardness of his body. In fact Sanei loved him with an intensity that would have frightened Corrigan if he had known about it; she knew that if he ever left her she would hate him just as much.

And as she watched him now with the white woman she vowed that if Rachel ever came between them she would kill her.

Patrick Corrigan felt in a benevolent mood. He had just finished a bottle of the whisky he had won from Manning and the previous evening's feelings of gloom and defeat had been dispelled.

They had made camp in a jungle-covered gully away from the tracks normally used by the natives. From the upmost branches of a tall teak, the ridge commanded views over The Slot and Marmari Point.

After the previous day's slog up the tortuous muddy slopes they had all been exhausted. Only Manning remained unbowed by rain or fatigue. At first light he had set Lavella and his men to work building a new hut for the radio, and constructing a new lookout in the trees.

The camp had been finished before sundown; three huts had been fashioned from the rudimentary materials of the forest under the steep walls of the gully; one for Manning and the radio; one for Lavella and his men; and one for Corrigan, Rachel and her uncle.

The storm had eased during the day but as twilight fell another squall moved in from the south; Corrigan huddled further into the corner of the hut and shivered while the rain cascaded from the eaves of the thatched roof, splashing on to the ground outside. A smoked-glass hurricane lamp swung from one of the rough-hewn bamboo rafters.

On the other side of the hut Rachel was trying to feed her uncle some tinned soup. Despite the privations of the trek through the mountains, he had rallied; the fever had broken and he was fully conscious.

Worse luck, Corrigan thought sourly.

Corrigan opened the second bottle of whisky, took a swallow, and ignored them. Despite what he had said to Rachel, the truth was that he was starting to regret his impulse to save Manning from the Japanese. He wondered if it was some previously undiscovered better instinct in him, or his contempt for Heydrich that had made him do it.

Whatever it was, he was coming to realise that it had been a serious error of judgement.

Now he was trapped; trapped on a wet mosquito-infested island with a martyr and a priest, and he had no idea what he was going to do next. Instinctively, he cocooned himself in the roseate glow of the alcohol, and decided to make the best of it.

Manning came in from outside, his hair plastered in thin strands across his forehead.

"Still busy organising the war?" Corrigan said.

Manning ignored him, and picked up the empty Johnny Walker bottle lying at his feet. "My God, Patrick, old chap. You've drunk the whole bottle."

"A nice drop too, old son," Corrigan said, raising the new bottle to his lips.

"I think you'd better go easy on that stuff."

"I don't see why. I've got nothing better to do."

Manning squatted down, wiping streaming droplets of rain off his face. "Got a bit of a problem, old boy."

"I know. The radio won't work. Hardly worth unpacking it. Still, that's none of my business."

Manning lowered his voice to a conspiratorial whisper.

"I have to get back on the air, Patrick old boy. There must be somewhere on the island I can get some more batteries."

"Why don't you go and get some off Heydrich?" Corrigan said and gulped another mouthful of whisky.

"Heydrich?"

"He's got four new batteries in the boatshed. Saw them myself. Suppose he keeps them as spares for that yacht of his."

"Just what we need." He looked eagerly at Corrigan. "Well – will you help us?"

Corrigan stopped drinking and stared at him. "Help you do what?"

"I'm going to send Sergeant Lavella and his men to get those batteries. I want you to go with them. You know your way round the place better than anyone here."

Corrigan shook his head vehemently. "Not me. The place is swarming with Nips. If you want to play soldiers, that's up to you. But this isn't my war. Remember?"

Manning patted him gently on the shoulder. When he spoke there was no reproach in his voice. "All right, old boy. I understand. You've helped us enough as it is."

Corrigan shook his head in disgust. He knew Manning would go back himself to get the batteries. The man was obsessed with the damn radio. He was going to get himself killed.

It was only a matter of time before the Japanese caught up with him. If it wasn't for Corrigan and the freak chance that had brought him to *Marakon* two days before, he would be dead already. Soon the Japanese would send planes to seek him out; or one of the natives would betray his new hiding place – for money, or out of fear. It was inevitable.

He visualised the end for Manning. He would be hunched over the radio, and there would be shouts and a sudden volley of gunfire as the Japanese soldiers burst out of the surrounding jungle. Lavella and his men would put up a brief, bitter fight and then it would be all over. The

best Manning could hope for was a quick death by a bullet.
If the Japanese took him alive . . .

Corrigan looked across the dimly lit hut where Rachel was crouched by her uncle's stretcher. She saw him looking at her and she looked up and smiled.

Corrigan scowled and looked away.

"Look, I'm sorry Manning. I'd like to help, but that's the way it is."

"No need to apologise old boy," Manning said cheerfully and turned to go back outside. Then almost as an afterthought he turned back and said: "Pity though. Because it's probably your only way to get out of this damned mess."

"What do you mean?"

"Well, as soon as the radio is working again I'm going to arrange for Father Goode and his niece to be evacuated."

"How the hell will you do that?"

Manning squatted back down on his haunches. Corrigan recognised the practised look of innocence on his face. He regretted having felt sorry for him now. Manning was a cunning bastard.

"Submarine," Manning was saying. "The Americans have offered to evacuate me at any time. Of course I'll stay here as long as I'm useful. But Father Goode needs urgent medical attention and I can't allow his young niece to run the same risks as the rest of us. They were misguided to come up here in the first place, really."

"That's what I tried to tell them."

"You were right."

"So get to it, Manning. What's the deal?"

"That's such a crass word, Patrick old boy. It's not a deal, only a suggestion. I could go after the batteries myself, but then I'm not really talented at this sort of thing and there's a good chance I might not come back. In which case you could stay here and rot with Father Goode and his niece. I'm only suggesting that you might feel safer getting the batteries yourself."

"And if . . . if I go and get them for you . . . you can get us out of this bloody island?"

"That's about the long and short of it," Manning said cheerfully. "So – what's it to be, old chap?"

Corrigan screwed the cap back on the whisky bottle. "When do we leave?"

31

The plan had been for Corrigan, Sergeant Lavella and the six native constables to head back to Heydrich's plantation, while the Japanese were still searching the hills for them, and take the batteries before they got back to *Marakon*. But the next evening, when Corrigan and Lavella crept on their hands and knees through the coconut palms two hundred yards from Heydrich's bungalow, they realised it would not be quite that simple.

Heydrich and the Japanese were already there.

Corrigan couldn't understand it. He had assumed Heydrich and his men would still be combing the jungle; he couldn't know that Kurosawa had convinced Tashiro of the futility of that on the very first day.

Corrigan wondered how long the Japanese soldiers would be at the plantation. Christ, they might even decide to set up a temporary base there.

On the evening breeze Corrigan caught the smell of the Japanese; a curious scent, like musty hay. There were only about half a dozen of them in view, the rest were probably inside the bungalow having their evening meal.

Knowing the Japs, they've bivouacked in Heydrich's bedroom, Corrigan thought with dark satisfaction.

"Bugger it," Corrigan said aloud.

"We kill *Japoni* soldier?" Sergeant Lavella whispered hopefully.

"Sure. If we had a regiment of paratroopers behind us," Corrigan said. He looked round. Lavella's men lay on their bellies just a few yards behind him.

They were armed with an odd assortment of ancient bolt-action rifles, which would be of little use against the Japanese Arisakas in a firefight. Corrigan's Mannlicher was the only modern weapon they had. It was Corrigan's intention to avoid shooting at all costs, despite Sergeant Lavella's evident disappointment.

"We go house b'long battery?" Sergeant Lavella said.

"You're an eager little bugger, aren't you?"

Corrigan nodded and the six men crawled away towards the boatshed.

There were two guards. They slouched on the jetty, their rifles cradled between their knees, smoking cigarettes. Their voices carried to Corrigan on the faint breeze. It was a token detail. After all, they were the hunters. The last thing they were expecting was to be attacked themselves.

It would be a simple matter to take care of them, Corrigan decided. But they would have to wait for the cover of night.

Sergeant Lavella drew his knife and made an elaborate pantomime of drawing the blade across his throat.

Corrigan nodded. "Yes, okay. But we'll wait till dark. Then I'll let you loose."

Corrigan shook his head. He was glad Lavella was on his side.

As luck would have it, there was an early full moon. It hung over the ocean like a huge marble ball, bathing the boathouse and the rows of coconut trees in silver. It was like having a searchlight positioned on the promontory overlooking the bay.

Corrigan zigzagged silently through the trees, a long gutting knife clasped in his right hand. From the other side of the grove he heard a distant ululation, like a monkey chattering in the trees. It was Lavella signalling that he was in position.

The two guards chattered and laughed, relaxed in the knowledge that their enemy was miles away somewhere up in the mountains. After an hour one of them wandered away into the trees to relieve himself. It was the moment Corrigan had anticipated; Lavella was waiting among the palms, ready for him.

His companion sat on the end of the jetty with his rifle cradled across his legs, and lit yet another cigarette. Corrigan crept around the edge of the clearing hidden by the lee of the jetty, the man's back towards him.

Corrigan hesitated. Killing wasn't in his line. The thought of cold-bloodedly cutting another man's throat with a knife didn't appeal to him. Instead he upturned the knife in his hand to expose the hard ivory handle with the blunt steel tip. That ought to do the job just as well.

Corrigan rose slowly to his feet and was just two feet away from the sentry when his blood turned to ice. Through the shadows of the trees he saw Sergeant Lavella grab the other Japanese by the shoulders, the steel of his broad-blade knife flashing in the moonlight.

The soldier on the jetty saw it too.

Corrigan scrambled over the last few paces slapping one huge hand over the sentry's mouth to stop him shouting an alarm, and bringing his knife down in a shallow arc from his shoulder.

But the Japanese was too quick for him. He brought the rifle up from his lap with both hands and in a reflex action he threw it up over his head.

Corrigan's wrist came down across the barrel, knocking the knife out of his grasp. It span through the air and landed silently in the carpet of vines under the palms.

Grunting with pain Corrigan kept his left hand over the man's mouth, as he squirmed and gasped underneath him, and with his injured hand he tried to wrestle the rifle out of the man's grip.

Suddenly the Japanese released his hold of the rifle, throwing Corrigan off balance; at the same time he brought both his elbows down and behind him, into Corrigan's ribs. Corrigan doubled over, winded, and he dropped the rifle as two more blows caught him just below the heart.

The sentry pulled his body away, and Corrigan fell sideways into the grass.

When he looked up the soldier had hoisted the rifle on to his shoulder and Corrigan found himself looking down the barrel of the Arisaka as the soldier's finger closed around the trigger.

Corrigan felt something hard under his left hand. It was the knife! Desperately he grabbed for it and threw it as hard as he could; in the same movement he rolled sideways away from the gun.

The knife flew at the soldier's head. Instinctively he ducked away, the rifle firing wildly into the trees. Before he could aim the rifle once more a dark hand clamped around his mouth and a silver blade flashed in the darkness. He slumped face down on to the ground, Sergeant Lavella kneeling over him.

Corrigan struggled to his knees, and picked up the rifle. He was surprised to find his hands were shaking. "You were supposed to wait for me to hit first," he growled at Lavella.

"You take him too long," Lavella complained. "*Japoni* he finis. Shake off drops. Have to kill im finis then."

Lavella's men raced towards the boathouse, their boots drumming on the wooden jetty. "We'd better hurry," Corrigan said. The instruction was unnecessary.

There were shouts from the main bungalow as the Japanese soldiers were routed out of the kitchen. Corrigan saw a large man in a white suit run out on to the verandah, pointing frantically towards the boathouse.

"And all I ever wanted was to be left alone," Corrigan muttered, and he hoisted the rifle on to his shoulder. It was too late for recriminations now. They would have to battle their way out.

By the time they reached the boathouse the Japanese were already swarming along the pathway from the bungalow towards them. Rifle fire splintered the wooden planking next to Corrigan's head and a native constable running next to him screamed and fell.

Corrigan grabbed his arms and dragged him inside, a dark stain smearing the wooden planking behind them.

Lavella and the rest of his men were already crouched inside the boatshed, one on each side of the doorway, returning fire into the grove.

Corrigan grabbed Lavella. "The shit's really hit the fan now. There's no way we're getting back out through the plantation."

"We bugger up properly orright," Lavella grunted. He bent to examine the wounded constable. A froth of crimson-stained bubbles erupted between the man's lips. "Very bad," Lavella said. "Lung shoot."

The man's eyes fluttered open. Lavella broke the news to him as gently as possible. "You for die," he told him.

The large silver moon was framed by the open seaward doors of the boatshed, shimmering on the indigo waters of the bay like a framed picture. It cast an eerie luminescent glow around the small wooden building and in that moment Corrigan thought he was hallucinating, for there, side by side with the *Deutschland*, was the *Shamrock*.

"The Japs must have sailed up in her," Corrigan said aloud.

"We finis here," Sergeant Lavella shouted at him. "No good very mus!"

As if to emphasise Lavella's summation, one of his men screamed and fell sideways on the planking, blood streaming from his left shoulder. Another man took his place at the door as rifle fire continued to smash into the flimsy walls of the boathouse.

"Get your men to load the batteries on to the *Shamrock*," Corrigan shouted at Lavella. "We're going to sail right out of here!"

Lavella shouted out a stream of commands. Two of his men jumped to their feet and dragged the batteries on to the stern of the *Shamrock*. When it was done, Corrigan ordered the rest of the men into the back of the launch.

Corrigan handed Lavella the Mannlicher. "Hold them off with this," he shouted.

He leaped into the cockpit of the *Shamrock* and started the engines. Lavella threw himself on the planking of the boathouse next to the wounded constable and emptied the Mannlicher's magazine at the line of advancing soldiers, keeping them pinned down by the first line of coconut palms.

Corrigan unhitched the ropes on the bows and the stern and ran back to the boathouse doors for Sergeant Lavella. "What about him?" he shouted, pointing to the man with the lung wound.

"Corporal Bingiti volunteer for hero," Lavella said simply.

Bingiti was lying on his back, his teeth and lips stained with his own blood. His eyes fluttered open and he raised his right hand for the Mannlicher.

Lavella reloaded the magazine, passed it to him and rolled him over on his belly.

Lavella whispered something to him and then he and Corrigan leaped to their feet and vaulted into the boat. Corrigan pushed the motor to full throttle and pointed her nose out of the boatshed; he had the sudden curious sensation that he was heading her prow straight for the moon.

As soon as the small craft hit the open water the night seemed to explode. Rifle fire cracked through the air around them. Corrigan ducked down in the cockpit, as bullets smashed the glass windscreen and splintered the solid mahogany of the bulwark.

He crouched down, with one hand on the wheel of the

Shamrock, and peered back over the stern. Already the Japanese soldiers were running up the jetty towards the boathouse. There was no answering fire from Bingiti. Poor bastard must be dead, Corrigan thought.

Any moment the Japanese would start the diesel motors of the *Deutschland* and come after them. If there'd only been time to scuttle Heydrich's yacht . . .

At that moment the boathouse exploded in a ball of bright orange flame, a mushroom of black smoke imploding and swirling up into the night sky.

"Christ," Corrigan muttered.

"Corporal Bingiti," Sergeant Lavella said at his shoulder. "I tell him to shoot benzene drums. No more boat. No more *Japoni*."

The rifle fire from the shore had become sporadic now. Already they were motoring through the reef that guarded the bay. In a few more moments they would be beyond the headland and safe from the Japanese snipers along the shoreline.

"Well, that's the worst bit over," Corrigan said. "All we've got to do now is carry the batteries five miles back through the jungle with the Japanese combing every inch of coastline. Should be a breeze."

Corrigan knew every inch of the waters around Santa Maria; the Admiralty charts were imprinted with absolute clarity in his mind. He headed north, hugging the coastline to Marmari Point. He could beach the *Shamrock* there, in the shallow bay to the east of the village. Mount Tahunga was just five miles to the southeast.

As they entered the bay Corrigan immediately sensed something was wrong; perhaps it was in the altered action of the waves, or perhaps it was just a sailor's sixth sense. He strained his eyes into the blackness, every nerve in his body screaming at him to turn back.

He slowed the engines and crawled ahead through the reefs.

"Which way?" Sergeant Lavella said, realising something was wrong.

"I don't know," Corrigan said. "Something's just not right."

Lavella and his men stood waiting in the stern, their eyes turned fearfully towards the black shore. Slowly the *Shamrock* inched her way forward, the chug-chug of her motors echoing around the lagoon.

Then through the glinting moonlight Corrigan caught a glimpse of something shining in the waves.

A shark?

Flying fish?

Corrigan strained his eyes into the blackness and suddenly he saw it.

"Wreck!" he gasped.

32

The full moon reflected on the submerged wreckage of the Japanese bomber, shining like whalebones in the shallow waters. Corrigan whipped the *Shamrock* around to starboard, to try and steer the launch around it.

The passage was too narrow for the manoeuvre. Corrigan heard the terrible crunching of metal and wood as the *Shamrock*'s hull ground over the coral. Then she lurched violently and swung round on her beam.

The *Shamrock* slammed to a halt, throwing them all on to the deck. Corrigan fed power full astern and tried to reverse her off the reef. The hull shuddered as the water around the stern churned and boiled, but the *Shamrock* did not move.

Lavella appeared beside him. "Bugger up finis?"

"Looks like it," Corrigan said. "We're stuck fast on a falling tide."

He looked at his watch. In another couple of hours it would be dawn and the Japanese spotter planes would find them.

"Which way we go?" Lavella said.

"Only one way we can go," Corrigan told him. "It looks like we're going to get our boots wet."

Rachel stood in the doorway of the radio hut and watched as Manning sat down on one of the crates, staring at the radio, now silent and useless. He took the binoculars from around his neck, and laid them on the trestle table next to him.

It was still early morning, but already a large sweat stain had spread across the back of his khaki shirt. He sagged forward, cradling his head on his arms.

"Are you all right?" Rachel said.

Manning turned, startled. He saw her and forced a smile. "Yes I'm fine. Just tired, that's all."

"I heard the bombers."

Manning nodded. "Three squadrons and a flight of Zeros. And there's five transports and a destroyer escort steaming down The Slot." He slapped the radio with the palm of his hand. "Looks like the Americans are on their own today."

"Nothing you can do?"

"Not without the batteries."

Rachel came and sat down on one of the packing crates next to the trestle table. She nodded her head towards the radio. "How much is this hurting the Japanese?"

Manning gave her a thin smile. "Oh, it's hurting them all right."

There was a long silence. Then Rachel took a deep breath and said: "I don't want to go."

Manning shook his head. "I don't understand."

"I don't want to leave the island. Put my uncle on the submarine. Corrigan too, if he wants to go. But let me stay here and help you. I'm not afraid."

Manning stared at her, shaken. What was she? Nineteen, twenty? He couldn't allow it. She had her whole life in front of her. Besides, he had been brought up to believe that war was a man's work.

"It's out of the question," he said simply.

"There's nothing you do here that I can't do."

Manning smiled grimly. "You're probably right. But it's still out of the question. Nevertheless I admire your courage."

"My uncle always told me never to run away from anything."

"I wish he'd tell that to Patrick."

Rachel stiffened. "Mister Corrigan doesn't lack courage."

"Oh, I know he doesn't," Manning said easily, surprised at how quickly Rachel had leaped to the big Irishman's defence. "I didn't mean it that way."

"Then what did you mean?"

"Perhaps it's better if you ask Patrick that question."

Rachel studied Manning carefully. "You seem to know an awful lot about him."

"Perhaps. That doesn't mean I understand him. I've been on this island a long time. He talks to me sometimes about the devils in his head. We each of us have them. Patrick's are perhaps a little more vicious than most."

Manning fell silent and Rachel knew better than to pry further. Manning was far too English to ever break another man's confidence.

She went to the door of the hut. "Do you think he'll be all right?"

"Oh, don't worry about him on that account. He'll be back, and he'll have the batteries. Whatever else he may be, Patrick's a survivor."

*

They arrived back at the camp early the following afternoon.

They had walked all day and half the night, the precious batteries on their shoulders; their skin was chafed raw, and two of the men had burns on their arms and hands from spilled acid.

Corrigan had waited on the outgoing tide. Soon, the waters around the *Shamrock* were only waist deep and they had waded ashore with their precious cargo, the batteries wrapped in an ancient waterproof Corrigan had salvaged from the saloon of the launch.

By the time they reached the camp they were exhausted. They had had to leave the wounded corporal behind them on the jungle track where he had fainted from loss of blood.

When they arrived Manning was in the radio hut, noting down the shipping movements he had spotted that morning along The Slot, jotting his notes in the small leather-bound notebook he carried with him.

As Corrigan reached the mouth of the gully, he came out of the hut, his hands on his hips, a faint smile of satisfaction playing round his lips.

"We've got the batteries," Corrigan told him.

"Jolly good show," Manning said. "I knew I could count on you."

And without another word he turned and went back inside the hut.

33

Wolfgang Heydrich looked over the smouldering ruins of his boathouse and wanted to weep. His lower lip trembled in self-pity as he stared at the charred stumps of the pilings and the skeleton of the *Deutschland* now lying in fifteen feet of shimmering water.

He cursed Corrigan softly in the harsh bitter tones of his mother tongue. Then he hawked up the bile in the back of his throat and spat into the water.

The bodies of the five dead Japanese soldiers had been laid out at the foot of the jetty. Already they were beginning to stink. A heavy khaki ground sheet had been thrown over the corpses and the flies swarmed around it in lazy black clouds.

Heydrich wrinkled his nose in disgust and walked back down the path to the bungalow. He found Tashiro on the verandah with Kurosawa. The Japanese officer was white-lipped with rage but Heydrich was too absorbed with his own loss to notice.

Kurosawa saw the German planter first. He stopped in mid-sentence and stared at him.

"Yes?"

"Ask him what he's going to do about my yacht," Heydrich said.

Tashiro turned and glared at him. There was menace in the small, dark eyes but Heydrich was determined they would not brush him off this time. He was an Aryan, one of Hitler's master race. He would not allow these yellow barbarians to treat him like one of the natives.

"Tashiro-san not speak now," Kurosawa said.

Heydrich ignored him. "Ask him what he's going to do about my yacht."

Kurosawa remained stubbornly silent. He had no intention of translating Heydrich's demand to Tashiro. He knew what his colleague's reaction would be. He didn't like the fat planter, but his stomach had seen enough violence for one day.

Unfortunately for Heydrich, Tashiro didn't need Kurosawa to interpret for him. A soft smile played around his lips for a few moments. There was no humour in it. Suddenly he drew his sword from the leather scabbard at his waist and the heavy polished blade flashed in the early morning sunlight. Heydrich shrieked as the razor-sharp tip sliced into the cleft under his chin.

He fell back against one of the wooden posts; Tashiro held him pinned there, with the point of the sword.

The point of the blade had penetrated the skin and the planter felt his own blood running down his neck and on to his shirt. He hardly dared breathe; his eyes did not move from the steel under his chin. He knew that Tashiro need only flick his wrist a few inches to the right or the left to slit the arteries in his throat.

It could have been seconds, or minutes. Finally Heydrich lifted his eyes into those of his tormentor. Tashiro was watching him, his eyes glittering with amusement. Heydrich realised with cold horror that he was making up his mind whether or not to kill him.

The German had never experienced such terror before. He tried to speak, but no words came; they bubbled in the back of his throat like the final gasp of a dying man.

He felt something hot and wet flood down the inside of his leg as he emptied the contents of his bladder down the front of his trousers.

Heydrich's involuntary act saved his life. Tashiro saw the stain spread across Heydrich's groin and down the white cotton of his trouser leg and he started to laugh.

Satisfied, he lowered the sword and put it back in its sheath. Then with one sudden motion he took hold of the lapels of Heydrich's shirt and threw him bodily down the steps of his own bungalow.

Babbling with fear, Heydrich scrambled to his feet and hurried away down the path towards the copra sheds. Minutes later Kurosawa and Tashiro heard a girl screaming somewhere in the servants' huts. It was Alice Melema'a.

Heydrich had found a sacrifice with which to exorcise his own humiliation.

34

It was exactly six o'clock.

Mitchell sat by the radio. Shoup had his earphones on, and was anxiously turning the dials. They had been joined by a half dozen other pilots from the squadron. They were already in their flying gear, ready for their missions that morning.

Mitchell was sipping a canteen cup of bubbling Navy issue coffee. Somehow the aluminium rim always seemed ten degrees hotter than its contents, but it was warming against the effects of the chill tropic dawn.

There was an air of expectancy in the room. After nearly six dark weeks, the men on Guadalcanal had their first stirrings of hope. They had just faced their sternest test. It had come just after sunset with a blistering twenty-minute barrage from the Japanese destroyers in Skylark Channel, the whip-like crack of the five-inch guns pounding the Marine positions on the ridge to the east of Henderson Field. An uncanny silence followed. Slowly a red flare drifted down over the ridge, bathing the surrounding jungle the colour of blood. Then the *banzai* screams and the bang of the firecrackers rent the night as the Japanese attacked Red Mike Edson's Baker Company; the deadly chatter of the Brownings answered them.

For two nights Mitchell and his men lay in their tents listening to the sounds of the battle as it came closer and closer to the field. The Marines were almost thrown off the ridge; Edson finally beat back the Japanese by having his howitzers fire through his own lines, butchering the enemy with his artillery from just fifty yards, the big guns side by side with the infantry, the same tactics that had been employed eighty years before at Bull Run and Pittsburgh.

The next morning Mitchell watched the survivors of Baker Company straggling back from the line, their eyes red-rimmed and etched with horror, staring vacantly ahead, too exhausted to pursue their defeated enemy. The Japanese left six hundred dead behind them on what the Marines now called Bloody Ridge.

The next day the Navy broke the siege. Admiral Kelly Turner lost an aircraft carrier, the *USS Wasp*, but he finally arrived in Iron Bottom Sound with the Marines Seventh Division and one thousand tons of rations.

The other factor that began to swing the balance back in the Americans' favour was The Weatherman.

The Grumman Wildcats of the Cactus Air Force were no match for the Japanese Zeros. They were neither as fast or as manoeuvrable. But the Japanese planes always arrived at Guadalcanal low on fuel after their long flights from Kavieng or Rabaul, slowed down by the extra belly tanks of fuel they were forced to carry.

More important, Mitchell and his men always knew when they would arrive. The only way to overcome the superior performance of the Zeros was by attacking them from above; the two-hour warning they received from The Weatherman gave them time to scramble their fighters and climb to their attack altitudes of 30,000 feet. When the Japanese finally arrived over the island, Mitchell's squadron was already in the air. They would then swoop down on them out of the sun, and cut them to pieces.

Even if the Japanese realised what was happening, Mitchell knew there was nothing they could do. If they tried to fly around the islands to the north they would not have enough fuel to reach Guadalcanal; if they flew too high they would betray their presence to the American radar.

While The Weatherman stayed on the air, they had the Japanese fighters cold.

Suddenly the radio crackled to life.

"Good morning, Allies. This is The Weatherman. There's some cloud over Bougainville and New Georgia today, but it seems to be clearing to the north-east. Three formations of bombers passed to the east of here thirty minutes ago. About ten thousand feet is my guess. Fighters are moving in to support them from Bougainville. I can see them from here. You're going to be busy today. Good luck Americans. Over and out!"

Shoup scribbled the message on to his pad and reached for the field phone. When he turned round the hut was empty. He guessed the pilots were already running out towards the revetments and climbing up the olive-drab fuselages of their fighters.

They were in for a big day.

35

Colonel Nakamura leaned forward on the desk in front of him, both hands splayed across the smooth mahogany surface. His voice had the soft menacing quality of a snake.

"How could this have happened?"

"My men did not expect such an attack, Nakamura-san," Tashiro said. "We were caught by surprise."

"Obviously," Nakamura interrupted his lieutenant.

He got to his feet and paced the room, his hands clenched into fists behind his back. Finally he turned to face the large map of the island that hung on the wall behind him. "They must be up here," he said, slapping the open surface of his hand on the dark green shaded area to the north of the island.

"My men are conducting a sweep of the jungles there at this moment."

Nakamura allowed himself a chill smile. "What about the natives?"

"They say they have not seen the Englishman. They will not help him. They know what will happen to them if we find him in one of their villages."

Nakamura turned away from the map and glared out of the window, across the neatly kept square of lawn and beyond to the breakers frothing in the bay.

He stood for a long time, the thick black eyebrows bunched into a frown. Tashiro waited in respectful silence.

"The battle for Guadalcanal does not go well for us. The Americans are putting up strong resistance. Furthermore, the High Command believes the enemy is still receiving news of all our movements between the islands by sea and by air. The damage that may already have been done is incalculable. We cannot allow this to continue!"

"We will catch him, Nakamura-san," Tashiro said.

"It has already taken us too long," Nakamura snapped. "How many men did you lose?"

"Five dead, three wounded," Tashiro said mechanically. The bitter shame of being defeated by these guerrillas was gnawing into his soul. Beneath the calm exterior he was consumed with a burning desire for revenge.

"How many of them were there?"

"It is impossible to estimate Colonel. In the darkness . . . there was much confusion."

"The Englishman had seven armed native policemen on the island. We must assume they have remained loyal to him. In addition the Irishman and the priest may have joined him. That makes ten men, at most. Hardly a formidable foe."

"We found the body of one of the native police in the remains of the boat shed, Colonel."

"A great victory! Nine men, then. I will give you another two platoons. Use whatever means is necessary to track the Englishman down. But find him. We have to find him!"

36

"How is he?" Manning asked.

"He needs expert attention. Far more than I am able to give him."

Rachel bent over her uncle's emaciated body and loosened the dressings on his leg. Father Goode muttered and tossed as he lay on the bamboo cot, bathed in his own perspiration. His face was as pale and waxen as a child's doll.

Manning watched her work, and grimaced. The leg was swollen fat and the area round the wound had turned an ugly blue-black colour. As Rachel removed the dirty dressings he sniffed the air and his stomach churned at the ugly taint of putrefaction.

Manning put a hand on Rachel's shoulder. "The Americans have promised to send a submarine as soon as possible."

"We have already waited almost a month. Every day he is worse. If we wait any longer it will be too late."

Momentarily Manning lost his patience. "There's a major battle going on at Guadalcanal. They don't have the submarines to spare just for a . . ." He stopped himself.

"Just for a sick priest and his stupid niece."

"I wasn't going to put it quite like that."

Rachel smiled an apology. "I'm sorry. You didn't ask us to come here."

Manning shrugged. "The Americans really will come as soon as they can."

"I know. It's just watching him die like this, by degrees . . . even if he lives, he's going to be a cripple."

Manning did not know what to say to her. He had long ago decided that his initial estimation of her had been wrong. Despite the fact that she was so young, she had strong nerves. He spent every minute of every day terrified to the depths of his soul, yet this young slip of a girl seemed only concerned for her uncle's health.

It made him only more determined to keep going.

He would be relieved to see them all on the submarine. Their presence in the camp was only an additional responsibility and burden. Father Goode's delirious outbursts often shattered the night silence, and Manning knew that if it ever happened when there was a Japanese patrol nearby, the nerve-shattering cries would lead them right to them.

Then there was Corrigan; morose, unpredictable and drinking heavily. And Sanei – silent as a shadow, with those dark, sullen eyes. Each of them threatened his mission in their own way. Most dangerous of all was the tension between Sanei and Rachel, subtle yet pervasive. But what was the reason for it?

He looked at Rachel and wondered.

"You should have left while you had the chance," he told her. "I tried to warn you."

"We stayed for the same reasons you did."

Manning gave a hollow laugh. "Oh, I don't think so."

"No man risks his life just for King and Country. My uncle thinks he's doing this for God. I suspect there may be a personal motive."

Manning frowned. "That's a very cynical view."

"Uncle Matthew needs to prove something to himself. Is it cynical to say that?"

"I suppose not. We all have something to prove, I suppose."

He watched her finish dressing Father Goode's leg with the last strips of muslin she had torn from her dress. She stood up, smoothing down the tapa cloth she now wore as if it was her best Sunday frock.

"Tell me one thing," Manning asked her. "Why did Corrigan help you?"

"You underestimate him, Mister Manning."
"I don't think so. I've known Patrick ever since he came to this island. The man is a rogue and a charlatan, and I say that as a friend of his. God knows what his enemies say about him."
"I appealed to his better nature."
"He doesn't have one."
"Then how else do you explain it?" Rachel asked him.
Manning looked down, embarrassed. "I suspect there may have been a personal motive."
The blood rushed to Rachel's cheeks and she turned away. "Well if he has one, I'm sure I've no idea what it might be," she said, and she turned and left the hut.

About four hundred yards from the camp, one of the mountain streams that fed the Ngulinni River broke across an outcrop of hard basalt, forming a ridge across the softer clay of the hillside. Here it had formed a waterfall, some thirty feet high, that dropped clear and sparkling into a wide, black pool.
The water here was ice cool, hidden from view behind a thick curtain of ferns and hanging creepers. Rachel went there often to wash away the sweat and grime of the steaming jungle.
That afternoon, as she made her way along the narrow path along the ridge, she heard voices. She recognised them at once. It was Corrigan and Sanei.
She hesitated. She knew she should turn back. They were probably bathing together in the pool. But instead she found her feet carrying her on along the trail. It was as if there was a powerful magnet, drawing her on.
The waterfall drowned out the sound of her footsteps through the jungle of ferns. She was only a few yards away from the water's edge when she saw them, their bodies brown and sleek against the limpid greens of the pool. They were both naked, waist deep in the water.
Rachel sank down on to her haunches, the breath catching in her throat.

Corrigan had his back to her. Sanei was facing him, her arms around his shoulders. She splashed his face with water, teasing, then ran away from him through the shallows with the water bursting like a shower of gems around her long brown limbs, the thin boyish body slim and svelte and brown.

Corrigan caught up with her and with a bellow he pulled her down into the pool and they both went down, yelling and laughing. Sanei tried to wriggle free but Corrigan gripped her wrist and pulled her towards him. Suddenly he lowered his head and began to kiss her neck and Sanei's laughter bubbled and died in her throat, changing instead to a soft moan.

She gasped, pulling Corrigan's mouth to her bare breast.

Rachel felt her cheeks blush hot as she watched Corrigan move his hands hungrily over the girl's body, caressing her. She could feel the ache in her own breasts and in that dark, guilty place between her legs and the force of her sudden longing made her cry out softly.

It was then she realised with the force of absolute clarity that she wanted Corrigan for herself. She wanted him more than she had ever wanted anything. She didn't care about her uncle, about God, about anything.

She wanted him.

Sanei's eyes were bright slits of pleasure, her mouth open in that same, silent animal scream that Rachel had first seen that morning outside the church, on another woman's face. Suddenly her eyes opened wide and she looked directly into Rachel's eyes in surprise and triumph.

Rachel gasped. She turned and stumbled back through the jungle, running blindly until she was exhausted, finally sinking to her knees by the side of a moss-covered tree, her breathing ragged and fire-hot in her chest.

The panting became deep sobs of despair as she finally wept for herself; a release of all the fear and aching terror of the last months, and tears for the utter emptiness of living with herself for twenty years as a total stranger.

37

Kumasi had wrestled with the dilemma all night, like a dog worrying a bone. He was confused, unhappy and frightened. The previous afternoon one of the young men had come back from a fishing expedition and told him that he had seen Japanese soldiers camped in the next bay. That could mean only one thing. They were hunting for the *kiap*.

The villagers at Marmari Point had known that Manning had made camp in the surrounding hills within two days of his arrival. Since then they had been up to the ridge many times, trading their field fruit and fish and sometimes a wild chicken.

But then the *japoni* soldiers had come and threatened them. They had told them that they must not help the Europeans. They said that if they knew where any white man was hiding they should tell them straight away.

Kumasi had shrugged his shoulders and pretended not to understand.

The islanders still did not know what to make of the Japanese. They had lived under the protection of the British government for almost fifty years, and it had brought many benefits. The British had brought medicine, and Cargo and the imposition of "Guberment" law had ended many of the bloody internecine conflicts.

It was hard for the islanders to like their new masters. The Japanese frequently recruited their help as carriers and labourers, but they were never paid for their work, as they had been by Manning and the other British *kiaps* before him. But what really antagonised the islanders was the way the Japanese looted their gardens.

It took them months of toil each year to create their gardens from the virgin jungle. They cultivated a new plot each year, just clearing enough land to feed their families, only harvesting enough sweet potato, yams, taro, bananas and papaya that was needed for each day's meal.

But when the Japanese came they pillaged their gardens needlessly, taking everything; even their coconut trees, which took up to fifteen years to grow, were chopped to the ground for just one crop of nuts.

One old man in Kumasi's village had found the Japanese looting a garden which he had recently planted with taro. The plants were so young that the edible bulbs at the base of the plant had still not formed, so they were useless for food. Outraged at the senseless act, the old man tried to stop them.

They had shot him down like a dog.

It was a barbaric action that the islanders found difficult to understand or to forgive.

Yet they were frightened. The Japanese had threatened to execute anyone who helped the Europeans. If, as the *kiap* said, other white soldiers were close by, why was he hiding himself away in the jungle like a fugitive?

Perhaps it was true what the *japoni* said – the war was over and Santa Maria was now part of the empire of Nippon. The white man Heydrich was working with the Japanese, so perhaps it could be true after all.

The islanders had all been profoundly shocked by the sudden departure of the whites, whom they had believed until then to be invincible; and although they still felt a certain loyalty to the British *kiap*, they wanted primarily to be left in peace.

The village elders had gathered to discuss the problem. Some of them had wondered if the *kiap* had become a liability; if the *japoni* discovered his camp so close to Marmari Point, they might be punished for harbouring him. It might be better if they killed him themselves and took his body to the *japoni*.

They looked to Kumasi for guidance.

Kumasi was the *luluai* – the headman of the village, appointed by Manning himself. He had won the position largely because of his ability to speak good English, which he had learned as a young man working as indentured labour on the Queensland sugar fields.

But this was not the real source of Kumasi's influence. Although Manning had not known it, Kumasi was also the village Big Man, or *mumi*. To achieve this, Kumasi had spent much of his wealth on lavish feasts, and spectacular sacrifices to the spirits after the death of the previous chief. Because of this, others in the tribe deferred to him, laughing loudly at his jokes, concurring with his opinions, ingratiating themselves with him. Influence and leadership had flowed to him naturally.

Aside from his wealth the *mumi* could also use his influence to focus praise or scorn upon anyone in the village; and so it was as *mumi*, and not as Manning's *luluai*, that the people of the village listened to Kumasi.

Kumasi had already decided that they could not betray the *kiap*, despite the dangers involved in tacitly assisting him. Aside from the fact that the *japoni* had done little to endear themselves to the islanders, Kumasi had other, more personal reasons. The *kiap* had the white woman with him; and it was the white woman who had saved Kumasi's life when he had the fire in his belly.

Forcefully and eloquently, Kumasi enumerated all the reasons why they should not help the *japoni*, ending his discourse with the two most persuasive reasons of all; if they did, they might have to answer to King George again one day.

Worse, the *kiap* had Father Goode with him so they might have to answer to the Virgin Mary as well.

As both these beings had assumed a mythical importance rivalling that of their own spirit ancestors, the people of Marmari Point agreed that their *mumi* was a man of great wisdom, and the decision was made. Besides, they reminded themselves, there was also the mysterious matter of the Cargo.

Ian Manning was safe. For the present, at least.

After the meeting, Kumasi sent his son Wesu to Manning's camp to warn him of the Japanese presence at Marmari. Early the next morning Wesu set off, striding nimbly up the familiar jungle trails towards the hills.

A bright coloured parrot shot through the dappled sunlight ahead of him, the blues and yellows of its feathers vivid in the misted bolts of sunlight that burst through the canopy of the trees overhead. Wesu never broke stride as he made his way through the hanging vine-ropes and the drooping parasites, and up the dim passageway leading to the lip of the gully where Manning had his camp.

Suddenly one of the ferns in front of him sprang into the air and pointed a long rifle at him. Wesu yelled and fell to his knees.

The fern began to walk towards him. It had white eyes and long brown arms. It spoke to him.

"What name you?" the fern said.

With a shock Wesu realised the fern was Sergeant Lavella, one of the *kiap*'s policemen. He had fern branches stuck all over his body. Wesu was amazed. He had never seen camouflage before.

"My name Wesu. Want talk-talk longa *kiap*," he said. "*Japoni* he come."

Sergeant Lavella lowered his rifle. He pulled Wesu roughly to his feet. "Come quick," he said, and led him back towards the camp.

Ian Manning felt the familiar cold thrill of fear deep in his stomach. There were days when he could forget that the Japanese were out there hunting for him, when he could pretend it was all some fantastic game on this beautiful jungle island. Sometimes he could blot out the terrible reality, damming the nightmare of his own imagination.

But now as he listened to the terrified native's story, the suffocating dread threatened to overwhelm him. For a moment his throat was too dry to allow him to speak.

He heard Corrigan's voice. "We haven't got a chance. Those bastards will tear up every tree on this island to find us. Tell the Americans to get us off here tonight."

"That's not possible, old boy," Manning said, surprised at how calm his own voice sounded. He didn't feel it.

"So what are we going to do?"

"We'll have to move the camp."

"Jesus, we've only just got here."

"We've no choice."

"Are you out of your mind? The bloody vicar's leg's going to drop off on the ground any minute. If you try and shift him he's going to snuff it."

"Delicately put, Patrick." He turned to Sergeant Lavella, who was waiting for instructions with his hand eagerly hovering on the trigger of his rifle. "Take your men and watch the trail leading up from Kumasi's village. But don't fire unless you have to."

Sergeant Lavella shook his head vigorously. He understood. He would not fire unless he was forced to.

That is, unless he saw a Japanese soldier.

38

Lieutenant Kurosawa stood at the rail of the launch, watching a flight of belama, the frigate birds of the Pacific, wheel away from the bow of the sampan with effortless grace. Ahead of them, an emerald finger of land pushed out into the blue-green coral water, where the green fronds of the tall statuesque palms bent to the offshore breeze.

The wind brought with it the distinctive smell of the village at Marmari Point; the smell of woodsmoke, and roasted pig, the taint of rotting vegetation and the sickly sweet scent of betel nut flowers.

But Kurosawa derived no pleasure from the scene. He was troubled by a vague sense of unease, irritating but insistent, like the buzzing of a mosquito in a darkened room. For the first time since he had joined the army, he was afraid; it was as if he sensed his own death.

He found himself thinking again about the pilgrimage he had made to the ancient capital of Nara, near Kyoto, before he had left for the war. Nara was the ancient town where Buddhism first took root in Japan, and to climb to the top of the steps to the ancient wooden temple was meant to bring good luck.

It was here that the sutras were first chanted by the Chinese monks in the eighth century. They could still be heard, ringing through the clear mountain air and the crowding cypress trees . . .

> *. . . the human body is frail and mortal . . .*
> *. . . it has no power as the earth has none,*
> *It has no durability as the wind has none,*
> *It is transient and sure to die . . .*

"So solemn, Kurosawa-san?"

He turned, startled. It was Tashiro.

"I was thinking."

"You think too much. That's your trouble."

Kurosawa turned away. "You're probably right, Tashiro-san," he murmured.

He knew Tashiro resented him. Although they were comrades, they were of vastly different backgrounds.

Tashiro's father was Samurai; Kurosawa's father was a well-off farmer from Hachioji, on the other side of Tokyo. His family even had a racehorse, and he had gone to Keio senior college, a school with westernist influences. He had even spent some time in the United States, at the University of Michigan.

Tashiro had no college education. He had received his

early training at one of the *rikugen yonen gakko* – a government military preparatory school – when he was twelve years old. The army was his life.

Tashiro was a volunteer; Kurosawa was a conscript. Tashiro wanted battle; Kurosawa wanted to avoid it. And while Tashiro wanted glory, Kurosawa wanted to survive.

Yet Tashiro despised and feared Kurosawa's intellect; in his comrade he saw reflected his own weakness. Kurosawa's doubts disturbed him more than he would admit.

"Soon we shall have them," Tashiro said. "They will not get away from us this time."

"We must step carefully, Tashiro-san. We need the natives to co-operate with us."

"The natives! They will co-operate – they have no choice!"

Like many others of his generation, Tashiro believed that anyone who was not Japanese was *kichibu* – a beast, and less than human. It was the rationale behind the atrocities the Japanese Army had already committed in China.

Kurosawa was silent. He knew it was pointless to argue. He lapsed into the dark reflections of his own thoughts.

The sampan was just a few yards from the beach. The muffled throb of the engines echoed around the lagoon and the jumble of thatched roof huts among the palms. As they reached the shallow sandy waters, the soldiers jumped out and waded ashore, Tashiro leading them, his sword drawn.

But when they reached the village it was deserted. Only Kumasi was there to meet them.

"It's no good," Sam Doo said to Lieutenant Kurosawa, as Tashiro stood by scowling, "he says he doesn't know anything about the English *kiap*."

"Ask him where the village people have gone," Kurosawa said.

"They are frightened. They have run away."

This was in fact only half the truth. Most of the young men of the village were helping Manning carry the teleradio to a higher base somewhere in the mountains. The old people, the women and the children had been sent away to hide in the jungle. Kumasi had stayed behind, hoping to prevent the Japanese from burning down the village, as they almost certainly would if they found it deserted.

Tashiro sent some of his men to search the huts, while Kumasi watched them fearfully, the wizened head bobbing and his eyes rolling in his head. The two Japanese officers turned their attentions back to Sam Doo. They had conscripted the little Chinese from the settlement to act as their interpreter. He spoke Pidgin, a little Japanese and enough of the many island languages to make himself understood; his facility with languages was the result of many years of running a South Seas' drinking and gambling establishment with a cosmopolitan clientele.

"Ask him again where *kiap* is," Kurosawa said to Sam Doo. "He must tell us."

The little Chinese grinned and bowed and turned to Kumasi, and spoke to him in the local dialect.

"He wants to know where the Englishman is. You must tell him. Say you don't know!" Sam Doo had no love for the Japanese.

"I don't know," Kumasi said.

"He says he doesn't know," Sam Doo said.

Kurosawa translated for Tashiro. The first lieutenant frowned.

He was convinced Manning was somewhere very close. If he was right this man must know where. No one could move through the mountains without the natives knowing – especially when they were loaded down with radios and supplies.

No, Tashiro thought grimly. *I must make an example of this one.*

There was a shout and Tashiro's sergeant ran out of

Kumasi's hut with a white muslin scarf clutched in his right hand. He handed it to Tashiro.

The missionary's niece!

Tashiro turned to the old man and held it under his nose. "Ask him where he got this!"

"He wants to know where you got it," Sam Doo translated for him. "Tell him to go fuck a monkey!"

"It belongs to the missionary's niece," Kumasi answered truthfully. "She left it behind many months ago. She saved my life!"

"Well?" Tashiro said.

Sam Doo thought quickly. He decided the old chief was not a very good liar. "He said one of the villagers traded a shark's tooth for it in Vancoro."

Tashiro's face flushed to the colour of old bronze, his eyes burning in his head like coals.

"Tell him to kneel down," he said.

Kurosawa hesitated, then repeated the order.

Sam Doo stared, not comprehending. He turned to Kumasi and translated. The old man trembled. He looked up into the Japanese officer's eyes, anticipating what was about to happen.

He thought about the white girl who had cut the evil spirit out of him that night many months ago. The fingers of his right hand crept to the cicatrice of thick scar tissue just above his right groin as he remembered. His own life was not his to save anyway. The girl had given it to him. He would repay his debt to her.

He slowly dropped to his knees.

Tashiro barked out a command and two soldiers ran across, seized the old man's arms and forced them behind his back. There was the rasping of steel as Tashiro drew his sword from the sheath at his belt.

"Tell him," Tashiro said to Kurosawa. "Tell him if he does not tell me where I will find the Englishman, he is going to die."

Kurosawa turned to his colleague. "We don't make war on old men. Put away your sword, Tashiro-san."

Sam Doo understood enough of what was spoken to understand. "He doesn't know where they are," he said desperately.

"Tell him!"

The old chief was trembling, his body shaking so violently it seemed his reed-thin arms would be pulled from their sockets where the soldiers held them fast. A thin trickle of saliva split from his betel-stained lips and hung suspended halfway to the ground. He began to wail.

"What is he saying?" Tashiro said.

Sam Doo, also terrified now, shook his head. "It's a prayer to his ancestors," he mumbled. "He is getting ready to die."

"Very well," Tashiro said, and raised the sword over his head.

39

The steel blade flashed the colour of blood as it caught the rays of the late afternoon sun before scything down in a swift arc on the back of the old man's neck, slicing cleanly through the tendons and bone. The headless body went into a brief spasm and then the two soldiers who had been holding Kumasi's arms let the torso slip to the ground, gouts of blood spouting horribly from the neck.

Sam Doo turned away and vomited.

Kurosawa looked at his colleague, stunned. "This is not war," he said.

"You talk like a woman," Tashiro said. He wiped the blade carefully on the broad leaf of a palm and sheathed his sword.

"We will have to teach these people how to co-operate with us. We will find this Englishman. Now they have seen how we treat disobedience, the natives will tell us where he is."

Sergeant Lavella raised his head above the shelter of the coconut bole and watched them come. There were about two dozen soldiers, and two officers, spread out in single file along the trail. Three of the soldiers were carrying a Nambu machine gun and tripod.

Manning had insisted that no shots were to be fired unless the Japanese were on top of the camp. Lavella had allowed himself some licence with these instructions; he had posted his men in ambush alongside the trail leading away from Kumasi's village. In his mind it was better to take the battle to the enemy than wait for them to bring it to you. Lavella came from a long line of warriors, and the concept of tactical withdrawal was entirely foreign to him.

Besides, what he had just seen had convinced him. The *japoni* had killed the *mumi* in cold blood. It was unthinkable that they should let the act go unpunished.

Lavella realised he and his men were outnumbered almost four to one. But he would have the initial advantage of surprise and by the very nature of jungle combat, the Japanese would not immediately realise that they had just six men ranged against them.

They would spring the trap, then quickly melt away into the jungle before the *japoni* had time to mount the machine gun against them. The *kiap* called it "shoot and scoot".

Lavella had chosen the site of the ambush very carefully.

Halfway up the high jungle-covered ridge above Marmari Point was a small clearing. It was here that Lavella and his men had taken up positions behind the ferns and trees. The wily old islander knew that men walking uphill in damp heat always stopped for a rest in any open space, and at such a time that they would bunch together and lose their alertness.

This would be the time to strike.

Lavella waited, his face pressed against the warm stock of the gun. The jungle trail passed just fifty yards below him. He knew that somewhere in the impenetrable mass of green his five men were similarly poised, waiting for him to fire the first shot. The Japanese would not be expecting this. The hunter would become the hunted.

The soldier on point was very close now. He was walking with his head down, struggling up the steep path with his rifle slung over his shoulder, sweat gleaming on his face, his tunic drenched with sweat.

He reached the clearing and stopped, swinging the rifle off his shoulder and leaning it against a tree. Panting, he reached for his water bottle.

Soon he was joined by the rest of the platoon; they milled around in the clearing, some sinking down thankfully against the trees, others swinging their packs off aching backs and fumbling for water bottles.

Lavella watched them, choosing his target. Finally he found him. He lined up the sights on the chest of the officer with the sword. Lavella grinned, a grimace of cold anticipation. Now the *japoni* would pay for the life of the old man.

His finger squeezed the trigger of the Enfield.

But Lavella had never been quite the expert marksman in reality as he supposed in his own mind. As he fired, he jerked the barrel with his left hand, as if trying to propel the bullet faster by his own strength. And despite all of Manning's patient coaching through the previous months, he pulled at the trigger, instead of squeezing it gently with his forefinger.

So his first shot went wildly clear of its intended target; but the Japanese soldiers were huddled so closely together in the clearing that the bullet still found its mark, ripping through the chest of one of the machine gunners, killing him instantly.

Lavella's second attempt hit Tashiro in the arm, and he fell screaming backwards into the undergrowth.

At once there was a deafening cacophony of rifle shots as Lavella's men joined his fire from their positions. Lavella saw more soldiers fall as the hail of bullets tore into them.

The rest of the Japanese threw themselves into the thick undergrowth, searching desperately for cover. In their panic some of them even abandoned their rifles.

There were six bodies strewn across the clearing. Lavella heard another Japanese screaming in pain somewhere in the tangled undergrowth below him. Lavella was satisfied. It was time to head back for the camp before the Japanese had time to recover and regroup.

A bullet splintered the trunk next to his head, adding urgency to the decision. In seconds the air around him was alive with the deadly whiplash of bullets as the Japanese fired blindly into the jungle around them.

The firing continued for some minutes before the Japanese realised their enemy had gone. Sergeant Lavella and his men had melted silently away into the thick jungle and returned to face the *kiap*'s wrath.

Rachel entered Corrigan's hut and found him with one of his sandals off, peering at the pad of his left foot. He had his ivory-handled gutting knife out and was carefully wiping it on the leg of his shorts.

"Ian said you'd hurt your foot."

"Got a thorn in it."

"You're not planning to cut it out with your knife?"

"I've washed it."

"The knife?"

"My foot."

"That isn't going to help very much."

"Got a better idea?"

Rachel didn't answer. She snatched the knife away from him and threw it on the ground. Then she bent down, took his foot in her hands and examined it. She could see the head of the thorn under the curl of his middle toes.

"Start slashing your foot with that knife and you'll get an infection. I'll get it out for you."

Corrigan leaned back on his elbows and grinned at her. "And how do you propose to do that?"

"With my teeth."

Corrigan speculated with his eyes. Finally he said: "That should be rather interesting. It will be a new experience for me, at least."

"There aren't many of those left for you to have, are there?" Rachel murmured and suddenly sank her teeth into the flesh around the thorn, biting down as hard as she could.

Corrigan tried to jerk his foot free. "Jesus!"

Rachel paused to examine her handiwork. The marks of her teeth showed pink against the tender white underside of his foot.

"You believe in savage medicine, and no mistake," Corrigan grumbled.

"Not always. It depends on the patient."

Corrigan grinned at her. "Do you treat all your men this way?"

Rachel resumed her study of the foot. "I think the sun has addled your brains, Patrick Corrigan."

"Boyfriends, then. You must have had boyfriends."

"I came here to remove a thorn from your foot. Not to discuss my personal life."

Suddenly Corrigan reached down and ran his hand along her arm. His touch was surprisingly gentle, and she was shocked by the sudden intimacy she felt with him. She looked up. He was leaning forward, his face now very close to hers. He was smiling, but not with that crooked, mocking grin she had seen so often before. There was a warmth and tenderness there that caught her quite by surprise.

She pulled away, startled by the possibilities of the moment and sank her teeth as hard as she could into Corrigan's foot.

Corrigan yelled again but this time his protests were drowned out by shouts from outside the hut.

Sergeant Lavella had returned.

40

Manning sat on the wooden crate in the radio hut and wiped the perspiration off his face with the handtowel he wore at his neck. The weakness and nausea had been affecting him more often in the last few days. He wondered how long he could keep going.

He listened to Sergeant Lavella's account of the battle with increasing tiredness. He did not share his sergeant's pride in the achievement. So he had killed some Japanese. They would always send more.

"How many casualties?" he asked again.

"Seven dead, fifteen wounded," Lavella said. As a warrior he was prone to exaggerating his prowess.

Corrigan laughed easily, as he lounged nonchalantly against one of the bamboo poles. "Halve that and he'd still be exaggerating. He probably nicked one of them in the hand."

Sergeant Lavella glared resentfully at Corrigan. Although he was terrified of Corrigan's massive physical presence he resented the way the big man underestimated him.

"I told you not to fire unless you had to."

Sergeant Lavella was silent. He still did not understand how the little black box that Manning spoke into every day was helping them beat the Japanese. In his experience there was only one effective way of getting rid of unwanted intruders.

"Well that's done it now," Corrigan said. "Now they know where we are they'll comb every inch of jungle round here with every man they've got."

"Did you lose any men?" Manning asked.

"One fella he no come," Lavella said shame-faced. "Corporal Volulu."

"My God. If they've taken him alive . . ."

"Him he no talk," Lavella said. "Good fella that one."

Manning shook his head. "We can't take any risks. We'll have to move camp. Now – tonight."

"I agree with you for once, old son."

Manning looked up wearily. "Thank you Sergeant Lavella. That will be all."

Sergeant Lavella snapped off a smart salute and marched outside.

After he'd gone Corrigan pulled up one of the wooden crates and sat down next to Manning. The Englishman was staring at the ground with his head bowed and his shoulders hunched in fatigue. The strain was beginning to show.

Corrigan put a hand on his shoulder. "You can't keep this up, you know. You're not looking well."

"Worried about me, are you Patrick?"

"Look, it's your funeral. I'm just giving you the benefit of my great wisdom. You've done your bit. Time to call it a day. Get this submarine here, and we'll all get on it and head for greener pastures."

"I can't do that."

"Why not, for God's sake?"

"I just can't. I have to stay. I can't run away from this."

Corrigan shook his head. "Well I'll be damned if I understand it. Still it's . . ."

"Yes, I know. It's my funeral."

Corrigan studied Manning's grey sunken cheeks, and the strained and yellow-shot eyes. "Sure, and a lot sooner than you think," he said.

*

Corporal Volulu's spirit ancestors had deserted him that morning. Wounded in the upper thigh by a stray bullet during the ambush, his companions had melted away into the bush before any of them had realised what had happened.

For almost an hour he had lain in agony, unable to move the leg, the femur shattered by the bullet. He had tried to staunch the flow of blood by thrusting his thumb deep into the wound, refusing to cry out for fear of luring his comrades back into danger.

Finally he had passed out from loss of blood.

When he regained consciousness, he found himself staring into the savagely grinning face of Lieutenant Tashiro.

Tashiro's arm was strapped across his chest, the sleeve of the tunic ripped away, his arm below the shoulder thickly encrusted with blood.

He was trembling with rage. Five of his men were dead. Three more were badly wounded.

Tashiro drew his sword. "Tie him to the tree," he whispered, and two of the soldiers forced Volulu to his feet, despite his agonised screams, and tied his arms behind him around the trunk of a callophyllum tree.

"Now you will tell me where the Englishman has his camp," Tashiro said. He reached behind him and grabbed the terrified Sam Doo by his shirt and threw him at the feet of Volulu. "Tell him he can die quickly or slowly. It is up to him."

Volulu looked back at the Japanese through a red mist of pain and with great precision he spat in his face.

41

The bloodied writhing thing tied to the tree was no longer recognisable as a man. Tashiro's sword had ripped away all resemblance. But Volulu had uttered not a sound. Now, near death, he could not have spoken if he had wanted to.

Tashiro lunged with the sword, plunging it so savagely into the islander's chest, that it embedded itself in the wood of the trunk. Volulu's eyes stared suddenly white from the bloodied mask of his face and then the mutilated body sagged against its bonds. A long sigh escaped his throat and then he was quite still.

His anger spent, Tashiro finally allowed himself to feel the humiliation of his defeat.

He would catch this Englishman. Nothing would stop him now.

Nothing.

Nothing.

The sudden darkness of the tropic night settled on the palm groves, and a huge yellow bomber's moon rose like a spectre out of the quiet sea. It cast an eerie light over Henderson Field through the fronds of the swaying palm trees, and the skeletal shadows of the control tower.

A flare burst against the velvet-black of the sky and as it faded, there came the cacophony of klaxon horns, the din of hands beating empty diesel drums and the babble of voices.

The lights went off in the tent area as if extinguished by a single hand, and there was the sound of catcalling and whistling from the movie tent. For the seventh successive night, the men would not see the end of the film.

On the field the planes were already warming up, the slipstreams churning up choking clouds of black dust. The Grummans struggled to get into the air to meet the bombers, while the Douglas Dauntless dive bombers and the P-400's were taking off too; their job was to stay out of the way until it was all over.

Mitchell left his tent at a run and started to sprint towards the nearest foxhole; his own plane had been riddled with bullets in a dogfight that afternoon, and was still too badly damaged to fly. He would have to sit out the bombing with everyone else.

Then he heard it, that distinctive desynchronised sound of the Japanese bombers; Betty's probably, he thought, searching for their silhouettes against the night sky.

"Here he comes," he heard someone say, from a foxhole very close. "Washing Machine Charlie."

Searchlights stabbed and searched the sky, the long white tendrils searching out their prey, suddenly converging on one plane. From the edge of the strip he heard the steady boom-boom of anti-aircraft fire.

Then he heard the shrieking whistle of the bombs, and he curled himself into a ball, trying to make himself as small as possible. He remembered to open his mouth to reduce the risk of concussion in case the bomb landed close by. Then there was nothing to do but wait and pray.

"Here it comes!" he heard someone yell.

A thudding roar followed by the boom-boom-boom as the rest of the stick hit. The ground shook and rocked underneath him, and he heard the echoes of the blasts reverberate away, across the jungle towards the mountains.

As the bombs continued to fall he huddled further down into the split trench. The splinters shrieked overhead, the concussions sucking and tearing at the air around him.

He was surprised to find that through the clammy, sweating fear, he wasn't thinking of himself. He was thinking of The Weatherman.

That morning the calm, measured voice had reported the weather as usual, and the Japanese movements. But then he had said something else. He had been forced to move camp again. The Japanese had sent two planes flying low over the island, looking for him. For the first time Mitchell had detected a note of desperation in the clipped, precise voice.

For Mitchell, The Weatherman had become an intensely personal affair. He wondered where he was. Choiseuil?

Bougainville? Mitchell guessed Bougainville. Up on one of those peaks at the north of the island overlooking Buka Passage.

The Japs would be desperate to find him. In recent weeks the tide had begun to swing against them. Just two nights ago the Navy had kicked their asses for the first time in a night action. They met the Tokyo Express off Cape Esperance and sunk two cruisers and crippled another. The Japanese could no longer call The Slot their own.

And now Nimitz had sent them the American division. They were just raw kids, lumberjacks and Minnesota farmhands who had spent the last few months lying in the sun on New Caledonia. They would get a taste of the war soon enough, Mitchell thought grimly. And until then Vandergrift had three thousand extra men to bolster his defences.

The Guadalcanal fortress was getting stronger. And they still had The Weatherman, their ace in the hole. By now the Japs would be combing the jungles on every island in The Slot trying to track him down. What sort of man could live under that sort of strain, Mitchell wondered. A professional. He had to be. Probably a Naval Intelligence man dropped behind the Japanese lines by submarine.

Whoever he was, they wouldn't have a chance without him. The Zeros would have shot them out of the skies long ago.

That afternoon had been another lurching, sick memory. The Weatherman had warned them that two squadrons of bombers and a Zero escort were on its way, headed for another attack on Henderson Field.

Mitchell's squadron had been waiting; they swooped down on them like gulls on a school of fish trapped in a net. They hit them time and time again, and any that managed to get through lurched into a barrage of exploding shell from the Navy cruisers and destroyers in Purvis Bay.

For almost an hour the air over Guadalcanal had been scorched to a cauldron of screaming death, filled with swooping planes and the smoking pyres of aircraft ploughing into the seas and jungles below.

Mitchell wondered how many of them they had taken out that day. His own personal tally was three. Already he had nineteen "meatballs" – the small Rising Sun flags that were painted on to the fuselage to indicate a kill – to his credit. Three others already had over twenty. Surely the Japs couldn't take much more of that.

More and more of his pilots were willing to dogfight with the Zeros now; many of the Japanese front line pilots had disappeared from the skies and their replacements were younger, much less experienced. The American Navy pilots were chewing them up.

Mitchell closed his eyes to try and blot out the memory of it. Like most men he was frightened to death. Although he inflicted it, he didn't enjoy watching it. Like some of the other pilots he didn't cheer when one of the Japanese went down.

When he landed his plane at the end of another mission, the only emotion he felt was one of relief. He had cheated death for another day.

But there was always tomorrow . . .

The shelling had stopped. A green flare burst in the sky overhead, appearing almost white in the bright moonlight. Around the field, lights began to wink on again. Already Corporal Cates was roaring across the airstrip in his bulldozer to fill in the fresh craters.

As he climbed out of the trench, Mitchell realised that The Weatherman had become his own personal talisman. While he survived out there in the jungle, day after day, surrounded by enemy soldiers, with the odds stacked so heavily against him, then Mitchell believed that he too could survive.

He dusted the dirt off his jacket. Shoup's head bobbed out of a foxhole close by.

"Bit of a pounding tonight, eh Major?"

"What's the matter with you? Want to live for ever?" Mitchell said.

"Sure do."

"Yeah," Mitchell told him. "Me too," and walked away grinning.

42

Father Goode lay on the tiny bamboo cot, moaning and shouting at the spectres that haunted the shadowy world of his unconscious, bathed in the sickly sweat of a raging fever.

The journey into the mountains had almost killed him. They had hiked for two days, by day and by night, using the Southern Cross as a guide. Manning had led them north again to his last fall-back camp, under the smouldering caldera of Mount Teatupa.

Here the mountains soared to razorback spines that fell away into deep brooding valleys; everything except the sheer black faces of the cliffs was covered in primeval forest, the treetops wreathed in swirling grey mist.

Here in the high inland jungle it rained each afternoon and as they squelched up the steep, winding tracks only the natives, with their broad, splayed-toed feet, were able to keep their balance on the slick mud. This was the domain of malarial mosquitoes and the giant centipedes whose single bite could leave a man writhing on the mud in swollen-limbed agony.

The verdant jungles filtered out the sunlight so that only a dim greenish light reached the tangled undergrowth of the jungle floor. The cathedral silence was broken only by the harsh screech of a mynah or a white cockatoo.

They had been forced to wade through dark patches

of mud that came up to their thighs, hacking through the drooping lianas and giant webs, as strong and fine as fishing line, spun by spiders as large as dinner plates.

The site Manning had chosen was high on a volcanic ridge, blessedly cooler and mosquito free, but by now it made no difference to the priest; he was gripped by the hot hand of malaria and septicaemia. It was a miracle he had survived so long. For a while it appeared that his leg was healing, but the trip into the mountains had re-opened the wound and another infection had set in. His resistance had been lowered by yet another bout of fever, and his condition had deteriorated with astonishing and frightening speed.

Now Rachel sat on the wooden crate beside him, bathing his forehead with a wet cloth. She was steeling herself for what she had to do. There was no other choice.

In her hand she had a bottle of whisky. It was the last of Manning's supply.

"Uncle. Drink some of this." She tipped a few drops on to his lips. The priest sat up choking and gagging.

"The Devil's brew!" he shouted. "Take it away!"

He threw out an arm spilling some of the contents on to the bare ground.

"You must drink some. It will kill the pain later," she said and tried to pin down his arms, leaning her weight across him and holding his wrist with her other hand. Quickly she tipped some more of the liquor into his mouth. He spat it out.

"There shall be weeping and gnashing of teeth!" the priest screamed and somehow he worked his left arm free and his hand smashed into Rachel's mouth, spilling her backwards on to the ground.

She sat there, feeling the tears filling into her eyes from the pain of it. She put her free hand up to her nose and felt the warm trickle of blood.

Father Goode turned his head towards her, his eyes glinting crazily from the effects of the fever and the poison in his body. She wasn't sure if he was conscious or in the throes of delirium, but she had the feeling he was somehow looking into her very soul.

"Lust," he muttered. "Lust."

"You have to drink the whisky. It will numb the pain."

"You women are all whores and the Lord shall rain down fire and destruction!" he screamed.

"If you won't drink it, I'll have to make you drink it."

But Father Goode did not hear her. The phantoms of Satan did not cease their torment and for the priest the world had become a hot and infernal place.

The late afternoon sun in the sky threw just enough light in the clearing for Rachel to make out Corrigan's silhouette outlined against the trunk of the bloodwood. He was lying on his back, apparently asleep.

Rachel approached him gingerly, still holding the bottle of whisky. She stood watching him for a few moments, studying the gentle rise and fall of the massive chest, the silent composition of his face. When he was asleep he looked like an angel.

"Is that bottle for me?" he said suddenly, and Rachel involuntarily took a step back. He had been awake the whole time.

She felt her cheeks burn hot. "It certainly is not for you."

"Pity."

"I've been trying to administer it to my uncle. He keeps spitting it out."

"Well, there you are then. The man has no appreciation for fine spirit. Let me have it."

"I have to get some of it into him. It will numb the pain."

"Let the bastard suffer. He enjoys it."

"Mister Corrigan, I am about to amputate his leg with a machete. I think a man deserves something to help him through such an ordeal, don't you?"

Corrigan sat up and stared at her. "Jesus, Mary and

Joseph but you're the damnedest woman I've ever met. Look at you. A girl your age ought to be wandering round in fields picking flowers and playing the piano."

"Perhaps one day I will. For now my uncle needs my help."

Corrigan leaned back against the trunk of the tree and observed her. He had been forced to revise his estimate of Rachel Goode in the last couple of months. Not only was she pretty, she was tougher than some men he knew.

The transformation had been astonishing. The prim and pale girl he had taken to Marmari Point – was it really less than a year ago?

She had been burned by the sun but now the redness had given way to a tan the colour of honey and she had long ago abandoned the tight bun with which she used to bundle up her hair. It now fell loose about her shoulders, thick and blue-black. She was wearing one of Manning's shirts, open at the neck, and a native tapa cloth. Her feet were bare.

She looked at once appealing and vulnerable, an impression Corrigan knew was utterly misleading.

He let his gaze drop down to the slim brown ankles beneath the wrap of the cloth. "Did I ever tell you you have pretty legs?"

Rachel blushed and her fingers moved self-consciously to the buttons of her shirt, almost as if she could feel him undressing her with his eyes. The man was completely incorrigible.

Since that afternoon when she had seen him and Sanei at the waterfall she had tried to avoid being alone in his company. Yet whenever she watched him with her – their easy laughter, the way the native girl leaned close to him and whispered – she could not fight back the waves of jealousy.

Sometimes she saw them together in a glade near the camp or walking back from the nearby stream. It disgusted her that they could be so brazen. Sometimes they were gone for the whole morning and once Manning was practically convinced they had been captured by a Japanese patrol. He was making preparations to leave camp when they had wandered back.

Rachel was at once repelled and attracted by this man who seemed to flaunt his own sexuality before everyone, even the other native men. She wondered if perhaps it was the constant danger, the ever-present possibility of death that made Corrigan so exciting for her.

For although her Catholic upbringing shrank in revolt, deep in her soul she wanted to change places with the tiny doe-eyed creature who shared his bed; yet now, when Corrigan flirted with her, she had no idea what to do.

She tried to concentrate on the task in front of her. "Will you help me get this whisky into him?" She was surprised at the hoarseness of her own voice.

"Sure I'll help you. I'll even help you operate on the poor man's leg if that's what you'd call an act of barbarism such as you're proposing. I'm getting used to it by now, so help me. If you can stand it, then I reckon I can."

Rachel watched him shamble slowly to his feet, his hands thrust belligerently into the pockets of his calico trousers.

She smiled. "Thank you Mister Corrigan."

Corrigan laughed, a happy, bubbling sound that made Rachel feel suddenly weak at the knees. "My pleasure, young lady," he said and followed her across the clearing to where Father Goode was still railing against the evil in the world and the jezebels of Gomorrah.

"We will have to tie his arms behind his back."

Corrigan nodded. "Whatever you say. You're the doctor."

"If you lean on his shoulders it will hold him." She turned to Manning and Sergeant Lavella, who both stood, hesitantly in the doorway. "If each of you put your weight on his legs, I'll get to work."

Manning's face was the colour of alabaster. "Isn't there any other way?"

"Look at him," Rachel said quietly. "The poison is

working through his whole body. Unless I remove the leg he will be dead within forty-eight hours."

Manning looked down at the priest. He was sleeping fitfully, each breath sawing in his throat. His skin had the sickly grey-green patina of a corpse. There were dark shadows under his cheekbones and eyebrows where the flesh had been eaten away by fever.

"What are his chances?" Manning asked.

Corrigan answered for her. "Let's put it this way. Don't put any money on him unless you can afford to lose it."

"I'll do what I can," Rachel added. "But he's already very weak. If he doesn't die of shock in the first few minutes, he'll probably die of infection tomorrow. It will be a miracle if he survives."

"And a blessing if he doesn't," Corrigan muttered.

Rachel turned towards him, her eyes glittering angrily. "Think what you will of him, Mister Corrigan, he cared for me for ten years when I was alone in the world. I will always love him for that."

"All right, I'm sorry," Corrigan mumbled. "Let's get on with it."

Rachel picked up a length of rope and turned the priest on to his side. Crossing his wrists behind his back, she tied them, as gently as she could. Then she rolled him on to his back.

When it was done, Corrigan knelt down and placed one massive hand on each of the priest's shoulders. Manning and Sergeant Lavella squatted down at Father Goode's feet and leaned forward, putting their weight on his shins.

Rachel produced the bottle of amber spirit.

"We must force some of this down his throat."

Quickly she knelt down beside Father Goode and cradled his head in the crook of her right arm. She pinched his nose shut with the thumb and index finger of her right hand, and with the other she forced the lip of the bottle in his mouth.

The priest gasped, and his whole body writhed under the weight of the three men. Finally he managed to turn his head to the side and force a spray of warm whisky into Corrigan's face.

"Jesus," Corrigan gasped. "I can stand the blood, girl, but I can't stand to see good liquor wasted. He doesn't want it."

"It's not important what a man wants, but what he needs," Rachel said and she forced her uncle's head back once more and upended the bottle in his mouth.

It took almost half an hour, but finally Rachel had succeeded in forcing half of the bottle down the priest's throat. Now he lay, in a drugged sleep, snoring deeply.

"He might die of alcoholic poisoning," Corrigan said. "But he's not going to feel any pain."

"I pray you're right," Rachel said, and she got to her feet and went outside to fetch the machete that waited in the froth of boiling water in a pot on the camp fire.

43

Tashiro stood to attention in front of Colonel Nakamura's desk.

"How are your wounds?" Nakamura said. His hands were folded neatly on the desk in front of him, his face a dark, impassive mask.

"They are nothing, Nakamura-san," Tashiro said.

He could not meet Nakamura's gaze. He stared stoically at the wall behind the colonel's head.

In fact Tashiro was still in considerable pain. The bullet had lodged in his shoulder, shattering the head of the humerus in his left arm. It was strapped now across his chest, under his open tunic. But he had lost a lot of blood, and the bullet had yet to be removed from the wound.

The Japanese had now set up a forward post at Marmari Point, but it had fallen to Tashiro to return to Vancoro and report to Nakamura personally the latest reverse his force had suffered at the hands of the English bandits.

He had allowed the surgeon to attend only briefly to his wounds at the hospital. Then with supreme effort of will he had marched up the slope to the Residency bungalow in the scorching midday heat, the bullet burning and aching in his body like a living thing. The pain had already etched the agony into his eyes; they were glassy and streaked with yellow.

"Once again the enemy has caught you by surprise," Nakamura was saying.

Tashiro's face showed no expression at this criticism. Nakamura studied him for a few moments in silence.

"What were your losses?"

"Five men killed, three wounded, Nakamura-san. One has a serious chest wound. He will not live."

Nakamura took a deep breath. It rattled in his chest like the growl of a bear, as he attempted to control his anger.

"What am I to tell the Imperial Command?" he said. "It now seems certain that the Englishman has been operating in our area as a spy for many months. We do not know the extent of the damage he may have caused by giving the enemy advance knowledge of our movements. And now he is even ambushing our own soldiers . . ." Nakamura's voice trailed away to a long sigh, like a death rattle.

Tashiro said nothing. Another spasm of pain hit him with the speed and force of an electric shock. He bit into his tongue, tasted the salt taste of his own blood in his mouth. He swayed slightly on his feet.

"You walked into their trap and they gunned you down like dogs," Nakamura continued, mercilessly. "They are just natives! How can such a thing happen?"

There was another long silence in the room. Perspiration

dripped from Tashiro's forehead and ran stinging into his eyes. He fought to hold himself rigid to defeat the giddiness that threatened to send him sprawling on his face.

"I have asked the Imperial Command to send us tracker dogs. Meanwhile you will continue to conduct your operations from Marmari Point, concentrating on the northern mountains. Another company of soldiers under Major Harada will be arriving there shortly and he will assume command of the operation himself."

"*Hai*, Nakamura-san."

"In the meantime, I must report truthfully on your performance to your superiors." Nakamura looked up. "You are dismissed. Have your wounds attended to, and return to your duties."

Tashiro felt the hot tears of pain and humiliation brimming in his eyes. He saluted, wheeled about and marched out of the room.

Rachel made her way up the narrow rocky path that led to the top of the ridge. From the spine of the ridgeback, looking west, Kangava Passage sprawled across the far horizon in breathtaking panorama, the vast ocean dotted with the emerald green of the islands. It was evening, and the first pinpoints of stars were appearing in a watery pearl-shell sky.

The greens and blues of the ocean were fading to steel-grey, and the shrill cries of the parrots in the tall trees of the jungle on either side were giving away to the night cries of the insects.

Rachel sat down on a rock, shivering. The night wind was warm, but inside she felt chilled to the heart. She wanted to blot out the memory of the last half an hour of her life.

Her uncle was dead. She had done everything she could but he had been too weak to withstand the shock. After she had removed the leg, she had tried to cauterize and bandage the wound, but he had died within minutes, mercifully without regaining consciousness. It had been a bloody and messy end to his long struggle with the poisons in his body. She wished now that she had left the leg and let him die whole, in peace.

"You did your best."

She turned. It was Corrigan.

"I shouldn't have attempted it. He was too weak." Her voice sounded strangely hoarse in the twilight.

"He was going to die anyway. You did everything you could."

Rachel nodded, unable to trust her voice. She realised she was trembling. Corrigan sat down next to her and put his arm around her shoulders. Suddenly her body began to shake with uncontrollable sobs. She put both her arms around his neck and clung to him.

She had no idea how long they were like that. It could have been minutes, or hours. She allowed the horror of the amputation and the agony of watching her uncle die by degrees to tumble out of her; and all of the emotions she had tried to keep in check in the past months and weeks to spill out, all of it, all the fear and confusion and aloneness.

When it was over, she lifted her face and was surprised by the look of tenderness on Corrigan's face. Suddenly he bent his face to hers and kissed her.

"Corrigan . . ."

"No, don't say anything," he whispered.

"I shouldn't be doing this."

"You want someone to hold on to. There's nothing wrong with that. We all need a bit of kindness now and then. Even you, Miss Goode."

But the part of her that was the missionary's niece was overwhelmed with horror and shame. Her uncle was still warm and she was making love with the man he had most despised. Feeling like a whore and a traitor, she pulled away from him and ran back to the camp.

44

Mitchell and Shoup sat alone in the dugout, listening to the rain dripping through the roof, and falling in dark puddles on the mud floor.

They had carefully positioned two wooden crates in between the cascades of water, and sat on them smoking cigarettes. Somewhere out on Edson's Ridge they heard the hammering of a Browning. Probably just one of the Americans getting trigger happy.

"They say he's a local, you know," Shoup said suddenly.

"Who?"

"The Weatherman. I always thought he must be from Intelligence. But they say he's just a government man. Small-time official who volunteered to stay behind. No special training, nuthin'."

"Which island is he on?"

"No one seems sure. Maybe New Georgia or Choiseul. What do you think?"

Mitchell shrugged and lit another cigarette. The rain was getting on his nerves.

"Must be one hell of a guy," Shoup said. "I wonder what he looks like?"

"I never thought about it," Mitchell lied.

"I don't know how he stands it day after day. Having the Japs all round him, not knowing when the natives might decide to hand him in. I wonder how he handles that kind of fear?"

Mitchell was silent. He didn't want to talk about The Weatherman. Not tonight. Sometimes it seemed to him as if they were talking about a dead man. And he wanted very much for The Weatherman to make it. If he could survive, with the odds stacked so heavily against him, then maybe he could too.

"Do you ever think much about it?" Shoup said.

"Not much," Mitchell said, and they fell silent.

They buried Father Goode in a clearing in the jungle just below the ridgeback.

They wrapped the body in a canvas tarpaulin and lowered it down with ropes. Rachel read the short service from her uncle's thick leather-bound Bible and one by one they threw a handful of the black wet soil into the grave.

Rachel went back alone to the camp.

"Don't look so sour," Corrigan said to Manning. "Could have been worse. Could have been you or me."

"For God's sake, Patrick."

"Look, just because I'm not a hypocrite and don't pretend I'm grief-stricken. I never liked the old bastard."

"Whatever you say about him, Patrick, he was a man of great courage. He did what he thought was right."

"And look where it got him."

"Everyone has to believe in something. If you don't, you may as well be dead."

Corrigan rubbed his chin. "Well, he's dead anyway. And what's changed? The Japs are still here, and the islanders still pray to sharks. He might just as well have come with me on Heydrich's boat."

"Why? Everything he lived for was here."

"One place is much the same as another."

"There's more to life than women and booze, Patrick."

"So I've heard you say. Like what?"

Manning felt himself getting angry. Sometimes Corrigan's devil-may-care attitude to life amused him. But there were other times – like now – when it filled him with black rage.

"I feel sorry for you, old boy," he growled and he turned away and followed Rachel back up the hill.

Corrigan watched him go, surprised at the quick and red-faced anger he had seen on Manning's face. Then he shrugged, and turned back to watch Sergeant Lavella and two of his police boys shovel the pile of moist clay into the hole. The rhythmic scraping of the shovels made a melancholy sound and the slap of the heavy earth on the priest's canvas-covered body left him feeling curiously uneasy.

He looked down into the hole and crossed himself; an involuntary reaction to death he remembered from long ago, in the church in Dundrum Bay. Despite himself he found himself saying the words that had been on each of their minds that morning.

"I wonder which of us is next?"

45

Manning was getting desperate.

A few days before he had sent Chomu into Vancoro to work as a labourer for the Japanese and report back on what was happening there. Chomu had sent word that the Japanese had built a giant steel bowl on top of one of their huts. Manning immediately realised what it was. The Japanese had installed radio direction-finding equipment.

From then on he kept his transmissions as brief as possible.

Manning had chosen the site for the camp well. The huts had been built in the lee of a dry gully, invisible from the air because of a natural overhang of rock and the dense vegetation that grew on its flanks.

The air currents moved upwards over the mountain

so that whenever they had to re-charge the teleradio's batteries, the noise of the diesel engine was carried away on the wind.

The only track into the camp led up through a fissure in the rock wall, scarcely wide enough for one man to squeeze through; above them the gully led to the ridgeback, protected on both sides by eighty-foot-high teak trees. Manning had built his observation post in the canopy of one of the teaks, and it afforded unobstructed views over Kangava Passage and westwards to The Slot.

The only way the Japanese would find them was if they walked in right on top of them. Even so, they all knew it was only a matter of time before the Japanese finally hunted them down. Now every day at dawn, and again late in the afternoon, a Japanese Zero flew lower over the mountains, looking for them. Once it flew almost directly over their heads.

Manning wondered how long they could evade the Japanese search. In his mind he measured his survival in terms of days rather than months.

Twice more, he had tried to organise an evacuation from Jervoise Bay; each time it was called off because the submarine that was to take them off the island was needed for vital combat operations elsewhere.

And so they had settled down to wait, the tension now almost a tangible thing between them.

The Japanese were not the only cause of the tension in the camp. Sanei had become silent and withdrawn, her brown, hooded eyes watching Rachel with sullen malevolence.

Sergeant Lavella watched Rachel gloomily, as if she was a *tabu* curse.

"No good too mus," he muttered to her one day. "That Sanei she want for killim you, missy."

Rachel shuddered and prayed that the submarine would come soon.

*

But each day there was another terror to deal with; ever since she had been a little girl Rachel had suffered from vertigo. Like all phobias, her fear of heights was unreasoned, unreasoning. A flimsy rope bridge led across the gorge below the ridgeback to a clear rock pool; and every trip across was a swaying, sickening nightmare. But each evening Rachel forced herself to cross it.

It was more than just the need to bathe away the damp sweat of the jungle. It was almost a ritual; a regimen that forced her dark terrors to the surface and focused them. Every day she forced herself to conquer them again.

The evening was cool, the dark thunderheads over the mountains shot through with shafts of gold, soaking the surrounding greens of the jungle in a soft light that accentuated the deep shadows of the valleys.

As Rachel climbed out of the pool she shivered as she quickly dried her skin and shook the droplets from her hair. The brown V at her neck and the polished mahogany of her legs contrasted with the creamy white of her body. She quickly shucked the loose-fitting shirt over her shoulders and fastened the tapa cloth at her waist.

She made her way back along the path, her long black hair falling wet and heavy around her shoulders, the cold water still dripping on to her shoulders and her cheeks. She walked quickly; she was eager to have the ordeal of the bridge over for another night.

She had a regimen she followed faithfully; at a certain point along the path she began to take deep breaths; ten breaths and she reached the bridge. Twenty and she was across to the other side.

But then she saw something that stopped her in her tracks, breaking the rhythm of her litany.

There was a figure squatting under a mahogany tree, on the far side of the bridge, waiting for her.

It was Sanei.

Rachel remembered what Sergeant Lavella had said to her. *That Sanei she want for killim you, missy.*

She hesitated, feeling a rush of oily fear deep in the pit

of her stomach. She remembered the day Corrigan had come to the mission, blood streaming from his shoulder where she had cut him with a knife.

Sanei got to her feet and started to walk towards her across the bridge.

That Sanei she want for killim you, missy.

Rachel kept her head held high and kept walking.

She's not going to intimidate me, she told herself. I won't let her frighten me.

When they reached the middle of the bridge Rachel realised Sanei was not going to let her pass. She also realised that Sanei had the advantage. She was a mountain girl, accustomed to the perilous swaying of the rope bridges. If Rachel tried to move past her she could easily tip her into the wild rushing waters a hundred feet below.

Rachel stopped. "What do you want?"

Sanei didn't answer. She stood watching her, and then, quite unexpectedly, she began to smile. She gripped the bridge ropes in each hand and began to rock. Instinctively, Rachel's hands tightened around the rope spans as she tried to keep her balance. The white waters of the gorge frothed and boiled a hundred feet below.

Sanei began to rock harder now, her feet splayed across the wooden slats, swinging the bridge through a huge arc in a wild giddying rhythm.

"Stop it!" Rachel screamed.

"Corrigan b'long me!"

"Stop it!"

The walls of the gorge and the white water of the gorge began to blur together in Rachel's vision. She knew that if she lost her purchase on the wooden slats beneath her feet, she would spill headlong into the yawning chasm underneath her.

Rachel closed her eyes to fight the vertigo that threatened to overwhelm her. Through the red mists of her panic she heard Sanei screaming at her. "Corrigan b'long me! You no take 'im! He b'long me!"

"STOP IT!"

Rachel could feel her knees starting to give way. She clung desperately to the ropes, her fingernails biting deep into the flesh of her palms.

"STOP IT!"

"Corrigan b'long me!"

Sanei screamed at her over and over. Rachel closed her eyes and clung on. Finally it stopped.

When Rachel opened her eyes, the rope bridge was rocking gently with the wind, the only sounds the creaking of the cordage, and the murmurous roar of the waters below. She gulped in long, deep breaths, her whole body shaking violently.

Sanei was standing just a few feet away, grinning in triumph. "You fright you for die?"

"Get away from me," Rachel murmured.

"You no for die," she said, as if she was speaking to a little child, "bridge good too mus. You no for die."

"Get away."

Sanei reached out and began to stroke Rachel's hair, taunting her. "Corrigan b'long me. You savvy, missy?"

Rachel wanted to snatch the girl's hand away from her, but she dared not release her hold on the rope. "Get away from me," she repeated.

Sanei laughed once. Then she skipped away along the bridge, her feet moving easily over the treacherous wooden slats.

For many long minutes Rachel dared not move, unable to control the trembling in her arms and legs. She closed her eyes again, and her chest heaved with racking sobs as the terror drained out of her.

In the back of her mind she heard Sanei repeating over and over: "Corrigan b'long me."

The strain of the past few months had taken a terrible toll on Ian Manning's health.

Already plagued with the congenital weakness in his lungs that had threatened to incapacitate him all his life, the constant fear and the damp rot of the jungle had brought him to the point of collapse. His eyes were shrunken into his head, and the flesh had wasted off him.

"You can't stay here, Manning," Corrigan was telling him. "If you do, you're going to die."

"I had already considered the possibility, old chap."

"Well then, let me put it another way. When are you going to get the rest of us out of here? You may want to be a hero, but I don't."

"I'm doing what I can, Patrick. I've asked them for an evacuation on a number of occasions. You must realise the problem."

"I don't give a damn about the problems. You and that bloody priest got me into this. Now you can bloody well get me out."

46

It was almost three weeks after Father Goode's death that Corrigan got the news he had been waiting for.

It was dark, Manning was in the radio hut. The others were outside, sitting on the packing crates, next to the smouldering ruins of the fire. They had eaten a sparse meal of rice and salted fish, and now they shivered in the cool night wind.

Suddenly Manning emerged from the radio hut, a scrap of paper held triumphantly in his hand. "Well, it looks like I'm going to get rid of you at last," he said with forced joviality.

Rachel looked up eagerly. "The Americans?"

Manning handed her the message. "Two nights' time. They'll pick you up in Jervoise Bay, to the north. This time next week you'll be in Australia."

"That's what you said before," Corrigan muttered.
"It's definite this time."
"I'll believe it when I see it."
"Boat she come?" Sanei said to Corrigan.
"So he says."
"We go?"
"Well, I'm not volunteering to stay."

Their expectations had been dashed too many times for any of them to show much excitement. Embarrassed, Manning shuffled back inside his hut and they fell silent once more, staring at the glowing embers, each lost in their own thoughts.

Rachel woke once during the night and shivered, drawing the rough blanket up around her shoulders. She couldn't get back to sleep. Fear and sadness conspired to keep her tossing restlessly, alone in the darkened hut.

Framed in the doorway, she could see the lightning flash silently across the night sky. Curious, she got up and went to the door of the hut. The broad white flashes came from the horizon far to the south-west and she realised it wasn't lightning at all; it was cannon fire.

Guadalcanal.

She remembered then; the war, and the vast and terrible battle that was raging so close to the anonymous drama they were playing out on this remote island, and the darkness in her own soul deepened.

The climb to the top of the swaying observation platform took Manning ten long and painful minutes. He looked down. Sergeant Lavella was watching him, his forehead knitted in a frown of concern. Manning knew he was getting weaker every day. His cough was worse, and when he looked in the broken shaving mirror he saw a haggard ghost with hollowed cheeks staring back at him.

He fought to drag the air into his lungs. The distant hills and oceans swam in and out of focus in his vision and a cold, panicked sweat broke out over his body as he fought to keep his tenuous hold on the rungs of the bamboo loops.

For long seconds he closed his eyes and tried to ride out the wave of nausea that swept over him. A part of him wanted to simply let go. It would be so easy to die, much easier than going on; he forced the notion aside. No, he would not give up. He couldn't. Not now.

Slowly his vision began to clear and the breath came easier to his lungs. He kept climbing.

The situation was desperate. Sergeant Lavella's tiny force was now down to three men; they had lost Constable Anea. He had been wounded in the arm during the raid on *Marakon* and then he had caught a fever. Manning had wanted to evacuate him with Corrigan and Rachel but a few days ago he too had died.

Another bamboo cross had been erected by the side of Father Goode's grave below the ridgeback.

For the first time Manning was considering evacuating with the others on the American submarine. He knew only too well his days on the island were numbered. God knew, no one would blame him. He had already served almost nine months behind enemy lines and it was obvious to himself and everyone else that he wouldn't be able to operate effectively much longer.

Carefully, he ascended the last few feet to the platform and stopped to get his breath. Then he bent over the field glasses on their tripod, concentrating on the distant strip of ocean to the west.

Out in The Slot there were five Japanese destroyers, low and grey and wolf-sleek, their bow waves throwing up a moustache of white foam. They were making their way south, seven transports lumbering along with them. They looked like toys against the backdrop of mountains and clouds over the islands beyond.

Manning made a careful notation in his leather-bound book and slipped it back into the breast pocket of his shirt. Then he started to climb slowly back down the tree.

He was still ten feet from the ground when he realised he was not going to make it.

The world started to spin around him, and there was a loud roaring in his ears. He groaned, trying to grip his fingers around the trunk of the tree but they refused to respond.

He was falling.

He thought: *this is it. It's all over.*

Then the earth rushed up to meet him and there was silence.

47

"He has three cracked ribs and a broken wrist. He also has concussion. No internal injuries as far as I can tell." Rachel finished bandaging the splint around Manning's left arm and straightened, brushing a lock of hair away from her face. "It's a miracle he's alive."

Corrigan and Sergeant Lavella had joined Rachel in the radio hut where Manning lay semi-conscious on his bamboo cot.

Corrigan grunted and sat down on one of the metal boxes in the corner. "Well, that's his war over. We'd better all get out of here while there's still enough of us left to carry the wounded."

"I don't know if he'll take the rigours of a long journey," Rachel said.

"He certainly isn't going to blossom back to health up here, now, is he? The submarine will be here tomorrow night. We'd better all be on it."

Rachel avoided his eyes. While she had been treating Manning for his injuries another notion had struck her;

a thought which was both terrible but irresistible. She wondered how she could tell Corrigan. He would probably try to stop her, but there really was no other choice. She would have to make him see that.

Manning's eyes flickered open, and he groaned.

"Pity we gave the vicar the last of the booze," Corrigan said. "Poor old Manning could probably do with some right now."

"Americans . . ." Manning murmured. ". . . must tell them."

"What's he saying?"

"*Japoni* ship he come," Sergeant Lavella said pointing towards the ocean. "*Kiap* want talk-talk longa bockis."

"The radio," Rachel said. "There must be more ships coming down The Slot."

"Well, that's not our worry any more."

"Americans . . ." Manning groaned. "Must know . . . must tell them . . ."

"What's he talking about?"

"I think he wants us to tell the Americans what's happening in The Slot."

"Then he must have a chronic brain injury as well. You've done your fair share and I've done a lot more than that considering I'm just a poor bloody Irishman who's supposed to be neutral. For a fella who says he's not taking sides I've been breaking a lot of Japanese heads just lately."

"I agree."

"Good. Well then, we'd better start getting ready to get away from here. It's a full day's hike to Jervoise Bay."

Rachel sat for a long time by Manning's cot, studying his face. It wasn't the sort of face that she would have associated with courage. Weak and broken as he was now, he looked like a frail schoolteacher or a clerk. Yet he had stayed, when others had run. He had held on, surrounded and alone, until the last of his strength had gone.

Now her own fears found themselves pitted against her

conscience. Someone had to take over Manning's job at the radio. If Corrigan wouldn't do it, then she would.

After all, she had watched Manning operate the radio many times; she was sure she could use it herself, and anyone with two arms and legs could climb to the top of the observation tree. There were the tear sheets from *Jane's Book of Ships* to help identify the warships along The Slot and there were the pencilled silhouettes of Japanese warplanes that Manning had drawn.

There was no practical reason to stop her.

Yet it would be so easy to walk away from it now; there was the promise of real food instead of the endless rice and taro, and the lure of sleeping between cotton sheets again. Most of all, she longed for just one night without the fear that every monkey's scream, every crash of a falling tree might be death approaching through the jungle . . .

It would be so easy to think only of her own safety. Yet just a few hundred miles away men were dying in the jungles and on the water and in the air, fighting to keep the islands from the Japanese. She did not know how important the radio on Santa Maria was to those men but she was sure in her heart of one thing.

She could not run away now.

It was almost an hour later that Corrigan stomped back into the hut and found Rachel still by Manning's cot, staring at the radio transmitter.

"Well? Are you ready?"

"I'm not coming."

Corrigan stared at her. "What?"

"You may go, of course, Mister Corrigan. I'm staying here."

He gave a raucous dry laugh. "You're not serious, now?"

"Perfectly."

"You're out of your mind!"

"Perhaps."

Corrigan looked into the pale green eyes and suddenly recognised that look of steely determination he had first seen the night she had asked him to take her on his boat to Marmari Point.

She really meant it.

"My God. You're really going to do it, aren't you?"

"I have been watching Mister Manning operate the radio every day for weeks. I think I can master it. Sergeant Lavella and his men will stay here to help me."

"Do you have any idea what you're doing? Do you know what will happen to you if . . . no, *when* the Japanese find you?"

"We are all born to die."

Corrigan felt the rage boil up inside him. This was senseless, totally senseless. Everyone around him seemed to be hell-bent on throwing their lives away. He grabbed Rachel by the shoulders and shook her.

"Don't be so bloody stupid! This isn't a game! If they find you here with this damned radio they'll take turns to rape you and then they'll tie you up to that tree and cut little bits off you till their arms get tired! Then they'll leave you there for the ants and the birds to finish you off! That's what will happen! There won't be any band of angels to help you ascend to the heavens on a cloud, no trumpets playing Land of Hope and Bloody Glory! The best you can hope for is they shoot you by mistake first. Is that what you want?"

Rachel was shaken as much by the force of Corrigan's anger as by what he had said. She tried to pull away from him but he was too strong.

"Please let go," she said mildly.

Corrigan stared at her, his face dark with anger. Finally he released her. "You're coming with us."

"No."

They stared at each other in a silent test of wills. It was Corrigan who turned away first. "Why, for God's sake?" he asked her.

"For the same reason I could not let the native chief

die, Mister Corrigan. Unlike you, I cannot turn my back on the world."

"But you're just going to get yourself killed! It's not going to change anything!"

"I disagree."

Corrigan sighed. "I could make you come with us," he said.

"You could. If you tied me hand and foot and carried me, I would be helpless. Or you could destroy the radio. But then you'd be taking sides, wouldn't you?"

"Damn you then! If you want to tie yourself to a cross, it's up to you."

"I'm sorry."

"Don't be. I don't give a damn."

And he stormed outside.

They had loaded just enough supplies for the day's march to Jervoise Bay. Sergeant Lavella was to act as guide, and another of the constables, Beni, was to come with them.

The other two constables were to stay behind with Rachel.

Manning, still in considerable pain, had recovered consciousness. He lay in the shade of a banyan, on a stretcher Sergeant Lavella had put together from bamboo poles and some tent canvas. Corrigan knelt down beside him.

"How are you feeling?"

"Don't waste your time carrying me anywhere, Patrick," he whispered. "I'm not going to make it."

"Don't talk daft. You'll be all right. Just a few scratches, that's all."

Manning blinked slowly. Even that seemed to be an effort. "What about the radio?" he croaked.

"No offence, but fuck the radio. I want you to talk to the girl. She's got it in her head to stay behind here."

"Thank God."

"What are you talking about?" Corrigan hissed at him. "She'll get herself killed! She's a bloody woman, for Christ's sake!"

Manning turned his head away. "Someone's got to do it, old boy."

Corrigan stamped away in disgust. He found Rachel in the radio hut, studying the notes in Manning's leather-bound note book. She looked up as Corrigan entered.

"Ready to go?"

Corrigan nodded. "Sergeant Lavella said you ought to have this." He put Lavella's precious bolt action Lee-Enfield on the crate next to her.

"Thanks."

Corrigan shuffled, embarrassed. "Lavella and Lavoro will head straight back here after the rendezvous. They shouldn't be gone more than a couple of days."

Rachel nodded, but said nothing.

"It's not too late to change your mind," Corrigan added.

"It's not too late for you to change yours, either."

Corrigan stiffened. "About what?"

"You could come back and help me."

"I could also put a gun to my own head and blow my brains out. It would be quicker."

Rachel shrugged. "I've been up on the platform, watching The Slot. Manning is right. There's a lot of boats massing out there. Destroyers, I think."

"They can launch a massed assault on the South Pole for all I care," Corrigan said. "Christ, what a waste."

Rachel looked up at him, puzzled. "What is?"

"You. A waste of beautiful legs and God knows what else you've got moving about under that skirt. In other circumstances I probably wouldn't be saying this, but you're not a bad-looking woman."

Rachel turned away. "You'd better be going, Mister Corrigan. Good luck."

"Miss Goode . . . Rachel . . ."

"Please. Just go."

Corrigan stood in the doorway, his hands clenched into fists. Anger and shame and bitterness burned in his throat like bile. It reminded him of that other time, long ago, when he had to turn his back on futility. But this time it took a far greater effort of will to tear his eyes away from the slim and stubborn girl by the radio and turn away without hearing her say goodbye.

48

Lieutenant Mashita Tashiro leaped out of the rubber dinghy and into the sandy shallows of Jervoise Bay. When he reached the white sloping sands of the beach he waited for his men to beach the raft and form a ragged line along the beach.

Behind them another raft, with Lieutenant Kurosawa and the rest of the platoon, ran up on to the strand.

"Which way do we go, Tashiro-san?" Kurosawa said.

"I will head south towards the mangroves," Tashiro told him. "Take your men and head north. If you see any natives bring them back here so I can question them."

Kurosawa nodded. For almost two weeks now they had patrolled the western coast of Santa Maria. Everywhere it had been the same. The natives had been sullen, unco-operative. Kurosawa was tired and dispirited.

"We will never find them this way, Tashiro-san," he said softly to Tashiro, so that their soldiers would not hear. "The Englishman would not come near the coast. He will be miles away from here, somewhere in the mountains."

Tashiro ignored him. "We will rendezvous back here. Leave two of your men to guard the boats."

Kurosawa nodded. "It is not the way," he muttered.

"We have our orders," Tashiro reminded him.

"Yes, Tashiro-san," Kurosawa said formally and went back to the beach to organise the patrols.

*

It bobbed in the middle of the lagoon, looking almost innocuous against the shimmering backdrop of the lagoon and the emerald fringe of coconut palms. The bay was silent except for the distant boom of breakers from the reef and the faint sighing of the sea breeze. It was just this one malevolent presence that indicated danger.

"Holy hell," Corrigan murmured in frustration at the incredible chance that had brought the Japanese patrol boat to the same bay where the submarine was supposed to surface that night.

Corrigan focused the field glasses on the strip of dazzling white beach away to his right. It was deserted, a solitary callophyllum tree leaning away from the line of palm trees, stretching its long trunk out over the shimmering water, as if shrinking from some unnamed horror in the hidden jungle beyond.

Corrigan put down the glasses and swore again.

He had left Lavella and the others back in the forest while he went ahead to scout for a way through the mangrove swamp that surrounded each flank of the bay. Until now, the Japanese patrol boat had been obscured by the sweep of the point.

There was nothing they could do. They would just have to wait and sweat it out.

Corrigan wondered what the submarine commander would do when he found the Japanese patrol boat in the bay. Would he wait? Or would he conclude they had been captured and head back to Noumea?

"Christ, I'll never get off this damn island," Corrigan muttered. He climbed to his feet and headed back through the swamp to break the news to the others.

The mangrove swamp was a dark and evil place. The gnarled roots of the trees writhed and twisted on the low, muddy banks like the tortured fingers of some ancient harridan, and the thick tangle of branches and leaves overhead blocked out the light from the sun.

Corrigan made his way back along the creek, trailing

the Enfield over his right shoulder, the dark, cloying mud sucking at his legs. Mud skippers darted away from him in surprise. The fetid stench of the mud seemed to pervade everything.

Crabs with bright orange carapaces clicked and squelched hideously along the banks of the channel, and occasionally Corrigan glimpsed a bright-coloured beetle, red and blue and yellow, crawling laboriously up one of the spindly mangrove roots. Once he heard the splash of a much larger creature dropping out of sight in the dirty water of the creek.

The silences of the jungle have qualities that have to be learned, and Corrigan's ear had become vitally tuned to them. Even the ordinary hush of the swamps contains some small sound – the cry of a king parrot perhaps, or the *tonk-tonk* of the frogs.

But when there were people moving close by, even they stopped their rumbling complaint.

It was this absolute hush that brought Corrigan instantly alert. He looked up and saw a white cockatoo high on the branch of an ivory nut tree, looking intently downwards, watching something.

He stopped and listened. There were voices coming from the mangroves, directly ahead of him.

He dropped on to the mud, and lay quite still, hardly daring to breathe. He felt the cold greasy hand of fear tighten around his stomach.

Japs!

Corrigan crawled to the shelter of a hollow log lying among the jumble of mangrove roots along the bank. Cautiously he raised his head and peered ahead.

There were a dozen of them, at least. Probably a landing party from the patrol boat he had seen in the bay. They were coming straight towards him along the bank of the creek.

"Holy Mother of God and all the Blessed Saints in Heaven," Corrigan muttered.

He could see them plainly now, their khaki uniforms

visible through the mottled greens of the surrounding jungle. In a few moments they would be walking right over the top of him. With a dry gasp of horror and frustration Corrigan looked back and saw his own footsteps outlined clearly in the soft mud; he was to be his own Judas.

Desperately he looked around.

The black waters of the creek were on one side of him, the jungle behind him. He considered trying to circle around behind the advancing soldiers through the swamp. But he knew it was pointless.

"Those big feet of yours plastered all over the mud will lead them straight to you, Patrick my boy."

The only way was to go back along the creek, covering his tracks, and then cross to the other bank.

He slithered silently across the mud on his belly and began to lower himself into the water.

Then he saw it.

There was a crocodile, floating on the surface less than fifty paces away. Its small malevolent eyes watched him, unblinking.

Corrigan felt the breath catch in his throat. He was trapped.

He scrambled back out of the water, and crawled back behind the log. He raised his head a few inches and saw the first Japanese soldier walking towards him, just fifty yards from where he lay.

"That's it, Patrick old son," Corrigan whispered to himself. "All roads lead to the Devil now."

49

The cold pig-like eyes continued to watch him, unblinking.

There was a tiny ripple around its snout as it began

to stir, edging closer to the bank. Its back glinted in the dappled sunlight; finally it began to emerge from the water, almost a ton of cold armoured flesh. It was a big one, perhaps eighteen feet long, its short bowed legs sinking deep into the stinking black mud.

As it raised itself on to the bank the gaping jaws opened a fraction, and Corrigan glimpsed rows of yellow razor-sharp teeth. There was an overpowering smell, something like dead fish.

The soldiers were very close now. Corrigan could hear them talking to each other, their voices harsh and staccato.

Suddenly the crocodile started to run towards him. It moved faster than Corrigan had expected. He braced himself against the log, and raised the rifle. In that instant he knew he had to choose between this terrible death and a bullet in the back from the soldiers.

"Better to die clean," Corrigan thought. He raised the gun, aiming between the beast's eyes. His finger squeezed the trigger. Nothing.

He fired again.

Nothing, nothing.

The trigger mechanism was jammed.

Christ, no, Corrigan thought. Some water must have seeped into the firing mechanism. He was defenceless.

He froze.

This was it. He was going to die.

Corporal Hiroo Haniguchi had no warning of the attack. He had been given the responsibility of taking point on the patrol and at that moment he was more concerned with negotiating the glutinous mud of the swamp, and the tangled, writhing roots of the mangroves.

He did not even see the crocodile until it was on him.

He heard the ugly slithering sound of the beast's belly as it raced across the mud towards him, and he looked up in time to see the great scaled head and spine glinting briefly in the dappled sunlight of the swamp.

He tried to raise his rifle but the creature was on him too fast, the massive jaws snapping shut around his thigh. He screamed and fired at the same time, the bullet ricocheting harmlessly away among the mangroves.

His comrades were slow to react. The huge beast began to drag the screaming man across the shiny mud towards the creek. It would drown its prey in the fetid waters of the swamp before taking its meal back to its underwater lair to consume at leisure.

But it had strayed too far from the sanctuary of the waterway. The Japanese soldiers quickly overcame their surprise and a volley of rifle fire tore into the heavily armoured flesh of the giant crocodile. It released its hold on its victim as it writhed and contorted under the impact of the bullets.

Volley after volley ripped into the crocodile. It attempted to flee into the creek but the bullets stopped it in its tracks halfway to the water, flipping it over on its back, exposing the soft white flesh of its belly, its huge tail beating the mud in rage and agony as it died.

A few feet away from the crocodile's body, Corporal Haniguchi clawed at the shattered stump of his right leg, his face taut with horror. Half his leg had been scythed away in the animal's jaws, and bright red arterial blood was spurting on to the slimy patina of the mud.

Lieutenant Tashiro ran forward, stripping off the webbing belt at his waist. He held the screaming man down with one knee while he wrapped the belt around his thigh as a tourniquet.

"Get him back to the beach!" Tashiro shouted. There was a medical officer on the patrol boat. Haniguchi had a chance if they could get him back to the bay before he bled to death.

Two of Tashiro's men threw their rifles over their arms and lifted their injured comrade under his arms. Another two took his legs; or what was left of them. They started to scramble back through the swamp, back the way they had come.

Tashiro stumbled after them. Silently he cursed the crocodile. There would be no way he would get his men to go back through the swamp now.

As the beast had lumbered out of the water towards him, its huge body driven by the squat, powerful limbs, Corrigan had reversed his grip on the rifle, hoping to use it as a club. It was only at the last moment that he realised it was not coming for him at all.

The first Japanese soldier had presented a far more inviting and easy target. He was closer to the creek, and he was upright, fully visible. Corrigan, hunched behind the log, could not see him but he heard his screams, and the terrible crunching sound of the beast's huge jaws clamping on to bone.

The man's frantic screams were drowned out by the sharp crack of rifle fire and the flat thump of the bullets as they struck the scaly body again and again. There was a sound like a whip cracking as the beast's huge tail slapped the mud in its death throes just feet away from him.

Corrigan held his breath and waited.

Finally there was silence except for the desperate sobs of the injured soldier. Then the Japanese all began shouting at once.

Corrigan imagined them clustered round the wounded man, applying tourniquets to the shattered stump of a limb. The sound the injured man was making made Corrigan's blood run cold; it was like no sound he had ever heard in his life. The first numbing shock had worn off, and the agony of the wounds would be ripping through the soldier's body.

Corrigan huddled closer to the log and struggled with a moment's indecision. Should he try and escape now while they were distracted? Or should he gamble on staying where he was?

No, the Japanese were too close. The moment he moved away from the log one of the soldiers must see or hear him.

He decided to wait it out.

The man screamed again over the voices of his comrades as they picked him up; but then the moans and the urgent babble of voices began to fade. They were going in the other direction, Corrigan realised, taking the injured man back to the boat.

He waited for long moments before peering cautiously over the top of the log. He saw the Japanese scrambling and slipping back through the steaming tangle of the swamp. They had their backs to him, but one of the soldiers looked back briefly and Corrigan was shocked to realise he recognised the face.

"Tashiro!" Corrigan murmured. "Pity it wasn't your leg the bastard chewed off."

After a few minutes the shrieks of the wounded man faded away and Corrigan was left with the brooding silence of the mangroves.

He got slowly to his feet. The dead crocodile lay on its back just a few feet away, the weed-green body ripped through with bullet holes. Further away on the shiny black mud there were ugly gouts of dark blood where Corporal Haniguchi had bled.

Corrigan sat down on the reptile's carcass, and shook his head, wondering at his own good fortune. "Well, Pat me boy, your old man was right. Stay away from women and you'll live to be ninety!"

That night the party huddled together in the jungle, watching the small fire on the beach where the Japanese were camped. Occasionally the sound of their voices carried to them on the breeze from the other side of the bay.

Unable to light a cooking fire, because it would give away their presence to the Japanese, they ate a few bananas and the flesh from a papaya and then huddled together on the ground and tried to sleep.

Manning lay beside Corrigan. His breathing was shallow and ragged. Corrigan wondered if he would survive till the submarine arrived; he had the same smell about him that Corrigan had recognised on the priest near the end; the sickly taint of death.

"How are you feeling?" Corrigan whispered in the darkness.

"The girl," Manning said, his voice cracked and hoarse. "I can't stop thinking about the girl."

"That makes two of us."

"You must go back for her. You can't leave her to carry on alone."

"You can go back if you like. I'm not stopping you."

"If you were any sort of man you wouldn't have allowed such a thing to happen. You're a monster!"

"I didn't force her to stay behind. If she wants to kill herself, I'll not have her drag me down with her."

Manning gave a muted sigh of distress. The thought of Father Goode's young niece alone and unprotected in the jungle had driven him to the point of complete despair. The pulsating rhythm of pain in his chest receded as he tried desperately to reason with Corrigan.

"I cannot believe you could be such a coward as to leave that brave young girl to her fate."

Corrigan felt his outrage boil over inside him. What did these people want from him?

"Look, it's her own stupid fault. I'm not responsible for her life or anyone else's. Christ knows I've done my best for you bunch of idiots. If she wants to commit suicide, that's her affair!"

Manning turned his head away to hide the tears of anger and helplessness that were burning down his cheeks. It was a pointless gesture. In the blackness that enveloped them, Corrigan could not even see his own hand in front of his face.

"You have to go back, old boy. You have to," Manning begged him.

"Go to sleep."

"My chest is on fire. I can't sleep."
"Well, I can. So shut up."
Manning couldn't understand men like Corrigan. They didn't see beyond themselves in the scheme of things. Manning was a man who believed in duty, and Corrigan's intransigence bewildered him.
"What are you running from, Patrick?"
"Blokes like you."
"You cannot run forever. Some time you will have to stop and commit yourself to something, or to someone. Otherwise life is meaningless."
"It's meaningless anyway."
"If that's what you think, I feel sorry for you."
"So you've said. And I feel damned sorry too. Sorry I ever let myself get involved with this whole crazy mess. Now for Christ's sake, shut up and leave me alone."
Sergeant Lavella took first watch that night. Corrigan huddled under a blanket with Sanei and tried to sleep. But he couldn't. He lay staring up at the blaze of stars in the night sky, and two hours later when he relieved Sergeant Lavella he was still wide awake and he felt an ache deep in his soul. He didn't know why.

50

Rachel lay in the darkness on Manning's narrow bamboo cot in the radio hut, and prayed.
Her uncle had always taught her that prayer was a means of devotion, that it should be used for worship, and nothing more. It had meant nothing to her then, and even less to her now.
Rachel was not even sure that there was such a thing

as God. But now, by some instinct she did not understand, she prayed as she had never prayed in her life; not as Father Goode had taught her, but for her own deliverance.

Already she was regretting her headstrong decision to stay. The day before she had felt with unerring conviction that she was doing the right thing, the only thing. Now, every night owl calling in the forest, every falling branch, each boom and tonk of the tree frogs, jarred her nerves and made her curse her own impetuousity.

Her first doubts had set in when she realised that the two native constables might not remain as loyal to her as they were to Manning. There was Silas Tenpound, the stocky little islander from the Rendells, with "£10" mysteriously tattooed on his left forearm, and Corporal Solomon, a lanky slow-moving Malaitan, sullen-faced and silent. Since Corrigan had departed neither of them had spoken to her, but occasionally she had caught them muttering darkly to themselves under their breath.

She realised that the two men owed their allegiance to Manning, the *kiap*, not to her. She was, in their eyes, just a woman. There was no guarantee they would still be with her in the morning. And she began to grow afraid.

Corrigan had been right. She had tied herself upon her own cross. It had been an arrogance to believe she could survive in the jungle alone.

Now Chomu had sent word from Vancoro that the Japanese had landed tracker dogs. The net was closing in around her; one day very soon the trap would be sprung.

The worst of it was not knowing when death would come. It might come creeping in the night, the innocent snap of a twig her only warning; or it might come in the heat of the day, as she sat hunched over the radio. A Japanese patrol might stumble across the clearing, or a patrol plane flying low over the trees might spot the aerial, or even one of the local natives might betray her. Every black face was a potential Judas.

She tried to shut out the dark thoughts and cocoon herself in sleep.

As she closed her eyes she saw a submarine sinking below the waters of a bay; as the blue waters closed over the conning tower, Rachel found herself whispering one word to the night, like a benediction.

"Corrigan."

Patrick Corrigan put the field glasses to his eyes and looked out over the shimmering water of the bay to the long white strip of beach. He had been there since dawn, waiting and watching.

It had been a bad night. The mosquitoes had surrounded them in dense clouds, swarming towards them from the swamp, scenting the warm blood. Around midnight Manning had become delirious again, and they had had to use blankets to muffle his shouts, knowing the sounds would travel on the night wind across the bay to the Japanese.

Corrigan had not slept. He couldn't stop thinking about the girl. Why couldn't she have done the simple thing and made it easy on all of them?

What was it Manning had called him last night? A monster, Jesus! He had risked his damned neck for them time and time again. Now they wanted him to stay behind and become a martyr for a cause he didn't believe in.

You have to go back for her. You have to.

Corrigan felt confused, bitter and angry. Confused by the curious cold ache deep in the pit of his stomach that refused to leave him; bitter at the responsibility he felt for all their safety, a responsibility he had never wanted; angry that Manning expected more from him.

It was a hot morning, and the moist, thin air was scented by the sea and the heavy musk of flowers. Above the island, the trade winds had flung the clouds in a mackerel pattern across the sky, in grand sweeping strokes of pure white.

A thin skein of smoke rose behind the first line of palms, where the Japanese were camped. There was a lot of movement on the beach and on the grey patrol boat that bobbed in the middle of the sparkling blue lagoon.

"Come on, get going you bastards," Corrigan muttered to himself as he focused the lens of the binoculars.

He knew the submarine might wait one night for them. If the Japanese didn't move off today, there was no chance the submarine commander would risk a second night in enemy waters.

As he watched, he heard the faint chatter of an outboard motor and saw a rubber dinghy set off across the lagoon from the patrol boat. A few minutes later it beached on the white sand, and the Japanese began loading equipment aboard. He saw two of the soldiers carry a stretcher towards the dinghy, a blanket thrown across the shapeless bundle on top of it.

Corrigan remembered the crocodile attack the previous day. So the man had died.

"Rather him than me," Corrigan said to himself.

"What name?" Sergeant Lavella whispered from Corrigan's side. "*Japoni* he go?"

"Looks like it," Corrigan said. "We're still in with a chance."

Corrigan and Lavella crawled slowly back through the undergrowth until they were out of sight of the beach. Then they scrambled to their feet and began to trudge back through the twisting roots of the mangroves.

As soon as the Japanese had gone, Corrigan decided, they would move Manning down to the water's edge and make camp there. They would have to wait till nightfall to discover if the submarine captain had kept his nerve.

But with any luck it would soon be all over, the endless weeks of sweating and hiding, eating watery rice and drinking foul water. This time next week he could be drinking an ice-cold beer in the front bar of the George Hotel in Circular Quay.

He should have been elated. To his surprise he felt curiously depressed.

*

Mitchell looked out of the cockpit and saw the squadron of Zeros many thousands of feet below, their metal skins shining in the afternoon sun, their silhouettes framed against the ocean by the cotton puff clouds. Mitchell followed them, leading his squadron of Grumman fighters into a thick cirrus haze, watching hundreds of rivulets of water trickle down the bullet proof glass of the windshield as they flew through the squall.

A few minutes later, they came out of the thick band of cloud. Mitchell looked down over the port wing. They were still there.

He turned to his right and saw his wing commander signalling thumbs up.

"This is Arrow leader. Zeros at seven o'clock. Let's hit 'em fellas!"

Mitchell pulled the Wildcat over on its port wing and started the dive, picking out the Zero in the lead of the formation, at the neck of the 'V'. As the Grumman went into its dive, Mitchell felt himself being thrown against his seatbelt. It was the only thing keeping him from being pitched through the roof of the cockpit.

The roar of the engines rose to a deafening shriek as the Wildcat picked up speed, closing on its target.

The Zeros kept their formation. Mitchell had kept the sun directly behind him, and the Japanese pilots didn't see them until it was too late.

Mitchell waited till he had closed to within three hundred yards before firing, saw the bright flashes as the Wildcat's cannons scored hits on the Zero's rudder and wings. Large pieces of the tailplane flew off, accompanied by bursts of black smoke; then the engine coolant blew leaving a white streamer of glycol pluming across the sky.

The Zero began to plummet out of control towards the sea. Mitchell watched, waiting for the blossom of the pilot's parachute but there was none. He must have been hit. The Zero smashed into the sea, creating a pyre of rich black oil-smoke that was swallowed up by the sea seconds later.

Suddenly he heard a clamour of alarm on his headset.

"Skipper, you've got a Zeke on your tail. Dive, dive!"

Mitchell twisted round in the cockpit and glimpsed the flash of red painted on the gleaming silver of the fighter and then the blinking flash of its machine guns. The Grumman lurched as shells punched holes in the wing and fuselage.

Mitchell pushed the throttle forward, and snapped away in a roll to starboard, one wing pointing directly at the sea far below, the port wing pointing straight up at the sky. The Japanese pilot followed him.

Mitchell heard the machine guns chatter again. Desperately, he rolled the Grumman three times then pulled up the flaps and dropped into a vertical spin to the left. It was a manoeuvre that had saved Mitchell's life dozens of times.

Mitchell twisted round in his cockpit. To his dismay, he saw the Zero was still right there on his tail. Whoever he was, he was good.

Mitchell held to the spiral, the G pressures pushing him down into his seat, his heart pounding wildly in his chest, and his head feeling as if it was being crushed by some enormous weight. A grey film clouded his vision.

Mitchell saw the needle on the Grumman's speedometer flickering at four hundred miles per hour. The two planes were locked together now in their embrace of death, spiralling down towards the blue pitching sea below.

Mitchell went round three times, four, five. Still the Zero clung to his tail. Hunter and hunted knew that the man who lost his nerve, the one who first turned in any other direction to ease the pressure, was finished.

Unless . . .

Instead of swinging into the sixth spiral, Mitchell pushed the throttle forward and broke away to the right and looped. The Japanese pilot, sensing victory now, went after him, cut inside his arc, and came out on his tail.

Mitchell kept flying loops, trying to narrow the distance of each arc but every time he went up and around the Zero cut inside the arc and lessened the distance between them. The Zero could outfly any other plane in the air in this type of manoeuvre.

Mitchell looked over his shoulder. The Zero was within range again. Bright tracer shells flashed past his starboard wing.

Now!

Mitchell dropped his flaps, chopping the power to his engine. He felt the Grumman shudder and almost stall. The Zero, closing from a hundred yards, overran him.

As it flashed past, Mitchell lined up the root of the Zero's starboard wing in his crosshairs, and fired a long burst from his machine guns. The tracers converged on their target. The Zero's designers had sacrificed armour for manoeuvrability. It disintegrated in front of his eyes, and the flaming wreck dropped out of the sky.

Rachel Goode saw it too, from her platform high in the trees in the shadow of Mount Teatupa. Minutes later she was crouched over the teleradio, speaking urgently and rapidly into the microphone.

"Good morning, Allies. This is The Weatherman. I'm afraid your regular weather reader has been taken sick. I'll try to do my best for you in the meantime."

"First, the weather. There are storm clouds over The Treasuries and Bougainville. We forecast rain from now till early afternoon. It's now ninety-five degrees."

"Now for the good news. You've really hit them hard! We watched eight Japanese planes go into the sea near here. I saw one American plane down a Zero right over our heads.

"There will be more for you to do today. Three destroyers and a cruiser are steaming down The Slot. Perhaps another landing attempt tonight! Be ready for them! Good luck, Americans. Over and out!"

Mitchell taxied his plane towards the gravel apron and the lines of dun-coloured tents on the edge of the field. As the plane rolled to a halt he pushed back the perspex canopy and peeled off the helmet and flying gloves, running his fingers through matted and sweat-soaked hair. Slowly he eased himself out of his seat.

The tension and fear of the previous hours had drained all emotion out of him. He sat for a long time, just staring straight ahead.

"Captain Mitchell!"

He looked round. It was Shoup. He had run across from the dugout on the other side of the field. His face was flushed with excitement.

Despite himself, Mitchell felt a smile crease his lips.

"The Weatherman?"

"Yes, sir! They're broadcasting again. The Japs didn't get him." He paused and then blurted out: "It's a dame this time, sir! A goddam dame!"

The black and jagged edge of the jungle fringing the bay was silhouetted against the purple of the night sky. A pale crescent moon shone above them, through the swaying fronds of the coconut trees. Gentle waves broke with a hollow thud, the silver flecks of foam hissing up the beach.

Five pairs of eyes watched and waited by the first line of trees, peering into the darkness beyond the reef. The only sounds were the rhythmic rush of the waves, the crackle of the burning wood of the signal fire and the occasional lonely cry of a night heron fishing on the reef.

Suddenly Corrigan saw the wink of a light flash on and off quickly from somewhere beyond the promontory of the lagoon.

The Americans! They were there! They had waited!

He looked round. He saw Lavella, his eyes and teeth appearing very large and white in the moonlight. "Boat b'long fish he come," Lavella whispered.

"You're damned right," Corrigan said and he pointed his torch across the bay, and flashed it on and off twice in the pre-arranged signal.

The answering wink of light confirmed the submarine had seen their signal. A boat would be sent ashore for them. In another few minutes they would be gone.

Corrigan turned round to look at the others. The native policeman Beni sat watching, impassive. Sanei came and stood next to Corrigan, gripping his arm.

"Me belong you," she murmured in the darkness.

"Don't worry. I'm not going anywhere without you," Corrigan said. "For all the good that does you."

"Patrick," Manning whispered in the darkness. His voice was weak and hoarse with pain.

"The war's over for you, old son," Corrigan said, squatting down next to the stretcher. "Another few minutes and you'll be on that submarine."

"What about Rachel?"

"For God's sake. Not that again."

"Go back for her, Patrick."

"Oh shut up, damn you," Corrigan snapped and walked back down to the beach to wait alone.

51

Corrigan had thought he would feel both relieved and grateful at this moment. Instead there was only a profound sense of loss. For the first time he wondered what he would do when he finally reached Australia and he had the curious sensation of peering into a vacuum. He realised that beyond the reef there might be nothing for him.

The wind was cool and Corrigan shivered in the thin, ragged white shirt he wore. Sensing something was wrong, Sanei gripped his arm tighter.

"Which way, Corrigan?" she asked him.

He didn't answer her.

He was finally jolted from his thoughts by the insistent throb of an outboard motor. He saw the tiny white moustache of a bow wave as the rubber boat shot through the shallow breakers, and up on to the beach.

There were two ratings and an officer.

A white-jacketed officer leaped out of the boat into the ankle deep water. He had a revolver drawn in his right hand. "Manning?" he said.

"Manning's hurt," Corrigan told him. "We've got him on the stretcher over there."

"All right, quickly. We must hurry. If a Jap patrol boat comes by, we're sitting ducks out there."

Sergeant Lavella and Constable Beni carried Manning down the beach and laid the stretcher in the dinghy.

Corrigan turned to the officer. "Right, that's it."

"Aren't you coming with us?"

Corrigan shook his head. Suddenly he knew with absolute clarity what it was that had brought on his mood of black despair, and there was only one thing he could do to end it.

"I've changed my mind," Corrigan said.

Sanei, standing ankle deep in the water beside him, tried to pull him towards the boat. "No," she hissed. "We go, we go!"

Corrigan shook his arm free. "Better get going, lieutenant," he said. "It's dangerous out here."

"It's your funeral," the man said. He ran back through the surf and jumped into the dinghy.

Within moments the dinghy was skimming back across the bay towards the distant silhouette of the submarine. The drumming of the outboard motor was swallowed up by the roar of the breakers and then it was lost against the dark indigo of the sea.

"We go, Iris," Sanei's voice was a murmur of bewilderment and disbelief. "You say we go."

"I changed my mind," Corrigan said.

He walked out of the shallows and up the beach to

where Sergeant Lavella and Constable Beni stood watching.

"Which way you not go longa boat?" Lavella said.

"Can't stand submarines," Corrigan told him, "they give me claustrophobia."

And he led the way back into the jungle.

Corrigan stood at the door of Manning's hut, watching Rachel turning the dials of the radio. She looked up. There was a soft smile on her face.

On the long trek back through the jungle he had asked himself a thousand times why he had done it. He didn't give a damn about the war. He didn't like the Japanese but he was damned if he was going to fight them to save the bloody Empire.

No, it wasn't that that made him come back. It was this girl. He just couldn't leave her behind, damn her.

She was still watching him as he slouched against the packing crates in the corner.

"Hello," he grinned at her.

"Hello Mister Corrigan," she said, still smiling. "I knew you'd come back."

PART THREE

52

While the battle on Guadalcanal was reaching its bloody climax, on Santa Maria Lieutenant Mashita Tashiro was busy waging a war of his own. The capture of the teleradio and its operators had become an obsession, one on which his future career – no, more than that, his honour – depended. For Tashiro knew that if he failed to capture them soon, he would not be able to endure the disgrace of his failure.

Tashiro was a desperate man. He had finally realised there were not enough soldiers on the island to do the job; Kurosawa had been right all along. Because of the danger of ambush, they had to go out in force; but this inevitably made their progress through the jungle far too slow.

The extra men Nakamura had requisitioned had not arrived. The High Command did not seem to appreciate the difficulties they faced and had diverted the men to Guadalcanal. Incredibly, they had all been cut down in one night on the Matanikau River.

But now, finally, they had the special tracker dogs they had been promised.

Tashiro stood on the beach and examined the rows of cages on the wharf at the end of the jetty. Even from twenty yards away Tashiro wrinkled his nose in disgust at the musky, fetid smell of the animals. The dogs were yelping and clawing angrily at the steel cages. They were Pinschers, trained tracker dogs that could hunt down the guerrillas by scent alone.

Some of the islanders stood in small groups close by,

watching with suspicious and frightened eyes. Every village had its own dogs but none of them had ever seen animals quite like these; slavering, red-eyed beasts with large yellow fangs and lean, muscled bodies.

Tashiro turned to them. "Now we will catch your English *kiap*!" he shouted at them. "We will hunt him down like an animal!"

They stared back at him, frightened and uncomprehending.

It was then that Tashiro heard the whine of aircraft engines overhead and looked up. Immediately some of the villagers started to run for the shelter of the trees.

Tashiro laughed. "No, no!" he yelled at them. "Sikorki Japan! Japanese plane!"

The villagers stared at him, uncertain. They all knew only too well the death and destruction that the big metal birds could cause. Tashiro again beat the palm of his hand on his chest to show them. "Sikorki Japan!"

He looked up at the sky, shielding his eyes against the glare of the early morning sun, looking for the approaching plane. It was circling over the island, coming towards them now from the promontory to the north.

As he watched a curious feeling of unease swept over him. There was something terribly unfamiliar about the fighter's lines. For the first time it occurred to him that the aircraft might be American.

But it couldn't be. Not this far north . . .

Then he saw the angry shark's teeth painted around the nose of the fighter and the olive green fuselage with the blue star on the side and suddenly he too started to run.

Seconds later the Wildcat started its first low pass over the beach. The tracer bullets kicked up sprays of sand, and as it dived towards the bay the death howls of the Pinschers were lost under the roar of the fighter's engines and the angry chatter of the cannons.

To engage, to destroy, to engage again – it was an obsession that left little time for introspection. The imminence of death was pushed to the back of the mind – it was the only way to stay sane.

As Mitchell sat in the cockpit of the Grumman there were now twenty-one red circles painted on the fuselage below the cockpit. Each represented a confirmed kill.

Mitchell had lost count of the endless days and weeks he had spent on that muddy malarial rock in the Pacific, the countless hours of mind-numbing monotony and boredom interspersed with sudden, shrill minutes of utter terror and intense concentration when one mistake would mean certain death.

Every morning they were up an hour before dawn, warming up the single Pratt and Whitney engine of their Grumman Wildcats. They would take off at first light, to pursue the destroyers and transports of Rear Admiral Raizo Tanaka's Tokyo Express, as they made their way back up The Slot; or to intercept the inevitable bombers and their escorts on their way down from Kavieng.

Taking off and landing at Henderson Field had become a nightmare. After each storm it was a sticky porridge of glutinous mud; but in hours the water would drain away through the porous black coral underneath the strip to leave a black dust bowl that choked a plane's engines.

There was no mess hall; just a musty, sodden tent where they served Spam, sausage or the indigestible dehydrated mashed potato. They took vitamin pills to keep up their resistance to disease but malaria and dysentery still took a terrible toll among the young pilots and Mitchell's squadron was always well below full strength.

Fatigue became their natural state; sucking oxygen day after day, hour after hour, at high altitudes, sapped their strength and made them groggy. They never got enough rest. More than good food or the company of a woman, what Mitchell longed for most was sleep.

But as the battle for Guadalcanal reached its climax, he spent more and more of each daylight hour in the air; by night, rest was impossible as shells and bombs crashed on to the airfield. Instead he snatched fragments of sleep in slit trenches and sometimes found himself dozing in the mess hall; once he even fell asleep in his cockpit, while the ground crew refuelled his plane.

It was this constant fatigue he feared most; it slowed reactions, made a pilot prone to daydreaming or elementary mistakes that might eventually cost him his life. Because that was the hardest thing to live with; the aching uncertainty they all lived with, never knowing if this dawn would be the last one.

The gnawing fear that asked: Is this my day to die?

The Japanese had thrown everything they had at them. A few days before – or was it weeks? Time had become blurred in his memory – they had given the newly arrived reinforcements of the American division a baptism of fire and steel. Two Japanese battleships in Iron Bottom Sound had rained fourteen-inch shells on Henderson Field for hours. Mitchell could remember the sound of that bombardment even now, like hundreds of railroad cars screeching down from the air, ploughing the airfield apart in spasms of dust and orange flame. The next morning, the pilots scrambled out of their trenches and found the airfield littered with twisted and shredded steel matting and mangled cans of Spam – the result of a direct hit on the supply dump. The main and auxiliary strips were pocked with craters and the Cactus Air Force had been decimated. Only eleven of the ninety planes could still fly.

Yet still they managed to force the remains of their air fleet into the sky that morning to harass the Tokyo Express in The Slot.

The Japanese came the next night from the jungle, across the sandpits of the Matanikau, where the Marines beat them back with first their Howitzers, then their machine guns, and finally their bare hands. Even the signalmen and bandsmen and cooks rushed out through the mud and rain to meet them.

The following night they came from the other side of the field, and the Marines' Brownings scythed them down in the long Kunai grass, piling their bodies in windrows. The hollow-eyed survivors later told Mitchell how they had to clear away the bodies with grenades to leave their fields of fire open. One young gunner fired twenty-six thousand rounds that night.

The next day was Dugout Sunday. Mitchell huddled, muddy and soaked, in a slit trench while his fighter was being repaired, and Japanese mortars thudded monotonously on to the base each ten minutes. Then that night, up on Bloody Ridge, the Japanese attacked again. Another thousand died.

No matter how many Japanese soldiers fell, how many planes they shot down, they still kept coming. It seemed endless. The rain, the mud, the shelling, the fear.

But now, as Mitchell circled Vancoro harbour, there was no fear; when he was behind the controls of the Wildcat he could at last fight back. And today there was a deep, cold hatred in his heart such as he had never felt before.

He was thinking of the long lines of dead bodies he had seen laid out on the beach at Lunga Point, most of them not more than boys. He thought about two of his pilots he had seen strafed and killed as they hung helpless in their parachutes over Savo Island.

He thought of The Weatherman.

There were two of them now. A young English girl and an Irishman. He had heard via the scuttlebutt that the Navy had evacuated the original Weatherman; somehow the other two continued to survive. Now one of their native scouts had found out about the arrival of some tracker dogs and they had asked for help.

Mitchell had volunteered for the mission.

Below him he could make out a motor launch nestled against the beach in the arm of the bay, and figures running towards the trees. He threw his aircraft into a turn and dived towards the harbour, his wingtips almost skimming the branches of the casuarinas and the coconut palms.

As he swooped along the line of trees, he saw the three large cages on the wharf. He lined them up in the cross-hairs of his target finder and fired his wing cannons. One by one they exploded and splintered into fragments, killing their live cargo instantly.

Mitchell banked at the far end of the bay, returning to strafe the length of the beach, grinning as the Japanese soldiers ran for cover into the coconut palms, while others threw themselves off the sampans into the bay.

As Mitchell roared back to Guadalcanal he left behind three sampans resting on the shallow sandy bottom of the lagoon, plumes of black smoke belching from the superstructure of another, shot through with orange flame.

Behind the mask of his flying helmet, Mitchell grinned, baring his teeth in cold satisfaction.

"One for The Weatherman," he said into his closed face mask and headed for home.

53

From the platform high in the trees below Mount Teatupa, Rachel and Corrigan watched the armada of planes pass overhead. The drone of their engines was deafening.

"Jesus, Mary and Joseph," Corrigan said in amazement.

Almost without thinking, Rachel made the sign of the cross. "This is it." Out on the horizon they had already counted an armada of sixty-one Japanese ships, all heading south.

Corrigan squinted upwards into the bright morning sky. "Never seen so many planes in my whole bloody life. How many do you reckon there are?"

Rachel took out Manning's leather-bound notebook and started to count the formations. Nine planes in a formation. Ten formations. Eleven. Twelve. More coming. More to the west now, over The Treasuries.

By the time the drone of the engines had begun to fade to the south they had estimated a hundred and twenty heavy bombers and eighty fighters.

"What altitude would you say they're flying at?" Rachel said.

Corrigan rubbed his chin with the palm of his hand. It made a rasping sound, like someone dragging an iron file over a piece of wood.

"Five thousand feet. Maybe thirty. Christ, don't ask me."

"I'll say fifteen thousand feet then," Rachel said. "It's halfway in between."

"Better get back and crank up the radio then. The Yanks aren't going to believe this."

Corrigan watched the burning Zero splutter and dive towards Jervoise Bay. The pilot tried to land her belly down on the water but at the last moment the nose spilled forward and the fighter pitched into the water, and exploded. The burning wreckage was quickly swallowed by the calm blue waves of the lagoon.

Across the sky he could make out the stragglers returning to Kavieng and Rabaul. He had already seen two heavy bombers, glycol vapour trailing from their wings, drop into the sea to the west.

Two hundred had flown north. He had counted fewer than fifty making their way back.

Corrigan clambered effortlessly back down the trunk, into the steaming heat of the jungle. Rachel was waiting for him. Neither of them spoke. They both knew what it meant.

Rachel put her arms around him and held him.

Corrigan felt curiously elated; it seemed almost a personal victory. A part of him even wished that Manning had been there to share the moment.

On the ridge Sanei watched them. She sat alone behind

a moss-covered rock, hugging her knees to her chest, rocking on her haunches like an abandoned child. She felt the hot, bright tears of her anger spill down her cheeks.

She hated Corrigan at that moment, as she had never hated anything before.

She hated him even more than she hated Rachel.

She knew why Corrigan had come back, why he had not taken them away on the boat when he had the chance. He would not admit the reason to her then, but she had known.

Now all she could do was watch and wait. The war was not important to Corrigan, she knew. It was this woman. He would give her what he had always denied to her. He would let her have his babies and he would buy her a proper house. And Sanei would be thrown away, like an empty bottle.

There was nothing she could do. She could not compete with a white woman.

She watched Corrigan take Rachel's head in his hands and kiss her softly and tenderly. He had never kissed Sanei that way before. He never would.

Unable to watch any longer she got up and ran away into the jungle, her eyes swimming with the tears of her anguish.

For the past few weeks Wolfgang Heydrich had been in a foul temper. Two of his houseboys had run away in terror. No longer able to vent his rage on them, he turned his attentions to Alice Melama'a and the old cook, Mary.

Alice's crime had been to neglect to strain the rice that accompanied his midday meal. Snatching a handful of the jet black hair at the side of her head, he dragged the young girl along the verandah and threw her screaming down the steps.

"Useless nigger!" he cursed her.

"I look out longa you, mastah!" Alice pleaded. "I make good *kai-kai* for you now!"

Running down the steps, his belly bobbing inside the

crumpled white shirt, Heydrich aimed a kick at her rump. Sobbing, Alice twisted away from him. She scrambled to her feet and ran away along the path.

Heydrich watched her go, his anger temporarily relieved. Damned natives. Not worth two *Pfennigs*, the lot of them.

He looked round at the garden. Since the houseboys had run away it had been untended. It was unkempt, overgrown now with weeds and the fast-approaching tentacles of the jungle. Two wild pigs were rooting at the base of the frangipani trees, undisturbed.

Heydrich's face creased into a scowl. He didn't care a damn. Everything was all to hell anyway.

The *Deutschland* was gone and the Japanese gave him a pittance for his copra. The Colonel had even hinted that he was lucky they paid him at all.

"South East Asia Co-Prosperity Sphere," he snorted. "*Scheiss*!"

They had eaten his food, slaughtered his chickens and his pigs, looted his gramophone and his radio. He felt like weeping when he thought of it.

They were animals, all of them. Now he was trapped on this island with them, having to suffer their humiliations and their petty thieving. *Gott in Himmel*! Without his boat, he was virtually a prisoner.

But Wolfgang Heydrich wasn't finished yet.

He would think of something.

Sanei climbed up the sandy path that led to the *tabu* hut on the outskirts of the village. A few women returning from the gardens with yams watched her with open curiosity.

The *vele* man was sitting outside his hut, under the overhang of the thatch roof; he was very old, his skin was scaly with disease and there was the yellow film of a cataract over his left eye. Crimson betel-stained saliva hung from the corner of his mouth.

"You are Lobo?" Sanei asked him.

The rheumy eyes gazed back at her with disinterest.

"I want you for helpim me. I want to talk-talk longa shark fella. I want for fixim this white feller."

Lobo mumbled something under his breath and looked away.

Sanei reached into the fibre bag she carried at her shoulder and brought out a large pouch of twist tobacco. She had taken it from Manning's store of trade goods. She bent down and held it under the old man's nose.

His head jerked up and the shadow of a smile passed across his face; he snatched it from her with his long bony fingers.

He nodded. "You gottim *mana* longa this white feller?"

Sanei nodded. She reached into the bag and held out a lock of Corrigan's hair, tied with fibre. She had cut it from Corrigan's head while he slept.

Lobo grinned. "You come longa me now."

Sanei hesitated a moment, then pushed aside the screen of thatch palm-leaf across the doorway and followed Lobo inside.

There was a nauseating stench inside the hut; it emanated from a large flat stone in the corner. As her eyes grew accustomed to the light she made out the shape of a human skull resting on a small platform of lashed sticks on top of the stone.

It was the *vele* man's *padagi tidatho* – the shrine of his guardian spirit.

A hardened paste of titi nut was spread across the bones of the skull, and its markings of charcoal and lime made it almost appear to have skin and flesh.

It was fixed in a wickerwork frame and there was a small hole cut in the top of it. Inside were pieces of areca nut, taro and yam.

Next to it lay two stones, one slightly larger than the other. The bigger stone was marked on its flat surface.

Lobo took the lock of hair and dropped it inside the open skull.

"I fixim for you very good," he giggled, "I fixim for you. You see."

54

The sow was tethered to a post outside the hut. She was a huge beast, her obscenely pale flesh scarred and smeared with mud, and the huge dugs that hung from her belly brushed the ground as she walked. Lobo took the long curved machete from his belt and started to move towards her.

The sow stood very still, the small pink eyes watching him suspiciously. It was as if she sensed the old man's intention. He was just a few feet away when she uttered a terrifying high-pitched squeal and tried to run. The rope around her neck jerked tight round her neck and pulled her back.

Lobo moved with surprising agility, catching hold of the rope and throwing his thin, matchstick legs astride the pig's bucking and writhing body. He slashed with the machete and bright blood spurted from the sow's neck.

The animal bucked in terror with sudden desperate violence. Lobo was knocked to his feet and as he scrabbled away through the dirt, the sow rushed at him, bold now with the despair of death. But Lobo scrambled clear.

For long minutes the pig thrashed and writhed convulsively, the fine spray of blood staining the dirt at her feet into a pink-grey slush of mud. Twice she sank to her knees, and Sanei thought she was dead. But each time she recovered, charging once again at her tormentor, who stood cackling inches from her reach.

Finally she sank to her haunches and keeled on to her

flanks; she lay there grunting and twitching. A final violent motion of her bowels signalled her death.

Lobo sprang forward and ran the machete along the soft cream underbelly, slicing clean through the tough thick skin and membranes. The intestines fell steaming on to the dirt. Lobo reached inside the cavity of the pig's stomach and pulled out the remainder of the entrails, hacking them clear of the abdominal walls.

Then he went to the head of the animal and started to hack at the neck.

Sanei watched dispassionately. She had seen animals slaughtered many times before; it was only the old man's desperate urgency that revolted her.

Lobo chopped through the remaining ligaments and muscles of the neck. He picked up the pig's severed head, gripping it by its ear; he threw it to Sanei.

"You takim. Quicktime."

Sanei did as she was told, holding the ghastly severed head at arm's length, the blood still dripping on to the dirt.

Meanwhile Lobo stooped down and gathered the steaming pile of innards in his arms. He set off towards the beach, the intestines trailing behind him in the dirt. With a movement of his head he indicated that Sanei was to follow him.

When they reached the beach, Lobo waded straight into the water, up to his knees. Then he dropped his grisly burden into the water and reached into the small pouch at his waist. He produced the two small stones Sanei had seen beside the spirit shrine.

He held the larger of the two stones in his right hand and beat it with the other. The sound was hypnotic, high-pitched, like a bell. Lobo began to chant in rhythm with the ringing of the stones, a tremulous wailing sound.

Suddenly Sanei saw a shape moving towards them through the limpid green water of the lagoon. A fin broke the surface, arrowing through the water. It was a shark, its dirty white body clearly visible in the shallow water. It was a big one, perhaps twelve or fifteen feet long, a Tiger. It beached itself on the sandy bottom, just a few feet away from where the old man stood.

Cackling with delight, Lobo reached down into the water and picked up the pig's innards with both hands. He threw them into the shallows in front of the shark's snout, like a man feeding a favourite dog. Sanei watched in awe.

Finally he turned round and indicated that she was to bring him the head. Terrified, Sanei waded towards him and held the grisly prize towards him, her eyes never once leaving the shark.

Lobo took the head from her and dropped it into the water at his feet. The shark's huge jaws opened wide and swallowed the head with one swift movement, making a terrible grunting, snuffling sound as it forced the offering down its gullet. Then it gave a flick of its powerful tail, and turned its huge body around in the shallows, sending an explosion of salt spray into the air. It sliced through the water, swimming back to the deep waters of the lagoon.

The old man turned and made his way back to the beach, his forearms slick with blood, the gore drying now with the sea-salt.

"All finis," he said in his strange sibilant whisper. "You makim good *vele*. White feller he b'long you now. He b'long you now till he die finis."

55

That evening Corrigan went to the waterpool to fetch water for the evening meal. He found Sanei sitting on the ledge of the rock at the water's edge, staring into the clear cold depths. Her eyes were puffed and red and when she saw Corrigan, her face creased into a bitter snarl.

"You make *pus-pus* with white Mary?" she demanded angrily.

Corrigan fixed his dark Celtic eyes on her and turned away. He started to fill the water canteens.

Sanei got up and came to stand behind him. "You belong me," she told him.

"I don't belong to anyone."

"We go. Go longa boat now, okay?"

"The boat's gone," Corrigan said patiently. "It won't be coming back."

"You want white Mary?"

"That's none of your business."

"You belong me, Iris."

Corrigan did not know what to say to her. She had been his girl for a long time, but he had had plenty of other girls too, islanders and white women, and he thought she had understood. Understood what? Fool, he cursed himself. Of course she expected more.

"You didn't think I was going to live with you for ever, now, did you?" Corrigan said. "I thought I'd made myself quite plain on that account."

"You belong me," Sanei repeated.

"Go back to your village. That's the best thing for both of us. The Japs will catch up with us here sooner or later anyway. Go back to your village and look out for yourself. I'm a dead man now."

Sanei suddenly threw herself forward and tried to claw his face with her nails. Corrigan caught her arms easily. She tried to kick him, spitting and hissing at him like a wildcat. A well aimed kick caught him in the groin.

Grunting with pain, Corrigan twisted one of her wrists and threw her to the ground.

Sanei fell backwards, and lay there, watching him. "You belong me, Corrigan, I savvy for to look out for you."

"You crazy bitch," Corrigan muttered. He groaned and doubled over, gasping for breath. "Jesus, I think you've kicked them right up around my kidneys."

"I stay longa you."

"No you don't. You go back to your village, all right? You may not realise it but I'm doing you a big favour. It won't be very pretty around here when those little yellow heathen find us."

As Sanei lay on the ground her fist closed around a smooth basalt rock. Suddenly she jumped to her feet, and tried to swing the rock down on the back of Corrigan's head. If he had moved a fraction of a second slower, she would have succeeded.

But he had anticipated the blow and in a moment he had taken a step towards her and brought the back of his hand smashing across her forearm, knocking the rock out of her hand. He grabbed her by her shoulders and shook her.

"For God's sake, listen to what I'm telling you! It's only a matter of time before the Japs find us! Go back to your village!"

"You b'long me, Iris," she repeated softly.

"I don't belong to anyone. I never did. I'm sorry . . ." His voice trailed off. "I didn't mean to hurt you," he mumbled.

Sanei's face was drawn in the agony of shame and defeat. "I stay longa you. Please, I stay longa you?"

"No. Go back to your village."

He finished filling the canteens and started to make his way back to the camp.

"I go for killim you, Iris," Sanei said.

Corrigan didn't answer her; and Sanei didn't try to follow.

The full moon rose out of the jungle, a huge blood moon that seemed almost close enough to touch as it crept over the towering slopes of Mount Teatupa. Rachel and Corrigan sat by the glowing coals of their fire, watching.

"Tell me about yourself, Patrick," Rachel said.

He looked up at her, surprised. It was the first time she had called him by his first name. "What do you want to know?"

"I want to know all about you."

"Why?"

"You intrigue me."

He laughed easily. "Do I now?" He stirred the hot ashes with a stick. Rachel watched him, silently. Finally, he spoke again. "I was born in County Down. In a little village on Dundrum Bay. You can see the Mountains of Mourne from Dundrum Bay."

"It must be beautiful."

"It is if you don't have to live there. That's why the Irish always sing about it after they emigrate."

"When did you leave?"

"We moved to Dublin in the winter of 1913. The old man bought a damp little house in Dun Laoghaire. Soon after that he got mixed up in de Valera's crowd. Started raving on about a united Ireland. Lot of good it did him. In the Easter Uprising the English stood him up against a wall and shot him."

He paused. Rachel felt he was waiting for her to comment, but what was there to say? She understood now why Corrigan could never see the war as his own.

"What happened?" she asked finally.

"One of his pals in the Sinn Fein traded the old man's life to save his own neck, damn his bloody eyes. Names, addresses, everything. So much for a united bloody Ireland." He paused, staring off into the darkness. "I was there in the house when it happened. I looked out the window and I saw the soldiers in the street. My old man ran and got his revolver and pulled me down on to the floor by the window. And do you know what he said? He made me promise to carry on the fight after he was dead. What fight? I mean, what was it that was worth dying for, will you tell me that? Jesus . . . I've never been so frightened in all my life. He stuck his gun out of the window and started firing at the soldiers. When the bullets ran out he tried to run for it. They shot him in the leg and took him away in a police van. That was the last I saw of him. A fine, glorious death my father died. My uncles still talk about him as if he were a bloody hero."

Rachel laid her hand on his arm. There was nothing to say.

Corrigan cleared his throat. "It was the last time I ever cried. He was still my old man, even if I did hate his guts. Your uncle would have liked him though. He was a good Catholic. Went to church every Sunday and beat the living Christ out of us the other six days a week."

"Did you join . . . like your father?"

"Did I hell! What for? Ireland's still not united and the old man's been dead these twenty-six years. What did it achieve, tell me that?"

"So you ran away to sea."

"It's one way of looking at it, but it wasn't quite like that. The point was the old man was gone and if we didn't go out and get a job we were going to starve. It's not a difficult choice, even when you're only thirteen. Like you say, Ireland's a beautiful place but there's nothing for a sensible man to do there. All my life I'd lived on top of the sea and I had a certain affection for her. So I took crew on the first boat that would have me. She was a cargo steamer, working the Atlantic run between Dublin and America."

"It sounds romantic."

"It isn't. You're wet and cold and terrified all the time."

"Santa Maria's a long way from Dun Laoghaire."

"Further than you'll know."

"So what brought you here?"

"Want the whole sordid story, do you now?"

Rachel waited, resting her chin on her hands.

Corrigan shrugged. "It's not so far, really. Not if you

run. And I've spent my whole life doing that. You'd be surprised how many places it's taken me."

"What about women, Patrick? You're a handsome man and . . ."

His face creased into a sudden grin, his white teeth flashing in the darkness. "Is this a confession, Miss Goode?"

She felt herself blush. Thank God he couldn't see it. Damn him. It was always as if he knew what she was thinking. "No," she stammered, "I just meant that I find it strange that . . . well, there must have been . . ."

"They have a special place reserved in Hell for me. They're going to chain me up in a room with all the women I've known in my life and leave me there. I dare say that most of them won't think that eternity's long enough to make me suffer for what I've done to them."

"My uncle used to say that no man was beyond redemption."

"Yes, he used to say that to me a few times as well." Corrigan threw the stick into the fire, watched it crackle and burn. "But you're right, Miss Goode. There was a woman once. In Dublin. She had the perverse pleasure of calling herself my wife for a time, and gave me a couple of daughters."

Rachel caught her breath. "What happened?"

"Well, not to put too fine a point on it, Miss Goode, I abandoned her. Went off to sea again and didn't come back for five years. By that time she was dead – pneumonia I think they said it was – and her brother was looking after the kids. When he saw me he came out with a shotgun and told me if I ever set foot near the place again he'd blow my brains out. I've always respected him for that. As for my wife, I'm sure she's down there in purgatory somewhere, keeping the irons hot for me." Corrigan fell silent. Neither of them spoke for a long time. Finally Corrigan got to his feet. "So you see, Miss Goode, this unpolished diamond of yours is nothing more than a bit of driftwood. Your uncle was right. I'm a physical and emotional coward.

Wherever I go the fact of it remains. I've never forgiven myself for what I did, and I don't expect anyone else to, either. We are what we are, I suppose."

"So why didn't you run away from here when you had the chance?"

"God knows. I must be crazy."

"Perhaps everyone has to stand up and be counted some time."

"Bloody hard standing up when you're dead."

The night had grown dark. Towering thunderheads rose from behind the volcano, and black clouds were racing across the moon. The air had become very still, and even the noises of the jungle had become muted.

Corrigan looked up at the sky. "There's a storm on its way," he said.

Rachel stood up, her heart hammering in her chest. There was something that had been on her mind constantly since he had come back. Tonight, she knew, she had to end the dilemma. "Are we going to die, Patrick?"

"Everybody dies. It's a question of timing."

"We're not going to get off this island, are we?"

"Your uncle believed in miracles. I don't."

She hesitated. "Then will you do something for me?" she said finally.

"And what's that?"

Rachel looked away. How many ways were there to say it? Yet it didn't really matter now. They were going to die; and knowing that gave her a kind of freedom.

"Miss Goode?"

She took a deep breath. "The thing is – I don't want to die a virgin. I don't know of any other circumstances where I'd be saying this to a man, but I don't think I can face dying without knowing what . . . well, what it's like. I know it's a sin, but I think God would forgive me in the circumstances."

Corrigan stared at her. She was unable to fathom his expression in the darkness.

"Are you shocked?" she whispered.

His voice was strangely hoarse. "You have a talent for doing the unexpected, that's for sure and certain."
"Well?"
He reached out and took her hand. "Miss Goode . . . Rachel . . ."
She put a finger to his lips. "No, don't say anything. You don't have to. Tonight, let the Devil look after his own."

56

Rachel woke with the full moon shining on her face through a hole in the thatch roof of the hut. She opened her eyes, wondering at the almost impossible brilliance of it, a full and perfect circle of pure white light. The storm had passed quickly, but the distant thunder still echoed around the mountains.
Corrigan's head lay on her breast. She ran her fingers through the thick black-rust curls. In sleep the rough face had the vulnerable sweetness of a boy, the lips slightly apart. She noticed for the first time the long dark lashes on his eyes. She stroked the muscles of his shoulder with her fingers, enjoying the feel of him, and the delicious warm smell of another body close to hers.
Poor Uncle Matthew. He must be spinning in his grave. But she wasn't sorry. Not now. Corrigan had been slow and gentle, not at all as he had been that morning outside the mission church. She could not understand why her uncle had been so obsessed by it. Love had made her feel more alive than she had ever felt before, and she didn't care what happened to her now.
She felt Sanei's presence before she heard her; it was no

more than a slight breath of movement but it was enough to make her turn her head, and she gave a small gasp as the native girl's shadow fell across the makeshift bed.

Sanei was watching them from the doorway of the hut. Her face, illuminated by the phosphorescent glow of the full moon, looked pale and macabre.

A frisson of fear ran through her. "Sanei?" Rachel said. Her own voice sounded hoarse and distant.

In that moment something flashed in the girl's hand. Rachel screamed.

If it had won its target, the gleaming ivory-handled knife would have certainly pierced her chest just under her heart. Rachel, still in the dream world of a half-sleep, was too slow to react and her right arm was pinned by Corrigan's body.

But in that moment Corrigan sat upright and the razor edge of the knife glanced off the bone of his left shoulder, deflecting it away from her.

For a brief moment it seemed to Rachel that the silhouettes of Corrigan and Sanei had blended into one. Corrigan gasped with pain and then his right arm struck out and Rachel heard the knife fall with a soft thud on the beaten earth floor of the hut.

Sanei gave a whimper of pain as Corrigan's fist hammered into her shoulder and then she was gone, her dark shadow running out of the hut and into the night.

Her footfall crashed through the undergrowth and faded, lost in the night sounds of the cicadas.

"Corrigan?" Rachel sat up and threw her arms round him.

"She stuck me with the knife," Corrigan muttered. There was no anger or pain in his voice; just indignation. "Bloody woman."

Rachel felt something wet and warm on her hand. "You're bleeding."

"What did she do that for?"

"It was meant for me."

Still drugged from sleep, Corrigan didn't seem to fully

understand. "That's the second time she's tried to stick me with a knife," he mumbled. "When I get hold of her I'll give her a bloody good hiding."

But Corrigan never carried out his threat. Next morning Sanei's small bundle of possessions was gone and they never saw her again.

57

The knife had entered Corrigan's body between his left shoulder and the thick band of pectoral muscle on his chest. It had left a gaping wound two inches long just below the collarbone. Rachel washed it with alcohol and stitched it as best she could, without anaesthetic. Corrigan made no sound as she worked on him, drawing the lips of the wound together as quickly and as skilfully as she could.

"I can't believe she did this," Corrigan said.

"She put a knife in you before, didn't she?"

"That was nothing. That was just temper. Heat of the moment. But she must have spent a lot of time planning it this time. She must really hate me."

"Or love you."

"It's the same thing in the end, isn't it?"

"Anyway, I told you. It was meant for me."

"How can you be sure of that?"

Rachel shrugged. "I just know."

Corrigan waited while Rachel put another suture into the wound. She saw his hands clench into fists in his lap as she drew the needle through his flesh.

"I'm almost finished."

"I'm all right. A little bit of pain never hurt anyone." He gave her the familiar crooked grin.

He reached out and tried to touch her. She pulled away.

"You're not going to get maidenly on me again, are you?"

Rachel ignored him. Everything she had felt the night before had evaporated with the dawn. Now she was embarrassed and awkward in his presence. But how was she supposed to feel? She had bared her soul as well as her body to a man she knew she could not afford to love. She felt dirty and sullied, and it didn't help when he teased her.

Rachel closed the final suture, deliberately giving the brown thread a final tug that raised the lips of the wound in a tight peak. She smiled with satisfaction as Corrigan gave a grunt of pain.

"It hasn't done any permanent damage," Rachel told him. "Just another scar to add to your collection."

Corrigan started to pull his shirt back on. "What's the matter, Miss Goode?"

She avoided his eyes. "Should anything be wrong, Mister Corrigan?"

He grinned knowingly. "You've consorted with the Devil and now you're feeling rotten. You've been human for half an hour and now you can't forgive yourself."

"That's got nothing to do with it," she said petulantly, and for a moment he thought she was going to stamp her foot. She snapped the medical bag shut. "Damn you," she hissed and stormed out of the tent.

58

Wolfgang Heydrich was a broken man.

He sat slumped in the cane chair on the verandah of

Marakon, in brooding contemplation of the cards that Fate had dealt him. The remains of the *Deutschland* lay rotting by the charred stumps of the jetty, and now the Japanese refused to pay him for his copra. He suspected that the Japanese colonel and his vicious first lieutenant somehow blamed him for the débâcle with Corrigan.

He was trapped on this stinking island, among barbarians.

The servants had deserted him. In mortal terror of the constant beatings and his volatile tantrums, they had gone back to their villages. Only Alice Melama'a still remained.

He looked around miserably. The bungalow and the outbuildings were in need of a coat of paint; chickens pecked at the coral sand and an old sow, rooting under the steps, seemed to add to the feeling of desolation.

He scratched irritably at his crotch. Sweat itch again. Sweat. It was the only thing in abundant supply at *Marakon*, now. It seemed to ooze out of every pore, soaking the voluminous and stained cotton shirt that flowed and bulged over his body, stinging as it flowed over the sores under his arm, behind his knees and in his groin.

Tiny ulcers had formed under one armpit. They would get infected he knew, and fester. Everything became infected here.

He was shaken from his miserable contemplation by the sound of footsteps on the verandah. He looked up.

It was Alice. She looked cowed and miserable. "What do you want?" he spat.

"Mary come for see you, boss."

"What Mary? What does she want with me?"

Alice shook her head.

"If she can cook, she can start right away in the kitchen. Anything would be better than the slop you serve me."

"Mary say she want talk-talk longa you."

"All right. Tell her to come here."

Heydrich wondered what the girl might want. If she

thought she would get higher wages just because he was down on his luck, she was sadly mistaken. He'd give her a good slapping and send her on her way back to her village, to remind the others who was master here.

But the native girl who stepped on to the verandah of *Marakon* a few moments later had not come to beg for work. She had much higher ambitions.

Wolfgang Heydrich was prepared for anything except the vision that greeted him. When he saw who it was his jaw gaped open in astonishment.

"*Mein Gott*," he whispered, slowly getting to his feet. "A miracle!"

Colonel Nakamura sat at his desk studying the latest field reports from Lieutenant Tashiro. Somehow the Americans had found out about the tracker dogs. Worse than the loss of the animals were the implications of the incident; it emphasised how important the radio on Santa Maria must be to them.

He heard the sound of horse's hooves outside the window and his nose twitched involuntarily. It was the German planter. Now whenever he came into the settlement he was forced to ride an ugly piebald horse; the horse in turn was accompanied by a legion of flies. It stank.

The door to his office opened and one of the guards stepped in.

"The fat planter is outside, Nakamura-san. He asks to speak with you."

Nakamura leaned back in the cane chair. It squeaked in protest under his weight.

"Fetch Kurosawa," he snapped. A few minutes later the soldier returned with the young Japanese officer.

"All right," Nakamura growled at the sentry. "Send the German in now."

When Heydrich entered Nakamura did not bother to look up. For long moments he enjoyed the German's discomfort as he hesitated between the door and the colonel's desk.

"Colonel Nakamura," Heydrich said finally.

Nakamura made no attempt to disguise his contempt for the German. He despised any man who continued at his work when his country was at war. In Nakamura's opinion, Heydrich should have left his plantation and returned to serve with the *Wehrmacht* in 1939.

"Ask him what he wants," Nakamura said to Kurosawa.

Heydrich smiled obsequiously. "I have come here to help you."

Kurosawa translated this information to the colonel.

"Tell him I consider that unlikely."

"You want to catch the Englander, don't you?"

"He asks us if we are still looking for the English bandits," Kurosawa repeated.

Nakamura got slowly to his feet and came to stand in front of the German, his eyes boring into the other man's. "More native gossip?"

Heydrich understood the tone of the colonel's voice, if not the meaning. "Look, what happened last time was not my fault," he said to Kurosawa. "It cost me dearly. My schooner, and my boathouse, both turned to cinders. To mention nothing of the food your soldiers took."

The young Japanese knew how Nakamura would react to this impertinence. Still, he was only there to translate. He told Nakamura what the Austrian had said.

Nakamura's eyes glinted angrily. "It seems my men did not have the time to also teach you some respect. I would find it a pleasure."

"You cannot treat me like this! I have information, and I can help you. I am a very influential man among the natives on this island."

"You must tell Nakamura-san what you know," Kurosawa snapped.

"First I must know what this information is worth."

"You want money?"

"I will lead you to the English bandits. In return you will give me a boat and pay me for everything your soldiers stole from me. And then I want a good price for my copra."

"He wants to bargain," Kurosawa said. "A new boat, compensation and an agreed price on his copra."

Nakamura smiled, a slow dangerous smile, revealing the gold eye tooth beneath his upper lip. "He is suddenly very brave."

"Is it a bargain?" Heydrich said eagerly.

"How can we know you not waste time again?" Kurosawa asked him.

Heydrich drew closer to the young officer, theatrically lowering his voice. Kurosawa sniffed at the taint of Heydrich's body. "Not this time. I have a great prize. Come outside – you will see."

"He says he has something to show us outside."

The two Japanese walked slowly to the door and Nakamura threw it open. Nakamura folded his hands imperiously behind his back.

Heydrich's horse was untethered and was chewing contentedly at the small patch of lawn around the flagpole. It occasionally flicked lethargically with its tail at the swarm of flies that hovered and crawled across its flanks and its rump.

Then Nakamura noticed the girl. She was squatting on her haunches in the shade below the bungalow steps, her arms folded across her knees in the patient attitude so distinctive of the islanders.

She was a pretty girl, with an oval pouting face and a slim, coffee-brown body. Nakamura wondered why he had not seen her in the settlement before. She would make a handsome addition to the stable of young girls he had already collected.

"What is her name?" Nakamura said.

"Sanei," Heydrich said. "Last night she came to *Marakon*. She asked me to bring her here. Until two days ago she was with the English on Mount Teatupa."

Kurosawa wheeled round in shock.

"What did he say?" Nakamura asked.

"He says she has come from the camp of the English bandits, Nakamura-san."

Heydrich nodded eagerly. "*Ja, ja*," he said. "She will lead you right to their camp." He put his head on one side, and gave Kurosawa a sly grin. "Now you will ask the good Colonel if we have a bargain, *ja*?"

59

Mitchell studied the handful of young men grouped around the room. They were all very young; but this morning they looked very old. They were the surviving pilots from Marine Air Group Twenty-Three, the Cactus Air Force of Guadalcanal. Now they sat on the wooden trestles and leaned against the earthen walls in the stifling heat of the dugout, waiting.

It seemed to all of them now that the battle for Guadalcanal was all but over. A week ago Uncle Dan – Rear Admiral Daniel Callaghan – and Rear Admiral Norman Scott had died aboard their cruisers off Suvo Island, trying to stop the Japanese launching another naval bombardment on Henderson Field. Their tiny force had been smashed to pieces by the big guns of the Japanese battlewagons, *Hiei* and *Kirishina*. Callaghan's fleet had sailed so close to the enemy battleships that at times the Japanese could not depress their guns low enough to hit them.

Somehow, despite terrifying losses, the Americans beat them off; but they paid the full price for their courage. On that hot, still night two admirals and one thousand American sailors died in just half an hour.

At dawn Mitchell and his men took off from Henderson

Field to exact their revenge. They caught the crippled *Hiei* in The Slot; they swooped down on it like birds of prey around a sick and injured animal. Mitchell and his men strafed the decks while the Douglas Dauntlesses from the *Enterprise* attacked with torpedoes and bombs. By four o'clock that afternoon the huge Japanese battlewagon had gone down.

Then they went after the Tokyo Express, now sailing unescorted towards Tassafaronga on the western tip of Guadalcanal. They attacked, returned to Henderson to refuel, then attacked again. On and on all day. Mitchell could still see the ugly black puffs of flak bursting around his canopy, the towering columns of spray and smoke as the dive bombers swooped down on the lumbering transports, the panicked Japanese foot soldiers rushing on to the decks of the sinking ships, leaping to their deaths in the burning sea.

The next day they tracked them again to the beaches of Tassafaronga, and went in for the kill. The Wildcats strafed the soldiers with their machine guns and cannons as they scrambled down ropes into the surf. The beaches became the killing fields of the crack *Hiroshima* division; Mitchell and his men went after the helpless Japanese soldiers on the boats without mercy, knowing that the young Marines around Henderson would have to face every one that got away from them. By the afternoon the seas around the stranded boats had turned crimson.

One by one the beached transports with their precious supplies and equipment blossomed with orange flame and when Mitchell turned his squadrons back to Henderson for the final time, they left behind them a pyre of black, oily smoke to mark the graveyard of the largest ever Tokyo Express. In those few days Mitchell's men and the handful of pilots from the *Enterprise* smashed an entire Japanese division.

The strain of those deadly hours was etched in grim lines on every face in the room. The horror of too much death, of dealing it out with such venom, of seeing friends broken and consumed by cannon shell and flaming glycol, had turned each of them into shuffling cadavers. In time, perhaps days, perhaps weeks, they would recover. Mitchell knew that some never would. In any fighting squadron, there were always casualties that would never show up on the combat reports.

But today it was quiet. The Japanese were still out there but the steady flow of warships and bombers heading down The Slot had slowed to a trickle. The feeling was growing among the men of Henderson Field that the worst was over. They had won.

Now they waited for news of the last of their number that was yet to make it back, a buddy they had never seen, but who had lived with them through the worst of the nightmare, for three long months. They waited in silence, as the minutes drifted by into an hour. One by one they drifted out.

Finally, only Mitchell and Shoup remained.

"That's the fifth day they've missed the sked," Shoup said.

Mitchell said nothing.

The radio silence had cast a gloom over all of them. There had been nothing from The Weatherman – as they still referred to the young woman who had taken the Englishman's place on the radio – for almost a week.

They had all heard the latest scuttlebutt. The Coastwatcher's Headquarters in Townsville had requested an urgent evacuation by the US Navy. Intelligence had reported that the natives on the northern islands, fearing reprisals, and disillusioned by word that the *kiap* had left for good, were turning against The Weatherman. It was only a matter of time now.

"Maybe they're just staying off the air to keep the Japs off their tails," Shoup said, breaking the long silence.

"Yeah," Mitchell said. "Maybe."

60

The office of the Supervising Intelligence Officer in charge of the Coastwatchers in the North-East Pacific area was housed in a back room in the Area Combined Headquarters in Townsville. It was into this room that a slight pale man in an ill-fitting naval officer's uniform was shown, one day late in the November of 1942.

The SIO rose as the man entered the office. He held out his hand. "Ian. Good to see you. How are you feeling?"

"Better thank you, sir."

"Good. Glad to see you on the mend again. You had us worried for a while. Sit down."

Manning sat down opposite the tall grey-haired man in the naval commander's uniform. Outside the monsoon rains murmured on the lush banana palms and ferns that grow in rich profusion along Australia's Queensland coast.

"The quacks put everything back together?"

"I've still got half a mile of plaster round my ribs. Arm's knitting nicely though and they say there's no internal damage, thank goodness."

"You were jolly lucky."

"I suppose so, sir."

The SIO's air of jovial bonhomie fell away. He knew why Manning had asked to see him. "I take it you've heard the news?"

Manning nodded. "No radio contact for eight days."

The SIO lowered his eyes. "Doesn't mean the Japanese have them. There are a hundred other reasons."

"I know, sir."

"Who are they, Ian? This Corrigan – is he a planter?"

Manning shook his head. "Trader. Did a run up the coast every now and then when he felt like it, ferrying supplies and the occasional visitor. Owned the trading post in Vancoro, but that was never open unless he was sober, which wasn't very often. The girl – only been on the island a couple of years. Her uncle died of a bullet wound a few weeks before you took me off."

The SIO shook his head. "Remarkable."

"Very."

The older man opened the ornate silver-engraved box on his desk. "Cigarette?"

"No thank you, sir." Manning patted his chest. "Doctor's orders."

The Commander took one of the cigarettes and put it between his lips. He lit it with a heavy silver lighter. As he exhaled the grey-blue smoke he regarded Manning thoughtfully. "What do you want me to do?"

"Let me go back and look for them."

The SIO sighed. "If only we'd known, Ian. We could have sent another man in at the time. Someone with experience."

"I didn't want to leave, sir. I thought I could hang on." Manning fidgeted impatiently in his chair. "Couldn't we have sent someone else in anyway?"

"No point. We have other men up there now, Ian, in the Rendells and on Choiseul and Bougainville. Besides, we don't even know if they're still alive. We haven't heard anything from them for a week."

"Let me go back and look for them."

"You? Sorry, Ian. I've seen the medical report. You've done your share. Your war's over."

"Mine perhaps. But theirs isn't. No one knows that island like I do. I know where they're hiding and I can find my way back up that mountain blindfolded. It has to be me."

"What if they're dead?"

"Then we'll know. If they're not . . . we can get them off. We can't abandon them now. Not after what they've done."

There was a long silence, broken only by the rhythmic beat of the fan, stirring the hot, moist air.

The SIO sighed. "I don't know, Ian," he said finally. "The Americans haven't even got a mess spoon to spare right now, and the old man will scream blue murder if we try and take one of his precious subs off combat duty. He finds that sort of thing hard to justify."

"Harder than abandoning a man and a woman who may have helped us hold on to Guadalcanal?"

The Commander raised his eyebrows in surprise at the brusque tone of Manning's voice. He encouraged the atmosphere of informality among the men in his branch of the service, but he also expected their respect.

But he let Manning's remark go without comment. After all, the bastard was right.

"I'll do what I can, Ian," he said evenly. "Meanwhile you'd better get some rest. If you're going to go back up there, you'll need it."

61

If he lived to be a hundred Heydrich knew he would always savour the look on Nakamura's face when he had told him who the girl was. Now there would be no more arguments over the price for his copra. There would be another boat for him, to replace the *Deutschland*. Fate had repaid him for the sufferings it had brought him.

Now as he stood on the verandah at *Marakon*, he allowed himself a smile of satisfaction. It was indeed a fortunate day when one was able to do oneself a good turn and revenge yourself on an old enemy at the same time.

He watched the Japanese soldiers unloading their equipment at the end of the wrecked jetty. *Gott in Himmel*, there were almost a hundred of them. For one Englishman and a girl!

Soon they would be crawling all over *Marakon* again. He consoled himself with the thought that it would be for just one night.

And it would be worth it.

He heard footsteps on the teak boards behind him and he turned. It was the girl, Sanei. "I want my money."

Heydrich put his hands on his hips and looked at her. There was a sullenness that spoiled the dark beauty of her face. It was a pity. He would have to beat it out of her.

"You got what you wanted," he growled. "You wanted Corrigan dead. I've arranged it for you."

"You promised me money."

Heydrich took a step towards her and slapped her once, hard, across the face. Sanei took a step back, stunned.

"Corrigan was too soft with you."

Sanei spat at him.

Unexpectedly Heydrich's face split into a grin. For the first time in many years he felt a tingling excitement in his groin. He had grown bored with the accustomed compliance of Alice Melama'a and the others. This little spitfire would be very different.

But first he would do the Japanese colonel one last favour. He had heard that Nakamura had a particular liking for the brown girls of the islands.

A gift like this would help to cement the bargain.

Corrigan and Rachel sat on two packing crates in the radio hut, staring gloomily at the teleradio. The back panel of the radio lay on the trestle table, where it had lain for over ten days. One of the valves had blown out, and they had no spare. Without it their last contact with the outside world was gone.

Rachel put her head in her hands. "What are we going to do?"

"We don't have a lot of options."

"We can't just sit here like this, day after day."

Corrigan said nothing.

"Perhaps they'll send someone to look for us."

"It doesn't do to trust the English, girl. Take it from an Irishman."

"They can't leave us stranded here."

"Why not? We always were."

"Perhaps they think we're dead."

"There's a war going on, girl. People are dying everywhere. What's a couple more?"

"Don't be so gloomy. If the Americans take Guadalcanal, they could be here within a few weeks."

"Maybe. I wouldn't count on it."

"We can survive. We've managed so far," Rachel got to her feet and walked over to him. She touched the thick bandage around his chest. "How is it?"

"It's fine."

She bent to examine it. "I'd better change the dressing."

He pushed her hand away. "It's not going to get better if you keep fiddling with it, now is it?"

That night, while the night owls screeched and the monsoon rumbled and crashed against the dark walls of the volcano, she lay alone in her hut and wondered just how much longer their luck could hold out.

Two of the crew undogged the after hatch and Manning followed them out on to the bows of the *USS Grampus*. The moon disappeared behind a dark cloud and only the foam breaking over the distant reef provided colour in the pitch black of the night.

Manning turned his head towards the deep booming of the breakers. Somewhere just beyond them lay the beach at Jervoise Bay, the same beach where they had carried him into the rubber boat almost six weeks before.

Manning gulped in deep lungfuls of the salt air, relieved to be away from the cramped unnatural world of the submarine, the smell of sweat, and diesel fumes, the insufferable heat, and the quickly melting ice cream that the sailors devoured by the gallon. There never seemed to be enough air below decks; Manning had had to struggle to control his own claustrophobia through the whole journey. At times, he thought he was suffocating.

They were a week out of Townsville; they travelled underwater by day, only surfacing at night to recharge the batteries in the comparative safety of the darkness, and to take deep lungfuls of the salt air.

The night before a Japanese destroyer had spotted them and Manning had learned at first hand the unspeakable fear of depth bombing; waiting silent in the clicking nightmare world of the submariners, hearing the hollow boom of the depth charges, then pitching into utter blackness as the lights flickered off and the metal walls of the submarine groaned under the concussion. He hoped he never had to go through that again.

The big submarine rolled gently as an oily swell passed beneath it, breaking a minute later on the dark reef. Meanwhile the crew brought two rubber boats from below, inflating them and launching them over the side of the *Grampus*.

Before they had sailed, Manning had seconded four Australian navy men to go with him as riflemen. Silently they emerged from below decks and jumped into the waiting boats. Manning jumped in after them, and they began to row silently for the shore.

As the silhouette of the *Grampus* faded into the night, Manning wondered yet again whether his mission was a fool's errand; they must all surely be dead. But no one could be certain. And while there was yet hope he owed it to Rachel and Corrigan to do all he could.

The dark mass that lay along the distant horizon might have been cloud; but as they came closer to the reef Manning could make out the outlines of the palms. A coconut bobbed in the water close by and then drifted past with the current. Manning felt suddenly charged with sadness and fear.

He wondered what lay ahead for him in the coming day. Were Corrigan and Rachel and Lavella all dead? Had they been captured by the Japanese? Perhaps the natives were now against them, ready to betray any white man who set foot on the island. Perhaps even now the Japanese were waiting for them on the shore.

Somewhere on the beach, above the deep boom of the surf, he heard the cicadas beating out their endless Morse; he had no cipher for their code.

62

The rising sun had already thrown a crimson stain over the eastern horizon when they reached the beach. It was the quiet time before dawn when even the rush of surf across the coral reef seemed hushed. The dark shadows of the palms overhung the beach in brooding silence.

They would have to be deep into the jungle at first light; they could not risk being caught on the beach and being seen by a Japanese spotter plane. As soon as they reached the shallows Manning leaped out of the rubber boat and helped two of the sailors drag it up on to the strand.

One of them, a beefy petty officer with a clipped ginger beard, trudged up on to the sand beside him, his rifle slung over one shoulder. His name was Hogan, a laconic Queenslander with a tattoo on his right forearm; it said "Mother".

"We'll go inland half a mile and store the gear," Manning told him. "Then we'll set off for the camp."

Hogan nodded. Behind him one of his ratings tripped

getting out of the other boat. There was a loud splash as the man fell headlong into the water.

"Is that you, Foster?" Hogan hissed at the man in the darkness.

"Sorry, chief."

"Christ, you're a clumsy bastard."

Manning groaned. It wasn't an auspicious start.

Alice Melama'a had heard the girl's screams from the bungalow the previous evening, from her hiding place in the forest overlooking the plantation. She had hidden there as soon as the Japanese had arrived at *Marakon*. She knew that Heydrich would not hesitate to offer her to the soldiers.

She waited there all that following morning until long after the Japanese soldiers and the little Malaita girl had set off into the hills for Teatupa. It was almost noon when she finally ventured up the steps of *Marakon*.

Heydrich was still not out of bed, and there was no sign of the girl. She tiptoed along the balcony and began to make the breakfast. When it was ready she waited a while, then went softly to the end of the verandah and peered through the French windows into Heydrich's bedroom.

He was still in bed. Puzzled, she crept into the room and pulled aside the mosquito net.

Heydrich lay naked on his back in the middle of the bed, his bulging eyes staring sightlessly at the ceiling, his face frozen in a mask of sudden, bewildered terror. A thick ivory-handled knife protruded from the middle of his chest, dark jelly-like masses of blood congealed around the wound. The bloodstains on the white cotton sheets gleamed in rich profusion against the marble-white of Heydrich's cold flesh.

Alice smiled grimly. So the little Malaita girl had had her revenge!

Alice shrugged and went back to the kitchen to finish her breakfast.

*

It had been almost a full day's march from the coast, but now Lieutenant Tashiro felt an eager thrill of anticipation as he watched the thin skein of smoke drift up through the trees ahead.

At last. He had them.

He had amused himself on the long march up from the coast by deciding what he would do with them. His men had been instructed to take the one called Corrigan alive if they could. Tashiro's wounded pride would not be satisfied by a single bullet.

The woman was of no consequence. He would let his men have her, while he attended to the big Englishman. He would die slowly, inch by inch, a piece at a time. He would attend to it personally. He had taken special care that the edge of the blade at his side was honed to razor-sharpness.

He smiled in anticipation of the moment.

Afterwards he would put their heads on bamboo poles and leave them in the jungle as carrion for the birds and the ants, and a warning to the natives of what would happen to enemies of the Emperor.

He stopped and turned to the native girl walking behind him with Kurosawa. "Which way?"

"You go there," she said, pointing to the narrow valley leading to the jungle-covered gully ahead. "Very narrow. Two soldier."

Tashiro pulled the plan she had drawn for them at *Marakon* from his pocket. He pointed to the ridgeback.

"Ask her how we can get up here," he said. "We have to cut off their escape." Tashiro had waited too long to allow them any avenue of escape.

"I show you," Sanei said when Kurosawa told her what they wanted.

He turned to Kurosawa. "Take your platoon and the Nambu and follow the girl. I want the machine gun to cover the ridge. We will flush them out for you. But remember – I want the white man alive."

Kurosawa saluted and went back down the trail to

where the soldiers were squatting among the trees, gulping gratefully from their water bottles, their rifles cradled across their knees. He barked out Tashiro's orders, making a mental reservation about the Englishman being taken alive. He hoped they would meet a quick end in the heat of the battle. He had had enough of Tashiro's brutal amusements.

63

Tashiro watched as Kurosawa led his platoon after the Malaita girl into the tangle of liana and ferns at the base of the gorge. Soon they were gone, swallowed up in the dense forest of green.

He looked away, and saw Nakamura still struggling up the steep trail behind him, his face shining with sweat. Tashiro grinned. The old bastard was out of condition. But it was fortuitous he would be on hand to witness the action this morning. It was his chance to vindicate himself.

Tashiro looked at his watch. He had given Kurosawa an hour to get his men into position. Then they would attack.

Eager with anticipation, Tashiro settled down to wait.

Rachel and Corrigan sat back to back on one of the packing crates outside the hut.

Above them the swirling banks of cumulus swirled across the blue canvas of the sky, billowing in the wake of the monsoon. This morning the birdsong was unbroken by the angry buzz of warplanes, and the blue waters of The Slot were clear and empty.

"It's been weeks since the Japanese have sent anything. It must be all over."

Corrigan got up and pushed the long lock of hair from his eyes. He grinned. "Took a woman and an Irishman to save the damned Empire. Wouldn't you know it?"

Rachel did not answer him. Instead she cradled her head in her arms, one finger tugging distractedly at the ragged threads on her shirt. There were dark rings under her eyes. Ever since the radio had broken down she seemed to have lost her will.

"You're not going to give up on me now, are you?" he asked her.

"We're stranded here, Corrigan. They've forgotten about us."

"I'll think of something."

"You're a good man, Patrick. No matter what you've done in your life, I'll always remember you as the bravest man I've ever known."

"Now that's something I haven't heard before. When we get away from here, I expect the King of England will be giving me a medal for saving his bloody Empire for him. Won't they just love that in Dun Laoghaire?"

She looked up at him. "How's your shoulder?"

"Just a scratch, I told you."

For the first time Rachel noticed the fever in his cheeks and the glaze to his eyes. She felt a sudden rush of alarm.

"Corrigan?"

She got up and tore away the filthy dressing he still wore over the top half of his chest. Immediately she smelt the taint of infection. The skin was swollen and hot and the wound itself was suppurating.

"It's getting worse." She tried to keep the panic out of her voice.

"I'm not surprised. I'd been using that knife to clean my boots."

The wound had refused to heal. Like her uncle's leg, Rachel reflected. Nothing healed properly here without drugs.

"We have to get help."

"How?"

The question was left unanswered.

The aftershock of the explosion shook the ground under their feet, and reverberated along the walls of the gorge.

"Get your head down!" Corrigan shouted. Instinctively, he threw himself at Rachel and dragged her to the ground, shielding her body with his own. There was a volley of rifle fire and Rachel heard someone cry out. It sounded like Silas.

A bullet ricocheted off the steep walls and smashed into the radio transmitter in the nearby hut. Rachel heard the valves splinter and explode.

Corrigan dragged her to the shelter of some rocks a few yards away.

Sergeant Lavella was running towards them from the mouth of the gully. "*Japoni* he come!" he shouted. "We go, we go!"

They had rehearsed this many times. They knew that if the Japanese attacked them they could defend the narrow neck at the end of the gully long enough for the others to get away.

Silas Tenpound and Corporal Solomon had enough ammunition to hold off the Japanese for perhaps as long as ten minutes. From the gully mouth Rachel heard the crack of the Japanese Arisaka rifles, and the booming response of the Enfields.

Corrigan pulled Lavella towards him. "Take the girl!"

"I won't leave you!" Rachel screamed.

Lavella hesitated, looking at Rachel, then at Corrigan.

"Get her out of here, damn you!"

Lavella made up his mind, Patrick Corrigan was not a man to argue with. Slinging his rifle over his arm he pulled Rachel to her feet and began to run, dragging her after him.

"Corrigan, what are you going to do?" Rachel shouted.

But Corrigan didn't answer. He grabbed the spare rifle from the radio hut and ran back down the gully, towards the sound of the gunfire.

64

Manning's party had been delayed that morning because Able Seaman Foster had tripped on a log in the first hour of the march and gashed his calf on a cacao thorn. It had bled profusely and by the time Hogan had dressed and bandaged the boy's leg they had lost almost a quarter of an hour.

It had seemed inconsequential at the time. Later Manning realised that those few minutes had saved all their lives.

They had crossed the swaying rope bridge behind the gorge and were heading up the steep path to the ridgeback. Manning had taken up point position and was the first to see the familiar straw coloured uniforms in the splash of green above them.

He raised his hand and fell flat on to his stomach. The others dropped to the ground behind him.

Hogan crawled up beside him. "What is it?"

Manning pointed to the hill above them, where the soldiers were taking up their positions among the palms and ferns at the foot of the ridge.

"Japs!" Hogan whispered.

Manning felt a thrill of relief and terror. Corrigan and Rachel must still be alive . . .

"They know they're in the gully," Manning whispered. "It's a trap. They're setting up a machine gun on the knoll over there."

A Japanese officer in a soft peaked cap signalled his men into position on either side of the track that snaked up the side of the ridge ahead. Through his field glasses

Manning could make out the figure of Constable Beni higher up the ridge. He was squatting down with his rifle across his knees. He still hadn't seen the Japanese.

"How many?" Hogan said.

"I count about a dozen."

"What do we do?"

"I'm not a military man, Chief Petty Officer."

"Neither am I, mate. I'm a bloody sailor. If they were in boats I'd fire a torpedo at them, but we didn't train for this at naval school."

Manning looked over his shoulder at the three pairs of eyes anxiously watching him. Each face was drawn with fear and anticipation. They were waiting for him to take command.

"All right," Manning whispered to Hogan, "we have the advantage for the time being. Although they outnumber us, they don't know we're behind them, and they're not expecting to be ambushed themselves. Leave two men here in reserve. You bring the other man and come with me. If we take out the machine gun, we can turn it on the Japs before they have time to react."

Hogan nodded. He turned to the others. "Okay, Kennedy, McFaul, stay here, Foster, it's time you did something useful for a change. You come with us. Stick close – and for Christ's sake try not to shoot yourself in the foot."

Corrigan ran, crouching low, along the gully, the cacophony of the firefight drowning out every other sound. He found Silas Tenpound lying face down in the middle of the rock strewn path.

Corrigan snatched up the dead man's rifle and ducked for cover.

Corporal Solomon lay on his stomach a few feet away, halfway up the rock spur that blocked the mouth of the gorge. A box of cartridges lay beside him.

"Too mus *japoni*!" he gasped. "More better we go, quick time!"

Corrigan threw himself down beside the corporal, bullets whipcracking through the air inches above his head.

"You go," Corrigan shouted. "I'll keep them busy. Leave me your ammunition."

Corporal Solomon hesitated for only a moment, then darted away, up the trail. He was in no hurry to die.

The hail of bullets stopped suddenly. Cautiously, Corrigan raised his head a few inches. Two Japanese soldiers were rushing up the scree slope from the shelter of the jungle below. Corrigan fired, reloaded, and fired again. One fell, and lay screaming on the ground. The other ducked for cover.

"This won't hold the bastards for long," Corrigan muttered, working the bolt on the Enfield. But he knew every second bought Rachel and the others time to get over the ridge and into the jungle. He would hold them as long as he could.

He grunted at a sudden spasm of pain in his chest. His fingers strayed automatically to the filthy dressing that covered the knife wound. Why not? He was a dead man anyway.

"Who would have thought it? Bloody Patrick Corrigan dying for a cause."

Then he heard the unmistakable staccato of machine gun fire. *Behind him.*

"Christ!" he gasped. "Rachel!"

And he threw himself away from the rocks and ran blindly back up the slope.

When Rachel and Sergeant Lavella reached the brow of the ridge, Constable Beni was waiting for them, wide-eyed with alarm.

"We go!" Sergeant Lavella yelled at him. "Quick time!"

"No!" Rachel screamed. "Wait!"

Lavella shook his head. "Come now, missy. No good too mus you stay here now. All bugger up finish properly."

"No!"

She looked back down the track. There was still no

sign of the Japanese. Solomon and Silas Tenpound must still be holding them off. Rifle fire drummed and echoed along the gully walls.

"Corrigan!" she screamed.

Sergeant Lavella tried to drag her away but Rachel fought him like a tiger. She swung her body round, clawing at Lavella's arm with her nails and kicking at his legs.

"No Missy! We go, we go!"

Lavella was too strong for her. He pulled her down the ridge after Constable Beni.

Suddenly the ground erupted as a hail of bullets slammed into the earth around them.

The first burst from the machine gun caught Constable Beni in the chest, sending him hurtling backwards through the air like a rag doll. He died without uttering a sound.

The second burst fell short. Sergeant Lavella screamed as one of the heavy shells shattered his thigh. He was slammed backwards on to the ground, his fingers clawing blindly at the air.

Rachel grabbed him by the wrist and pulled him back up the slope.

When they reached the lee of the ridge, Lavella threw himself on to the ground, gasping with pain. He clenched both his hands around the torn pulp of his thigh. The blood spurted and trickled through his fingers.

Another wave of shrill agony hit him and he arched his back and screamed.

Manning was just twenty yards from the Nambu machine gun when it opened fire. The noise of it was terrifying. Manning had never heard one fired at close quarters before and the sudden terrible roar of it paralysed him for a moment.

Then he looked up at the ridge and saw two small figures scrambling back up the slope. He recognised Rachel's long jet hair and the familiar figure of Sergeant Lavella.

They weren't going to make it.

Unless he silenced the gun . . .

There were three men behind the Nambu, their backs towards him. Manning lifted his revolver and fired. The man at the gun toppled forwards and the gun tilted back on its tripod, the heavy calibre shells spraying harmlessly into the air. The other two span round, and Manning was close enough to see their expressions change from surprise to sudden terror.

There were two more shots in rapid succession, and the two Japanese fell backwards down the slope into the thick mass of jungle. Manning looked behind him. Hogan stood up, grinning, a wisp of cordite hovering at the barrel of his .303.

"Used to do a spot of duck-shooting along the Diamantina when I was a kid. Haven't lost my touch."

Manning rushed towards the machine gun. He heard Hogan shout a warning behind him.

The gunner, his tunic soaked with blood where the bullet had passed through his chest, was sitting up, calmly removing a grenade from his belt. He already had the pin between his teeth.

Manning knew he could never bring up his revolver in time to fire, and he was directly between the wounded man and Hogan, blocking his line of fire.

There was nothing he could do.

Suddenly the man's face exploded into a pulp of cherry red. He jerked backwards, the grenade falling harmlessly away into the undergrowth, the safety pin intact.

Foster ran into the clearing, looking almost as shocked as Manning.

"Well done, son," Hogan shouted at him. "You did something right for a change."

Rachel crawled down the slope towards Lavella's fallen rifle. She could see the Japanese soldiers climbing up the path towards them. She grabbed the rifle and scrambled back up to the shelter of the rocks.

She heard the machine gun chatter to life again.

*

When the first burst from the machine gun cut down three of his men, Kurosawa had been too stunned to react. But as the second volley snaked up the jungle path towards him, he shook off his surprise and threw himself behind a palm trunk. Moments later the heavy bullets slapped into the wood a few inches from his head.

He dragged himself through the tangle of liana towards his corporal. "They must have taken the gun!"

"But that's impossible!" the corporal stammered. "How did they get out of the gully?"

"I don't know how! It doesn't matter how! Just get it back. Take half a dozen men and circle back! Hurry!"

Kurosawa made his way through the undergrowth towards the lee of the ridge. What had happened? Had they stationed some of their men at the bridge instead of on the ridgeback?

Or had the girl lied to them?

He realised he hadn't seen the Malaita girl since they reached the knoll. Could it all have been an elaborate trap?

He knew the answers would have to wait. He crawled on his belly through the clinging undergrowth and back towards the ridge, as the heavy shells whined and screamed through the air above his head.

"Me bugger up properly now."

Sergeant Lavella's teeth were clenched tight against the pain. Rachel had fashioned a tourniquet out of the shirtsleeve of his uniform and it had staunched the flow of blood. But the femur had been smashed and he could not walk.

Rachel looked down the path leading to the bridge. The machine gun was firing bursts into the undergrowth on each side of the path, and three Japanese soldiers lay face down, cut down by their own gun.

She didn't understand what was happening. All she knew was that somehow there was a way out.

"Try to stand up. I'll carry you," Rachel said.

Lavella shook his head. "No Missy. You go. You run. I for die finis now."

"No you won't," she screamed at him. "Get up!"

Suddenly Lavella sat up and pointed. "Missy!"

Rachel span round. She saw a Japanese officer scrambling up the path towards her. Rachel reached for the rifle, but she was too late.

He was just a few yards away from her. He raised his revolver and pointed it straight at her chest.

65

Rachel recognised Lieutenant Kurosawa from the day at the Mission, when she and her uncle had served him scones and tea. Kurosawa remembered her too, and the shock of recognition made him hesitate. Besides, it was not in his nature to make war on women and his finger relaxed on the trigger of the revolver in his right hand.

It was at that moment that Corrigan reached the brow of the ridge. He had overtaken Corporal Solomon, who was still scrambling up the trail behind him. Corrigan had two rifles and a box of ammunition clutched in one hand and instinctively Kurosawa looked up and turned the gun towards him. Corrigan stopped dead in his tracks and stared at him.

Corrigan was not sure, even then, if Kurosawa would have pulled the trigger. But the threat of the moment was enough and Rachel calmly raised Sergeant Lavella's rifle and shot him through the heart.

Suddenly Kurosawa found himself staring at the sky, the white mountains of cloud fading to a fuzz of pink gauze.

And he heard the monks chanting once again on the mountains of Nara . . .

The human body is frail and mortal . . .
. . . it has no power as the earth has none,
. . . it has no durability as the wind has none,
. . . it is transient and sure to die.

Ratings first class Ian Kennedy and Joseph McFaul had seen the squad of Japanese soldiers circling the machine gun position on the lip of the knoll while Hogan, Foster and Manning were concentrating their efforts on the path up to the ridge.

Silently the two riflemen slipped through the undergrowth to intercept them.

The thick vines and tangled lianas slowed their progress; they were almost too late. When McFaul spotted him, the Japanese corporal was just a few yards away from the gun. Hogan was facing away from him, intent on the Japanese officer who was making a zig-zagging run up towards the ridgeback.

The corporal lay on his side, almost invisible in the dense jungle. He removed a grenade from his belt. Kennedy raised the .303 to his shoulder and fired, the bullet blowing away the back of the man's skull.

The rest of the Japanese squad panicked. Shaken by this second unexpected attack, they scrambled to their feet and began to run. McFaul fired twice and saw one of them fall. Hogan, now alerted to the danger, swung the Nambu around and fired off two quick bursts. Three more fell, and the others disappeared into the jungle.

Kennedy, his finger still curled around the trigger of his rifle, advanced slowly down the slope to the body of the dead Japanese corporal and turned the body over with his boot. The grenade lay under the man's body.

He bent down and picked it up, stuffing it into the pocket of his tunic.

"Souvenir," he said to McFaul, grinning. "But what I really wanted was a sword."

Manning had seen the Japanese officer make the ridge and he was afraid that Rachel and Sergeant Lavella might already be dead. Abandoning Foster and Hogan to the gun he ran down the knoll through the *alang alang* grass to the path.

He heard someone crashing through the ferns towards him. He dropped on to one knee, aimed his revolver, and waited.

"Corrigan!"

"Manning! Christ, am I pleased to see you!"

Corrigan had Sergeant Lavella slung across his shoulders, and the left side of his shirt was soaked with blood. Rachel appeared from the jungle behind him. Corporal Solomon was taking up the rear, carrying the rifles and ammunition they had saved from the camp.

Manning grinned. "Thank God you're all right."

"I'd hardly call this all right. We've got half the Nip army breathing down our bloody necks."

"England's proud of you, Patrick. You've done a fine job."

"Bugger England. Get us out of here."

"You go, you go," Lavella was saying. "My turn for hero now."

"We're not leaving you behind," Manning told him.

"Yes, yes, *Japoni* he catchim you. This one Sergeant Lavella too heavy too mus. Leave me with that feller chatter-chat."

"What's he talking about?" Corrigan demanded.

"He wants to stay behind with the machine gun. Cover us while we get across the bridge."

"Somebody's got to."

Hogan came running down through the trees, Foster close behind him. "Let's get out of here!"

Sergeant Lavella turned to Corporal Solomon. "You

fella volunteer orright. You take me longa chatter-chat quick time!"

Corporal Solomon sighed. The slim hopes he had held for his survival had suddenly evaporated. But even now, he dare not disobey the redoubtable Lavella. "Yo-i sergeant," he mumbled.

Solomon put his arm under Lavella's body and lifted him to his feet. Resting Lavella's weight on his shoulder Solomon dragged him up the knoll towards the gun.

Manning watched him, hesitating. Lavella had been his ally and confidant through so much. He didn't want to leave him behind now.

The whine of rifle fire smashing into the trees a few feet away shook him from his indecision. Corrigan pushed him roughly ahead down the path and they started to run for the bridge.

When Lieutenant Tashiro reached the crest of the ridge he stared around in utter disbelief. Kurosawa lay a few feet away, shot through the chest. He was dead. The bodies of half his platoon lay sprawled on the twisting path leading up from the valley.

"No," he whispered. "No."

What had gone wrong?

He could make out running figures in the jungle below him. Somehow they had escaped.

Tashiro had been frustrated for almost ten minutes by the native sentries at the mouth of the gully. With no cover on the bare scree slope below the gorge, they had been unable to get close enough to blast their way through with grenades.

When Tashiro had finally drawn his sword and led his men in a desperate *banzai* charge up the face of the slope they had met no resistance. They had found only the dead body of one of the native constables. The Englishman and the others were gone.

Even then, Tashiro had been confident that they had succeeded in flushing them straight into the guns of Kurosawa's men.

What had gone wrong?

He raised his field glasses to his eyes. He could see the English bandits clearly now, about half a mile away, heading for the rope bridge that led across the gorge. He screamed at his men to hurry. Once they reached the bridge they could cut it down behind them and he would lose them in the jungle.

Tashiro set off down the slope after them and suddenly the trees and bushes around him erupted into singing, crashing fury as Sergeant Lavella opened up with the captured Nambu machine gun.

Sergeant Lavella had never fired a machine gun before. It was the crowning achievement in a life dedicated to the random discharge of firearms, and if it was to be his last act, he considered it a fitting and glorious end.

Unfortunately, he knew nothing about the operation of such a weapon, and Manning had had no time to coach him. It is doubtful whether Sergeant Lavella would have paid much attention to him even if he had. Lining up his target in the sights along the barrel he squeezed the trigger – and kept it there.

He did not know that an automatic gun jerks upwards and that he should sight the gun lower than the target to compensate. All he knew was that it made a wonderful noise and he blasted away at the scurrying figures below him, his finger clamped on the trigger.

But his efforts were enough to keep them pinned down for valuable minutes, as the bullets whined over their heads, smashing down saplings and spraying the jungle with tree bark, leaves and dead birds.

Down by the bridge, Manning heard the long uninterrupted hammering of the gun and he turned in anguish to Corrigan. "He's going to jam it," he said.

On cue, the gun fell silent.

"Get across!" Corrigan shouted at Manning. "Hurry!"

Corrigan pushed Manning and Rachel ahead of him, but Rachel suddenly froze.

"I can't!" she screamed.

She looked down at the swirling angry waters a hundred feet below.

"Jesus, not now!" Corrigan swore at her. "Get across that bridge!"

Manning took her hand and started to pull her across. Rachel closed her eyes to the swaying, yawning vertigo, stumbling blindly after Manning. Terror urged her on. She heard other footsteps clattering on the wooden slats behind her.

When they reached the far bank Rachel sank to her knees, her limbs shaking so hard they would not support her. She looked around. Japanese soldiers were swarming down the path on the far side. She saw the puffs of smoke from their Arisakas and a fraction of a second later heard the echoes of the rifle fire.

Hogan and Foster were just a few feet away but Corrigan and the other two seamen were still struggling up the slope of the swaying, creaking bridge.

There was no way they could make it across now. There was nothing to do but watch.

66

Hogan and Foster threw themselves on to the ground and started firing back across the gully. Meanwhile McFaul reached the end of the bridge. Corrigan and Kennedy were still ten yards behind him.

"Use your knife," Corrigan screamed at McFaul. "Cut the rope!"

McFaul pulled the knife from his belt just as a bullet slammed into him, sending him hurtling backwards, the knife still clutched between his fingers.

Manning crawled towards him, reaching for the knife. They had to cut down the bridge. It was their only chance of escape.

Kennedy screamed once and pitched forward, his body sprawled across two of the slats of the bridge. Corrigan saw him stumble and went back for him.

Kennedy looked up at him, a froth of blood appearing at his lips. The bullet had destroyed his left lung. He rolled slightly to one side and reached into his pocket and pulled out the grenade he had taken from the Japanese corporal. He held it up for Corrigan to see and his other hand tightened around the pin.

"Go," he croaked.

Corrigan knew what he was going to do.

"Jesus," Corrigan muttered and scrambled the last few yards to the end of the bridge. He threw himself forwards just as the grenade exploded.

When he looked back the bridge was snaking and splashing down into the raging torrent of the river a hundred feet below. Kennedy – what was left of him – followed it in.

Manning turned to Corrigan, the knife still clutched in his right hand; his face had drained of all colour. "My God. He blew himself up."

"He saved our skins is what he did," Corrigan growled. "Now let's get out of here."

Two hundred yards away, around the bend of the gorge, unseen by the Japanese or any of Manning's band, Corporal Solomon carried a bleeding Sergeant Lavella on his shoulders to the edge of the gorge. He hesitated only briefly on the brink of the yawning, roaring chasm. Then he jumped, and the two men disappeared in the frothing, raging waters below.

"She's not coming," Hogan said, echoing the thoughts of each one of them.

By the time they reached the beach it was already dark. They had watched for hours in the darkness, under the velvet and diamond sky, their eyes turned to the black horizon, searching for the flicker of light that was their signal.

It did not come.

Nerves, already raw from the battle on Mount Teatupa, were now stretched past breaking point as they huddled together in the sand. They had each thought that the ordeal was over. Now, without help, with little ammunition and no food, all hope had quickly evaporated.

"Maybe the Japs spotted it," Manning said.

Hogan nodded. "I'd say that was certain. The skipper was a good bloke. There's no way he would have left us here."

There was a long, brooding silence. "What do we do now, sir?" Foster said.

"If you're a rating you shut up and wait for someone to give you an order," Hogan growled.

"What he means, son, is he hasn't got the faintest idea. And neither has anyone else," Corrigan said.

"It will be all right," Manning said. "They'll be back. We just have to sit tight and wait."

"That's what I love about you, Ian. You're an incurable optimist," Corrigan said, and exhausted beyond even his own prodigious resources he collapsed on the sand to sleep.

That night, with Rachel huddled under his arm for warmth, he slept fitfully, the wound in his shoulder burning into his flesh like a brand. He knew what it meant.

There was a sense of unreality to it all. Death had brushed against him before, but somehow he had always managed to wriggle free of its embrace. But he had ridden his luck pretty hard lately; now he wondered if his stock of it had finally run out . . .

67

Wesu found the small group huddled beneath a callophyllum tree a hundred yards from the beach. Two of the villagers, out hunting wild pig, had spotted them earlier that morning. Crouching behind a large fern, Wesu examined them closely. There were five of them, four white fellers and a white mary. Two of the men were dressed all in white, and had shooting sticks, and stood on guard on the perimeter of the coconut grove. Their eyesight, he realised with disappointment, was almost as bad as the *japoni* soldiers. He was only a few yards away – he could have reached out to touch the young one – but they still had not seen him.

He studied the others, and recognised the white *kiap* straight away. He almost did not recognise the white missus who had saved his father's life almost a year before. Then she had been a pale, sickly creature who had always frightened him with her resemblance to a ghostly spirit. He remembered her in her long white calico dress, and enormous hat; nothing like the brown-limbed creature in the *tapa* cloth and ragged white blouse now sleeping with her head against the trunk of the tree, her long hair falling around her face.

He knew the other white feller too. It was the big man from Vancoro, the one who had brought her to Marmari Point on the mysterious Cargo boat.

Satisfied, Wesu stood up.

Foster, standing on guard a few feet away, yelled in shock and raised his rifle. Wesu grinned, bobbing his head.

"You belong King George and Virgin Mary?" Wesu said.

"Bloody hell, a nig-nog. I thought you were a Jap," Foster said. His hands were shaking. He put down his rifle and urinated urgently against a nearby tree.

"Wesu happy too mus," Wesu said, beaming. "*Japoni* say you for die."

"Not yet," Rachel said. She held out her hand in greeting. "They will have to try harder."

"Oh, *japoni* he try very hard, missus," Wesu told her, and he grinned at the group of pale, tired faces now clustering around him.

"Who is he?" Corrigan said.

"Wesu. Don't you remember him?" Rachel answered. Corrigan looked blank. "That time you took me to Marmari Point . . . the operation we performed in the village there? It was his father."

Corrigan raised an eyebrow. "How is the old bugger? Dead, I suppose."

Wesu shook his head. "He not die from sick. But *japoni* they come. They kill him dead."

"They murdered him?"

"Cut off him head b'long sword. We fright for *japoni* here."

"Why did they kill him?"

"They lookim for *kiap*." Wesu nodded his head in Manning's direction.

The Englishman bowed his head. "Your father was a good man. I'm sorry."

Wesu looked back at Rachel, then at Corrigan. "You wantim boat?"

"What boat?" Corrigan said.

"Boat belong you. Gods they bringim for you, plenty cargo too. We look out for him."

"I don't understand," Rachel said.

Wesu jumped to his feet. "You come. Village not far. I show you," he said.

*

The palm trees on Marmari Point were reflected in the blue waters that lapped at the white fringe of beach. The tree line was broken in places where the canoe houses jutted out from the green jungle over the water itself. From where he stood Corrigan could make out a lazy tendril of smoke spiralling into the air from the village compound and the small, square food gardens in the hills beyond. He remembered the first time he had come here, that night of the first monsoons, almost a year ago; and recalled another dark night, just a few months before, when he and Lavella had escaped from *Marakon*. Neither of the memories were pleasant, and he was unprepared for the surge of pleasure he felt at seeing the village again. It seemed to give an illusion of sanctuary, at least.

The canoe house appeared suddenly and unexpectedly from the jungle as they followed Wesu along the jungle path. It had been constructed behind the first line of palms, invisible from the beach or from the bay, built like most native canoe houses from sago leaf and sturdy teak poles. But Corrigan knew immediately that this was no ordinary canoe house. What was it doing so far from the village? Corrigan wondered. And there were walls on all four sides. Why?

Wesu stopped and pointed proudly towards it. Corrigan found a small opening at the rear of the hut, lowered his head and walked inside.

"Jesus, Mary, Joseph and All the Blessed Saints of Heaven," Corrigan murmured.

It was the *Shamrock*.

"You see how our good deeds return to bless us tenfold?" Rachel said somewhere behind him.

Corrigan turned and looked at her. She had that infuriatingly benign expression on her face. He supposed it ran in the family. "I don't understand," he said.

"Wesu says they found her drifting in the lagoon. It must have been the morning after you raided *Marakon*. They recognised the boat but they couldn't understand why it was deserted. They thought it was a warning from the gods not to betray the *kiap*. But they were frightened of the Japanese so they dragged her up on to the beach and built the boathouse around her. They knew the Japanese would never think to search their houses."

"But why for God's sake?"

"You know how superstitious they are. They found her just floating there one morning, like a ghost ship. What else could they make of it? Besides, she brought cargo. They found the stores the Japanese had left on board – bags of rice, tinned meat, cigarettes. They think it all came from their ancestor gods. The *Shamrock*'s almost become a holy shrine. When Wesu's brother got sick they laid him out on the deck. Next morning he got up and walked away."

Corrigan shook his head in wonderment.

Wesu came in and grinned at Corrigan's astonishment.

"Can you get it back into the water?" Rachel said to him.

"Yes, missus. But first you take *kai-kai*. Then Wesu helpim you. Anything for you, missus."

Later that afternoon Wesu led the young men of his village through the jungle and back to the boathouse that concealed the *Shamrock*. They had with them strong ropes made from liana vine to drag the launch back down to the beach. By dusk, they had the *Shamrock* back in the water, drifting in the shallow waters of the lagoon.

Corrigan and Rachel stood side by side on the beach and watched Wesu's men wade back towards the shore, strong brown bodies glistening and slick with seawater.

Rachel looked up at Corrigan, expecting to see the characteristic crooked grin. Instead Corrigan's face was drawn tight with distress. He swayed on his feet and reached for her shoulder with his good arm, leaning against her for support.

"Corrigan . . .?"

"This damned shoulder," he muttered, through his clenched teeth.

That morning Hogan had fetched the medical kit from the cache of supplies they had hidden in the jungle the night they landed. He had put clean dressings on Corrigan's wound and packed it with sulphonamide. But Corrigan had grown weaker during the day and now his face was flushed with fever.

The spasm passed and he pushed himself away from her.

"Hold on," she whispered to him. "We'll make it."

"We'll wait until nightfall," he said, ignoring her. "Then I'll plot a course south-west for Moresby."

He stumbled away from her towards the lagoon.

As she watched him wade through the water and climb aboard the *Shamrock*, she felt a terrible sense of dread that had nothing to do with the perilous journey that lay ahead of them.

68

First Lieutenant Mashita Tashiro carefully removed his father's sword from its sheath and held it in front of his eyes. His own reflection stared back at him from the polished steel, distorted by the curve of the blade. He stood this way for a long time before slowly replacing it in the lacquered scabbard and laying it reverently on the *tatami* mat. He placed his ceremonial short sword beside it.

He undressed slowly, removing his boots first, then his tunic and trousers, folding his uniform neatly on the bed. He removed the one thousand stitch waistband last, rolling it around the fist of his left hand and placing it on the table beside the bed.

Then he picked up the incense holder, removed the black sandalwood stopper and placed a stick of incense inside it. He lit it, reverently.

Then, clad only in his shorts, he knelt down on the bamboo *tatami* and looked up at the framed photograph of the Emperor beside the bed.

He inclined his head in prayer.

Nakamura's words still echoed around his head, like the rifle shots that afternoon in the gorge. "You have disgraced yourself, Tashiro. You have utterly failed in your duty! A handful of English bandits and you lose half of your men and allow them to escape you once more! You have brought shame upon me and upon your regiment!"

Tashiro flinched at the memory, each word still stinging in his brain like a lash. Now there was only one honourable way.

He picked up the short sword from the mat. He took a deep breath and then, gripping the long rope-bound handle, he held the sharp point against his own stomach.

It was cramped hot in the tiny room and the sweat burst from the pores of his skin and ran in tiny rivulets down his body. Images began to form in his brain, of crisp summer mornings in the mountains, when he and his brothers went to tend the charcoal kiln.

It was the time of the *Bon* festival dances. The men would strut about the wooden stage in their kimonos to the steady beat of the drum, and then join the women and dance round in a circle while the drums beat out their heavy, arcane rhythms.

In a dreamy, faraway voice he began to murmur the words of a song he had learned as a youth:

The only ones who aren't dancing tonight
are the old stone Buddha and me.

As he slowly exhaled the breath he felt the razor tip of the sword part the tight skin of his abdomen. A small trickle of blood sprang from him and snaked down his groin, staining his shorts.

The muscles of his arms contracted, rippling on his bronzed skin like whipcord. He clenched the muscles of his jaw, tensing his whole body so that it seemed to vibrate, imperceptibly, like telegraph wire in a storm.

Then, suddenly, his arms jerked inwards.

His eyes bulged from their sockets, the scream catching in his mouth so that his cheeks bulged like small pink balloons.

Slowly, very slowly, his left hand pushed against his right fist, drawing the sword across his abdomen. The slick grey of his intestines popped and oozed through the scarlet gash blossoming across his stomach. An almost imperceptible vapour of steam drifted from the entrails as they spread on to the mat in front of him.

But Tashiro did not look down. His eyes were fixed on some distant vision that helped him endure this, the moment of his death.

A spray of blood spurted from the wound, signalling the end of the deadly act. Tashiro's fist loosened its grip on the short sword.

The trembling of his limbs was uncontrollable now, and the scream in his throat erupted little by little through clenched teeth, an unearthly, high-pitched sound.

Slowly Mashita Tashiro, son of a Samurai, fell sideways, his knees drawing themselves up to his chest. His body contorted twice, writhing amongst its own innards, and then he subsided into the soft and slow dance of death, and waited for the night to come.

It was morning. A roseate stain soaked into the steel-blue of the horizon, inching slowly up across the sky. In the distance the mountains of Santa Ysabel stood in dark silhouette against the backdrop of cloud.

Corrigan stood at the wheel, looking east.

Manning came to stand beside him.

"Feeling better?" Corrigan asked.

"A little. Not as rough now, thank God."

There had been a heavy swell the previous night and the pitching of the boat had affected them all, even Hogan and Foster. Rachel had been affected worst of all and now she lay in an exhausted sleep in the shade of the deckhouse.

"Where are we?" Manning said.

"We're in The Slot, west of Santa Ysabel. We're probably only a hundred miles from Guadalcanal."

"What's our chances, Patrick?"

"They were never very good. Let me put it to you this way, Ian. They haven't got any worse."

Rachel opened her eyes and groaned. Manning crouched down next to her. "How are you feeling?"

"Awful."

"Cabin boy will be around in a minute with some bacon and eggs," Corrigan said.

"That isn't funny, Corrigan."

Manning helped her to her feet. She swayed against the rolling of the launch, her fingers gripping the guardrail. "Where are we?"

"As I was just saying to Manning here, the current's carrying us south. If we don't meet anyone on the way, we'll pass to the west of Guadalcanal Island some time tomorrow night. But someone's bound to see us, probably in the next couple of hours. We're sailing right into the middle of the biggest battle the South Pacific's ever seen."

"We can only hope the Americans see us first," Manning said.

Rachel turned to Corrigan. She suddenly realised that he was keeping himself going now by willpower alone. He looked terribly ill. His skin was drawn tight across the bones of his face, as shiny as wax. His fists gripped the wheel of the launch, to support him.

"Corrigan?"

She touched his cheek. His flesh was fever-hot.

"We have to get you to a hospital."

"I don't want to spoil everyone's day, but I think it might be a bit late for that."

Rachel put her cheek on Corrigan's shoulder. "You can't die. I love you, Patrick."

Corrigan would not look at her. "Now that's the damnedest thing I ever heard. You must have got too much sun."

"I mean it."

"You don't know what you're saying. A leopard doesn't change its spots, girl. A year with me and you'd be sticking me with a knife too. If I was still around."

"I'm not talking about what might happen in the future. I'm talking about now."

"That's good. Because to be honest with you, the future doesn't look all that rosy."

"You're enjoying this, aren't you, Corrigan? You enjoy wallowing in hopelessness."

Corrigan sighed. "Christ, woman, what do you want from me?"

"I'm sorry," she said, and laid a hand on his arm. "If it wasn't for me none of this would have happened. You could have got away."

"Well, at least you finally realise that. You can carve it on my headstone."

"Are you sorry?"

Corrigan scowled. "Yes."

"I don't believe you." Suddenly she grabbed his hair and pulled her head towards him. She kissed him hard on the lips. The other three men looked away, each finding something of sudden and intense interest on the blue monotony of the sea.

"You're a terrible judge of character," Corrigan whispered.

It was Manning who heard it first.

"A plane," he said.

Corrigan stiffened. He pulled away from Rachel and switched off the engines.

They all listened. For a few moments there was only the lapping of the swell against the hull; but then it came, the throb of aeroplane engines, rising and fading in circadian rhythm. It grew gradually louder. Corrigan saw it first; he pointed to the north-east.

"There!"

There was a tiny black speck in the sky, outlined against the powdery white banks of cumulus clouds over Ysabel. As it got closer they made out the familiar silhouette of a flying boat.

"A Japanese Betty," Manning whispered.

"Are you sure?"

"Afraid so, old boy. I've been spotting the damn things every day for six months."

"Looks like they've seen us too," Hogan grunted.

69

Wing Commander James Mitchell was about to turn for home when he saw the flying boat, low in the sky to his west. Fatigue almost caused him to miss it. He had taken off from Henderson Field at first light that morning on a routine patrol, looking for Japanese ships straggling too far to the south. He had found nothing.

Here at least was a consolation prize.

Mitchell dipped the port wing and started to dive towards the Betty. The sun would be directly behind him.

It would be an easy kill.

The flying boat made one low pass over the *Shamrock*, so low that Rachel felt that she could reach up and touch the wings. She saw the machine gunner in the perspex bubble in the nose of the plane, saw him pointing, the face mask flapping wildly against his leather jacket.

Then the shadow of the Betty passed over them and she watched it roar on into the west. For one brief moment, she thought it was going to keep flying. Perhaps they were small fry, too inconsequential to bother with.

But then, inexorably, the huge aircraft began its turn, banking to starboard and returning in a wide arc towards them, the red sun on its fuselage in vivid contrast to the steel grey of the wings.

Rachel watched it come, without fear now. There was only a numbing bitterness.

We've come too far to die this way.

"Into the water!" Corrigan screamed. "Get into the water!"

Corrigan grabbed her by the arm and pulled her towards the port gunwale. He threw her over the side. When she surfaced, she saw Manning and Hogan leap into the water from the deck of the launch. Corrigan was still struggling with Foster. The boy had raised his rifle to his shoulder and was firing off single rounds at the oncoming plane.

Corrigan was shouting something at him; she could see his mouth working but the roar of the flying boat engines had drowned out every other sound. Corrigan wrenched the rifle from the boy's hands and dragged him towards the side of the boat.

Suddenly there was another sound, harsh and staccato; it was the flying boat's forward machine gun. Corrigan pulled Foster over the side of the boat and they dived into the water, as the heavy bullets sprayed and cracked across the decks of the *Shamrock*.

Another burst from the machine gun in the nose of the Betty slapped into the hull of the *Shamrock*, igniting the fuel tanks. She exploded in a sudden rush of heat and cracking timber, and was instantly consumed by a ball of orange flame.

A plume of choking black smoke mushroomed into the sky and when Rachel looked again, the *Shamrock* was gone.

Corrigan surfaced beside Rachel in the water.

"Are you all right?" he gasped.

"I'm okay," she shouted back. "Where are the others?"

Corrigan looked around. Foster had drifted about fifty yards away. Nearby Manning was slapping ineffectually at the water as Hogan fought to keep the Englishman's head above the waves.

"I can't swim," he shouted.

Corrigan began to swim towards him but then Rachel reached out and grabbed his shoulder, pointing to the east.

The Japanese were coming back for them.

Mitchell was still a mile away from the Betty when he saw the stricken launch in the water below. He watched the Betty turn and make its second pass, then saw the *Shamrock* explode into flames.

"What the hell is that?" Mitchell asked himself.

The Betty was banking to the west now, getting ready to make another pass. He could guess why. There would be survivors in the water.

"No you don't, you son of a bitch!" He dropped the flaps on the Wildcat and started his dive.

He was wrong about the Japanese pilot. He thought he would not see him coming out of the sun, but when Mitchell was about a quarter of a mile away he could see him gesticulating wildly out of his cockpit window.

He pulled the flying boat into a tight turn to port, to try and make a smaller target.

Mitchell's right hand tightened on the control stick as the wing stem of the Betty filled the cross-hairs of his target finder. He felt the Grumman shudder as he fired the first burst from the 8mm cannons on the wing-tips.

"Get ready to dive!" Corrigan shouted.

Rachel took a deep breath, summoning her strength for one massive effort. She knew they would have to dive deep, ensuring the bullets would spend themselves in the water.

But at the last moment the Japanese pilot altered his course, pulling the nose of the flying boat so sharply to port that it seemed it would stall.

"What's he doing?" she screamed.

Corrigan pointed towards the sun, and then she saw it too, a flicker of silver through the drifting plume of black smoke from the sinking wreckage of the *Shamrock*.

"A fighter!"

The gunner in the cockpit high amidships of the Betty got away one short wild burst before the Grumman's wing cannons ripped into his plane. Almost stalled in mid-air, she presented an inviting target. Pieces of fabric and steel flew away from the port wing; Rachel saw the forward machine gunner writhing like a marionette as the perspex in front of him sprayed with blood.

More shells tore open the fuselage and the cockpit and then one of the Grumman's fifty calibre shells exploded in the Betty's fuel tank. Even from four hundred yards away Rachel felt the searing heat of the explosion as the plane vaporised in mid-air.

Wreckage began to splash into the water around them. Rachel felt the shockwave as one of the Kasei engines landed in the water just fifty yards away.

Then the Grumman was overhead, its wingtips skimming the surface of the waves. Rachel watched it as it made a slow climbing turn and came back towards them.

She raised one hand out of the water and waved.

James Mitchell looked out of the perspex window of his cockpit, and frowned, puzzled. At first he had thought that the Japanese had been attacking a PBY torpedo boat. He was surprised to see the ungainly lines of a civilian launch this deep into the war zone.

As he buzzed the water for the second time he made out the four white faces in the water below him and he remembered the rescue party that had disappeared on Santa Maria just a few days before.

"Jesus, it can't be," he muttered but he reached for his mask and began to radio his position to Henderson Field.

"Get a PBY out here as soon as you can," he said. "Looks like we've got some Coastwatchers in the water."

By the time the PBY appeared on the horizon Mitchell calculated he had only thirty minutes' fuel left in the tanks, barely enough to get him back to Henderson Field. Reluctantly he set a course for Guadalcanal.

He continued to circle the four people in the water, watching with rage and frustration as the first dark, lithe silhouette sliced through the green waters of the ocean towards them.

Soon it was joined by a second, then a third. Now there were almost a dozen sharks circling them.

He looked towards the white moustache of the PBY's bow wave and silently urged them to hurry.

Then dipping his wings once, he turned south-east and in minutes he had disappeared over the horizon.

70

Corrigan did not have such a clear view of the shark pack as Mitchell, but he too knew they were there. He saw the dark shadows around him in the water, and then a dorsal fin broke the surface, close by. Another fin appeared, fifty yards to the right. They were unpredictable killers; they might circle for a few more minutes or a few hours, but they would come.

Hogan was getting weaker, the effort of keeping Manning afloat in the water had almost spent him; Corrigan too was at the point of surrender. His left arm was stiff and aching and useless.

The wound in his shoulder burned like a white-hot brand embedded in the muscle of his chest. He had to fight to stay conscious. His strength was deserting him, and twice his head dipped below the waves and he almost surrendered to the salt embrace of the sea.

It was Rachel who dragged him back to the surface each time, grabbing a fistful of hair in her fingers and forcing his head back to the surface.

"You can't die!" she screamed at him. "I won't let you die!"

It was then that he saw the PBY, a small dark shape on the brilliant shimmering surface of the sea. In his delirium he had thought it was another shark, but now he could make out the white fleck of the bow wave and the tall, thin lines of the bridge.

Suddenly something hit him very hard, just by the right thigh. He twisted around, startled, and saw the sunlight glitter for a moment on the erect dorsal fin as the shark surfaced, then dived out of sight once more below the waves.

It had been a dry run. The next time it would come with its jaws gaping, and there was nothing he could do.

Foster was the first to reach the PBY and hands reached out for him, hauling him on to the deck. The American commander then manoeuvred his craft towards Hogan and Manning. The seaman, although exhausted, pushed Manning ahead of him and two of the American crew pulled his limp body from the sea.

Hogan dog-paddled in the water, waiting for the sailors to haul him up.

They took just seconds too long.

He didn't even see it; a big mako, powering through the water from below him. It reached the surface just a few feet away, its jaws gaping and one black eye staring straight down into his face before it took him around the chest.

In moments he was gone.

A few seconds later Hogan – or what was left of him, the torso and the stump of an arm with "Mother" tattooed on the forearm – surfaced on the water a hundred yards away. The rest of the pack moved in for the easy pickings. The water turned into a bloody, bubbling cauldron as the sharks closed in, snapping over the morsels in feeding frenzy.

By then Corrigan and Rachel had reached the PBY.

Corrigan summoned the last reserves of his will to grasp Rachel under the arm with his right hand and lift her out of the water. Eager hands grabbed her, pulling her on to the deck.

Rachel screamed, her hands reaching back for Corrigan. The crew were yelling frantically. Two of the American sailors manning the machine gun at the bow of the PBY loosed off round after round into the churning water in an angry futile effort to stave off the pack. "Corrigan!" Rachel screamed. One of the sailors leaned right out over the side and reached for Corrigan's one good arm. He began to lift him out of the sea but then the water seemed to boil as a huge, dirty-white body flashed along the port side and came for Corrigan, its terrible slit mouth gaping. The rows of needle sharp teeth slammed shut like a steel trap.

Epilogue

September 1944

Cormorants swooped and dived over the ocean, hunting fish. Breakers frothed in silver showers over the reef and the ice-blue of the sky melted into a sapphire sea.

Mitchell closed his eyes. It was so silent now, without the guns.

It was hard to remember that two thousand Japanese had died on this island; hard to picture the quiet lagoon as it had been when the Americans landed that morning, pouring on to the white beach through a deadly swathe of bullets and shrapnel.

In a few minutes the ferry nudged the jetty and the airman stepped off and made his way along the creaking wooden planks towards the settlement. He walked slowly, nursing the three broken ribs he had earned when he had jumped out of his burning plane over Rabaul. He had spent two days in a rubber raft, tormented by the same sun that now seemed so warm and benign.

Unlike some others he did not itch to get back to war. They were winning now. He had seen enough of death.

It was on the point of the bay, not far from the old Residency bungalow, with the Pacific breakers booming like distant cannon on the reefs below, that the Seabees built the cemetery.

It was surrounded by a white picket fence. The Stars and Stripes fluttered from a steel grey flagpole at one corner. Here, among the warm tropical green, the air redolent with frangipani, were rows upon rows of neat white crosses. There were almost three hundred here, each silent grave someone's personal tragedy, anonymous now.

They stood at attention in neat white lines, the dead mustered for inspection on their final parade, the colonels, the captains, the sergeant-at arms. The husbands and brothers and lovers.

The airman stopped at the gate and lit a cigarette. They were here on the island somewhere, he knew. Shoup had told him.

It was then he noticed a native policeman shambling towards him. He wore a *lava-lava* and broad leather belt with a heavy metal buckle. He carried an old Enfield rifle over his left shoulder.

A large slice of muscle was missing from the thigh of his right leg and there was an ugly purple scar above his knee, tight and round as a nickel. The wound had left him with a pronounced limp, the right leg stiff and almost useless; but it did not detract from the man's air of polished dignity.

The native stood watching him, his head cocked to one side. "What name you?" he asked finally.

"My name's Mitchell. I'm with the US Air Force. I was looking for someone. A woman. Rachel Goode."

The man nodded. "I know that one orright."

"Perhaps you could take me to see her."

"Mebbe," the man said. He seemed suspicious. "How you know white missus?"

"I don't . . . I mean, we never actually met. I was with the Air Force on Guadalcanal. She meant a lot to all of us on the island. I guess I just wanted to say thanks."

A slow smile creased the man's pug features, revealing the white tombstones of his teeth. "Good you come," he said. "Good too mus. You walk longa me. I show you."

Mitchell followed the man up a winding path through the ferns and banyan. The scent of frangipani hung heavy and warm on the air.

Mitchell wiped the beads of perspiration from his forehead. "What's your name?" Mitchell asked the man.

"Name belong me Sergeant Lavella," the man said.

"What happened to your leg?"

"*Japoni* he kill me," Sergeant Lavella said, "but not kill finis. Sergeant Lavella too much big man for *japoni*."

"Were you one of Manning's men?"

Lavella nodded his head vigorously. "Damn good *kiap*, that one," he said, using the strongest oath he knew. "Damn good."

They had reached the new mission building at the top of the hill. The sound of children's voices came from inside a big thatched hut that dominated the compound. They were singing a hymn; "Onward, Christian Soldiers".

On the other side of the compound was a bungalow, the verandah wreathed with purple flowering bougainvillea. Outside there was a small white cairn of stones and a white cross. Mitchell bent to examine the inscription:

PATRICK CORRIGAN
1907–1942
If it wasn't for me
he would have got away

Mitchell straightened, frowning. He turned to Sergeant Lavella. "But I don't understand. I thought that . . ."

The singing had stopped inside the hut. Naked brown children swarmed out, laughing and shouting. In the midst of them was a white man, his huge frame towering above them, his dark curls glistening with perspiration. A lock of hair fell into his eye and he pushed it away with a practised sweep of his hand.

Sergeant Lavella said something in his ear. The man looked over at Mitchell and his darkly handsome face split into a broad grin. "Patrick Corrigan," he said, extending his huge hand, "welcome to Santa Maria."

"Captain James Mitchell," the American said. He

pointed to the cross, confused. "But the inscription says . . ."

"Oh, take no notice of that. She put that there. A symbol, I suppose you'd call it. Maybe I'll tell you the story later, if you've got time. So you're one of the Yank pilots?"

Mitchell shook his hand. "And you must be The Weatherman."

"No, not me. She's in the church there, collecting the missals." He lowered his voice to a whisper. "I still don't lay a great store by it myself but Rachel thinks it's doing the children a bit of good and everybody likes a sing-song, don't they?"

He led the way towards the mission church. Mitchell noticed the limp. "You tangle with the same Japanese marksman as the sergeant over there?"

Corrigan shook his head. "Shark," he said. "Nearly had me, but one of your American sailors managed to get me out of the water just in time. Still, it kept half my leg as a souvenir." He patted his left trouser leg. "Not much meat left. It's slowed me down a bit, but Rachel reckons it was about time. Talk of the Devil, here comes your Weatherman now."

She was one of the most beautiful young women Mitchell had ever seen. She was wearing a white muslin dress, but her arms were bare and very brown, and her feet were also bare, displaying her slim ankles. Her jet black hair fell heavily around a perfect oval face. She moved with an easy feline grace.

She put a proprietary arm around Corrigan's waist and stood on tip toe to kiss him lightly on the cheek. Mitchell could not suppress a pang of jealousy.

"This is Jim," Corrigan said, as if he had known the pilot all his life. "Jim, this is The Weatherman."

Mitchell held out his hand. "I'm glad you made it. I'm glad you both made it."

Rachel's hand was soft and warm. She offered him a dazzling smile. "Not quite. We left parts of ourselves behind. Anyway, I'm delighted to meet you. Come inside. I don't know about you but I could do with a good, stiff drink right now. Join me, Patrick?"

"Not me," Corrigan said, "I've reformed."

And he gave Mitchell a broad wink and left the American to wonder what it meant.

COLIN FALCONER

VENOM

'I will survive', he promised the black silence.
'I will survive and I will come back to haunt you. All of you . . .'

It began like a page from the Kama Sutra. A beautiful French girl and her Indian lover locked in the white heat of illicit passion.

The result was Michel. Thrown out on to the dangerous streets, he grew to ferocious manhood in the alleys of Saigon. He survived to wreak the most extreme vengeance for every beating and all the betrayals. Possessed of a raw sexuality and the flair of a master criminal, driven by a pitiless hidden violence, he left a trail of blood that stretched from the backstreets of Bombay to the boulevards of Paris.

When the judge's gavel cracks across a Delhi courtroom and the world waits for justice, his destiny will hang on one last ironic twist of fate . . .

'Exotic, exciting, darkly suspenseful – a splendid novel'

Campbell Armstrong

CAMPBELL ARMSTRONG

MAMBO

Frank Pagan was sitting beside the world's most notorious terrorist.

Over the years Gunther Ruhr had left a trail of carnage behind him from the Mediterranean to Japan. Now he had been captured. But why had he been in Cambridge of all places?

Frank Pagan had good reason to be uneasy, for a conspiracy of unprecedented scale was under way.

From the foggy flatlands of East Anglia to the steam heat of Cuba, from the chic streets of Paris to the Scottish countryside, the search for answers turns into a race against time as a world-threatening plot comes to a climax . . .

HODDER AND STOUGHTON PAPERBACKS

TERENCE STRONG

SONS OF HEAVEN

They are the *Pessarane Behesht*. The Sons of Heaven. Secret sword of Islam.

Spawned in war-torn Beirut from the seeds of legend. Nurtured in revolutionary Iran to wreak vengeance on the enemies of Allah.

A secret arms-for-hostages deal is threatened when a ship vanishes in mysterious circumstances.

And the *Pessarane Behesht* respond with kidnap and assassination.

Only one man can stop the rising tide of terror – a former SAS major with a personal score to settle.

Sheer human courage struggles against insidious odds to save the innocent victims whose lives hang by a thread.

'Well-plotted and genuinely exciting'

Sunday Telegraph

'Belongs to the action-man school of writing, backed up by hands-on research'

The Times

ROBERT MARKHAM

COLONEL SUN

With a special introduction by
KINGSLEY AMIS

A dozen oysters with a chilled rosé, then silverside of beef. In the afternoon; a convivial round of golf at Sunningdale.

But just as complacency threatens to creep up on Bond, comes the news: M has been kidnapped.

The violence has been extreme. M's servants are dead, coldly shot down without mercy.

And on a deceptively calm Greek island, a most ungenial Colonel Sun is waiting to welcome Bond to a new game . . .

To be played without rules.

To be played to the death.

'First-class'

Daily Telegraph

'All the ingredients are here'

The Standard

HODDER AND STOUGHTON PAPERBACKS